GERBER WATCHED THE ENEMY SOLDIER

He was unaware of the rest of the jungle. The heat and humidity had ceased to exist for him. He concentrated on the soldier, afraid that he might communicate his presence to the enemy through ESP. He kept the knife low, the blade pointed at the ground.

The NVA continued his approach, swiveling his head, but not searching hard. He stepped past Gerber, then stopped, his feet next to Gerber's equipment. He didn't see that, either.

Without warning, Gerber struck. He stepped up behind the man, grabbing him under the chin, lifting. There was a splash of blood, then the odor of copper overwhelmed everything around them.

"Evocative... Nam as it most likely was..."
—Ed Gorman, *Cedar Rapids Gazette*

"The Vietnam warrior has distinguished himself as none other in the history of America."
—Don Pendleton, creator of
The Executioner

"Vietnam: Ground Zero... books to linger in the mi... ng."
—... *west Book Review*

D0974006

VIETNAM: GROUND ZERO™

THE RAID

A GOLD EAGLE BOOK FROM
WORLDWIDE®

TORONTO • NEW YORK • LONDON • PARIS
AMSTERDAM • STOCKHOLM • HAMBURG
ATHENS • MILAN • TOKYO • SYDNEY

First edition June 1988

ISBN 0-373-60501-3

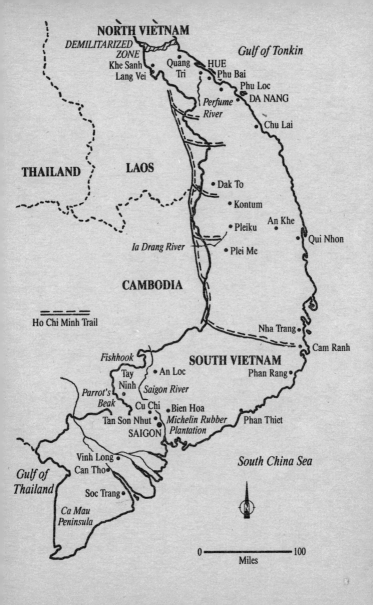

VIETNAM: GROUND ZERO..

THE RAID

PROLOGUE

OFFICE OF GENERAL
GRIGORI BUKHARIN
COMMANDER OF THE
DIVERSIONARY TROOPS
OF DISTRICT 1
(SPETSNAZ), MOSCOW
USSR

The office was huge, even by the standards set in the Politburo. Arrayed on shelves against the walls were scores of American books. The mix of literature included a lot of history, covering the social unrest and civil disobedience of the 1960s, the Indian Wars and the Civil War. It was the most massive collection of American writing gathered anywhere outside the United States, and it surpassed anything held by the many public libraries in the Soviet Union. Ownership of some of the books was considered a crime against the state.

Colonel Fyodor Tretyak, a large, rotund man, sat in a high-backed leather chair and studied his manicured fingernails. He was fleshy with huge jowls, a round pink face, bushy eyebrows and thinning hair. Although it wasn't hot in the office, Tretyak wiped a hand over his forehead. Whenever he was in a room with General Bukharin, Tretyak sweated heavily.

Tired of studying his fingernails, he turned his attention back to the bookcases. He wondered how Bukharin had managed to obtain such a collection of forbidden literature, but he would never ask the question. To do so would be to violate the strict military system of customs and courtesies. A subordinate assumed that everything his superior did was acceptable and to question would signal a lack of respect, a lack of faith in the system. And Tretyak was all too familiar with the treatment of anyone under suspicion. He shuddered involuntarily at the thought.

Tretyak sat quietly, waiting for the general to complete the paperwork centered on the red felt blotter that lay on his huge, ornately carved rosewood desk. A gold-and-green lamp at the front of the blotter threw a pool of light onto the papers. To one side was a telephone that contained three lines. Two of them were monitored by the KGB and the third was supposedly free of electronic bugs. Opposite it was a pen-and-pencil set that had been a gift from the head of the Politburo and the General Secretary of the Communist Party.

Tretyak's gaze was drawn to the window. Outside, the spires and towers of Red Square poked into a gray sky like some Hindu mystic's bed of nails. The gunmetal cloud cover threatened more snow. The temperature was far below zero, and there were shortages in the city because of the cold and snow.

Bukharin closed his file folder and opened the middle drawer of his desk, dropping the folder inside. As he closed the drawer, he looked up at Tretyak. "So, Fyodor, it has been a long time."

"Yes, Comrade General."

"So formal, Fyodor." Bukharin smiled. He pushed a button on the intercom. "Sergeant, I would like some refreshments." He glanced at the other man. "I assume a little vodka would be welcome."

"Of course, General."

The silence was disquieting. Tretyak listened to the wind howling outside. He listened to the sound of the clock ticking and relaxed slightly. Tretyak knew that if he had been in trouble, the general wouldn't have bothered with vodka or small talk.

The door opened and the sergeant entered. He held a small silver tray with two crystal glasses filled with clear liquid. Specks of black pepper floated on the surface of the vodka. The sergeant served the general first and then Tretyak. When both officers had a glass, he retreated quickly, never saying a word.

Bukharin swallowed half the contents of his glass in one gulp, smacked his lips and set his glass on the blotter to avoid damaging the surface of the desk. He cleared his throat, then spoke. "Now we can talk."

"Yes, Comrade General."

Bukharin laughed. "This isn't a punishment session, Fyodor. I'd have thought you perceptive enough to have deduced that."

Tretyak felt like wiping his face again, but didn't want to betray his nervousness. He smiled weakly and tried to think of something witty to say, but all he could think of was, "Yes, Comrade General."

Bukharin stood and moved from behind his desk. He glanced out the window and then stepped to one of the floor-to-ceiling bookcases. "Do you know what all this represents, Fyodor?"

"I'm afraid I don't, Comrade General." He had to twist around to face Bukharin.

"This is the result of years of study. Years of work. Years of learning everything I can about our enemy, the Americans. I've read each of these books. First I had them translated into Russian, but that isn't the same. We lose something in the translation, as they say. Words, meanings, inflections aren't conveyed well in translation."

He turned, pulled a book from one of the shelves and held it up like an offering to a god. "To truly understand the meaning, it must be read in the native language. It must be read in English. It must be studied in English. Only then is it possible to understand exactly what is meant by the written word."

Tretyak nodded his agreement because he didn't know where the conversation was leading.

Bukharin returned to his desk and dropped the book onto it. He sat down and resumed speaking. "Because I've studied these books I understand the American mentality." He waved a hand and added quickly, "Oh, I'm not referring to their mentally deficient leadership. I'm talking about the American people. The American society." He stopped long enough to pick up his glass and drink again. Then he stared at Tretyak. "You have no idea what I'm talking about, do you, Fyodor?"

"I'm afraid I don't follow."

"No matter. I have some special orders for you. An assignment that will hurt the Americans without their knowing we're hurting them. A secret assignment that will make the inept American leadership seem truly incompetent. Are you interested?"

Tretyak drained his glass and felt the vodka explode in his stomach. His head spun for a moment and then cleared. He nodded. "Very much, Comrade General."

Bukharin pulled out a drawer and removed a file with a red leather cover. He set it on the desk before him and opened it. "I have here a report on the American effort in Vietnam. It's a projection of the cost in terms of equipment, percentage of gross national product . . . and in lives. It's a suggestion that the American military machine can easily defeat our comrades in North Vietnam, if they're willing to do so."

"Not a surprise," ventured Tretyak.

"No, not much of one," agreed Bukharin. "Now, we factor in the protests and civil disobedience in the United States. We add the pressure exerted on their elective bodies and the pressure of the unrestrained press and we have a different outcome. No, not a victory for our comrades, but the next best thing. The Americans will capitulate."

"You believe this?"

"Most assuredly. Think it through, Fyodor. Look at the riots in the streets. The Americans don't want the war in Vietnam. A little special guidance from us and their defeat will be ensured."

"I fear that my Spetsnaz soldiers lack that type of training. But assassinations, surprise, special operations behind enemy lines, then, yes..."

"No, no, Fyodor, you leap to unwarranted conclusions." Bukharin sipped at his vodka. "You won't be sent to the United States to add to that confusion. That would be a grave political error on our part. Any taint on those riots by us would have disastrous effects and drive the majority of Americans into the administration's camp. Communist agitation from the outside is the last thing we want."

"But—"

"Hear me out, Fyodor. These Americans are afraid of the stain of communism. Even the assumption of communism is enough to sink the most trusted of leaders. And if a line could be drawn from a riot-torn campus to the Soviet Union, the whole structure of civil disobedience would collapse."

"But, Comrade General, there are Communists involved in the riots and demonstrations."

"Yes, but they're Americans, not Soviets. No, we must be more subtle. We must be cleverer than the Americans expect us to be. We must do everything we can to undermine their war effort in Southeast Asia so that the protestors and demonstrators will have more to protest." Bukharin grinned broadly. "And of course we can organize a few demonstrations in Western Europe to fuel the fire."

Tretyak crossed his legs and picked at a bit of imagined lint. "Again, my soldiers aren't trained for that."

"Forget the riots," snapped Bukharin. "That is so much window dressing. We have other plans in mind. One of them involves your Spetsnaz troops."

Tretyak sat up straighter. "They're ready, Comrade General. We look forward to the opportunity to engage the Americans in combat."

"No, Fyodor, that wouldn't be the case, either. We don't want the Americans to have the body of a Soviet soldier to show the world."

"That won't happen," said Tretyak, swelling with pride. "The Americans are no match for my Spetsnaz. They are in peak physical condition, stronger, quicker and smarter than any soldiers in the world."

"No doubt," said Bukharin. "But we aren't going to confront the Americans in South Vietnam. That could only draw us into the conflict, and the dangers of escalation into a worldwide war and possible nuclear confrontation are too great."

"I don't understand."

"We're going to send a unit of your Spetsnaz troops into North Vietnam to set up a special training center. You will, or they will, instruct the best of the North Vietnamese on the specialties of your troops. Teach them the techniques, train them in the methods and show them how to disrupt the Americans for maximum damage."

"How is that going to help them win? There's only so much the Spetsnaz can do."

"Fyodor, don't underestimate the value of a well-timed assassination. Do not underestimate the value of a well-conceived ambush. A few disasters for the Americans and more of the American media, more of the American people, will begin to clamor for an end to the war." He smiled slyly and added, "Most Americans don't understand the importance of military secrecy or a massive battle. They only see the end results and misinterpret them. We shall give them something more to misunderstand and misinterpret."

Tretyak looked into the bottom of his empty glass and wished he had more vodka. "You believe this is going to help our North Vietnamese comrades?"

"Of course. I want you to pick the men and instruct them personally on the design of the training program. Ground them in all aspects of it until you have a team of twelve or thirteen men, each trained in one speciality and cross-trained in another. There will be one officer to lead and one to work as his deputy. There will be men who are experts with weapons, demolitions, communications, medicine and gathering intelligence. These skills will be taught to the North Vietnamese."

"Yes, Comrade General."

"As the teams of North Vietnamese are trained, they'll be sent into South Vietnam to destroy American supplies, kill their leaders, kill the South Vietnamese leaders and create havoc. When enough teams are trained and operating in the South, the American war machine will grind to a halt and the war will end with their defeat."

Tretyak sat back and thought about it. A dozen Spetsnaz teams, two dozen, operating in South Vietnam would be a blow the Americans would find devastating. Tretyak had to smile. It was a brilliant plan because it involved a limited number of Soviet soldiers, none of them in danger in the South. They would stay on friendly soil and direct the missions, letting the North Vietnamese take care of the problems. And it would give the Soviets exactly what they wanted: destabilization in the United States. How long would the Americans support a policy that was failing so badly?

"I see, Comrade General. I shall begin designing the program at once."

"Very good, Fyodor. I want our men in Vietnam within sixty days. Everything will be waiting for them by then."

Tretyak got to his feet and came to attention. "Yes, Comrade General."

"Keep me informed, but don't send anything to me in writing. I only want oral communication with you."

"Yes, Comrade General."

"Good luck."

Tretyak saluted, waited for it to be returned and then left the office. Done correctly, everyone would be promoted. Done poorly and a lot of men would end up in Siberia or be shot. As he hurried down the hall, Tretyak decided he would do it correctly because he didn't even wish to contemplate a stint in Siberia, nor did he want to be thought of as a traitor.

1

**AIR TECHNICAL
INTELLIGENCE CENTER
WRIGHT-PATTERSON
AIR FORCE BASE
DAYTON, OHIO**

Sitting in the small cinder-block building, which had no windows and was surrounded by a twelve-foot-high chain link fence with restricted access, Air Force Lieutenant David Rawlings pored over the week's photo recon package. Rawlings was a young man, having been on active duty with the Air Force for just under two years. Prior to that he had been a college student who had been drawn into the Air Force ROTC program by the promise of a job on graduation, and by the promise of money for attending classes. Now, with the Vietnam War in full swing, with just over half a million men in the field, Rawlings wasn't sure his choice had been a wise one.

Then he remembered that a broken eardrum had kept him out of the flying career fields and those were the ones that were using up the other young men. Young men whom he'd gone to college with had learned to fly airplanes, or navigate them, and were now flying over North Vietnam and getting shot at. All he had to do was dodge the demonstrators who occasionally came out to protest the Air Force presence at Wright-Patterson Air Force Base. These incidents were few since civilians in the community realized just how much money was pumped into the local economy by the military.

Rawlings pushed back his chair and stood up. He walked around the sparsely furnished room. There was a massive filing cabinet shoved into one corner. A combination lock secured the middle drawer, and it would take three men and a hand dolly to steal the cabinet. There was a gray metal bookcase containing black loose-leaf binders with unclassified information, a worktable in the center of the room with eight chairs around it, and a single, stuffed chair shoved into another corner. In front of that chair was a throw rug, giving the office its only homey touch. The cinder-block walls were painted light green and were covered with posters showing Soviet-built aircraft, surface-to-air missiles and automatic weapons. Each week a package with new posters arrived from the DIA, the CIA or one of the Air Force intelligence schools.

Rawlings moved to the door and unlocked it. Outside was an empty hallway. No one seemed to be interested in working on a Sunday morning. Rawlings wished he had a Coke, or a cup of coffee, but the machine was empty and there was no one around to brew coffee. Besides, he had his safe open, and if he left the office, he would have to lock everything. It was too much of a hassle.

Closing the door, he sat down at the table, pulled a packet of photos over and opened it. There were bright red Secret stamps on the cover of the file folder and at the top and bottom of each picture. Rawlings knew the photos were classified only because no one wanted the Soviets or the enemy in North Vietnam to know how good the cameras on the spy planes were. When pictures were released, they were always of fuzzy prints, purposely printed slightly out of focus so that labels had to be placed on them to indicate the locations of missiles and launchers, or trucks, or enemy installations. People didn't know how sharp and clear the real things were.

He set the first photo in front of him and scanned it quickly. It showed a walled compound near Lang Mo in the North, a small camp nestled in hills and surrounded by jungle. Because of the wall around it, the compound was on the Air Force list of priority targets. For over a year the Air Force had been regularly flying over these locations, looking for changes, indications that American prisoners of war had been moved into them. In that year Rawlings had never seen anything to indicate they had.

To the unaided eye, the photo showed nothing unusual. Rawlings pulled over a magnifier, a small eyepiece on a thin black metal tripod, and peered through it. With his left hand he moved the magnifier slowly over the picture, studying the shapes, the different areas of dark and light, the buildings, the trees inside the wall, the shadows and the surrounding countryside.

The first thing he noticed was that the track that led to the gate on the south side seemed to be deeper than in earlier photos, more distinct, as if a number of vehicles had used it recently. Sometimes that happened because of the seasonal changes, he knew. When the hot and marginally dry season hit, the vegetation wasn't quite as thick as during the hot and wet season so that it seemed that an abandoned dirt road had been used.

Then he noticed what he thought was a new guard tower, constructed in the northeast corner. But he realized that that wasn't quite right. It appeared as if the existing tower had been repaired. Rawlings drew the magnifier down against the photo and examined the tower again. There was evidence of recent work there.

The lieutenant began studying the compound carefully. He decided that there had been quite a bit of recent activity on the site, so he got up and went to the safe. From it he took another packet of photos, all of them six months old. At the table, he sorted through the stack until he found another that showed the compound outside Lang Mo. But the angle of the shot was different so that comparisons were difficult.

But not that difficult. Even with the unaided eye, he could see changes had been made. Repairs were obvious to a number of the buildings. One looked as if it had a new roof. Another had had a new wing built onto it. A pile of dirt in one photo wasn't in the next. A pile of dirt had been moved. A new

well had been dug. A couple of small buildings, hidden under
the trees, had been built. Yes, thought Rawlings, there *had*
been quite a bit of activity.

He took out a couple of the other pictures from the most recent run and studied them, looking for signs of people. Sometimes they got good shots of the enemy as they worked. He
remembered one where a North Vietnamese soldier stood in
the open countryside flipping the bird at an American aircraft, a gesture he must have learned from an American. That
notion had caused quite a stir in U.S. intelligence circles. A
number of people were sure that POWs were being held
nearby, but they couldn't locate a probable site.

For the next hour he studied the pictures. He didn't seem
to hear the rattling compressor in the air conditioner, which
sometimes drove him to distraction. Neither did he hear the
quiet ticking of the clock on the bookcase, nor the footsteps
of another Sunday worker walking down the hallway outside
the door. Instead, he hunched over the photos, comparing,
searching, making notes.

At one point he slipped the pictures into acetate sleeves and
got out a black grease pencil. He began to write on the acetate, drawing on it and labeling different features so that he
could show his boss the changes in the camp in one quick
glance.

When he finished, he got out of the chair and walked to the
wall phone near the door. Picking up the receiver, he dialed
nine for an outside line and then dialed the number listed next
to Major Richard Booth's name on the sign-out sheet. When
the ringing was answered, he said, "Sorry to bother you at
home on a Sunday, Major, but I have something here that I
think you'd better see."

"Can you tell me what it is?"

Rawlings grinned. Whenever he called Booth, the major
asked if it was something that could be discussed on the phone,
knowing that it wouldn't be because if it could, then it could
wait until morning.

"No, sir, afraid not."

"Okay. I'll be there in about twenty minutes." There was a short pause. "This better be good, because John Wayne is about to attack Iwo Jima."

"It is, sir," said Rawlings. "Besides, we know John Wayne will take the island."

Thirty minutes later, with Major Booth standing behind him, Rawlings was pointing out what he had found. Using the grease pencil, he circled an area. "Notice that this dirt, obviously part of the construction here, has now disappeared. I see construction or evidence of it here and here and right here. Couple that to the improvements on the guard tower here, and I think we can conclude that the North Vietnamese plan to use this as a POW camp."

Booth, a tall, skinny man with thick black hair greased to the top of his head, slipped into the chair beside Rawlings. The major had a pasty white complexion, bright blue eyes and a nervous habit of clutching his throat periodically as if to straighten his tie whether he wore one or not. Now he rubbed his forehead with an index finger as if he had the world's worst headache. "Okay, where exactly is this camp located?"

Pulling a map across the table, Rawlings pointed at Lang Mo. "As you can see," he said, "it's not that far north of the DMZ."

"Yeah. That's what bothers me about it. Why would they build a camp so close to the DMZ, almost as if inviting a raid from us, or an escape by the prisoners?"

"We know," said Rawlings, "that they've captured a number of our men, mainly Army and Marines, in the South. Maybe they're going to bring them all north and this is a way station or a collection point."

"No," said Booth, pushing the map away. "I don't like that. It's too close to the border. It invites escape. A guy gets out and only has to make it forty or fifty miles to safety."

"Do you deny that there's been construction at the site?"

"No," said Booth, looking at the pictures again. "That much is fairly obvious from these."

"Our directives say we're supposed to watch for and then report this sort of thing."

"I know that," agreed Booth. "I just don't want to jump to conclusions. Besides, you know as well as I do that there are probably a dozen other offices examining this material so that nothing gets overlooked."

"Then you're going to ignore it." Rawlings felt his stomach turn over in disappointment. He had envisioned the Air Force Commendation Medal and a letter of appreciation. It was one of the reasons that he gave up his Sundays. After all, he could have been visiting one of two young women he knew, or watching John Wayne as Booth had been.

Booth took the magnifier and studied the pictures quietly. Finally he pushed everything away. "No, I can't ignore it. The evidence is too clear to ignore. I don't like it because it doesn't make sense. But they are trying to conceal the work."

"How do you mean, sir?"

"I mean they haven't brought any heavy equipment in to help them. The road shows almost no use and it suggests something is going on that they don't want us to know about. Therefore, I think we should bump this up the line."

"Yes, sir."

Booth looked at his watch. "If you don't mind working this afternoon, I think we can have something for the colonel at the morning Intel briefing. And I'll want a package ready to forward either to DIA or to SACSA at the Pentagon, though I suspect they must be onto this already."

"Yes, sir," said Rawlings. He didn't mind working on Sunday, because he had nothing else planned. And he doubted that anyone else was onto the camp yet. Lang Mo, as Booth had pointed out, wasn't a likely place for POWs. It was too far from Hanoi, where the press and the peace activists were taken to see how humane the enemy was, and it was too close to South Vietnam. That was why he always searched in that area first. Everyone else would look at it last.

Booth stood, looking at his watch again. "Do you want me to stay around here?"

Rawlings looked up at the major and shook his head. The man didn't like giving up his weekends for anything. It was strange, the way so many career officers in the military looked on their responsibilities as a nine-to-five, Monday-to-Friday proposition. They failed to remember that almost every major assault ever undertaken had begun at about dawn and that Pearl Harbor had been attacked on Sunday. The Air Force was breeding managers, not leaders.

"No, sir," he said. "I'll have a package ready for you in the morning, and one ready so that you can brief the colonel."

"Oh, no," said Booth. "This is your baby. You came up with it and you're developing the briefings. I think you should be responsible for giving them."

"I'll be ready, sir."

COLONEL THOMAS A. JEPSON sat at the head of the long wooden table and waited for the men to finish rustling the papers and folders in front of them. At the other end of the room, on the screen pulled from its hiding place in the ceiling, was a slide showing the organizational crest and a title that indicated they were involved in a briefing.

Jepson was a short, pudgy man who liked to have his short, pudgy fingers in each of the pies of his command. Unlike some Air Force managers who let each section of a unit run until someone screwed up, Jepson watched everything everyone did, making suggestions that wouldn't work because he didn't understand. It sounded suspiciously as if he believed the manager's handbook, which demanded he take an active interest in each of his subordinates.

Before anyone spoke, Jepson reached into the shirt pocket of his sweat-soaked khaki uniform and took out a pen. Like most Air Force officers, Jepson wore only a set of wings, a name tag and his rank insignia on his uniform. Ribbons were reserved for official functions and the Class A uniform.

"I have a number of announcements to make," he said, opening the thick leather-covered folder in front of him.

Rawlings wasn't happy about that. He looked at the two dozen officers at the table with him, each listening to the colonel. There were some young men, captains and lieutenants who headed small departments. There were older men, majors and lieutenant colonels who headed the larger ones. These were men who had spent their lives in the military, concerned with the workings of the bureaucracy that the military machine had become.

Rawlings wondered if anyone realized how closely the Air Force resembled a large corporation. The only difference was that the Air Force had everything, to the tiniest detail, spelled out for its members in its vast set of regulations. And, of course, everyone wore a uniform that immediately told everyone else his status in the organization. Rawlings knew there were corporate "uniforms" but they were harder to judge than those of the Air Force. A general's stars were easier to spot than a president's five-hundred-dollar suit.

But all this was just the clutter that Rawlings used to keep from getting nervous. He didn't like speaking in front of groups, especially when nearly everyone in that group outranked him. So he didn't hear what the colonel was talking about, neither the new Air Force fitness program designed to make sure everyone in the service could walk a mile and a half in fifteen minutes, nor the uniform change that would come about in six months. All he could think about was the order of the slides, the classified nature of the briefing and whether he should actually ensure the doors were locked as regulations demanded.

Finally Jepson looked around the table at the assembled officers. "If there are no questions about this, we'll get the Intel update out of the way so that we can move on to other business."

Rawlings stood and handed several vu-graphs to the projectionist. He then glanced at the door and asked, "May I have that locked, please?" An NCO, who was sitting behind the colonel, got up and locked it. "If you have a radio," he continued, "please turn it off." Again he waited, and then nodded to the projectionist for the first slide. "This briefing is classified secret. Please do not discuss the contents outside of this room."

Then he began telling them everything he had discovered the day before. He went into great detail, using a pointer against the screen as each slide came up. He knew this was exactly what they wanted to see and hear. It was stuff they wouldn't read later in the newspapers, *Time* or *Newsweek*. It made them feel as if they were in on something important.

When he finished, he asked for questions. Jepson had two, neither of which made any sense and one of which had nothing to do with the briefing. It was as if the colonel hadn't been listening to a word he had said.

Feeling that he had blown his big chance, Rawlings collected his slides and waited for the other classified briefing to be completed. When it was over, the door was unlocked and Rawlings was dismissed. He was only too happy to get out because he didn't want to be around at the end of the meeting. He didn't want to have to look at any of these people.

Back in his office, he sat with the briefing package in front of him and wondered if anyone cared if he cried. Somehow it hadn't gone as planned. The staff thought of it as just one more boring briefing that they had to sit through.

A moment later the door opened and Booth entered. He had on a khaki uniform, his wings pinned above the left pocket. He looked at Rawlings. "How'd it go?"

Rawlings shrugged. "All right, I guess. They listened, but they didn't seem interested."

"They don't understand the value of the work we do. It's too abstract for them. Don't let it get to you."

"But I thought they'd want to hear this. They're always complaining because we don't give them anything they don't see on the evening news."

Before Booth could tell him that the members of the staff never knew what they wanted, the door opened again. Another of Booth's lieutenants entered. She was tall, thin and blond and had blue eyes, delicate features and tiny ears. She wore a blue uniform with a short skirt and black pumps. Her hair was piled on her head because Air Force regulations said that it must not touch the collar.

"Got a call, Major," the lieutenant said.

"A call from whom?"

"Colonel Jepson. He asked that we send Lieutenant Rawlings to Washington to brief General Steward on his findings. He'd like him to be ready to leave by one this afternoon."

Booth clapped Rawlings on the shoulder. "So, somebody *was* listening to you."

The woman checked her notes, then addressed the major again. "They want someone to go with him to act as liaison."

"Liaison?"

"Yes, sir. Lieutenant Rawlings will be too busy with his briefings to worry about the mundane. They want someone with him."

Booth smiled. "You want to go to Washington, Sheila?"

"Yes, sir."

"Fine. I'll see that the orders are cut. Rawlings, you're going to have to be the classified courier. Have you read the regulations on that?"

"Yes, sir. I'm even on the roster of acceptable couriers."

"I'll expect both of you back here in an hour packed and ready to go."

"Yes, sir."

THE SOVIET-MADE ANTONOV AN-12 touched down, bounced once and settled onto the runway of Gia Lam near Hanoi. Captain Yuri Kutnetsov looked out of the window with trepidation. The deep greens of the jungle outside the window contrasted violently with the whites of the snowdrifts outside Moscow when Kutnetsov had left the Soviet capital two days earlier.

When the plane finally rolled to a halt on a large black ramp, Kutnetsov got up from his seat. He glanced over his shoulder, into the rear of the plane where the NCOs on his team had been sitting. He eased his way forward, waiting for those in front of him to gather their carry-on equipment. They all stopped until a crew member opened the hatch to let them out.

Kutnetsov was standing close enough to the front so that when the hatch was raised he was hit by the humidity and heat of the tropics. There was a taste in the air, something almost physical. Kutnetsov didn't know what it was. He just knew

that it was different from the crisp, cold air he had been used
to when he had boarded the plane in Moscow.

He stopped in the hatch, blinking in the bright afternoon
sun, then jumped onto the ground. Putting a hand up, he
shaded his eyes and studied his surroundings. There were
metal and stone buildings, and a jungle that seemed to swarm
down the nearby hills in an attempt to overrun the airfield.

Already he was sweating heavily. He moved away from the
hatch and turned, waiting for the other members of his team.
Senior Lieutenant Andrei Ogarkov—a tall, robust man with
blond hair and eyebrows so fair, they seemed nonexistent—was
next out. He wore a fatigue uniform that had somehow survived the long flight and still looked fresh. It was hard to believe he had been on the aircraft.

Ogarkov saw his team leader and moved toward him. "It's
very hot, isn't it?"

Kutnetsov nodded. "Very hot. I don't think I'm going to
like it here."

"I'll get the men organized," volunteered Ogarkov.
"Where would you like to meet them?"

"Get the equipment located and take it over there." He
pointed to the edge of the ramp, near a modern-looking metal
building. It had two huge windows and there was a radio antenna on the roof. "I'll see if I can find our liaison officer. He
seems to be late."

As Kutnetsov turned, there was a roar behind him. He
stopped and saw a truck, which had been modeled after the
Soviet ZIL-150, coming at him. Behind the windshield there
was a driver and a single passenger. Then, from behind the
building, came a jeep. It looked American-made. There was
only one man in it.

"Maybe our ride has arrived," said Ogarkov.

The truck stopped near the nose of the aircraft, but neither
man in it moved. The jeep pulled up closer. The driver turned
off the engine and climbed out. He was small, with black hair
and olive skin. He wore a khaki uniform and the shoulder
boards of a major. There were no sweat stains on his uniform.
It looked as if he had worn it especially for the meeting.

He approached the two Soviets, stopped, but didn't salute or wait for them to salute. Instead he asked, "Captain Kutnetsov?"

"I'm Captain Kutnetsov."

"I am Major Vin Long Tran, the People's Army of North Vietnam. I have been sent to welcome you to our country." He spoke Russian with only a slight accent.

"Is the truck for us?"

"Yes. You may have your men toss their equipment into it and then they'll be taken to their temporary quarters. If you'll accompany me, I'll take you over to meet Colonel Thuy. He is most anxious to welcome you to our country."

"Ogarkov, have Sergeant Moskvin take charge of the men. Get them settled and then stand by. I'll see what the plans are here."

"Certainly, sir."

"Lead on, Major," said Kutnetsov.

Tran stepped to the jeep and climbed into the driver's seat. Kutnetsov sat on the passenger side. He noticed that the placard in front of him was written in English.

Tran saw where he was looking. "The Americans in South Vietnam donated this to us. They didn't know it at the time." He twisted the ignition switch and started the engine. Grinding the gears, he slipped it into reverse, backed up, spun the wheel and slammed it into first. They roared off the airfield.

Kutnetsov took the opportunity to examine his surroundings. There were low buildings with tin or tile roofs, and an expanse of concrete, some of it in runways and taxiways, was spread out on the grassy valley floor. Heat from the afternoon sun shimmered on the surfaces. Off to one side were several MiG aircraft. Unlike the pictures Kutnetsov had seen of the American base in Saigon, these weren't parked in revetments. They stood at the edge of the runway, lined up like sitting ducks.

Beyond them, at the approach ends of the runways, were antiaircraft guns. There were small 12.7 mm machine guns that could be manned and fired by a lone soldier. Near them were the twin-barreled 23 mm weapons that took a crew of three and which could knock down a fighter flying at twenty thousand feet. It also looked as if there were a couple of ZSU-23/4s, radar-controlled weapons that could throw up a wall of lead that would make it nearly impossible for fighters to attack the airbase.

As they wove their way between the buildings, Kutnetsov saw a number of sweating, tired men in uniform. A few of them carried the Kalashnikov, which was becoming the standard weapon of the Communist world.

They finally pulled up in front of a heavily guarded one-story building. There were sandbags around part of the structure, and the closed windows were fitted with iron bars.

"If you'll come with me, Captain."

Kutnetsov got out of the jeep and followed Tran. The guards nodded to him, coming to attention as he passed. Tran opened the door, which looked as if it were made of metal, then stepped back to let Kutnetsov enter.

The interior was cold. The floors were stone and swept clean. The walls were painted beige and cluttered with posters condemning the Americans, the South Vietnamese, laziness, capitalism and a dozen other crimes against the state. The doors that lined the hallway were all closed and the place seemed to be empty.

Tran took him to the end of the corridor, turned and then opened a door. Kutnetsov was surprised when he entered. He had expected something fancy, maybe carpeting, expensive furniture and curtains. Instead he found the same stone floor and beige walls, with the addition of cheap furniture. Colonel Thuy, wearing a short-sleeved shirt, sat at his desk. He looked up from his writing when the two men opened the door.

Immediately he got to his feet and came around his desk. Tossing his pencil onto the blotter, he held out a hand. "Captain Kutnetsov, we are so happy to have you here. Please, make yourself comfortable and we will talk." He, too, spoke Russian but it was harder to understand him.

Kutnetsov was taken aback. During his military career he'd had little contact with senior officers, and these had always been ass-chewings or rewards for a well-done job. They had always been short meetings with nothing like the warmth being expressed here. Thuy pointed to a couple of old, uncomfortable-looking wooden chairs.

"Sit," said the colonel.

Kutnetsov nodded and sat. He took the black beret from his head and twisted it in his hands. "Thank you, Comrade Colonel."

"Before we start, is there anything I can get you? Refreshment?"

"A cold beverage would be most welcome."

Thuy turned to Tran. "Major?" Thuy sat down in the other chair. "Now, let's see what we can learn about each other."

2

**WAR ZONE D
NORTHWEST OF TAY
NINH CITY, REPUBLIC
OF VIETNAM**

U.S. Army Special Forces Captain MacKenzie K. Gerber lay in the dense jungle vegetation, his eyes on the path that ran from Cambodia into South Vietnam. This was a minor off-shoot of the famous Ho Chi Minh Trail, which was more like a highway than a jungle path. Here, in South Vietnam, it had narrowed until it was little more than a single track through the thick jungle, detouring around the massive trunks of two-hundred-foot-tall teak trees.

Gerber had been lying there motionless for the better part of the day, letting the heat and humidity oppress him like a wet blanket. The rotting vegetation under him was damp, and water from an early-morning rain was just beginning to drip onto the ground. Triple-canopy jungle kept the rain suspended for long periods of time above the ground. Slowly it worked its way from the broad, thick leaves at the top, sliding from one leaf to the next, down the trunk of a tree, until it reached the ground to make Gerber's life more miserable than it already was.

Gerber's tiger-striped fatigues, the standard-issue uniform of the Vietnamese rangers, were soaked from his sweat, the dampness of the ground and the rain. His face was covered with green, brown and black camouflage paint to match the pattern of his fatigues. Sweat had soaked his hair under his boonie hat and dripped down his forehead to splash into his eyes, but he didn't dare move to wipe it away. The quickest way to be seen in the jungle was to move. But a soldier lying still could have an entire division walk right by him without seeing him.

Next to him was his pack containing his food, water and spare ammo. He held his weapon in his right hand, the barrel and the breech off the ground so that they wouldn't get wet or fouled with dirt.

Lost in the green gloom of the jungle, ten or twelve meters to his right, was Master Sergeant Anthony B. Fetterman. Fetterman was a small wiry man who claimed at times to be part-Aztec or part-Sioux and whose black hair and olive skin suggested he was part-Italian. Fetterman had joined the Army as a teenager during World War II, had landed with the American Army in France in 1944 and had stayed with them until the Germans quit the following year. When the Korean War broke out, Fetterman was in the thick of it from almost the first moment the United States entered that conflict.

After Korea Fetterman had found his way into the fledgling Special Forces and had been in it ever since. Like Gerber, he had done one tour in Vietnam already, and on his return to Southeast Asia he had been assigned to MACV-SOG.

Gerber had served a long time with Fetterman, had seen him in action in Vietnam, on R and R in Hong Kong and as an instructor in the World. Fetterman was the most dangerous man Gerber had ever met, his diminutive stature notwithstanding. If Gerber knew he was going to be in trouble, he wanted Fetterman nearby. The Special Forces captain had never encountered a cooler, more efficient combat soldier.

Gerber was hooked to Fetterman by a tiny length of string tied to his little finger on his left hand. A sudden tug would alert Gerber to a problem, so there was no need for verbal communication.

Fetterman, in turn, was hooked to Sergeant Justin "Boom Boom" Tyme. Like the others, he was on his second tour in Vietnam, but unlike them, had been assigned to an A-Detachment again. This meant that he and twelve others were allied with a South Vietnamese Special Forces team known as the Luc Luong Duc Biet. Together they trained the locals to fight the Vietcong and the North Vietnamese. Since Tyme had served with Gerber on his first tour, he had been plucked from Song Be for this mission.

Tyme was a young man who had sandy hair, freckles and a love of weapons that bordered on an obsession. He could tear down and reassemble any small arm in the world, many of them while blindfolded. And like most of the Special Forces, he understood the necessity of lying in the steaming jungle, bathed in sweat and not moving. He understood why they were watching the path with such intensity.

On the other side of him was Sergeant Andy Santini. Unlike the others, Gerber hadn't served with the sergeant on his first tour and only knew him as the sergeant major at the Fifth Special Forces Headquarters in Nha Trang. However, he had worked with Santini on his return to Vietnam, and when this assignment had been given to him, he'd asked that Santini be allowed to tag along.

Gerber's first impression of Santini hadn't been favorable. He had been confronted with a man who had all the earmarks of a real garrison trooper. The day they'd first met, Santini had worn starched fatigues that had shown no signs of sweat, although it had been late afternoon. A .45 in a holster had hung from his pistol belt with the first-aid kit in front so that he had looked like every TV combat soldier ever filmed and, in an attempt to look sharp, he had shaved sometime in the hour before Gerber had met him.

But Santini had also looked like Fetterman. He was a small man with black hair and dark skin. He looked mean but didn't act it. And it turned out he was a good soldier, too. The only reason he had been assigned to Nha Trang was that he had broken his ankle coming in from a combat operation and they hadn't wanted him in the field until he was fully recovered.

With this small team, smaller than it should have been because of the increasing pressure on the Special Forces to supply soldiers for various recons, training posts and direct-action operations, Gerber had been sent out to observe the enemy. He was not to make contact. He was not to engage in combat. He was to lie in wait and observe.

The words of the briefing came back with great clarity. He, along with Fetterman, had been sitting in the office of a Colonel Brown in Saigon. In the South Vietnamese capital there were more colonels than there were sergeants and each had his own air-conditioned office, complete with a huge wooden desk, a green felt blotter, pen-and-pencil set and In and Out baskets. There were always two stuffed chairs in front of the desk for visitors, along with a couch or settee against one wall. Opposite it would be a bookcase loaded with black binders, and above that a framed print, most showing some great moments from the Army's past.

This particular colonel, who looked like a college professor and not a combat officer, and who spoke like one, had explained that after Tet there had been a serious reduction in the number of guerrilla-induced incidents. That was exactly what Brown had called them—guerrilla-induced incidents, which meant the VC had attacked somewhere or blown something up. The colonel's thought, however, was that the incidents were down and he was suggesting that there were now more North Vietnamese in the war.

Gerber had smiled, only because Brown had seemed so serious and because he had removed battlefield casualties from the realm of dead and wounded men to the realm of statistics. Although Gerber didn't like the direction the war was going in, meaning it had become a political football where decisions were made because of politics rather than tactical or strategic necessity, he thought the colonel was right. The VC had become less of a threat after Tet, and their role was being taken over by the North Vietnamese Army.

Because of that, Gerber had said he would take a team into the field to observe. It was an interesting question and one that needed answering. If the Tet offensive had so badly depleted the ranks of the Vietcong that they now had to rely on help from the North, then things had gone better than even the optimists in MACV believed.

This was, of course, in direct opposition to what the American media claimed. But the longer Gerber remained in the Army, the more times he saw reality disagree with the perceptions of the supposedly friendly press.

Now he was lying under a lacy fern, water dripping from it onto his back as he watched a path no more than ten feet in front of him. He had to be that close or the enemy could slip by him unseen. A man skilled in the jungle, moving carefully, could get by anyone if he was separated by only a short distance. It was dangerous being that close to the path, but it couldn't be helped.

Gerber shifted his eyes and looked at his wrist where the black face of his watch was exposed. It was a long time until nightfall. Even without the rays of the sun beating down on him, it was hot. The wind, which sometimes rustled the branches overhead, was like everything else. It couldn't penetrate to the ground. All that was left was the steaming, wet jungle with its buzzing insects, screeching birds and chattering monkeys. It was a quiet, dead place that smelled of wet earth that would occasionally explode into noise as the animals came awake or fled from one another.

Gerber had tuned into the jungle so that when a troop of monkeys crashed through the trees overhead he knew it meant nothing this time. They were merely playing, chasing one another as they moved through the canopy. They weren't fleeing from humans. In minutes their screams and cries died away as they left the area. Gerber had only his own thoughts to keep his mind active so that he didn't relax and fall asleep.

But there was nothing that Gerber could do about it. He had to lie there quietly, his attention focused on the path and the jungle because he couldn't let his mind wander. He couldn't think of a cold beer in Saigon, or of Robin Morrow, the journalist he knew. He couldn't think of snow or swimming pools or of clean sheets in a cool bed. He had to watch the shifting patterns of dark and light around him, waiting for the enemy to show. The last thing he could afford was to let his attention wander.

But wander it did. He felt himself dozing, his eyes closing as if the lids were magnetized. It was the result of too many hours lying perfectly still, the only relief when he rocked onto his side to urinate. And even that wasn't as comforting as it could have been. He had to be careful not to make noise, which meant he had to control his bladder. It became a test of his willpower. Could he actually force the flow into a quiet dribble when he really wanted to let it all go? And he had to be careful he didn't foul his own hiding place. Lying on the damp earth, his uniform soaked was bad enough. He didn't want to add to the misery by wetting himself.

He spent the whole day, more than the day, lying there. They had quietly, carefully, slipped into position before dawn, having crawled through the jungle for most of the night. That in itself had been a chore—moving with the exaggerated slowness of a man crippled by arthritis. When they had finally reached the path, they had backed off it and taken up position, waiting for daylight. The dawn had proved them in the right place, though Gerber had never doubted Fetterman's navigation for a minute. The man seemed to have a sixth sense that guided him through the jungle.

As the sun finally faded, Gerber thought it would now be possible to pull out. They had seen and heard nothing. They would shift during the night, catch some sleep and then find a new hiding place in the morning. But just as he felt they should move, there was a quiet swishing noise in the distance. Not much of a noise, but enough that it alerted him. It sounded like someone walking.

He turned toward the sound and waited. The sunlight was fading fast, what little there had been. The green glow that had filtered through the trees all day was changing to a washed-out gray, then to a charcoal, so that the shadows and the trees merged into one solid background.

But that didn't stop the noise. It came closer. He stared into the advancing blackness, trying to see. He turned his head slowly so that he was looking out of the corner of his eyes, but he still couldn't make out anything. And, just as he was beginning to wonder if he had imagined the noise, there was a gentle tug on the string around his finger. After a hesitation, he felt two more tugs, which told him the danger was real. Someone was out there.

Gerber didn't move. He let his eyes shift right and left so that he could check the positions of his rifle and equipment. His knife, a Ka-bar sharpened to a razorlike edge, was taped upside down on the left side of his harness. By rolling slightly to his left, he could feel the hilt as it pressed into his ribs.

With the approaching darkness, the last thing he wanted was to get into a firefight. The muzzle-flash would give his position away. At night the best weapons were his knife and grenades. They could kill without telling the enemy where he was. And the knife was best if the enemy didn't know anyone was around. Men would disappear and no one would know why.

Now a long, hard pull came, telling him that the enemy was very close to one of his men. But Gerber still hadn't seen anyone, and the noise he'd heard had disappeared. All he could do was wait for the all-clear or until he saw the enemy himself.

He wasn't worried. He had been within inches of the enemy on past patrols and the VC had failed to spot him. It was a question of remaining quiet and calm. Think everything through. The enemy, with no clue that there were Americans in the area, would be sloppy. They always were.

But then, as he began to relax again, there was a single shout. The voice was loud, surprised and not American. It was answered by another and then a burst of fire. The staccato sound shattered the stillness. Gerber knew it wasn't an American weapon. An AK. A short burst. Gerber heard one round snap through the trees over his head.

He was up and moving, sliding to the right as he gathered the string in his left hand and jerked hard, breaking it. Ensuring that his equipment, especially his weapon, was only a foot or so away from him, he moved deeper into the jungle. Gerber knew he had to be careful; it was easy to lose a weapon in dense jungle.

He unsheathed his knife and held it in his right hand, then took a grenade, gripping it in his left, and waited. Around him everything had gotten quiet. The insects and animals had ceased their racket altogether. Then suddenly there was a second shout, and Gerber turned toward it. Because he was out of contact with his men, he couldn't move around. He knew where each of his men were, but now that they were out of touch, he couldn't afford to move. Listening, he silently watched the jungle.

Firing broke out to the left—single shots from an AK-47. There was a crash, more like a dull pop, as a grenade, probably Chicom, detonated. The dirt cascaded back to the ground, sounding like rain on the leaves of the plants. Gerber could smell the burnt gunpowder from the explosion. But still he didn't move. He knew the enemy was searching for him and his men. They were firing and throwing grenades, trying to draw return fire so that they could pinpoint the Americans.

Then there was a rustling of leaves near him. He backed up against a giant teak tree. He could feel the smooth bark against his spine. Huge leaves, now dark brown in the fading light, hung in front of his eyes. There were vines, some of them covered with thorns that snagged clothes, holding tight. Gerber ignored all that and waited patiently.

The first movement was little more than a vibration at the edge of his vision. The man was moving carefully, his weapon held in front of him at port arms. He walked with his knees bent, his head swinging from side to side, giving the appearance of a hunter looking for game. The weapon, just a dark silhouette against the grays of the trees, was an AK-47. The shape was distinctive.

Gerber noticed that the enemy soldier wore a dark green fatiguelike uniform. He had a chest pouch strapped on, and a helmet that looked as if it belonged on safari. He also wore boots. Definitely not VC. NVA. Just as the silly colonel in Saigon had said.

The soldier stopped, his head cocked to one side as if he had heard something. Far away someone shouted in Vietnamese, but the words were lost. The man looked over his shoulder, but didn't retreat. Instead, he continued forward, peering into the gathering gloom.

Gerber was sure the man would walk right by, but he turned and moved toward Gerber. The Special Forces captain slipped the grenade into the pocket of his jungle fatigue jacket and crouched, letting the man come to him.

He was unaware of the rest of the jungle. The heat and humidity had ceased to exist for him. He concentrated on the enemy soldier, letting his eyes slide away occasionally, afraid he was about to communicate his presence to the enemy through ESP. He kept the knife low, the blade pointed at the ground.

The NVA soldier kept coming. He swiveled his head, but didn't seem to be searching hard as he stepped past Gerber and then stopped, his feet next to Gerber's equipment, which he didn't see, either.

Like lightning, Gerber struck. He stepped up behind the man, grabbed him under the chin and lifted. As he did, he pulled the man to the rear. The NVA soldier's back was against the fulcrum of Gerber's knee. Arched there, he dropped his rifle and grabbed at Gerber's hand. There was a whisper like silk ripping as the man spasmed once. Then he kicked outward and tried to leap free.

But very quickly there was a splash of hot blood, and the odor of copper overwhelmed everything around them. Gerber kept up the pressure against the man's chin, feeling him buck once, twice, and then go limp. The odor of copper was replaced by the stench of released bowels.

Gerber rolled the body onto a fern, then picked up the enemy's weapon and slung it over his shoulder. He moved back to where his equipment was and crouched. Around him was the noise of the strange battle.

Coming through the trees were the quiet grunts of the fight—Americans using knives against the enemy. Then there was the rattle of automatic weapon fire, and Gerber saw the muzzle-flashes and bright green tracers. He pulled a grenade and jerked the pin. Hesitating, he listened, then saw the NVA fire again. This time he threw the grenade at the enemy position.

He heard it crash through the trees as he dropped to the ground. A few seconds of silence passed and then there was an explosion. Through gaps in the vegetation he saw the fountain of sparks, a flaming explosion that spread shrapnel over ten meters of jungle. There was no response from the enemy.

And then it was quiet. Gerber climbed to one knee, his hand on the pistol grip of his M-16, thumb on the safety. His eyes roamed over the blackness of the jungle. Now he couldn't see more than a foot or two in front of him. He sensed there was something moving somewhere just outside his range of vision.

Gerber stayed where he was, listening. There was movement to his left again, but this time he didn't attack. Instead, he waited until he heard the quiet call from Fetterman. They didn't need to bother with codes and signals because Gerber recognized the master sergeant's voice.

He said simply, "Coming in."

Fetterman stepped near Gerber and both men put out a hand. When Fetterman felt it, he moved closer and pressed his lips against the captain's ear. "We got twelve of them. Think that was everyone. No one escaped."

"All NVA?"

"Couldn't tell. A couple were wearing black pajamas, so they could have been Vietcong."

"But you don't think so," said Gerber.

"No, sir. I think they were NVA dressed as VC. That confirms the colonel's suspicions."

Gerber nodded, then realized Fetterman would never be able to see the gesture in the inky blackness of the jungle. "Okay, Master Sergeant, it's time to get out of here. If there's anyone else around, they had to hear the noise. We take five minutes, gather the weapons, then we scram."

"Yes, sir."

KUTNETSOV ENTERED the long, low building and heard a burst of laughter from the right. He turned in that direction and entered the squad bay. It was a large, open room that ran the length of the building. A series of windows under the roof opened into the dark, buzzing night to facilitate circulation of air. Overhead were three whirling fans. The wall that separated this room from the rest of the building didn't reach all the way to either the floor or the ceiling. It had been designed so that air would be able to blow around it.

The men of Kutnetsov's team were scattered around the room, sitting on cots or the floor, their equipment piled around them. The weapons expert, Sergeant Yuri Baykal, had a rifle broken down into small pieces on a white sheet in front of him. He was on his hands and knees, studying it closely.

Kutnetsov crouched beside him. He looked at the weapon's parts. "What do you have here?"

Baykal shot a glance at his captain. "What I have here is a poor copy of our Kalashnikov. A very poor copy indeed, manufactured by our Vietnamese comrades."

"What's wrong with it?"

"There's no quality control." He picked up the trigger housing group, broke it apart and pointed. "See here. And here. The edges are rough. They haven't been filed. The action isn't smooth and could get hung up." He dropped it onto the sheet and grabbed another bit. Gritting his teeth, he bent it. "I shouldn't be able to do that. The metal's inferior."

Kutnetsov nodded. "Where did you get this?"

"I traded one of the guards for it. Gave him one of ours, telling him I wanted one of theirs as a souvenir." Baykal grinned. "He was only too happy to trade."

"I can see why."

"No, sir, I don't think you do. He had no idea his weapon was of such poor quality." Baykal sat down and shook his head. "They stamp them out as fast as they can. These weapons probably wouldn't last in a sustained firefight."

"What about those made by our Chinese allies?"

Now Baykal nodded. "Better. Much better. They seem to understand the subtleties of making weapons. Not as good as those manufactured by us, but very good."

"So, first we must equip our teams with Soviet-made weapons."

"Either that or some of the M-1s or carbines they've gotten from the South. Those weapons are plentiful enough that I can find spare parts, and ammunition for them isn't hard to obtain."

"Good. Have you had a chance to examine the ammunition made here?"

"Not to the degree I'd like, but from what I've seen, the quality is as poor as that of the weapons. They don't pay attention to lab work. They throw bullets together as if they're baking a cake. A little of this, a little of that. Gives them some batches that are highly explosive and others that aren't much better than low-grade fireworks."

Kutnetsov stood. "So we must be careful of the weapons made by our comrades."

"Yes, sir. I'll look at their mortars and machine guns as soon as I have a chance."

"Hard to mess up a mortar."

"I think these people will find a way to do it. They refuse to understand that you must take care of details before you move into battle. They just want to charge into the South."

"Well, that's not our problem. When we get back home, you may write a report to be forwarded."

"Yes, sir, to be lost in the bureaucratic channels and then filed."

Kutnetsov shrugged. "Sometimes someone reads them and acts on them. After all, we're here."

"Yes, sir."

Baykal didn't look satisfied. He went back to work, slowly reassembling the AK as he searched for imperfections in the manufacture.

Kutnetsov turned and looked around the room for his operations sergeant. He found Moskvin at the far end, sitting on the edge of his cot in a sweat-soaked T-shirt. As Kutnetsov approached, he saw that the man was studying a checklist held in one meaty hand.

"How's it going, Sergeant?"

When Moskvin saw the captain, he leaped to his feet. "Just fine, sir."

"Sit down, Viktor. We're not trainees anymore."

"Yes, sir."

"Now, how are things going?"

"I checked on our equipment. Everything seems to have made it and is in good shape. Just a matter of loading it onto the trucks for transport to our permanent station."

Kutnetsov sat down next to the burly sergeant. "You sound surprised."

"Yes, sir. I was sure we'd lose some of it after we landed. Our Vietnamese allies tend to have sticky fingers, but I can't see where anything has been taken." He hooked a thumb over his shoulder. "Only young Yuri seems to have made a bad trade."

"I view that as a bit of intelligence gathering. Finding out about local capabilities."

"Then he should let Sergeant Salmonov know what he's found."

"Viktor, I came over here to—"

The sudden wail of a siren started as a low growl and built to a high-pitched scream. Kutnetsov stood and stared out of the window. He saw only blackness.

"What in hell!" cried Moskvin.

At that moment, Colonel Thuy burst into the room. "Come with me," he called. "We must head for shelter."

"What is it?" demanded Kutnetsov.

"The Americans. An air raid. Please come with me."

Just then a quiet popping began in the distance. The sound grew until Kutnetsov recognized it as the firing of antiaircraft weapons. First the noise seemed far away, but as the American jets approached, it became louder.

As they raced for the door, one of the men stooped to pick up a duffel bag of gear.

"Leave that," ordered Thuy. "We must hurry."

Thuy ran outside into the hot, dark night and stopped. As the men from the barracks joined him, he pointed to a low sandbagged wall. ''Air raid shelter.''

Kutnetsov halted beside him. The banging of the antiaircraft weapons had come closer. At the end of the runways were the orange-yellow flashes of the 23 mm weapons. Green tracers from the 12.7 danced skyward, seeming to climb lazily into the night. Those were quickly joined by others until the sky was alive with glowing green balls.

The Soviets ran past Kutnetsov and Thuy. One fell, sprawling on his chest. He came to his feet in a single, fluid motion, brushing at the dirt on his chest as he sprinted for the protection of the bunker.

As the men disappeared on the other side of the sandbags, the rumbling blasts began. They were far away but could be felt through the soles of the feet. As they came closer, though, they became deafening. Orange balls of flame burst upward, lighting the ground like giant strobes.

Thuy, who had seemed fairly calm, now tugged at Kutnetsov. ''They're coming at us.'' He took off, running across the tarmac and grass.

For a moment Kutnetsov stood watching the show, as if mesmerized. There were no spotlights stabbing into the sky because everything was radar-guided now. The hammering of the big weapons, combined with the rumbling explosions of the dropping bombs, created one long detonation. Kutnetsov felt the shock waves of the bombs as they split the air.

In the sky he could see only the green and white tracers from the North Vietnamese weapons. They swarmed into the night, tumbling upward, but striking nothing. Intermittently, he heard the roar of jet engines.

Finally he turned and ran. He leaped over the low wall of sandbags and was surprised to find a hole on the other side. Falling heavily, he landed on his hip with a grunt of pain. As he corrected himself, he noticed he was in a trench that angled downward into a tiny doorway. Keeping his head down, he scrambled forward.

When he reached the bunker doorway, the air vibrated with a huge explosion. The rattling of the weapons seemed right on top of him now. As the red-hot air of fiery explosion washed over, filling the trench, he leaped into the bunker.

The walls around him vibrated and shook, and the cascading dirt started men coughing and choking. One of his Soviet troops was mumbling quietly while a Vietnamese screamed. The air was hot and dank and filled with the smell of fear.

Kutnetsov sat up and looked around him. The space was crowded, the men jammed together shoulder to shoulder. Some were sitting on the floor, others standing, leaning against the wooden plank walls. A single naked light bulb hung from the ceiling on bare wires. It glowed dim yellow.

For a moment everything hung suspended in time. The roaring outside increased to a crescendo and then diminished. Dust hung heavy and the smell of burning fuel assaulted Kutnetsov's nostrils.

"How long will this last?" he asked Thuy.

"A few more minutes. These never last too long."

Kutnetsov nodded and moved back to the doorway. He noticed it was brighter on the field. Something was burning.

"Not our equipment," he prayed. "Anything but that."

3

THE OFFICE OF MAJOR
GENERAL WILSON P.
STEWARD, THE
PENTAGON
WASHINGTON, D.C.

Rawlings sat in a leather chair, the briefcase no longer hand-cuffed to his wrist now that he was inside a restricted area. He was waiting for permission to brief General Steward. The briefcase rested against his leg so that he would feel if anyone touched it. In his hands he held a recent copy of *Newsweek* that featured a long story on American involvement in Vietnam, including an analysis on the battle at Hue during Tet. But he wasn't reading it, nor was he looking at the plush surroundings. He wasn't interested in the thick blue carpeting or the huge wooden desk where a secretary sat typing. He didn't care about the wall of books, all hardbound, some of them expensive leather editions, nor did he care about the oil paintings on the walls.

When he had walked in, he'd noticed it all and been suitably impressed. During his short military career, he hadn't had the opportunity to visit many generals in their offices, and when he'd first entered Steward's office, he'd wondered if the taxpayers knew how much money was being spent to ensure the general's comfort. But, as he'd sat down in the leather chair next to the matching couch, he'd found himself watching Sheila Halliday instead. Until they had been thrown together on the trip, he had never really met her. She was just one of the lieutenants who worked in one of the other offices in the Intel section. Their paths had rarely crossed.

Now she sat there quietly absorbed in a copy of *Time*. She was wearing a Class A uniform that had a tight, short skirt. Rawlings found he couldn't keep his eyes off her legs. There was a run in her stocking that started at her knee. Occasionally, without looking, she reached down and scratched at it.

Rawlings tried to read his *Newsweek*. He was interested in what was happening in Vietnam because he believed that if they didn't get the war wrapped up fast enough, he'd find himself ordered over. But even with that incentive, he was busy watching Sheila's legs. And she didn't seem to know or care about it.

Finally he closed the magazine and spoke. "The hotel arrangements made?"

"Yes. I didn't have to do a thing. Someone here took care of it. We'll have transportation to the hotel as soon as we're finished." She smiled as if he'd asked her the dumbest thing in the world.

"And we have access to a safe for the classified material?"

"Yes, Dave, all of that's arranged." She closed her magazine and stared at him. "All you have to do is show the material to the general. That's all."

He wanted to say something more to her, but didn't know what. She was being patient with him, as if she were the senior officer and he the subordinate. That was the last thing he wanted. But before he could say anything witty, a major entered the office and walked over to him.

"Lieutenant Rawlings?"

Rawlings got to his feet. "Yes, sir."

"I'm Major Comstock, General Steward's aide. The general will see you now. Please remember that the general is extremely busy and has no tolerance for levity. Keep the briefing short and to the point. Do you have visual aids?"

"I have vu-graphs and photos. One duplicates the other."

"All right. Give me the vu-graphs and I'll have one of our people put them on."

Rawlings hesitated. "They're all classified."

"We're all cleared. You can't work in this area if you don't have a security clearance."

Still Rawlings hesitated. He knew all the rules and regulations about safeguarding classified material. He knew it was his responsibility to protect the material, and if it got into unauthorized hands, his head would be the one on the chopping block.

"Give me the vu-graphs," Comstock repeated.

Rawlings looked at Halliday. She just sat there watching the exchange. Finally Rawlings handed the package over to the major and asked, "How do I get the man to change them?"

"You'll be given a control. It signals the projectionist. Are these in the order you want them?"

"Yes, sir."

"Then let's go." He noticed that Halliday had gotten to her feet. "Will she be briefing, too?"

"No, sir."

Comstock nodded. "You may wait out here, Lieutenant."

"Yes, sir," she said.

Rawlings followed the major into the other office. As he entered, he saw what opulence was all about. The room was gigantic, and if they'd hung hoops on opposite walls, they could have played basketball in it. The carpeting was light blue with a crest woven into it that Rawlings didn't recognize. A desk, a massive thing of rich, dark wood, stood in the corner along with a wall lined with books, more of the same from the outer office. Models of airplanes and tanks sat on some of the shelves. There was a red flag with white stars near the desk.

At the other end of the room was a large conference table. A screen that pulled down from the ceiling was open, and the curtains had been drawn to cut off the outside light. The general sat there, his head bent as he read from a document.

General Steward didn't look up. He merely waved a hand, indicating that Rawlings and Comstock should enter. As they approached the table, the general closed his folder. "I don't have a lot of time today, Lieutenant. You'll have to impress me quickly or get out.''

Before Rawlings could say anything, the general added, ''Excuse my rudeness, it's an occupational hazard. Once you reach general, you tend to forget how it was at the other end of the spectrum. Today I'm swamped and I'm afraid they dumped you on me.''

''I'll be brief, General.''

''Jim, if you'll get the lights, we'll get this show on the road.''

''Yes, sir,'' said Comstock. Plucking a small box from the seat of a chair, he slipped it to Rawlings and whispered, ''When you want the vu-graph changed, punch the white button. Hit the red one if you want to go back. And please hurry.''

Rawlings suddenly started to sweat. He could feel it beading on his forehead and trickling down his sides. For a moment he thought he might be sick. He nodded dumbly and took the control from the major. As the aide moved across the room, Rawlings set his notes on the table in front of him and knew that he would never be able to read them. He couldn't see them.

Then the lights went out and Rawlings realized he would have to talk. He wanted to be out of there. Anywhere. Vietnam even. His throat felt parched. He needed a large glass of water, but all he could do was clear his throat and begin the briefing.

He spoke too quickly, stumbling over words, trying to get through the ordeal as fast as possible. Stepping to the screen once, he showed where a pile of dirt had been one day six months ago, and then pointed out the new well. When he finished, he moved back to the table and rushed through the rest of the briefing.

As soon as it was over, the general asked two questions. One was how sure Rawlings was of his observations.

Rawlings swallowed. ''They're right there for all to see, General. The modifications to the site have been made and the North Vietnamese have tried to cover them up.''

"What do you think is going on there?"

"I don't know, sir. I only reported my observations given the instructions and guidelines we use."

Steward stood. "Thank you, Lieutenant. Please stay in touch. Leave the name of your hotel with my aide before you go, in case I have other questions."

Rawlings gathered up his material and slipped out of the office. He stopped in front of Halliday. "We have to stay in town."

She nodded. "I thought as much. That's why they made the reservations. Can we go now?"

"Yeah, but we have to stay in touch."

AS SOON AS COMSTOCK returned to the office, Steward handed him a sheet of paper. "While you were out I put together this list of things to be done."

The aide took it. "They're not going to like it."

"I don't know where that idea came from," said Steward, shaking his head. "People in the military aren't required to like their orders. They're supposed to obey them."

"Into the valley of death?" questioned the major.

"If that becomes necessary. But this is only a minor inconvenience."

"Yes, sir, though I think a forced TDY move is more than a minor inconvenience."

"Jim, I want those people here. Both of them. And I don't want either returning to Wright-Patterson until this is resolved one way or the other. Now you get on it."

Comstock slipped into one of the chairs and leaned back. He waved the paper. "Not even an opportunity to collect extra clothes?"

"I think the order speaks for itself. I want them billeted on one of the bases around here or damned close to it. By tomorrow at the latest. Anything they need, they can buy and bill it to the government as long as they don't get too extravagant."

"Excuse me, General, but why is this necessary?"

Steward closed the folder in front of him and pinched the bridge of his nose as if he was very tired. "You heard the briefing. We've got a POW camp going up close to the DMZ. That gives us the opportunity to sneak in and grab some of our men. I don't want this compromised in any fashion, so I want those people kept here.''

''But Rawlings briefed his staff at Wright-Patterson. The people in his shop know what he found.''

''And orders will be issued to cover that. But I want them here and I don't want any more arguments about it.''

''Yes, General. Anything else?''

''As a matter of fact, yes, I want you to set up a meeting with General Wheeler as soon as possible. Then get in touch with someone at Fort Bragg, at the unconventional warfare school, and have him up here to answer a few questions. Then get hold of General Rydell of the Air Force and tell him I might ask for a special bombing mission.''

''Yes, sir. Anything else?''

Now Steward smiled. ''And call my wife to tell her I might be a little late for dinner tonight.''

''Of course.''

PROGRESS THROUGH the triple-canopy jungle at night was very slow. Gerber and his recon team had to move carefully, almost feeling their way along because there was so little light. No starlight, and very little moonlight, filtered through the various levels of canopy. There were some dim glows caused by the decaying vegetation, but for the most part it was dark, hot and humid. And quiet. Not even the insects buzzed.

Gerber let Fetterman find his own path through the vegetation. He had instructed the master sergeant simply to move in a certain direction and left it to Fetterman to get them out of the jungle so that they could be picked up.

The tiny patrol stuck together, none of them more than a foot or so apart. They almost had to walk with one hand on the shoulder of the man ahead in order not to become separated in the dark. It was slow work, moving carefully to avoid making noise or walking into a tree. They used a technique of setting the heel down gently and then rolling the foot forward until it was completely on the ground. The weight had to be shifted slowly so that any obstacle could be felt. They were actually trying to avoid snapping a twig or rustling the bushes, but the method also helped to find pressure plates on booby traps, and it gave each of the men the opportunity to hear the clicking as a land mine armed itself.

It was hot, nerve-racking work that strained all the senses. Gerber felt his eyes burn and his ears twitch. His breathing had begun to speed up and he consciously forced himself into a more rhythmic pattern. He heard nothing but the blood pounding in his own ears and damned it. He kept his eyes moving, only to see a solid blackness around him that was occasionally broken by dark grays or deeper blacks.

The muscles in his legs, especially his calves, screamed with each step. Moving so carefully demanded peak physical conditioning. And now the added weight from his pack and the extra weapon caused his shoulders and back to ache. He had ordered the men to pick up all the weapons and extra ammo carried by the NVA soldiers.

Gerber was certain they were NVA. Close examination had proven that. Although a couple were dressed as VC guides, it was obvious they were all NVA. Not one of them was a VC. The close-cropped hair and the perfect identity cards left no doubt in Gerber's mind.

Gerber wasn't sure they had proven the colonel's point with only one patrol, but it was indicative of something. In the past few weeks Gerber couldn't remember seeing any Vietcong; the enemy had all been North Vietnamese.

There was one other proof of that. None of the weapons they had picked up were of North Vietnamese manufacture. All were Chicom except for one AK that had Russian markings. Gerber knew, as did nearly everyone in Special Forces, that the NVA was equipped with the higher quality weapons made outside North Vietnam. It was only the VC who had the inferior AKs made in the North, or who had to pick up weapons after an ambush.

But all this was taking his mind away from the problem at hand. He had to concentrate on what he was doing, so he forced his mind back to the jungle, listening and looking harder for the enemy.

There was a sudden rush of cool air, a breath of freshness that had somehow penetrated the canopy, and then the jungle opened up and the sky blazed with stars. It was crystal clear overhead, like a wintry evening in the country, except that the season was anything but winter.

Fetterman dropped to one knee and waved a hand. Gerber slipped to the jungle floor and studied the clearing in front of him. There were a series of rice paddies that came almost to the edge of the jungle. Across the paddies, nearly a klick away, was more jungle. It was as if they had reached a river valley between two green granite cliffs. The alluvial plain had been cultivated, but instead of granite cliffs there were walls of solid jungle and the river was little more than a stream. The monsoon and some irrigation would keep the paddies full of water until it was needed.

Without a word the rest of the team spread out. Santini faced the direction they had just come while Tyme moved toward the edge of the clearing.

Gerber leaned close to Fetterman. "We can stay here until morning and then request a chopper."

"That's what I thought, sir. Plenty of room for them to land."

For a moment Gerber was going to suggest they break up into two teams so that they could get some rest. But he decided against it. Dawn was only a couple of hours away, and the chopper would be there within minutes of that. Everyone would just have to remain awake for another few hours and then they could spend hours in bed, some of it sleeping.

"Let's settle in, but stay alert. We're too far into this mission to get someone hurt now."

THE DAMAGE TO THE AIRFIELD had been limited to the row of jets and to two of the hangars. The jets, MiG-19 Farmers, were now little more than blackened rubble that resembled a scrap heap. The hangars were twisted steel skeletons that were still smoking. The fire fighting capability had been wasted trying to save the jets once the bombing had stopped. They had failed.

Kutnetsov stood in the early-morning sun, watching the Vietnamese scramble to get the mess cleaned up before the Americans could perform a bomb-assessment flight. He knew the Americans would want to know how much damage had been inflicted, and although photos of the raid would have been taken the night before, probably by the last aircraft in formation, they sometimes ran morning cross-checks.

"We have the trucks loaded now, Captain."

Kutnetsov turned and stared at Sergeant Moskvin. "Then we should get out of here before the Americans try to kill us again."

"You don't think the raid was directed against us, do you, sir?"

"No, of course not. It was a coincidence. If they had learned of our presence, they wouldn't have wasted their time on the jets and hangars."

"Yes, sir. Of course."

Kutnetsov wanted to check each of the trucks to make sure everything had been loaded properly, but knew he couldn't. The delay was one problem. The other was that the men would realize what he was doing and feel he didn't trust them. If that happened, they would start doping off because they knew that no matter what they did, he would check it so that there was no reason to do it right.

Instead, he watched Moskvin climb into the cab of the first truck. Kutnetsov moved to the front and got into the jeep. The driver nodded, but didn't speak. He started the engine and turned to look at Colonel Thuy, who was in the back.

"You may begin."

"What about the Americans?" asked Kutnetsov.

"They shouldn't be a problem. The daylight bombing raids are normally accomplished by their big bombers or carrier-based fighters operating from high altitude. They're not searching for targets of opportunity. They already have their targets assigned and rarely venture into this area. We're too far from the main targets farther north."

"Still . . ."

"Still," said Thuy, "we've learned how to avoid them if they appear. I think their restrictions make it hard for them to hurt us."

The convoy lurched forward, rumbling past the remains of the hangars where men now worked feverishly. They turned onto a paved road that was barely wide enough for the ZIL trucks. Kutnetsov looked over his shoulder once, as if to confirm that the rest of the convoy was behind him.

On both sides of the road were rice paddies as far as the eye could see. It was as if they were driving on a wide dike. Farmers worked in knee-deep water, bent over, their black pajamas rolled above their knees. All of them wore the coolie hats that looked like something from another age. A few men trudged behind water buffalo that seemed to be moving in slow motion.

It was quiet now, the only sound the rush of wind and the occasional pop of static from the radio. Kutnetsov put one foot up on the dashboard of the jeep and thought about the heat. It was much too hot for this time of year. At least it would have been if this were Moscow where he belonged. Fighting in the jungle was something that should be left to the low-ranking people. Soviet soldiers shouldn't be detailed to such a task.

The road branched and they turned south. In the distance was a solid wall of green. At first it seemed they were approaching heavily forested foothills, but as they neared it was evident that it was jungle.

The road entered the dense vegetation, narrowed and became a mud track. It was like driving through a living cave of deep greens with only an occasional flash of color—a bright bird or flower caught in the glowing green twilight of the jungle. Thick tree limbs and branches of leafy ferns brushed the sides of the vehicles. Progress was slowed until it was nearly a crawl.

Although it had been sunny when they had entered the jungle, the driver now turned on the windshield wipers. Water dripped from the top of the canopy, down the trunks of the trees to the big, shallow dish leaves and then to the ground, making the roadway muddy. They splashed along, the mud splashing up into the jeep, but the driver didn't notice.

Kutnetsov was surprised there wasn't a wider variety of color. He had envisioned the jungle as being alive with all kinds of plant and animal life that would add to the color, but everything was one or another hue of green. Incongruously the thought occurred to him that the army had designed the jungle and painted everything in it the same hideous color.

They rounded a corner and the driver slowed. Colonel Thuy leaned forward and tapped Kutnetsov on the shoulder. "We have to cross a river now."

They stopped at the edge of a wide stream. The jungle canopy stretched almost unbroken all the way from one bank to the other, but there were places where it was spotty over the river at the center. Sunlight poked through there, reflecting off the water like spinning lights in mirrors.

"Is there a problem?"

"No. Just wait."

The driver climbed out of the jeep and walked to the edge of the water. He hesitated there and then stepped off. Kutnetsov thought they were checking the depth at the middle, but the water never reached the man's ankles. When he got to the center, he stood, his head back, staring into the sunlight. He moved right and left and then returned to the jeep.

"What was that all about?"

Thuy grinned. "It's to fool the Americans. They like to bomb our bridges, so we've learned to build them under the surface of the water. From the air it's impossible to see the bridge. The driver was making sure there were no aircraft coming. We don't want to be caught in the middle of the stream with the Americans over us."

The driver, back behind the wheel, dropped the jeep into gear and rolled forward slowly. The front tires entered the water. He gave the engine a little gas, and they drove into the stream.

Over the sound of the engine was the buzz of insects. A cloud of mosquitoes seemed to be hanging in the air above the river. The cloud was stationary for a moment and then fragmented.

Some of the mosquitoes flew off toward the jungle while the rest swooped down on the convoy. Kutnetsov ducked instinctively and then swatted at his face. In the field, when it counted, he wouldn't have bothered, but now, riding in a jeep, it didn't matter.

He leaned over, scooped water from the river and wiped it over his face and hands. The mosquitoes didn't mind the water. They continued to attack.

With the water splashing up over the hood of the jeep, the driver tried to get out of the river quickly. Waving at the air, he ducked around, his eyes on the road. He kept speeding up until they pulled up on the opposite bank. As they left the river, the mosquitoes broke off the assault.

Once they were clear, they stopped long enough to make sure that each of the trucks of the convoy had made it safely. When all the trucks joined them, they continued on.

Late in the afternoon they pulled over to the side of the road. When the whole convoy was parked, Colonel Thuy said, "We rest for a while. It's another several hours to the camp. We eat some lunch and then move on."

4

MACV HEADQUARTERS
SAIGON

Gerber and Fetterman sat in a small conference room and waited for Colonel Brown to finish writing in his folder. The room held a screen at one end and a slide projector on a tiny table at the other. The walls were wooden and painted the same light green as walls on all Army posts around the world. The conference table was large enough for only eight people and was scarred with cigarette burns. There was only one picture in the room. It showed the U.S. Army in the Philippines.

Although the room was large enough for more people, it held only the three men. Gerber and Fetterman had taken showers, shaved and changed into clean jungle fatigues earlier. Tyme and Santini had been released as soon as they had arrived in Saigon and were waiting downtown at the Carasel Hotel.

Brown finished with his notes and looked up. Again he asked, "You're sure the men were North Vietnamese? All of them?"

Gerber nodded. "It was dark, so our examination wasn't as thorough as we would have liked, but they were North Vietnamese. The close-cropped hair, the uniforms, the discipline, all suggested they were well-trained regulars and not guerrillas of the Vietcong."

"Okay," said the colonel. "Could you tell if they were originally from North Vietnam?"

Fetterman shook his head. "Come again, sir?"

"I mean, were the men born in the North or the South?"

"There's no way to tell that, sir," said Gerber. "There are men in the South Vietnamese army who hate the Communists but who were born in the North before the country was divided. I'm sure the opposite could be said."

Brown made a note and began reading from another of the documents.

Gerber stifled a yawn. He blinked rapidly and wished he could get up to walk around.

Apparently Brown saw that and said, "If I'm boring you, Captain, I'm sorry."

"No, sir," responded Gerber. "I'm tired. I didn't get much sleep in the past few days."

Brown set his pencil down carefully, folded his hands and asked, "Why's that?"

"Wasn't much opportunity in the field."

"Why's that?" repeated Brown.

Gerber shrugged. "It was a short recon and there wasn't the opportunity to sleep. We needed to stay awake most of the time."

"In my experience, Captain, we had time to sleep during long patrols. Half the men stayed alert while the others napped."

"Yes, sir," said Gerber. "But this was a short patrol with only a few men. It seemed there were no opportunities for a lot of sleep."

"Yes, well," said Brown. He picked up his pencil and made a note. "Then, in your opinion, the men you saw were all North Vietnamese."

"Yes, sir. We saw no Vietcong," repeated Gerber. "Although some of the North Vietnamese were dressed as Vietcong."

"But you attached no significance to this?"

Gerber glanced at Fetterman, then turned back to face the colonel. "No, sir. We've seen it in the past. It's indicative of the North Vietnamese trying to slip people into the South."

Now Brown nodded. He added a note to his file and then rocked back. Lacing his hands behind his head, he said, "I think I have everything I need." Then he rocked forward and closed his file. Standing, he added, "There are things I might want to ask you, so don't get too far afield."

With that, he left the room. Fetterman watched the door close. "All right, Captain, let's get out of here and go find Tyme and Santini."

"Don't you ever think there might be someone else I'd like to find?"

Fetterman nodded. "Yes, sir, I do. But I figured Miss Morrow would have to work during the day. She must work sometime."

"Yes," agreed Gerber.

"So I figured you'd want to head downtown and have a beer with Tyme and Santini."

"You figured right," said Gerber.

They left the conference room and entered a corridor with a dirty green tile floor. The wooden walls were painted the same color as the walls of the conference room and were lined with posters. As well, there were bulletin boards covered with directives that no one read.

They turned a corner and moved to the double doors that led outside. Fetterman opened the first and Gerber got the second. As he opened it, the heat and humidity overwhelmed the air-conditioning. Gerber shuddered involuntarily as they moved outside.

"You arrange for a taxi?" asked Gerber.

"No, sir." But as he spoke an old Ford pulled into the parking lot. It seemed to be a dull red, but it could have been a coating of dust. Two men climbed out of the back and started for the building. The driver got out and looked directly at Fetterman. "I think we've found a ride," the master sergeant said.

Gerber nodded, but when he reached the cab he wasn't sure he wanted to enter it. There were cigarette butts, papers, beer cans and even a used condom on the floor. The back seat was stained and the rear window was cracked. "Maybe we should wait for the next one."

"Come on, Captain. You'll wash."

Gerber shrugged and climbed into the back. There was a slight odor of vomit. As Fetterman got in, the driver slipped behind the wheel. He twisted around and asked, "Where to, Joe?"

"Downtown," said Fetterman. "Carasel Hotel."

With a wide grin the driver gunned the vehicle. Gravel rattled under the fenders and threw up a cloud of dust. The driver barely missed a light pole, corrected the drifting cab, then burst out of the lot.

They rocketed down wide palm-lined streets filled with traffic. The roar of Army trucks and jeeps and civilian cars assaulted the senses. Lambretta scooters wove in and out of traffic. Some of them sported a flat bed at the rear to carry passengers. And everywhere there were bicycles, ridden by both men and women. Thousands of pedestrians lined the sidewalks, some dodging the vehicles. Men in lurid Hawaiian shirts and baggy pants intermingled with others wearing uniforms. There were Vietnamese in uniform and civilian clothes while the women wore traditional garb or short skirts and tight blouses.

Gerber let the roar of the trucks and the insectile buzz of the Lambrettas wash over him. Rock music from any one of a dozen bars challenged the less raucous country and western music from any of another dozen. There was the blare of car horns and popping sounds that might have been a weapon or a string of firecrackers.

They turned down a narrow street, dodging the White Mice in the traffic island. One of them blew his whistle and waved at the cab, forcing it to swerve.

When they slowed again, Gerber felt the heat and humidity of Saigon. It seemed to be even more oppressive here than in the jungle. Maybe it was because the heat was reflected from the concrete and stone of the buildings. The humidity hung heavy in the air without the slightest breeze to move it.

And there was the stench of the city. Open sewers that drew flies and disease, the smell of half-burned diesel and the odor of the humidity gave Gerber the sudden urge to wash.

He turned and saw a dozen men, some missing arms or legs or both, begging on the sidewalk. The crowd ignored them. Kids, not much older than six or seven, were following the pedestrians, demanding money or asking for cigarettes. Gerber shook his head as he watched it all, seeing it as the symptoms of a corrupt system. There were men in Saigon who sat in air-conditioned offices and made more money than they could ever spend while others crouched in rice paddies and jungles, hoping they would survive the day. Or the hour.

Saigon was no longer a city that could be called the Pearl of the Orient. There was too much sleaze, too much greed. There was an undercurrent in the city, something that drove the people to live life at a frantic pace. Maybe they expected it all to end soon, collapse into smoke and fire. Perhaps they were trying to get everything they could before that happened. People would do things in Saigon that they wouldn't do anywhere else. Rules and laws didn't apply in the South Vietnamese capital. The people sensed something ominous on the horizon and believed they had the right to take everything they could.

Gerber closed his eyes and tried to rest for a moment, but at that moment the taxi pulled to the curb. Before the doorman could get down the steps outside the hotel, Gerber had opened the car door himself. Fetterman followed him, but then bent down so that he could talk to the driver.

"I get you here, Joe. One thousand P."

Fetterman shook his head. "Two hundred P."

"Joe, you numbah ten. You cheat me. I call cop."

"Two hundred P," repeated Fetterman.

"You take food from my children. You make me starve. Eight hundred P."

Fetterman grinned. "Three hundred."

The driver returned the grin, showing broken yellow teeth. "Seven hundred P. You pay me now."

"No way," said Fetterman. "I'll give you four hundred and a tip of fifty P."

"You give me six hundred and a tip," said the driver.

Fetterman nodded. "Six hundred and no tip."

"Okay, Joe. Six hundred P."

Fetterman took out a wad of cash. The driver spotted the MPC and said, "You give me five dollars, MPC."

"No way," said Fetterman. "Four dollars."

"Okay, Joe," said the driver. "Four dollars, MPC."

Fetterman peeled off the four one-dollar bills and gave them to the driver. Four dollars was less than the six hundred piasters that they had settled on, but many of Vietnamese preferred the Monopoly money issued by the American military because they felt it was better than their own money. Fetterman didn't understand the feeling, but he didn't mind getting the reduced rate.

As he turned, Gerber asked, "You finished browbeating the locals?"

"Captain, I told you before that you have to bargain with them. If you don't, you inflate the economy and everything gets more expensive. The people can't afford to live, and runaway inflation is the result."

"Tony," said Gerber, "I'm in no mood for one of your lectures."

"All right. Then let's go drink."

They walked up the three steps that led to the huge brass-and-glass door, which was opened by the man standing there. As they entered, Gerber said, "I'll meet you in the bar. I want to make a phone call."

"Yes, sir. Tell Miss Morrow I said hello."

"Of course."

GENERAL WILSON P. STEWARD sat in his darkened office. The entire interior was lost in the gloom with the exception of a pool of bright light from a green-shaded lamp sitting in front of the blotter. Steward was reading from a file folder and making notes on a pad by his left hand. He had been there since before dinner, and the odor of the meal brought by his aide lingered. There was a tap at the door and Steward called out, "Come."

Major Comstock entered, crossed the floor and stopped just outside the pool of light. "Sir?"

"I'm drafting a message here that should go out over the secure network to MACV-SOG as soon as possible. I want you to take it to the message center."

"Yes, sir."

"Jim, sit down for a moment." Steward stood and walked around the edge of his desk. He leaned against it and asked, "What do you think of all this?"

Comstock shrugged. "I don't know, General. I haven't seen enough of the information to make a good guess, but I don't think the North Vietnamese would build a POW camp so close to the DMZ. It's almost as if they're daring us to mount a raid."

"Yes," said Steward, "but if it's a POW camp..." He let the sentence go unfinished. The implication was that they had to act. To let the enemy challenge them in that fashion was almost a slap in the face. It suggested that the enemy believed their territory was immune to American retaliation. It also suggested that the enemy didn't know how many cross-border operations were being run into the North.

Steward had seen a request from the CIA that claimed they had put agents, guided by Special Forces men, right into Hanoi. He had seen pictures of Hanoi that had been taken from the ground by the Special Forces. And he knew of one Army recon team that had spent four months walking to and from Hanoi.

But that didn't get him the information he needed. All he had was some photographs taken from altitude that suggested the camp was being prepared.

"What did General Wheeler say?" asked Comstock.

"He wasn't impressed with the information. He wants more information. As do I."

"Which means?" asked Comstock.

"It means you take the message down to have it transmitted. We'll put a team into the field and let them go take a close look at the camp. Once they're at the site they'll be able to tell quickly whether or not there are POWs there."

"And in the meantime?"

"We proceed as if we've been handed a valuable piece of intelligence. We get the ball rolling, a team assembled here and the logistics in place."

"Yes, sir," said Comstock. "Isn't that a lot of work if there's no one there?"

"It's quite a bit of work if no one's there. But if they are, if we can confirm it, then we have the people in place to do something about it."

Comstock stood. "If there are POWs there, just exactly what are we going to do about it?"

"Why, Jim, we're going to bust them out of there of course. What else would we do?"

GERBER CROSSED the huge marble floor, which was partially covered by ornate carpeting, of the Carasel Hotel. Chairs and tables were scattered around, and giant marble pillars climbed to the ceiling. The dark wooden walls had a rich look; palm trees and ferns in large brass pots squatted strategically on the floor, and a huge desk sat opposite the doors where the clerks worked. People were loitering in the lobby—men waiting for rooms and women waiting for men.

He dodged into a cloakroom that housed a bank of telephones. Picking up the receiver of one, he deposited money and dialed a number. He heard it ringing at the other end and was surprised when it was answered right away.

"Morrow."

"Robin, this is Mack. I'm in town."

There was a hesitation and then, "Oh, wonderful. You just get in?"

"Couple of hours ago. They had me locked up over at MACV for a couple of debriefings."

"Uh-huh."

"Robin, I'm sorry. I couldn't call you before I left. We were taken into isolation with almost no notice. Once in isolation, I couldn't call."

"Sure."

Gerber had to grin. He suddenly realized she wasn't mad at him. She was giving him a hard time, hoping he would tell her something about the mission and thereby give her a story. Instead of apologizing again, he asked, "You interested in some free drinks and a dinner?"

Again there was a hesitation. "What kind of dinner?"

"Let's say any kind you want. Money's no object. Well, let's not get ridiculous, but we can eat fairly well."

"I don't know, Gerber. You're pretty cavalier about all this."

"Well, give me a chance to make it up to you."

"Where are you now?"

"I'm with Fetterman and a couple of the boys over at the Carasel Hotel."

"I'll be there in twenty minutes."

"See you then," said Gerber. He hung up and drifted back into the lobby. For a moment he thought about waiting for her there, but then decided he shouldn't keep the others waiting, so he turned toward the bar and entered.

It was dark inside. One wall was dominated by the bar, which had shelves behind it that held dozens of liquor bottles. The bartender was Vietnamese. He wore a white shirt and a red bow tie. There were tables packed in and two walls held booths. As Gerber entered, he saw that Fetterman and the boys had secured one of the booths. A waitress wearing a short skirt, a white shirt and a tiny apron stood near them, waiting for their order.

Gerber slipped into the booth. He ordered a beer and the waitress took off.

"So, Captain," said Tyme, "what's the plan for the day?"

"I didn't know I was required to provide a plan. I thought Sergeant Fetterman had organized this."

"I just said we'd meet them here," said Fetterman.

"All right," said Gerber, "now when I was a young sergeant, the last thing I wanted to do was hang around with old master sergeants and captains. I'll buy the beers and then you're free to find fun wherever you can. I've already made plans along those lines."

"So what did Brown say?" asked Santini.

"Colonel Brown suggested that the information we supplied reinforced his theories. He asked that we stay in Saigon in case he has more questions for us."

"And, of course," added Fetterman, "we didn't argue with orders to remain in Saigon."

"That mean we're free to see the sights?"

Gerber held up a hand. The waitress appeared and set dripping wet bottles of beer in front of each man. Without a word, she turned and left.

"So," said Gerber, "I think we just hang around here as long as we can, telling everyone that Colonel Brown has ordered us to remain close."

Fetterman lifted his beer and took a long pull. He belched loudly, then set the bottle back on the table. "Aren't we exploiting the system?"

"Hell, yes," said Gerber. "I'm tired of sleeping in the jungle on wet ground with all kinds of nasty creatures running over me. I'm tired of waking up with aches in my back and knees, needing to shit and shave and not being able to do either. Someone wants me to stay in Saigon and live in a hotel, eat hot food and take hot baths, I'm not going to argue."

"Well," said Tyme, "there are worse ways to fight a war."

"Yeah," said Gerber, "and we're not Marines. We can be comfortable."

He took a drink of beer and glanced at the doors. At that moment Robin Morrow walked in. A tall, slender woman with light brown hair that hung to her shoulders, she wore her standard khaki-colored jumpsuit with cutoff legs. Her camera bag was over one shoulder. When she spotted Gerber, she waved and started toward the group.

"Ah," said Tyme, "no wonder the captain didn't want us hanging around with him." He stood up so that Morrow could sit between him and Santini.

She stopped at the end of the table and looked at the men. For a moment she didn't react, and then she smiled. "So you all got back safely."

Santini returned the smile. "Nice try, Miss Morrow."

She set her camera bag down next to the end of the booth and then sat down. She reached across the table and took Gerber's beer, drinking deeply from it.

"So, Mack," she said, "you going to buy me a beer or what?"

"I thought the deal was dinner."

"Was and is. Thought I'd hit you up for a beer and then go get changed and make you buy me dinner."

"Fine," said Gerber.

"And then you can tell me about your trip into the jungle."

"Nothing to tell. It really isn't very interesting. Nothing the press would be interested in."

"Then tell me and let me decide."

Gerber shrugged. "Maybe later."

5

THE FIFTH ESTATE
ROOM, CARASEL HOTEL
SAIGON

Gerber felt slightly out of place. His khaki uniform, though cleaned and pressed, didn't look like the tailored gabardine uniforms of most of the soldiers in the room. Other men wore suits made of silk by Hong Kong tailors. But these men were the Saigon commandos, men who spent their tours in Saigon running supply depots or officers' clubs, or as staff officers at MACV or USARV. Others were civilians assigned to the embassy, men whose contact with the war came about when the VC rocketed Saigon. Gerber decided he felt more than slightly out of place.

But Morrow fitted right in. She was wearing a low-cut silk dress of pale yellow. The short skirt ended well above her knees. She had brushed her hair until it shone and had waited in the air-conditioned lobby of the hotel until Gerber had arrived. Then, to avoid the humidity outside, she'd asked to be taken to the restaurant in the hotel.

Gerber thought she wanted to eat in the rooftop garden. They had spent several nights there before, drinking and dancing, but this time she declined. She'd seen enough of Saigon, even at night when the lights flickered in interesting and beautiful displays. And she made a point of telling Gerber that she didn't want to be reminded of where she was.

Now Gerber sat opposite her in The Fifth Estate Room of the Carasel Hotel. The air-conditioning failed to dispel the heat generated by the crowded restaurant. Besides, it was too close to the kitchen, and the day had been extremely hot.

Not that it wasn't an elegant room. The tables were separated by enough floor space so that the patrons could have some privacy and wouldn't overhear other diners' conversations. The walls were paneled in a rich dark wood, probably teak, and there were a dozen small chandeliers blazing with light.

Each of the tables was covered with a white linen cloth on which sat red napkins and a full set of silver cutlery and glassware. The waiters were dressed in dark pants and jackets and wore red bow ties. The waitresses wore costumes similiar to those of the waitresses in the bar downstairs.

Gerber found himself staring at Robin Morrow. He had forgotten how attractive she was. Most of the time he saw her in circumstances that were far from perfect—at Special Forces camps, in the field or at other Army bases, away from mundane conveniences such as hot water. Here, in Saigon, with an opportunity to dress up, she showed just how beautiful she was. He wondered how he could ignore her the way he sometimes did.

He noticed sweat beading on her upper lip, at her hairline and dripping between her breasts. He tried not to stare, but couldn't help himself. She was more exciting than anyone he had seen in a long time.

She was fiddling nervously with her napkin, pulling at the corners as if to unravel it. Finally she looked up. "So what were you doing in the field?" she asked, trying to fill the silence that was becoming uncomfortable for her.

"Truthfully?" he asked.

"Truthfully," she said. "But remember that I'm a reporter, so this will be on the record."

"Robin, there's nothing to tell. It was just a routine mission to watch a trail."

"You make contact?"

"Briefly. Nothing to it. After that we pulled out and came back here—to Saigon."

She was going to ask about that, but the waiter arrived. Gerber ordered a steak with a baked potato, the day's vegetable and a bottle of wine. Morrow followed suit because she wasn't interested in dinner. She was more interested in Gerber, and dinner was a hassle she didn't want to deal with.

When the waiter was gone, she asked, "When you made contact, why'd you break it off?"

Gerber picked up the crystal glass and drank deeply. He set it down almost on top of the wet ring it had left. "That's not exactly what happened," he told her.

"Then tell me."

"Why are you pressing me on this?"

"Because there's something going on here in Vietnam that isn't being discussed. I'm trying to get a handle on it."

"That's a vague statement. What do you mean by something going on?"

She lifted a hand and waved it around. "I mean that since the Tet the press briefings have changed. The military isn't telling us anything anymore. We have to drag it all out. Now you're doing the same thing."

Gerber looked her in the eye. "I'm not dodging your questions. Well, I am, but not for the reason you think. It's here, this room, that's causing the problem. I don't like discussing military matters in this environment." He smiled and added, "Especially with a beautiful woman."

"Trying to get away from the issue by throwing out compliments?"

"Not at all. I think of this as a date, not as an interview. If you want to conduct an interview, then we'll do that. But I'll let you buy the dinner."

"Okay," she said, nodding. "I won't question you about the mission now. But I reserve the right to return to it if I don't like the way the evening is progressing."

"Are you suggesting I might become boring?"

Before she could answer, the salad arrived and they both concentrated on eating. Gerber glanced at Morrow occasionally, realizing how comfortable he was becoming in her company. It hadn't always been that way. When he had first met her at the officers' club at Tan Son Nhut, he had mistaken her for her sister, Karen, whom Gerber once thought he had loved. But that was before Karen had returned to the World to be with her husband. It had been a bad situation that Gerber had made worse by not understanding all of it.

And then it was complicated by Robin's attraction to him. It was almost a high school romance confused by the lies told by Karen. Gerber had avoided entanglements with Robin, more or less, and now they were friends. Sometimes more than that and sometimes less. He wasn't sure of his status now because of the way he'd treated her in the past month. Not that it was all his fault. His orders and his mission made his life, and hers, difficult. So he moved slowly with her.

Gerber suddenly became aware that she had put down her fork and was now staring at him, her green eyes ablaze. He did the same, and he felt something change in the air. Looking at her, he knew she felt it, too.

"I wish we hadn't ordered dinner," she said.

Gerber used his napkin, patting his lips. Methodically he set it beside his plate. "It was your idea to eat a big dinner."

"I know. I can't imagine why I wanted to. There are so many other more important things to do."

But before either of them could act on the notion, the waiter was back with the main course. He set it in front of them, stared at them, then wiped a hand across his forehead. He was sweating heavily in the steaming atmosphere of the dining room. For a moment he stood watching them, unsure of what was happening. And then he retreated, looking back over his shoulder as he disappeared into the kitchen.

"Do we have to eat this?" asked Robin.

Gerber stared at the food, a steak broiled to perfection and a baked potato swimming in butter. It was a meal fit for a king, but he wasn't sure he could eat it.

"No," he said quietly, "we don't have to eat this."

She looked down at the plate and then back up at Gerber. "Mack, can we just get out of here? I'll pay for the dinner, but I'm not hungry right now."

Gerber stood and dropped a wad of bills on the table, not bothering to count it. He was sure it would cover the price of the dinner and probably include a healthy tip for the waiter. In Vietnam he found that money had little meaning to him. One day he might have a thousand dollars and the next he might be dead, so who cared about money? It was living life to the fullest that counted in the war zone. That was much the attitude he had seen as he and Fetterman had ridden through Saigon earlier.

Leaving the food on the table and the wine sitting in its bucket, they headed for the door, walking so close together that they bumped into each other. Neither seemed to care, and at the elevator they remained silent, both of them shifting awkwardly and impatiently from foot to foot.

Once the door was closed and they were alone, they turned to face each other. Gerber reached out for her, and she came to him. He felt her lips and then her tongue probing his mouth. Her body was warm, and he felt the sticky dampness caused by her perspiration when he rested his hand on her back. He wanted to talk, but couldn't think of the proper words, so he let the moment, the tension, build.

The bell rang and the elevator doors hissed open. They stepped into the hallway, a dimly lit corridor with dark carpeting and rows of closed doors. She took his hand and said, "My room is down here. We can go there, if you don't mind a slight mess." She laughed once and shrugged. "Or a big mess."

"Can't be worse than a foxhole," he said, and then wondered why. He hadn't seen a real foxhole since he had arrived in Vietnam.

They stopped at her door and she dug the key out of her purse. As she opened the door, she took his hand and dragged him inside. Then, before retrieving the key, she kicked the door shut. Grabbing him, she kissed him more fiercely than before.

Gerber didn't resist. He held her tightly, his lips grinding against hers, his left hand cupping her breast. He felt her nipple respond, pushing at his hand through the thin fabric.

She broke the kiss and took a deep breath. Without looking at him, she opened the door long enough to get her key, then relocked it.

He pulled her close and let his fingers work their way to the zipper at the back of her dress. As he tugged it down, she kissed him. Leaning away from her momentarily, he pushed the fabric from her shoulders. It slipped to her waist. Gerber worked the dress lower until it was pooled around her feet, leaving her nearly naked. Morrow now wore only a flimsy pair of bikini panties. He felt that he could watch her all day, dressed as she was.

She turned and looked at him shyly, and the expression excited Gerber even more. The perspiration on her body seemed to make her glow. As she held his eyes with hers, she hooked her thumbs into the waistband of her panties. Slowly, smiling demurely, she rolled them down her thighs, stopping at her knees. She straightened, let them fall to her ankles, then stepped out of them but didn't move closer to Gerber. Instead she sat on the bed, her knees together primly.

"Well, Mack," she said quietly.

He swallowed. "Yes, well." He moved to her and lifted her to her feet. Again he kissed her. This time his hand caressed her stomach and then dipped lower until he could tell she was ready for him.

The knock on the door, a quiet but insistent tapping, broke through the emotions of the moment. Morrow looked over his shoulder. "That someone for you?"

"No one knows where I am," he said. "Must be for you."

She shrugged and moved to the door. Gerber watched her walk away, thinking that there were some people who just shouldn't wear clothes. Their bodies, their skin tone, everything about them was so well constructed that wearing clothes spoiled the effect.

Morrow leaned against the door and yelled, "Who is it?"

"Sergeant Fetterman, ma'am," came the muffled response. "I need to find the captain."

She turned and stared at Gerber, raising her eyebrows in question.

Gerber shrugged and buckled his belt. Morrow shot a glance at the ceiling as if asking for divine guidance. She stepped away from the door, moving toward Gerber.

"Ma'am?" Fetterman's voice inquired on the other side of the door.

"What are you going to do, Captain?" asked Morrow. She took his hand and leaned against him.

"I'm going to have to answer it," said Gerber. "Tony wouldn't interrupt unless it was something very important."

She spun away from him and snatched a robe from the nearby chair. "More important than me," she said.

"No, Robin, not more important. Just more imperative."

"Meaning I can wait. Well, Mack Gerber, I might not wait much longer."

Gerber had no response to that. Things ran through his head, but they were either nasty or implied a long-term commitment. He wanted neither.

"Yes, Tony," he shouted, "what is it?"

"Sorry to bother you, sir, but Jerry Maxwell needs to see us. He said ASAP."

"Doesn't that mean in the morning?"

"Sir, I'd rather not stand out here and shout through the door."

"Let him in," said Morrow, her voice icy. "I have no secrets from anyone."

Gerber hesitated and then moved to open the door. Fetterman stepped inside, looked at Morrow and said, "I really am sorry, ma'am, but this is imperative."

She sat down on the bed, the robe falling open to reveal her naked legs. She closed it and held it with one hand. "Please, don't mind me."

"Sir, we're to report to MACV Headquarters in the next thirty minutes." He glanced at Morrow and added hastily, "That's all I know about it."

"Robin, I—" Gerber began.

"Hey! You don't owe me any explanation."

Gerber noticed that Morrow's tone was that of a wife who had just had her dinner party ruined because her husband had been called to the office by an uncompromising boss.

"Tony could tell them he couldn't find me," Gerber suggested. "Tony, you could head over there and I could join you in an hour or so."

"Hey, Gerber, don't do me any big favors."

"Sir, it sounded like it was very important. I don't think they'd take kindly to that plan."

"So what are they going to do? Send me to Vietnam?"

"Go ahead, Gerber," said Morrow.

"Sir?"

"Tony, wait outside for a moment. I'll join you there."

"Yes, sir."

As the master sergeant disappeared, Gerber moved to Morrow. He put his hands on her shoulders, but she shrugged them away. Her eyes were moist now.

"Why do you always do this to me?" she asked. "It's not fair, and I'm not going to take it much longer."

"When I'm finished over at MACV, I could come back here and buy you a late dinner."

"Don't make any promises you won't be able to keep." Then softening slightly, she said, "I know it's not your fault."

"I'll call you when I'm finished," he said.

Now she stood up and let her robe fall open. She pressed her naked body against him and kissed him hard, then took his hand and directed it inside her robe.

When she broke the kiss, she said, "That's just to let you know what you're going to be missing tonight. While you sit in hot offices with cigar-smoking men, you could have been here with me."

"Yes," he agreed. He moved to the door, one hand on the knob. He watched as she slowly closed the robe and then turned away from him. He left the room and looked at Fetterman, who was standing with an amused smile on his face.

"Not one word, Master Sergeant," said Gerber. "I don't want to hear one word from you."

THE NORTH VIETNAMESE and their Soviet advisers camped for the night, hidden from the sky by the thick jungle canopy. They had come to a wide spot in the road where it was evident others had remained overnight. The thick grasses had been trampled flat, and the ferns, bushes and vines had been cut back to leave a clean, parklike area. There were remains of campfires, and tin cans, papers and bits of cardboard lay scattered around.

The jungle canopy protected them from the prying eyes of American recon aircraft and spy satellites. Because they were far north of the DMZ, there were no American patrols to worry about, and the few big cats that inhabited the jungles had long been driven deeper into the trees. It was a safe, quiet camp with only the occasional, distant crump of antiaircraft or the detonations of bombs to disturb them.

At dawn they started again. Kutnetsov rode in the jeep with Colonel Thuy and the driver who hadn't spoken since he'd swatted the mosquitoes the day before. They continued through the jungle. Sometimes the road widened until it was big enough for two trucks to pass, other times it shrank so that the branches rattled against the jeep's sides. They crossed another bridge, this one barely out of the water and made of logs lashed together. It creaked and popped as they crossed, but it held up.

Finally they stopped, and after spreading out, they ate a cold meal. Kutnetsov walked around the perimeter of the camp, peering into the jungle. It was a solid cliff of green that extended from the ground to the canopy. There were thick, heavy leaves on bushes that looked as if they were made of wax. Some hung so that they brushed the ground. There were vines laced in there, ferns with huge, delicate leaves and then a few splotches of brown where the trunks of the trees showed through. Dull green moss grew on the trees.

He turned and headed back to the camp. He saw that Moskvin had the men checking the equipment to make sure the rough ride and humidity hadn't damaged anything. They had opened some of the crates, taken out the radios, machine guns or Starlite scopes stolen from the Americans and found that all of it was traveling well. He didn't bother to talk to them. Instead he returned to the jeep, where Thuy was sitting.

The colonel glanced at him. "Is the weather bothering you?"

Kutnetsov wiped at his forehead with the sleeve of his uniform. He looked at the wet smear. "It's hotter than I care for."

"And heading south won't help. I'm afraid we're going to stay on the plains here and not travel into the mountains."

"No relief?"

"None."

Kutnetsov sat down on the rough canvas seat and wiped his face again. His uniform was soaked. Not all of it was sweat. Some of it was the water dripping through the jungle. "Then let's get going."

Thuy turned. His uniform showed only the slightest traces of sweat. He was damp under the arms and down the back but looked almost comfortable. "As soon as your men are ready, we can continue."

"Is it much farther?"

"I think another two, three hours and then we'll be there."

Kutnetsov nodded and got out of the jeep. He walked over to where Moskvin was. "Let's get this wrapped up so we can get out of here."

Moskvin got to his feet. "That's it," he told the men. "Let's get our gear stowed." He watched quietly, his arms folded across his chest, as the men put their equipment away and then loaded it back into the trucks. In minutes they were finished.

Kutnetsov didn't wait for Moskvin. As the men finished and climbed into the trucks, he returned to the jeep. "Let's get going," he said to Thuy.

GENERAL WILSON STEWARD stood and stretched. He looked at the pile of papers and photographs littering the center of his desk. Once again he wondered if he had leaped to a conclusion that was unwarranted by the information at hand. He bent over, gathered the papers into a single pile and stuffed it all into a leather briefcase.

The door to his office opened and his aide entered. "Car's waiting outside, General."

Steward hit the button on his lamp. The room was plunged into darkness, the only light coming from the outer office. "Thank you. Did you get in touch with that lieutenant?"

"Yes, sir. Lieutenant Rawlings will be waiting for you at the White House. He mentioned that all his classified materials, including the report you read, were locked in the safes here."

"Well, that's just too damn bad," said Steward as he moved toward the door. "I'm not going to be the errand boy for some lieutenant. Not at this stage of the game."

"Yes, sir. I could have the papers delivered to you."

"No, I don't think that's necessary. I'll just tell the National Security Adviser—"

"I'm afraid the meeting will be with the deputy."

"The deputy then, that I've seen the materials and I don't believe Lieutenant Rawlings has misinterpreted them."

They moved through the outer office. Steward stopped at the door and waited for the aide to open it. As they passed through, the aide asked, "Why hasn't anyone else come forward with this?"

"Because," said Steward, pretending he was answering the question as if it had been posed by the NSA deputy, "no one else has checked the latest Intel pictures that far south."

"You think he'll accept that?"

"Doesn't matter," said Steward. "What matters is to get the ball rolling. Get everyone off their fat behinds and doing something." He stopped at a water fountain. After a few mouthfuls, he looked up. "Let me tell you a little story. I sat in on a simulated international problem. A super secret plane had crashed in a country that was aligned with the Soviets. We were given a list of assets available and given a time frame. The Soviets and their allies could get to the plane in twelve hours if we didn't respond."

Steward looked at his aide and then continued. "To me, the situation was easy. Everyone wanted to talk about it. Didn't want to ruffle feathers and create an international incident. I suggested that we launch the bombers at once and turn our fleet around. Everyone wanted to know why I'd do that."

"To blow up the plane, obviously."

"Not at all. The fleet was fourteen hours' steaming time away and the bombers were ten hours' flying time away. If the situation deteriorated, we'd need those assets. While we debated, they could be moving to a more advantageous position, but everyone disagreed with me. Said we didn't know if those assets would be of any use. I told them they were right, but if they were wrong, we'd need them quickly."

"So what happened?"

Steward grinned. "The problem was called on account of lunch, and when we returned there was another problem for us to deal with. But I'll tell you, Jim, I learned one thing on that problem. You move your assets around so that they'll be available when you need them. You can't wait until the last minute."

"And that means?"

"It means I get permission to move the assets. Put a team into the North and start the ball rolling. Start to look for the men who would go in on the rescue if it comes to that."

They began to walk down the corridor again. They moved from the inner ring of the Pentagon to an outer one and then to a door that overlooked an expanse of parking lot. Even this late at night there were hundreds of cars in it. The night shift was working to have information and briefings ready for the generals, admirals and politicians in the morning. These lower ranking men and women took the responsibility of seeing to the country's defense and readiness while the majority of people slept.

At the foot of the steps was a single car, the color lost in the darkness and the strange blue-white light of the parking lot lamps. A tiny flag flapped on the front bumper, and a tired-looking sergeant stood at the rear door holding it open for Steward.

Before he descended the steps, Steward said, "I want confirmation from Saigon that a team is being assembled to make a ground recon. I want that on my desk when I return."

"Yes, sir."

"And when you get it, just leave a note saying yes or no. I'll understand. Then you can go home for the night."

"Thank you, General."

Steward nodded and then climbed into the rear of the car. He sat stiffly, staring out the windshield, wishing Rawlings had kept his speculations to himself.

6

MACV HEADQUARTERS
SAIGON

Gerber and Fetterman entered through the double doors but didn't go into any of the offices on the ground floor. Instead they made their way along the tiled corridor and used the stairs to reach the basement. At the bottom of the steps they were stopped by a military guard armed with a pistol. An M-16 leaned against a nearby wall. The guard was posted in front of a gate of iron bars that ran from floor to ceiling. Although he recognized Gerber, he refused to let the captain and Fetterman pass until he checked their ID cards.

"You know," advised Gerber, "if you recognize someone on a personal level, you aren't required to check his ID each time."

"Yes, sir," said the guard as he examined the card to make sure no one had tampered with it. "But if my sergeant sees me let you through without checking your ID, he'll have my butt. I'll be on the street chasing whores or riding shotgun on convoy. This may be boring, but it ain't deadly."

"I understand," said Gerber, smiling.

The guard handed him a book. "If you and Sergeant Fetterman will sign in with the time and destination, I'll let you through."

The guard unlocked the gate and let them into the restricted area. They walked down a corridor lined with cinderblock walls that dripped with condensation. Rust spots where metal chairs and cabinets had been set and later moved stained the tile. Gerber stopped in front of a wooden door that had neither a number nor a nameplate. He glanced at Fetterman and then knocked.

A moment later the door opened. Jerry Maxwell, the local CIA representative, motioned them in. He then checked the corridor, as if to make sure they hadn't been followed. Convinced they were alone, he shut the door and turned.

"Took your own sweet time," he snapped.

"Hey, Jerry," said Gerber, "I have much better things to do. Don't get snotty."

Maxwell was a short man, with dark hair and dark eyes. Although he had been in Vietnam for over a year, he was still sunburned. He wore his normal uniform that consisted of a wrinkled and stained white suit, and a thin black tie pulled down from the open collar of his white shirt. He waved a big hand around the room. "Sit down and we'll get started."

Gerber dropped into a ripped leather chair. Although Maxwell had tried to mend it, the stuffing stuck out in a dozen places. Fetterman leaned against a bank of gray filing cabinets that lined one wall. The tops were covered with file folders, loose papers, notebooks, charts, maps and reference books.

Maxwell moved across the tiny office and sat in the only other chair. It was pushed in front of an old, battered, battleship-gray desk. One side was lined with empty Coke cans. Like the files, the desk top was hidden under a blizzard of paper and files.

"Now," said Maxwell, pulling still another file from the middle drawer. "I've got a couple of things we need to talk about."

Gerber glanced at Fetterman who shrugged. "Jerry, I have to tell you every time I come in here that you're supposed to be friendly. We do some small talk and then you launch into some impossible mission."

Fetterman ignored that, pawing through the stuff on top of the files.

"Come on, guys," said Maxwell, "I don't have a lot of time." He spotted Fetterman digging and snapped, "Don't do that. You guys don't have time, either."

Gerber stood up. "I don't know about this. I think you're just too irritable tonight. Tony, let's come back tomorrow."

"Sure, Captain."

"Okay, okay," said Maxwell. "Sorry. How have you been?"

Gerber dropped back into the chair, which groaned under his weight. "I've been a little tired lately. How about you, Tony?"

"Sick, Captain. I'm real sick. I think I need a week in the hospital to recover."

"Very funny," said Maxwell. "If you're done with the Mutt and Jeff routine, we have some serious shit to cover here."

"Tony, you finished?"

"Yes, sir. I'm finished. I have one question, though."

Maxwell turned to him. "What is it?"

"Where's your picture of the Wagon Box Fight? I miss that. I'm not sure you're the real Jerry Maxwell without it."

"Glass on the frame got broken, so I took it down."

"Again?" asked Gerber. "You get mad and throw another Coke can at it?"

"Gentlemen," said Maxwell, his voice weak. "We have a lot of material to cover before you draw your equipment for the field, so I think we'd better get with it."

"That's it, Jerry," said Gerber. "I'm not going out on another of these half-baked, CIA-inspired boondoggles. You people never have a clue about what's happening. You just throw people into the war and hope they come out alive."

"Before you shoot your mouth off, Gerber," snapped Maxwell, "I think you better listen to what I have to say."

Again Gerber glanced at Fetterman. The master sergeant looked relieved. He was waiting for the power struggle between the CIA man and his captain to end so that he could hear what the new problem was.

"Okay, Jerry, I may have been out of line. If I was, I'm sorry, but you've got to admit that some of the plans to come out of here haven't been thoroughly researched."

"Mack, this is something different. Now hear me out before you protest. This one comes from the highest levels, and I don't mean here in Saigon. This one's from Washington."

"You have my attention," said Gerber.

"Thank you. Now here's the deal. For the past year we've been flying regular sorties over everything in North Vietnam that has a wall around it. The thinking is that some of those places could be used as POW camps. If we could locate one that's isolated from a major population center, we might be able to free some of our men."

Gerber nodded and felt his stomach turn over. POWs and the missing in action were a sore point with all military men. The POWs and the MIAs were men who had done their jobs and lost their freedom while doing it. Gerber would do everything he could to help them. "Continue," he said.

Fetterman just nodded his agreement.

For the next thirty minutes Maxwell covered everything he knew about the situation. He read them the message that had been forwarded from the States and then showed them photos of the camp. "Aerial recon is good," he told them, "but it can't do everything. We need a team in there to gather data, a team that can verify what's going on, then radio us that verification. How many men do you need for that recon?"

"Wait a minute, Jerry," said Gerber. "It's not quite that easy. How long will we be in the field? Do we stay on-site as pathfinders, or do we pull out? Do we make contact, or do we avoid the enemy? This may be a noble effort, but we need a little more information."

"Okay," said Maxwell. "First, we'd want you in there for several weeks. Certainly no fewer than two and maybe as many as four or five."

"That takes real coordination," said Gerber. "We have to make provisions for resupply...."

Maxwell grinned. "I thought you Special Forces guys could live off the land, move through it like the wind and not be seen by anyone."

Now Fetterman spoke up. "We can live off the land, but then we spend the majority of our time searching for food and water and very little watching the target. It means we have to move around quite a bit, and the more we move, the greater the likelihood we'll trip over the enemy, especially in North Vietnam."

"Okay," said Maxwell, nodding. "You have to make provisions for resupply. How many men?"

"No fewer than four or more than eight. We don't want the force so small that the enemy could overwhelm us easily, nor do we want it so large that we'll be tripping over one another."

"When can you hit the field?" asked Maxwell.

Gerber looked at his watch and then laughed. "We need to know more about this, but I'd guess we could be ready in a couple of days. Give us a chance to pick the team and get the equipment coordinated. What you're not going to like is getting a second and third team ready for the resupply."

"What do you mean a second or third team?"

Gerber shifted in his chair and leaned on Maxwell's desk. "I mean that someone is going to have to bring us supplies, and that someone is going to have to cache them so that we can find them."

"We can't have a bunch of extra people in on this. The last thing we want to do is tip our hand."

"But," said Gerber, "we won't be able to carry in everything we need. That means someone is going to have to bring it to us." He held up a hand to stop Maxwell's protest. "They don't have to bring it right to us. We can meet them several klicks from the site, but there'll have to be a coordinated resupply effort, even if we're in there for only two weeks."

"Okay, okay," said Maxwell. "I can see you're going to complicate this way beyond what I wanted."

"Jerry," snapped Gerber, "it's not a question of complicating it. It's a question of mounting a recon mission that has a chance of success. We do it halfway and we're going to get caught and compromised. We do it right and the bad guys aren't going to know we're even in there."

Maxwell scratched his shoulder, then let his hand drop. "All right, I'll tell you what. Get a list together of what you want and when you want it. Plan to be in the field for a month. Get back to me with it in the morning and I'll present it to my higher-ups and see what they say."

"One thing," cautioned Gerber, "make sure you tell those clowns who's going into the field. It's me and Fetterman and the men we choose, not them. Everything we want is something we need to make this work. I don't want some bureaucrat thinking this is like camping in a state park. If we get into trouble, there won't be a ranger station a mile or two away to provide help. We get into trouble, we have to get ourselves out of it."

Maxwell stood. "I understand. I'll expect you back here by noon tomorrow with the information I want."

"Come on, Tony," said Gerber, standing. "Looks like we've got some work to do."

They moved toward the door with Maxwell following them. "Noon tomorrow," he said again.

As they moved down the hallway, Fetterman said, "There isn't that much to do, Captain. Sounds like a standard long-range recon into the North."

"Sure, but we don't have to tell Maxwell we can put it together in a couple of hours. Now we have some time. We can eat a good breakfast tomorrow, make a few notes during it and then come back here."

"Yes, sir," agreed Fetterman.

IT WAS EARLY in the morning when Kutnetsov and his team finally pulled up to the camp. They broke out of the thick jungle at the top of a ridge. The ground dropped away slowly until it formed a shallow valley. The other side was lost in the distance and the light mists of the jungle.

They stopped at the edge of the jungle so that Kutnetsov could examine the camp. It was a big, completely walled area.

There were a number of large tile-roofed buildings as well as several smaller ones, and guard towers had been placed on the walls to ensure civilians were kept away. A few trees grew in the compound, but they weren't tall or large enough to conceal the site from the air.

"We have a nice camp built for you," said Thuy. "Everything you could want, including a generator and a backup for electricity all night."

Kutnetsov got out of the jeep and looked down on the camp. It appeared to be new and it seemed clean. There was no sign of anyone living on it.

"Just a caretaker force," explained Thuy. "The trainees won't arrive until we ask for them. Then they'll be here in a matter of hours."

"Then we should take steps to get them here quickly. There's no reason to wait."

"I'll speak to my officers as soon as we conclude our business here," said Thuy.

"I'd like to cut down the trees and the bush outside the walls so that we have a killing field of three or four hundred meters."

"Captain," said Thuy, "this is North Vietnam. You won't be attacked here. The vegetation is our friend. It conceals us from the American spy planes."

"It's so thin that I can't see what good it's doing you here. Seems to me that if you're going to learn from us, we should erect our camp to fit the specifications of the mission. If we're not concerned with enemy assaults, then we can build a proper model."

"We must be concerned with air assaults," said Thuy.

"But the Americans wouldn't waste their time attacking a compound that's used strictly for training."

Thuy shrugged. "Who knows what the Americans might do?"

Kutnetsov decided this wasn't the time to worry about such things. Later, once the school was established, he could make the changes he wanted.

"If you're ready, Captain, we'll drive on down."

"Yes, Comrade Colonel," said Kutnetsov. He got back into the jeep. They drove down the hill, the road rough and rutted and partially overgrown by grass. From the air it would look as if it had been abandoned, and Kutnetsov was sure that was the impression the North Vietnamese wanted to give.

They rolled to a stop at a wooden gate on the south side of the wall that surrounded the camp. A ten-foot-high brick wall with no firing ports, it was built along the lines of those around forts of the old American West, where the defenders had to fire over the top. But that didn't matter here. Kutnetsov had to remind himself again that the Americans wouldn't be attacking them. He was as safe as he would be in Moscow.

Someone on the inside opened the gate, and they drove through. The interior courtyard wasn't very large. The driver pulled up beside a guard tower in the corner, just missing a small brick square that masked a well. Behind them, the trucks entered, spreading out so that the equipment carried in them would be close to the buildings where it would be housed.

Kutnetsov got out of the jeep again. This time he stretched, his arms high over his head. The journey was finally over, at least for a while. He watched as his men jumped to the ground. For a moment they looked confused or unhappy. They looked hot and miserable.

Moskvin didn't give them a chance to worry about it. He started ordering the men to pick up the equipment. Then he turned and faced the captain.

Kutnetsov in turn faced Colonel Thuy. The North Vietnamese officer said, "Behind us is the barracks. Personal equipment in there. Over to the north is a blockhouse. Weapons and ammo in there. And beside it is a hut for the radio equipment."

"You get that, Viktor?"

"Yes, sir."

"Get the equipment stored and we'll meet back here for a quick briefing. Then we'll get settled in."

"Yes, sir."

STEWARD SAT PATIENTLY in the small conference room used by the Joint Chiefs of Staff. It was a plush room with thick carpeting and ornate wallpaper. Large leather chairs were positioned around a highly polished mahogany table, which had a silver tea service in the center and green blotters in front of each chair. Each chief of staff had his respective service's crest embossed on his blotter. The lighting was muted and the doors on one wall were open to reveal a large screen.

For the past hour the men had been arguing over what to do about the information Steward had given them. Each had reasons why they should wait and see, and each was hoping that the others would make the final decision. The issue was so volatile that a mistake, even a minor one, could sink a career that had taken a lifetime to build. Steward, well aware of that, sat quietly, answering the questions as they were presented to him.

Finally, in response to a question about the lead time needed to put an operation together, Steward said, "Gentlemen, I suggest you give me a conditional approval. We can set the wheels in motion, but the final plan won't be approved until we have additional information."

"And just for the sake of argument," said the chief of the Air Force, "how will this additional information be secured?"

"Easily enough, General," said Steward. "Recon flights over the camp for one. We'll have to be careful since the camp is well away from any targets of strategic significance, but we can make a couple of flights. And we're going to put a team in there on the ground."

"Who approved that?" asked the Army chief.

Steward grinned sheepishly. "I've given tentative approval to it and sent a Twix to MACV-SOG, asking that a team be identified for the mission."

"Took quite a load of responsibility, didn't you?" inquired the Army man.

"No, General. I merely asked them to identify the assets and to be prepared to insert them into the North. We can cancel the mission at any time, but we've gained a ten-hour jump on it now."

"General Steward, would you please wait outside for a few moments?" asked the chairman.

"Certainly, General," said Steward. He got up and left the room. Outside in the waiting area, which was almost as plush as the interior of the conference room, he found his aide asleep on a couch. The major's feet were propped on a coffee table that looked as rich and ornate as everything else.

Steward moved to the console television and snapped it on. He flipped the channels until he found *The Today Show*. Pulling one of the chairs close, he watched the news. He learned how the fighting in Vietnam was going, learned of more student protests, saw a couple of victims from a murder and discovered that the space program had run into a few minor problems.

Comstock woke up, blinked and stretched. "How'd it go?"

"We'll know in a little while. They're debating in there now."

At that moment the door opened and Steward was asked to come back in. He stood at the end of the conference table and looked at the chairman of the Joint Chiefs. All he could see were the rows of ribbons on the man's service jacket.

"General," the chairman said, "if we give you a green light for the time being, what are your plans?"

"First, I'd want a team on the ground in the North. Next I'd want a couple of recon flights, and last, I'd begin to put together the rescue party—eighty to a hundred men who would actually take part in the raid."

"How much would these people know?"

"The ground team would have to know the location of the camp, and I believe the information about it being a possible POW compound has been communicated to them. The rest of the men involved, the recon pilots and the ground assault team, could be kept in the dark almost up to the end."

"Where would you train these people?"

Now Steward scratched his head. "First off, I'd choose somewhere isolated. There's a reserve or a National Guard training facility near Alpena, Michigan, that would be fine for the beginning. After that we'd need a more tropical environment, but to start it would cover us well. Then maybe to Elgin in Florida. I believe there's an ROTC training site that might work. Or maybe to the Jungle Survival School in Panama."

"What kind of staff do you envision?"

"I've already taken the liberty of placing Lieutenant Rawlings and his assistant on my staff. I'd like a few more intelligence types, photo interpreters and the like. And I'd like to select an overall mission commander to place in the field to find the men to make the raid."

"Thank you, General," said the chairman. He looked at the four other officers. "Any other questions? No? All right then. General Steward, inside the hour you'll have an order from me authorizing the formation of a special team whose purpose and mission will remain undefined. You'll be provided everything you need, and if anyone balks at this, you'll be authorized to use my name to grease the wheels."

"Yes, sir. Thank you, General."

"Now wait. Don't let this thing take on a life of its own. You'll clear every new phase of training and planning with my office. Colonel Jason Sheckley will be your liaison with me. I'll have him stop by your office later this morning. Now then, do you have any questions?"

"No, General. I understand my instructions completely."

"Please check in with me on a daily basis. Again, thank you for your time."

Steward saluted and then retreated. He moved into the outer office, waited until Comstock opened his eyes, then said, "Wake up, Jim. We have a great deal of work to do."

"Yes, sir."

7

THE CAMP OUTSIDE
LANG MO
NORTH VIETNAM

Colonel Thuy sat in his ground-floor office and wondered what he had gotten himself into. The office was Spartan. There was an old wooden desk that had been badly scarred, and two wooden chairs, one of dark wood and the other a lighter color, were pushed against the wall. Over them was a poster of Ho Chi Minh.

Thuy leaned forward and wished again that the Soviets would just go home. They had arrived on the scene, invited by the bureaucrats in Hanoi, to assist in the war against the American imperialists. Thuy wasn't convinced the Soviets were going to teach him anything he needed to know to fight the Americans. Nor was he convinced that the request for Soviet assistance had been made in Hanoi. He was beginning to suspect that the Soviets had offered to help, and the men in Hanoi had accepted with no thought about the possible consequences, no thought about the Soviet belief that only they understood true communism.

He opened the file that lay in front of him and read it carefully. It was Captain Kutnetsov's report on the forty-man platoon that had been organized. The captain wasn't pleased with the North Vietnamese response to close-order drill. They wanted to learn how to use their weapons and then go south to fight. They didn't want to spend hours in the hot sun marching in small squares and circles.

Thuy rose from his chair and walked to the window. An open hole in the wall without screen or glass, it showed him the small square of dirt that Kutnetsov had designated a parade ground.

The forty North Vietnamese, dressed in the black pajamas of the Vietcong, stood in four ranks of ten men. At the head of each squad was a man with a yellow band around his arm, indicating a squad leader. The Soviets moved among the men, checking their weapons.

Thuy shook his head as he watched the display. No, the Soviets simply didn't understand the way the war had to be fought. The Soviets thought they should be in charge. They would lead the world to communism, and no one could tell them anything different.

He returned to his desk, wondering how long he should allow this situation to go unchallenged. Then there was a tap at his door, and Major Tran entered. He had arrived earlier with the forty men, stood on the edge of the parade ground and watched as the Soviets had taken over, using interpreters supplied by the Vietnamese who spoke both Russian and Vietnamese. Thuy had noticed at the time that no one in the Russian party spoke Vietnamese. At least the Americans had taken the time to teach some of their soldiers the language.

"What is it, Major?" asked Thuy.

Tran looked around and then fell into the chair. He wiped a hand over his forehead and rubbed the sweat onto his khaki shirt. "The Soviets have begun their training program."

"I have seen."

"They want us to march in circles because it teaches us attention to detail and to obey orders."

"There's something to be said for that," said Thuy.

"But we've provided them with soldiers who are combat veterans, not children from schools. Marching won't help us in our fight."

"We must be patient. They have their own methods, and it allowed them to defeat Hitler in their great war."

"Those methods were fine twenty years ago, but this is a different war."

Thuy grinned and tented his fingers under his chin. "But, Comrade Major, you must remember that we're fighting the Americans now who fought in the same war the same way. Maybe the Soviet methods will help us defeat the Americans."

"I suppose this means we must listen to the lectures on the true Communist man and let them build their Lenin room."

"It's such a small price to pay for their help," said Thuy.

"But they think their way is the only way."

"Comrade Major, we shall allow them to train our soldiers in their way. We will watch and learn and we will take that which will help us and ignore the rest. For now our soldiers will just have to put up with Soviet methods. Soon they'll find something else to entertain them."

"Yes, Comrade Colonel."

"And don't let our allies hear you making critical remarks about them. We don't want to alienate them."

"Yes, Comrade Colonel."

Tran stood up and saluted. He left the room quietly. When he was gone, Thuy returned to the window to watch the progress outside. He wasn't sure of the wisdom of standing out in the open in a camp so close to the line dividing North and South. He wasn't convinced the Soviets understood much of anything, but he welcomed their help.

"Give me the patience I need to deal with these foreigners," he prayed.

GERBER SAT AT THE TABLE in his hotel room, letting the cold air from the aging air conditioner blow on him. He had returned from the briefing with Maxwell and decided that he was tired. Instead of having the breakfast he had told Fetterman about, he'd slept in. He hadn't had much shut-eye in the past week. Now, sitting alone in his room, he felt worse than he had in days.

His hotel room was better than the hootch he had lived in during his first tour. That had been little more than a plywood box with screening, and electricity that worked some of the time. Here there was power all night, air-conditioning, hot water and indoor plumbing. Granted the bed was lumpy, but there were clean sheets on it. The wardrobe against one wall held his uniforms and the few civilian clothes he had. A single chair, a little threadbare but in good shape, sat in one corner. Opposite, on a low table, was a small black-and-white TV he'd bought at the PX. He rarely watched it, but sometimes it was fun to sit there and isolate himself in front of it.

Gerber stood and groaned with the effort. Although he had just turned thirty a few months earlier, he felt as if he were sixty. His muscles were tight and his joints stiff. He padded to the bathroom and turned on the light. The sink had a rust stain where the faucet dripped, and the bathtub behind him crouched on feet that gave it the appearance of imminent flight.

He let water run for a moment and then splashed some onto his face. As he lathered his chin with soap, there was a knock at the door. Gerber looked in that direction and mumbled, "Give me a chance for Christ's sake." Wrapping a towel around his waist, he walked to the door. He opened it and spun without waiting to see who it was. "Come on in," he said.

"You never came back last night."

Gerber stopped and turned. Robin Morrow stood there dressed in her usual modified khaki jumpsuit. Over one shoulder was her camera bag.

Without a word to her, he returned to the bathroom, washed off the lather, then turned off the water. Back in the living room, he pointed to the chair. "Have a seat." As she moved toward it, he made sure she had closed the door behind her.

He sat on the edge of the bed, suddenly aware that he was only wearing a towel. It was a situation that was new to him. Normally it was the woman who was in the provocative state of dress or undress. Idly he wondered if women reacted to such a situation the way men did.

"You never came back," she repeated.

"No, it was too late when we finished. I figured to call you this morning and see if you were interested in lunch." He grinned at her.

"Lunch, huh? Nothing about last night."

"Last night didn't work out quite right," said Gerber. He pushed and pulled at the towel, trying to keep himself covered properly.

"I know that," she said, rolling her eyes. "I mean after it didn't work out. What was the big deal that you had to attend to?"

"You know how the military is. Everyone jumping through his ass without taking the time to think things through. We got the problem solved and came back here."

"You could have called," said Morrow. "No matter how late it was."

"I know," said Gerber. "But I needed to get some sleep." He clapped his hands once. "So you want some lunch?"

"You mean now, this early in the day?"

"I mean later. I've a few things to attend to, but once they're done we could eat."

She stood up. "Give me a call when you're ready."

"Okay." He escorted her to the door and opened it. He wondered if he should kiss her goodbye, but then she was in the hallway and someone was coming. He told her he'd be in touch and closed the door.

He went back into the bathroom and shaved. He dressed in starched jungle fatigues, feeling like one of the Saigon commandos. In the lobby he found Fetterman sitting on a sofa reading *Stars and Stripes*.

"You ready, Master Sergeant?"

Fetterman folded the paper and set it next to him. "I'm always ready."

"Then let's head over to MACV and get Jerry Maxwell stirred up. You thought of who you want on this boondoggle?"

"I think Tyme and Santini for sure. And then someone trained as a medic. Hell, I'd prefer a surgeon, but I doubt we'll get that lucky."

"Wouldn't be the first time a team went out with a fully qualified surgeon."

"Yes, sir. Anyway, failing that, I think we should try to find T.J."

"Is he back in-country?"

"I think so. He DEROSed with the rest of us, so he should be back unless he was discharged."

Gerber shook his head. "I think he still had a couple of years on his enlistment when we went home."

Fetterman stood and they began moving to the lobby doors across the expanse of carpeting and marble. Neither man was aware of his surroundings now. They were concentrating on the design of their team.

"I'd like to get old Eleven Fingers Kepler as the specialist," said Fetterman.

"If we're just thinking in terms of the old team, then why not Bocker for commo. I know he's in-country."

They stopped and let the doorman open the doors, then descended the two steps to the sidewalk. The heat and humidity of the day washed over them like a wave. Almost before they reached the sidewalk, they were bathed in sweat. It dripped down their faces and soaked the underarms of their uniforms. The starch seemed to wilt immediately so that no one would ever be able to tell that Gerber had been wearing starched fatigues.

At the curb they stared into the bright morning sun. There were hundreds of vehicles on the streets, honking, belching and rumbling along. The din from the vehicles and voices rose in a solid wall of noise.

"I don't need this," said Gerber. "A little quiet is a nice thing."

"It *is* a war zone, Captain."

"Yes, but no one's fighting the war right here."

Fetterman shrugged and raised a hand. A bright red taxi swooped in on them like a bird of prey. The driver leaned across the passenger's seat and asked, "Where to, gents?"

"You're not going to pretend you don't speak English?" asked Fetterman.

"Oh, no," said the driver. "I speak English very good. I studied in the United States."

Fetterman opened a rear door. "Then take us to MACV Headquarters."

"You are as good as there."

ROBIN MORROW MADE HER WAY to her desk in the city room of the press bureau she worked for. The city room was a massive area, almost like a warehouse with windows at the front and along one wall. The view overlooked the downtown area—neon blazing at night with the rhythmic thump of rock and roll pounding through the walls.

The inside of the city room was a collection of desks, most of them scrounged from the military and painted battleship gray. Morrow's was an exception. It was a pale green that would have driven a normal person insane if he stared at it too long. Her chair was a small, swivel model with a ripped back and a torn seat. She dropped her camera bag onto the floor and fell into her chair.

Behind her, along the wall with the entrance, was a bank of filing cabinets. Little of importance was stored in them. If anyone wanted to learn about Saigon nightlife, or what had happened in the war a month earlier, it was filed there.

Along the last wall were several glassed-in offices where the special correspondents and the editors worked. Morrow sometimes thought of it as working in a fishbowl.

She placed her elbows on her desk and felt the sweat bead and drip. She looked up and saw that the ceiling fans weren't turning. It was then that she noticed the electricity was out in the room. No one was typing, although most of them had manual typewriters. The power failure was an excuse not to work.

Without a word to the others, she got up and walked to the filing cabinets. On top of one there was a pot of coffee with a sign that demanded everyone chip in or the pot would be removed. She decided not to bother with it. Instead she stole a Coke from the refrigerator kept outside Mark Hodges's office.

Back at her desk, she pulled her shirt away from her body and slipped the cold can between her breasts to cool herself. It sent shivers up and down her spine.

"You need any help there," said one of the men, "you let me know."

Without looking, she answered. "You'll be the first I call."

Finally she set the can on her desk and looked at the papers stacked in the tray in the corner. There was nothing interesting in them. She got up, grabbed her Coke and opened it. Then she walked over to the editor's office and found Mark Hodges sitting at his desk reading *Playboy*.

"Got a question for you. Anything going on over at MACV late last night?"

Hodges closed the magazine and looked up. "Not that I know of. Why?"

"I know that a couple of men were called over there fairly late and I wondered if anyone around here had picked up any rumblings about it."

Hodges turned and took a clipboard from the wall where it hung among four others. He flipped through the pages, then shook his head. "Nothing here. No one else has heard a word. If there was any high-ranking people involved, someone would have noticed it."

Morrow scratched the top of her head. "Yeah. That's what I thought."

"Listen, Robin, you have something going, you pursue it. Even if none of the wheels were there last night, it could be something important. You know how some of those generals and colonels like to talk and see their names in the paper."

"Yeah, well," she said, "it could be nothing. I mean, I'm talking about a captain and a sergeant."

"The way this war is being fought, it could be a big deal. You want to follow it up, I'll take you off assignment for a couple of days."

She took a deep pull at her Coke and touched her mouth with the back of her hand. "What did you have me on?"

"Just a press briefing on the success of the program of defoliation being carried out. Think the code name for it is Ranch Hand. Doesn't seem like it's going to be much of a story."

"I can cover that, too, if you want."

"No," said Hodges, shaking his head. "We've plenty of people over here now. Tet got the press involved in the war again. You run down your leads. That might end up being the big story."

"Or it could be a big bust," she said.

THIS TIME GERBER and Fetterman didn't meet with Jerry Maxwell alone. And the meeting was held upstairs in another conference room, one as Spartan as Maxwell's office. The only furniture was a huge table, six chairs and a small screen. The table was old and scarred with cigarette burns and water rings. The chairs were torn and mended with mismatched cloth. Even the screen had seen better days.

But that meant nothing. The man at the head of the table was a lieutenant general—a tall, thin man with white hair, black eyebrows and a beak of a nose covered by hundreds of broken blood vessels. His skin was pale and sagged under his chin. He looked like an aged corporate executive who was in his last moments before retiring. But his starched khaki uniform showed a number of decorations for valor. The man had seen combat in World War II and Korea. He knew the score.

As soon as everyone was seated, he said, "Gentlemen, I won't bore you with a lot of unnecessary details. I have a coded message from the Joint Chiefs of Staff that came in late last night. I know Jerry Maxwell briefed you then. Now I'll tell you that Washington wants us to proceed on this."

"You mean, General," said Gerber, "that they've approved the recon into North Vietnam?"

"That's exactly what I mean, Captain. Is there a problem?"

"Just that we've caught some flak about cross-border operations into Laos and Cambodia."

"Only the ones the press learned about. You've read nothing about ops into the North. And you won't. But you may rest assured that we've run them."

"Yes, sir. I know that," said Gerber. He'd been on a couple of them himself. "That raises a number of questions."

The general opened a folder in front of him. "Maybe this will answer your questions. You'll travel into the North for the purpose specified by Mr. Maxwell. You'll travel using sterile equipment and you will not be captured alive. The enemy can have your dead bodies but not a live one. We can claim anything we want if you're dead, but if you're alive, you could make some embarrassing statements. Clear?"

"Yes, sir."

"I have the list that you prepared for Mr. Maxwell. The only item on it that bothers me is this resupply into the North."

Gerber looked at Fetterman, then returned his gaze to the general. "The only solution is to have part of the team go back to the DMZ to pick up the supplies if you won't drop them into the North...."

"I didn't suggest we wouldn't, Captain. I just want to make sure I understand how this will operate."

"Yes, General. Under ideal conditions, a drop would be made at a predetermined location. Guides from my end would be there and the supplies would be carried to our FOB. Once there, the men who brought the supplies could head south. To keep the number of men involved down, I'd advise using the same men for the resupply each time."

"How often?"

"Again, ideally, every two weeks. That gives everyone time to rest and doesn't set up anything for the enemy to spot. It would mean only one or two resupply missions."

"I buy it," said the general. "I buy it completely. How long to set all this up and get ready to go into the field?"

"Oh, no more than a week, I'd say."

"What's the problem?"

"Finding the people we want and getting them to Saigon. Getting their orders approved and arranging it so that we don't leave any of the A-Detachments undermanned."

"Shit, son, that's no problem. You tell me who you want and I'll have them here this afternoon. Anything else?"

Gerber shrugged. "Can't think of anything."

"Good. Be ready to hit the field tomorrow."

GENERAL STEWARD SAT in his office, making notes on a yellow legal pad. He was pleased with the list. First was a recon flight over the camp scheduled for late evening. An hour or so before sunset seemed the best time. If there were prisoners in the camp, they would probably be outside, or at least some of them would be outside, and the recon plane would be able to spot them. It would add to the confirmation of POWs in the camp.

There was a knock on his door and Comstock looked in. "General, there are a number of people here to see you. First is Alan Bates. He's the Special Forces officer you wanted. And then there's Lieutenant Rawlings and Lieutenant Halliday."

"Send the lieutenants in first. Give me about ten minutes with them. Then I'll see Colonel Bates. Make sure he has everything he wants."

"Yes, sir."

A moment later Rawlings and Halliday entered. Both stopped in front of the general's desk and saluted. Before either could report in a proper military fashion, Steward said, "Relax and have a seat."

When both were comfortable, Steward said, "Tomorrow morning I hope to have some photos for the two of you to look at. I'll want the same painstaking examinations of these that you've given the other pictures. You'll have full access to any data you might need, including the reference copies you brought with you. Please be here by 0900."

Rawlings looked at Halliday, then said, "Yes, sir."

"Now, if I may be so bold. We have quite a few interesting sights here in Washington. Libraries and museums and landmarks. Take the rest of the day and see them. Have fun. Drink. Even hit the strip joints if the mood moves you. But be here tomorrow."

"Yes, sir."

"That's all I have for you."

Both stood and saluted, then retreated. When they were gone, Alan Bates entered. He was a short, stocky man with graying blond hair, which he wore in a flattop. His features were broad and his nose looked as if it had been broken more than once. His skin was tanned, but not the deep tropical tan that suggested his recent tour in Vietnam. The ribbons on his chest said that he had been in both World War II and Korea. He was a paratrooper. Rolled up in his left hand was his green beret. As he walked in, Steward nodded and thought that this was exactly the man he wanted to put together the ground assault force.

Before Bates could salute or speak, Steward was on his feet, a hand stretched across his desk. "Welcome, Colonel. Sorry the notice was so short, but we've got quite a project to put together."

Bates stopped, hesitated and then reached for the general's hand. "Yes, sir" was all he said.

"Now get comfortable and I'll tell you what I need so that you can get busy."

8

MACV HEADQUARTERS
SAIGON

Gerber and Fetterman spent the morning getting ready for the move into the field. They checked their equipment and replaced anything that seemed to be even slightly worn. Gerber knew it wasn't every day that a three-star general gave them the juice to get new equipment if they felt they needed it. The captain drew a new weapon and Fetterman got an M-79 grenade launcher to go with the M-3 grease gun he sometimes carried. That, coupled with the .45 that used the same ammo, made him a walking arsenal. Of course neither man mentioned that the mission was going to be sterile. Gerber would have to store his brand-new M-16 and Fetterman would have to store the M-79.

That finished, Gerber drove them over to his hotel in the jeep the general had gotten for them. He checked his room, packed a few small items such as clean socks and his toothbrush and then locked up. At the front desk he paid his bill for the next month. Afraid that he might be compromising the mission by paying, he told the grinning clerk he had gotten a special assignment to Hawaii—three or four weeks in the lush, comfortable tropics surrounded by people who spoke English.

"You come back here?" asked the clerk, looking bored with the conversation.

"Probably, unless I can convince a general I'm more valuable in Hawaii."

"You don't have much for your trip."

"Man," said Gerber, grinning, "the last thing I want is a bunch of clothes that look like they're from Vietnam. Besides, we're not allowed to wear jungle fatigues stateside. I'll need new uniforms once I arrive."

He slipped the man a few extra dollars to keep an eye on his room and then hurried across the lobby to where Fetterman waited.

"What was that all about?"

"Paid for my room for the next six weeks."

Fetterman turned and looked at Gerber closely. "That a good idea? If the man's VC, he's going to know you'll be in the field."

"Uh-uh. Told him I was on my way to Hawaii."

Now Fetterman shrugged. "I guess he'd know you were somewhere other than Saigon when you didn't show up."

They reached the lobby door. "You have everything you require?" asked Gerber.

"I'm all set."

They went down the steps to the jeep, which was parked right in front of the door. Gerber dropped his gear into the back and started to climb behind the wheel. He stopped, nearly burning his hand on the top of the seat. Touching the fabric, now baked red-hot by the afternoon sun, he muttered, "Shit!"

"It's not that bad."

Gerber touched the steering wheel with his fingers as if he were touching a stove. "No," he agreed. "Not that bad."

He sat down carefully, keeping his back away from the seat. Finally he leaned back, unlocked the chain that held the steering wheel in place and started the engine. He held the steering wheel lightly, with the tips of his fingers, trying not to burn his hands.

Again they drove through the streets of Saigon, but this time Gerber didn't see them. He was concentrating on his driving, observing the traffic around him, dodging the bicycles and Lambrettas. The entire experience, the odors of partially burnt diesel, the horns and the shouts, the roar of the wind, seemed to isolate him from the sleaziness and squalor of the streets. He kept one hand on the gearshift and one on the steering wheel, using both frequently. Fetterman sat in the passenger seat, his eyes closed, looking as if he didn't have a care in the world.

At MACV Headquarters they parked in the gravel lot, walked past the MP, who saluted Gerber and nodded to Fetterman, and entered the building. Again they made their way to the small conference room, but this time they found a colonel there.

The colonel was a tall, heavyset man who needed a shave. His eyes, a light gray, peered out from under thick, bushy eyebrows. He had a broad, flat nose and a weak chin. His hair was cut close to his head, making it look like a black smudge. Unlike many of the others at MACV, he wore fatigues.

"Gentlemen," he said as Gerber and Fetterman entered, "have a seat. In a few moments I'll escort you to a chopper and you'll be on your way to Bien Hoa."

"Wait a minute," said Gerber.

"No, Captain. No need to wait. Everything's arranged. The men you've asked for are being assigned and will meet you at Bien Hoa."

Fetterman sat down but didn't say a word. Gerber remained near the door. He asked, "Do I have time for a phone call?"

"I think not," said the colonel.

Gerber dropped into the chair next to Fetterman. "Robin's going to be pissed." And then, "Oh, shit."

"What?" asked Fetterman.

"I was supposed to meet her for lunch."

"Captain," said Fetterman, "if I didn't know better, I'd say you were deliberately trying to alienate her. You keep taking her for granted like that and she's not going to hang around."

"Who is this Robin?" asked the colonel.

"She's a friend of mine," answered Gerber. "A very good friend who's a journalist here in Saigon."

"She going to cause trouble?"

"If you mean for me, possibly. When she's pissed, she's a tiger. If you mean for us and the mission, I doubt it."

"Captain," said Fetterman.

"Yes, well," he amended, "she has been known to dig deeply for a story. With just the smallest of clues she's found out some amazing things."

"Then she could be a problem for us on this?"

Gerber wanted to say that Robin Morrow was a fine, upstanding woman who would sit around quietly while Gerber pursued the war, but that wasn't true. Whenever he disappeared, as he was about to, she began to dig, searching for the reasons for that disappearance.

"She'll dig into this. Don't give her a false story because she'll see right through it."

"Damn it, Captain," snapped the colonel, "how could you let this happen?"

"Let what happen?"

"How could you get involved with a journalist? You know how they treat the military with their so-called objective reporting."

"Colonel, Robin Morrow has always been fair with us. She'll dig for a story and present it as accurately as possible. But she will dig."

"Then I suggest you get on the horn to her right now and do what you can to head that off. I don't want a reporter hanging around here looking for a story on some kind of a secret mission."

"Yes, sir."

"You make sure she doesn't suspect anything. This is just another mission into the jungle."

Gerber stood up. "Yes, sir." He left the conference room and made his way down the corridor until he found an office manned by a staff sergeant. He entered and asked the man if he could use the phone in private. The sergeant looked annoyed, but told him to go ahead because he needed a cup of coffee anyway.

As the sergeant disappeared, Gerber sat down at the desk, noticing there was a cup of coffee sitting there. He picked up the phone and managed to get through to the press office where Morrow worked.

When she finally came on the line, Gerber said, "Robin, it's Mack."

"Is this the Mack who was going to call for lunch?" she asked sweetly.

"The very same."

"Sorry, Mack, I had lunch a couple of hours ago."

"Yes, I'm sorry about that, but I got hung up in a couple of briefings."

"Going anywhere interesting?"

"No. Into the jungle for a few days, though. Going to see what the jungle looks like."

"Uh-huh," she said coldly.

"I thought I should let you know."

There was a hesitation at the other end. Gerber knew she was angry with him. First he had failed to call for lunch and now he was on his way out again—with no good explanation.

Finally she said, "Well, you be careful in the field, Mack. Where are you going?"

"North of here. Toward the Central Highlands." Even as he said it, he knew she wouldn't believe it. The last thing he would do would be to compromise his mission by telling her where he was going on the phone. COMSEC and Army regulations prohibited it, and she knew that as well as he did.

"Well, you give me a call when you return." Her voice was now icy.

"Sure, Robin. Be glad to."

"I've got to get back to work." She hung up.

Gerber cradled the phone slowly and sat staring at it. He hadn't handled that well, but thought it might work out. She was so mad at him that she might not even want to find out what was going on. She might push him and everything about him out of her mind. In the end it would mean he had managed to do what he had set out to do: prevent her from trying to learn where he was.

"You through, sir?" asked the sergeant.

"Certainly. Thanks." He got up and headed back to the conference room. No, that hadn't gone well, and he could see that his relationship with Morrow was turning into a problem. With her media connections, she didn't need much of a clue to begin searching for a story. The fact that he was going into the field again so soon was enough to set her off on the hunt. The colonel might be right about that. He'd better think about the relationship.

Outside the conference room he stopped and drained his mind. When he felt the tension was gone, he opened the door and stepped in.

"How'd it go?" the colonel asked.

"She wasn't happy about it, but I don't think there'll be a problem."

"Then grab your gear and let's go. Chopper's waiting at the pad."

Outside MACV Headquarters was a rubber helipad, the corners and sides held down by rows of green sandbags. The chopper sat in the center, its rotors spinning and the engine roaring. The crew chief, wearing an aviation helmet with the dark green sun visor pulled down so that he looked like an insect, was standing next to the cargo compartment door. He wore a Nomex flight suit, aviation gloves and combat boots. The only parts of his body exposed were his nose, mouth and chin.

Gerber and Fetterman hurried toward him in a crouched run so that they wouldn't be clipped by the rotors. They tossed their gear into the rear of the chopper and climbed in. When they were aboard, the crew chief got into the well behind his door gun and flashed a thumbs-up at the pilot, who was facing the rear.

Gerber glanced out at the colonel, who stood at the edge of the pad. As the noise from the engine increased and the rotors began to spin faster, the colonel put a hand to his head to hold down his cap.

The chopper picked up to a hover, the rotor wash snagging any loose debris and flipping it into the air. Dust and dirt swirled around and totally obscured the MACV building and the surrounding landscape. Slowly the chopper turned until it was facing the sun. It lifted gently then, the engine roaring and the rotors vibrating. They climbed up over the parking lot where the jeeps, trucks and cars sat baking in the afternoon sun.

Breaking to the west and then north, they flew over the Song Sai Gon and a large red slash in the earth that had been partially covered with concrete. It was a strange rosette-shaped area that looked almost like an SA-2 emplacement. Gerber had heard it described as the University of Saigon and knew that it was a national cemetery.

The ground dropped away into a swampy mess with a series of roads and bridges that connected Saigon with Bien Hoa and Long Binh. The windshields of the vehicles inching along winked in the sun and a few people waved at the chopper.

Gerber finally sat back, his head against the gray soundproofing, and let the cool air wash over him. He glanced out the windshield. The sky was becoming crowded with choppers. Fixed-wing aircraft, some like the tiny Cessna spotter planes, were low, while others, the jets and the big cargo planes, were higher. The sky seemed almost as congested as the roadways below.

They turned again and entered the traffic pattern at Bien Hoa, landing at a helipad and staying clear of the runways used by the fighters. As the skids touched the ground, a jeep broke from the cover of several buildings and raced toward them. It stopped short of the pad.

Gerber got out to see a man running toward him and shouting over the roar of the helicopter, "You Gerber?"

"I'm Captain Gerber."

"Yes, sir. I'm to provide a ride for you."

Gerber looked at the man. He was short, fat, balding and sloppy and looked as if he was waiting for nightfall so that he could go off duty and drink beer while he chased the club girls. His jungle fatigues were a reddish-green, which suggested they hadn't been washed in a while. This was a man who stayed in the rear, had a good job driving a jeep around and didn't care about his appearance. Gerber knew that an enlisted man in Vietnam with such a job would take steps to protect it.

Pointing at the equipment in the cargo compartment, Gerber said, "Why don't you grab some of that and take it to the jeep?"

The soldier looked as if he had been asked to build the Pyramid by himself. He said nothing to Gerber, but mumbled to himself as he made his way to the chopper. He grabbed a bundle and hauled it to the jeep.

Fetterman joined them. When everything was out of the chopper, it took off, leaving them in a silence that seemed to swell until the driver started the jeep's engine and drove off the field, angled between buildings and a couple of huge trees and passed an area of tents whose raised flaps revealed rows of cots. Men in various states of undress, looking hot and tired, lounged in the area playing cards, writing letters or trying to catch some sleep.

They continued on through a gate in a twelve-foot-high barbed wire fence. Thirty feet away was a second fence, this one with a guard hut near the gate. The driver slowed until the MP nodded at him. Then they drove through and turned toward a long, low hootch. The driver pulled up in front of it and said, "I was told to bring you here."

"Just where is here?" asked Fetterman.

"The isolation area. It's away from everything so that the press people and the snooping colonels and majors can't stick their noses into our business."

Gerber got out of the jeep and stared at the hootch. It was a single-story affair with a rusting tin roof that had been patched several times. Sandbags were stacked around the building partway up the wall, and above them were screens, which had been inserted below the roof for ventilation. The hootch had a dark, foreboding look that Gerber couldn't explain. He stepped up onto the boardwalk that led to the front door. "Anyone going to meet us here?" he asked.

The driver shrugged. "I was told to bring you here from the chopper. I don't know from nothing else." He grinned but didn't get out to help with the gear.

Fetterman grabbed the equipment and began piling it on the walk. When he finished, the driver slipped the jeep into reverse and backed away. He gunned the engine and fled the compound with a spray of loose gravel and dirt.

"Looks like we're home," said Fetterman.

"Looks like," agreed Gerber.

The interior was as gloomy as the outside. There was a dirty plywood floor and a ceiling fan that wasn't turning. Against the far wall was a table piled with uniforms. Next to it was another covered with equipment. There were rucksacks, canteens, knives and boots, but nothing was of American manufacture.

Fetterman stared at the tables. "Looks like the colonel or the general wasn't fooling. This will be a sterile mission."

Gerber spotted the locked racks of weapons against the other wall. Some of them were American-made. There were a couple of M-1 Garands, a few M-2 carbines and even a grease gun like the one Fetterman usually carried. But the racks also held weapons made outside the United States. There were a dozen AK-47s, a few SKSs and a single French MAS 49 7.5 mm self-loading rifle.

Next to the racks was a box of grenades that had been stolen from the enemy, at least that was what the writing on the outside indicated. Gerber would believe it when he had a chance to look at the contents.

Beyond all that was a doorway that led into another room. Gerber walked toward it and peered inside. The overhead fan turned with a quiet chirping sound. A man was sprawled on the first of the cots that lined one wall. A second man, stripped to his underwear, was opposite the first, also asleep.

Gerber turned to Fetterman. "We've got company."

As he spoke, the closest man sat up. "Howdy, Captain," he said.

"Glad to see you, Justin," said Gerber. "Who's your friend at the other end?"

"Sergeant Santini, just as you requested."

"Anyone else here?"

"No, sir." Tyme swung his legs to the floor and rubbed a hand through his hair.

"How long you been here?"

"Arrived this morning. Had time to inspect the weapons and even a chance to take some of them out to the range to check them out. They're in good shape."

"Anything else I should know?"

"No, sir. Except that there's supposed to be some major in here to coordinate everything. All we have to do is change into the sterile equipment and be ready to move out."

From the outside came the rumble of a diesel engine. Gerber turned and moved toward the front of the hootch. There was a deuce-and-a-half sitting at the end of the boardwalk. For a moment it looked as if it was abandoned, then the flap at the rear opened and two men dropped to the ground. Gerber recognized one as Sergeant Bocker.

Bocker was a big man, older than most of the men in the Special Forces. He had dark hair and massive features. As a commo specialist on his first tour, he had been assigned to Gerber's A-Detachment as the senior communications NCO. He was a good soldier who knew how to avoid backbreaking work while not seeming to duck responsibility.

Bocker picked up a duffel bag and an M-16, then said something to the other man, whom Gerber didn't recognize. Then a third soldier appeared. Again it was a man who had served with Gerber on his first tour.

Derek "Eleven Fingers" Kepler was an Intel specialist. He had spent his first tour running a string of agents and spies throughout the southern portion of South Vietnam. He was also the best man available for securing equipment that had been snarled in red tape. Once he had arrived at the camp dressed as a nurse but with a 90 mm recoilless rifle that he had "found." Another time he had "found" a boat they needed and delivered it while dressed as a Navy lieutenant commander.

Kepler was a stocky man with light hair, and nondescript features. But the thing that stood out about him was his hands. They were huge. The quickest way of describing him to someone who didn't know him was to tell the person to look for the man with the biggest hands imaginable. Kepler could hold a dozen hand grenades at once. His gigantic paw made a .45 look like a kid's toy.

Behind Kepler was another man whom Gerber didn't recognize. He was small and dark with black hair, and when he turned, Gerber realized he was Vietnamese. The man was obviously some kind of scout or interpreter. Gerber didn't like having a Vietnamese he didn't know assigned to them.

The four new men entered the hootch. They all dropped their equipment onto the floor. Kepler stood there, looked everything over and then called out, "Hey, Captain. How's it going?" He made it sound as if he'd last seen Gerber only a week or so before instead of over a year ago.

Gerber stepped forward and held out a hand. "Good to see you again, Derek. How goes it with you?"

"Better now, Captain. Glad to see you're on this and not some candy-ass fresh from school and the World who thinks he can win it all at once."

"Christ, who jerked your chain?" asked Bocker.

"Oh, those assholes at Nha Trang wouldn't know an Intel asset if it bit them square on the ass. I tell them something and they run off to confirm, and when they fail, they shitcan the info. Then a day later it turns out to be righteous. Fuck."

Gerber decided to ignore that. He stuck a hand out at Bocker. "Hello, Gavin."

"Captain."

"Who have you got with you?"

"Other man is an expert on the North Vietnamese and their methods of operations. Qualified as a medic. Second-tour man. Sergeant Davies, this is Captain Gerber."

The man came forward. Like Fetterman, he was a small, but he didn't have the air of confidence that Fetterman projected. Although Fetterman wasn't muscular, he had a wiry strength that deceived people. Davies didn't seem to have that. His skin was white, as if he hadn't gotten out into the tropical sun. His hair was red, and Gerber wondered if he sunburned easily. Of course, deep in the jungle, sunburn wasn't a problem.

"Sergeant Davies," said Gerber.

"David Davies," he said, nodding. "My mother thought it was cute. Davy Davies." He shrugged. "I don't know. Maybe it is."

"Fucking darling," said Kepler.

"And who's the last man?"

Kepler touched the Vietnamese on the shoulder. "This is Sergeant Lo Vo Van, late of the LLDB. I got him pulled for this because I thought he'd be an asset for us. Knows the country well just north of the DMZ." Now Kepler grinned. "Speaks the language like a native and has family in the area who might give us some help if we need it."

"I don't know, Derek. . . ."

"We can trust him, sir. Hates the Cong with a passion. Hates the Communists. One of them killed his sister. Dragged her into the bush, raped her and then gutted her. Left her to die with her intestines hanging out."

"I don't need all the details. I was more concerned with his being captured in the North. If someone recognizes him, the Communists will really work him over."

"I not be captured," said Van.

Gerber stared at the smaller man. There was a scar on his face that ran from his hairline across his right eye and down to his chin. It was a thin scar that looked as if he had lost a knife fight.

"You'll find him to be a good soldier," Kepler insisted.

Gerber held out his hand again. "If Sergeant Kepler trusts you, then we all do. Welcome aboard."

"Thank you."

With that Gerber turned his attention to everyone around him. Tyme, wearing only jungle fatigue pants, leaned against the doorjamb. Santini continued sleeping in the other room, unaware that the whole team had finally arrived.

"I have no idea what the plan is from here," Gerber told them. "I would imagine you people know as much about it as

I do. I suggest we get the sterile equipment organized and be prepared to move out on a moment's notice.''

"Any idea when that might be, sir?'' asked Kepler.

"No, but given the speed they got us here, I'd be surprised if we spent the night. I was hoping we'd get a briefing, but the way things are going it wouldn't surprise me if we don't.''

"And until then?'' asked Bocker.

"Until then, we wait.''

9

WASHINGTON, D.C.

Rawlings sat in a room that could have been a duplicate of his office at Wright-Patterson. There were no windows, and a military-style table, which meant that it was heavy, made of metal and painted gray, sat in the center of the room. On it were nearly a hundred black-and-white photographs, several magnifiers and two legal pads. Along one wall was a bookcase containing a number of black binders, and shoved into a corner was a massive safe. The walls were painted a light blue and there was a calendar on one of them. Another held a couple of posters reminding everyone that COMSEC was their job and that the enemy only needed a small piece of the puzzle from everyone before he had it all.

Near the closed door was a leather chair, complete with ottoman. Sheila Halliday sat in it reading a copy of *Playboy*. She had yet to get beyond the letters.

Rawlings, on the other hand, was searching through the pictures taken by a high-flying recon plane. He was studying them carefully, grumbling because Halliday didn't seem to be taking anything seriously.

Finally he said, "You know, with two of us working we'd get through this faster."

Halliday closed the magazine and dropped it onto the floor. She stared at him for a moment and then asked, "You really think this makes any difference?"

"What are you talking about?"

She stood and walked to the table. Grabbing a handful of the pictures, she flipped through them, letting them fall back onto the table. "I mean, they've now got fifteen, twenty people examining these pictures, looking at the stuff you're looking at. You've had your moment in the spotlight."

"No one ever found what I was looking at."

"That's right," she said. She slipped into a chair slowly so that her left leg was folded under her. It hiked her tight skirt up. "But now everyone knows where to look. They're keeping us in the game because we came to them with the information in the first place."

"But the general is going to ask us for a report."

"Of course he is. And what are you going to tell him?"

Rawlings pulled a couple of the photos closer. "I'm going to tell him there's more evidence of activity in the camp—a new building added and a new pile of dirt near the south wall."

Halliday couldn't help smiling. "Well, there's big news, I'm sure. We spend a couple of million dollars to learn that the enemy has built something and is moving his dirt around."

"It indicates more activity at the camp."

"But, David, don't you see? It doesn't mean there are Americans there, and unless we find something like that in the next few days, the bloom is coming off our rose."

Rawlings faced her. "How is sitting here reading magazines going to help?"

She shrugged. "How's it going to hurt?"

Before he could respond, there was a knock at the door. It opened slowly and an officer said, "General Steward wants to know if you've finished your examination."

"We're through," said Halliday hastily.

"If you'll follow me then."

"We have classified material scattered out here," said Rawlings.

"Don't worry. I'll have someone collect the photos and see that they're put into a safe. Now come with me."

The three of them moved from the enclosed office to a corridor that wound through the center of the Pentagon until they arrived at Steward's outer office. Here they were handed over to Comstock, who escorted them into Steward's office.

The general stood to meet them and directed them to the conference area where another man sat waiting. As they approached, Steward said, "This is Colonel Alan Bates. He wants to hear what you've learned from the new photos."

Bates nodded at them, but didn't speak. Rawlings suddenly felt naked. He had no notes, no visuals and no idea how to proceed. Every time he had been asked to brief someone, he'd had time to collect slides or vu-graphs and prepare a written report. In fact, he'd been told to never attempt a briefing without visual aids. Now he had to wing it, something else he'd been cautioned against doing by every one of his military instructors and supervisors.

"I'm afraid I don't actually have—"

Steward clapped a hand to his shoulder. "Son, you aren't being graded on your performance here. If you're a little disjointed, we'll understand." He dropped into a chair and nodded at another one, indicating that Halliday should sit down, too.

Rawlings stood in front of them and felt as if he were a child who had been asked to perform in front of his family at Christmas. He cleared his throat, then scratched the back of his head. "Okay, current information, provided by the recon flight of yesterday afternoon showed more activity in the camp. Another building's been constructed and they've created another pile of dirt. Other than that there's no evidence that anyone's been in the camp or is in the camp. No people were visible in any of the photos I saw."

Bates nodded. "Maybe the camera wasn't good enough."

"Oh, no, sir. There were several pictures taken during the approach that showed farmers in their fields or standing by their hootches. If there were people in the camp, we'd have seen them."

"Prisoners might have been confined to the inside," suggested Steward.

"Yes, General, I thought of that," said Rawlings. "But there would still be guards on the outside."

"Maybe they hid when the plane flew over," said Bates.

Rawlings looked at the colonel. "But there would have been something for us to see. And I don't think they'd have abandoned everything to fool us. If we saw some Vietnamese in the compound, would we have cared? No, it looks stranger not to see anyone."

"What's your conclusion?" asked Steward.

Rawlings wiped a hand over his face. Even in the near arctic temperatures created by the air-conditioning, he was sweating. He felt hot and sick.

"General," he said, "my conclusion is that there's no one in the camp yet. They're preparing for something, but they haven't finished the preparations yet."

Steward looked at Halliday. "You concur?"

"Oh, yes, General. I saw nothing on the photos to indicate anyone was in the camp."

"Okay," said Steward. "That's all I need from you two. I'll be in touch."

With that, Comstock came forward and took them out of the room. When they were gone, Steward said, "Well, Alan, what do you think?"

"I think it sounds like we're jumping the gun here. We're rushing around with the idea of rescuing American POWs when there are no POWs to be rescued."

Steward turned in his chair so that he was facing the windows. He pursed his lips and then rubbed them with his left hand. To Bates, he said, "You know that the President, along with the entire civilian chain of command, is very interested in this. They want the rescue."

"I understand that, but right now there isn't anyone to rescue."

"So what do you see as the next move?"

"Sit back and let the North Vietnamese put some people in that camp. Let them make the move. I don't understand this need to rush, rush, rush. It's not like the target's going to get away from us. Like I said, there is no target yet."

"So you're suggesting we do nothing."

"No, General, not at all. I'm suggesting we continue to proceed. I just don't see the need to drop everything else until we're sure that this camp is going to be used for POWs. Until that can be confirmed, there's no need to rush."

Steward rubbed a hand over his face and tugged at his lower lip. "What kind of team do you want for this if it's a go?"

"I'll need about a hundred specially trained men, people with training in communications, demolitions and weapons. And I'd like to take a couple of doctors, too. Not medics, but doctors. Of course we'll need the medics, too. The majority of the force will be grunts—men with combat experience who know the score."

"How long to put the team together?"

"Put them together?" echoed Bates. "I'd say two, three days. I can get personnel to help with a list of the qualified men, then maybe six or eight weeks to get them ready."

"We may not have that long," said Steward.

"To do it right, I'd need that long. We'll want to train them on seizing the compound, and we'll need a mock-up of the camp to do it right."

"All right, Colonel. You get busy building your team, but keep it low-key. I don't want to hear any rumblings about it. You'll report back to me here."

Bates stood up. "I understand, General. I'll be in touch when I know more."

BOTH COLONEL THUY and Soviet Captain Kutnetsov watched as the ZIL-150 diesel trucks drove from their hiding places in the trees on the ridge down to the gate on the south side of the wall. Kutnetsov didn't want to use them because bringing them in left tracks that could be seen from the air, but he didn't know what else to do. He needed the transportation and he didn't want to start the mission by making his men walk a kilometer or two in the hot, humid atmosphere if he could help it.

As the two trucks stopped under the large tree that protected the headquarters building from the sun's rays and the spying of the Americans, Kutnetsov turned from the window and sat down in one of the chairs.

"You think this is a good idea?" said Thuy, still watching everything outside.

"A very good idea," he answered. "First we get a chance at the Americans and second we provide our soldiers with some first-class training."

Now Thuy turned and looked at the Soviet officer. "And if you or one of your men is killed?"

Kutnetsov thought about his orders, given to him by Colonel Tretyak before he'd left the Soviet Union. *Don't let any of your men get killed or captured. Don't violate the DMZ yourself. Let the Vietnamese handle those duties.*

But now, in the field, he didn't see how he could obey those orders without making it look as if he was afraid of the Americans. He shrugged. "We bring the body out or destroy it. The Americans will never know. Besides, there have been rumors for years that white men have been aiding the Vietcong. Former French soldiers and even some Americans who defected."

Thuy sat down behind his desk. "Comrade Captain, I don't understand the necessity of going into South Vietnam so soon. You can practice your ambushes here, away from the Americans. You don't have to take risks."

"You yourself have said that each of the men provided is a combat veteran. Practice missions are of no help. We need the real thing."

"But to tempt fate by going into South Vietnam so early in the program seems foolhardy."

"Comrade Colonel, it isn't foolhardy, it's necessary. Only under the stress of an actual combat mission will I be able to evaluate each of the men."

Thuy shrugged. "You have the authority from my government to do what you think is right. I'm not supposed to interfere in your training or your methods."

Now Kutnetsov smiled. "We'll return in time for breakfast and have a celebration."

"Good luck then."

Kutnetsov rose and bowed slightly. "Thank you." He turned and walked out of the office. At the doorway he stood and watched the progress of the men loading the trucks. They weren't taking much in the way of equipment—a little food, canteens filled with water from the new well, knives, pistols and grenades. Each man carried a new AK-47 and each wore a chest pouch with spare magazines. They ignored radios, afraid that the Americans would be able to overhear their conversations. They took only what they needed for one night in the field, loading themselves down with ammo.

As the sun dropped toward the horizon, Kutnetsov, along with sergeants Moskvin and Salmonov, boarded the lead truck. The Vietnamese, nineteen men selected because of their aggressiveness during the first few hours in the camp, boarded as well. Kutnetsov leaned forward and rapped the cab, telling the driver to proceed.

Outside the gate they turned south, cutting across an open field. A kilometer from the wall, they entered the jungle, following a double path that was heavily overgrown. The North Vietnamese liked it that way because it made it impossible for the Americans to spot the road from the air.

Looking for a good ambush spot, they rocked and bounced along slowly, heading toward the DMZ, now less than thirty miles to the south. They would spend the night there, the Vietnamese preparing for the ambush in case they got lucky and the Soviets observing all their techniques.

Kutnetsov sat gripping his weapon in both hands, his head bowed. The humidity of the jungle seemed to hang in the air, making it difficult to breathe. He felt the sweat on his body dripping from under his arms and down his back. All he wanted was to get out of the jungle and onto an open plain where he hoped there would be a breeze.

Of course he knew that was impossible. As they approached the line dividing the two Vietnams, he began to hear the rumblings of war. Jets streaked overhead, or to the south. There was the pop of helicopter rotor blades and the boom of distant fighting. To leave the jungle now would be to invite attack.

And then the trucks rolled to a halt. Kutnetsov jumped from the rear and ran up to the cab. The Vietnamese driver sat there staring into the distance, a cloth in his hand. Kutnetsov asked what was wrong, but the man only answered in Vietnamese, and Kutnetsov didn't understand him.

One of the Vietnamese who could speak some English and French was able to tell Kutnetsov, using the English, that to travel farther would be to die. The Americans were too close now.

"Have the men get out of the trucks," Kutnetsov ordered. "Form a patrol."

The Vietnamese began to get out slowly. No one wanted to walk. No one wanted to go out on the ambush. Safe at home, or safe in the camp, they talked of nothing other than confronting the Americans and killing them. With the opportunity close at hand, they all began to move with the swiftness of a snail. Each waited for the other to take the initiative.

Kutnetsov stood near the cab of the truck, shaking his head ruefully. Moskvin was shouting at the locals, using a few Vietnamese words he had learned in the short time they had been there. He pushed them and struck them until one of their own men took over. Then Moskvin walked toward his captain.

"I want to see them do it themselves," Kutnetsov scolded. "I don't want us to provide the incentive."

"Sorry, Comrade Captain, but with daylight fading I thought it best to get a move on."

"Under normal circumstances, I'd agree with you. But this is a training mission. We must let them make their own mistakes."

"Being careful not to let them kill us in the process," he warned.

"Precisely."

It took another ten minutes, but the Vietnamese finally formed their patrol. The man who became the leader turned toward the Russians, and when neither of them moved, he gave a command in Vietnamese. The point man started forward, detoured around the massive trunk of a teak tree and disappeared into a wall of vegetation.

A moment later several other men started out, spreading themselves out to avoid ambush. They had good noise discipline. Kutnetsov, Moskvin and Salmonov fell in with the center of the line. They moved quickly, keeping the men ahead in sight. But as it got darker, the distance between them shrunk.

It struck Kutnetsov that even without the sun the jungle was hot. It seemed that the interlocking leaves forming the layers of the canopy conspired to hold the wetness and heat in. Even after moving only a few meters, Kutnetsov found himself soaked. His uniform, at one time a dull green, now looked black because of the moisture and sweat. He wiped at his face constantly, trying to keep the perspiration out of his eyes. He discovered that he wanted only to sit down and rest. His muscles ached and his nerves screamed. To make it worse, they had been walking in the jungle for only ten minutes. Suddenly he wondered if the Vietnamese were testing him. If the Soviet instructor couldn't keep up in the jungle, what good was he to them? He might understand the positioning of a tank division, or how to deploy an infantry company, but that knowledge wasn't any good in the jungle.

Determined not to falter in front of the Vietnamese, Kutnetsov closed his mouth and forced himself to breathe through his nose. He stopped wiping at the sweat and tried to ignore it. Gritting his teeth, he began to move forward with great effort of will. If they were testing him, he would surprise them. He would pass the test with flying colors, and even teach them a thing or two about the true Communist soldier.

ROBIN MORROW KNEW Gerber was involved in something important. She had been around long enough to recognize all the signs. First there were the midnight meetings that no one seemed to know a thing about. Then there were the broken dates and the late phone calls. If it hadn't been Vietnam, and if she'd been married to Gerber, she would have been convinced he was cheating on her.

Now, sitting alone in her room, she tried to figure out how to get a handle on it. From the things Gerber had said, she knew he was attached to the Studies and Observations Group at MACV and that SOG worked with the CIA. In fact, she knew that Studies and Observations was a cover name for Special Operations. It was something that no one spoke aloud. Everyone pretended that he or she didn't know.

She stood up and walked to the tiny alcove that doubled as her kitchen and took out a box of tea bags. As she ran water into a pot, she tried to think of her next move. Ever since Tet, the military and the CIA had been quiet about their operations. The military felt that the press had given them a bad rap because of the momentary gains of the VC.

She still remembered Gerber saying, "Give me a hundred thousand guys and no restrictions on casualties and I'll be able to gain any objective you assign. I won't be able to hold it, but I'll be able to take it."

At first she hadn't understood what he'd meant. And then she'd realized that a surprise attack where the deaths of the soldiers weren't counted as part of the loss seemed to have great success. But how could the Vietcong claim any kind of victory when their casualties were ten and twelve times as high as those suffered by the Americans? How could they claim victory when every one of their achievements had been reversed inside of a month? Now, because the military thought the American press failed to give them the credit they deserved, they didn't give the press anything.

But even without cooperation from MACV, Morrow was sure that something big was about to happen. Maybe it was just a gut feeling, or maybe it was because every time Gerber disappeared it turned out to be something major. His missions in Vietnam were the stuff of novels, and often the novels weren't nearly imaginative enough.

She set the pot on the hot plate and then took it off. Dumping the water, she went back to the combination living room and bedroom. In a single motion she unzipped her jumpsuit and shrugged her way out of it, letting it drop to the floor. Then she stepped to the wardrobe and stood for a moment in front of the air conditioner, letting the cool air dry the sweat from her body. After that she opened the wardrobe and selected one of her prettiest dresses.

As she slipped it on, she knew she wouldn't be able to fool Jerry Maxwell. He would be on guard against her probing questions. Once before she had gotten him to take her out and then pumped him for information. When the evening had ended, she'd felt sickened by what she had done. This time she would tell him up front that she wanted information. Maybe if she turned it into a cat-and-mouse game, she wouldn't feel as if she were violating his trust.

Fully dressed and wishing she had taken a shower first, although she'd already taken two since morning, she left the room. Outside the hotel she flagged down a cab. The driver put the car into gear and gunned the engine before Morrow even had the door shut. Weaving his way in and out of traffic, he found spaces barely large enough for the vehicle to fit into. He roared down one street, took the corner fast enough to send the rear wheels drifting off the asphalt, and then slid to a halt in the MACV parking lot, kicking up a cloud of dust large enough to obscure half the skyline.

Morrow got out gratefully and didn't haggle over the price. She wondered if that had been the driver's plan: scare the passenger so badly that he or she just paid to get away. Walking toward the front of the building, she flashed her press pass at the bored MP.

Inside the MACV building, she began to look for an officer to escort her to the lower level. She found a lieutenant who was working late. He wore wrinkled and sweat-stained jungle fatigues and looked miserable. When she entered his office, he smiled at her and then frowned when she asked him to take her downstairs.

"I'm not sure we can do that, ma'am," he said.

"Don't worry about it. I simply want to talk to the guard."

He stood and pointed at the papers scattered on his desk. "Anything to get away from this."

Together they went to the lower level. The MP informed them that no one was allowed beyond that point.

"Is Jerry Maxwell in?" asked Morrow.

The MP looked as if he had just sat on a pointed stick. He hesitated, wondering what to do. People weren't supposed to know about Jerry Maxwell.

"Check your roster and see if he's signed out," said Morrow.

The MP looked at his clipboard and then picked it up reluctantly. He scanned the names and said, "Mr. Maxwell is still in his office."

"Please tell him that Robin Morrow is here to see him and maybe feed him if he's nice to me."

The MP stared at her as if about to suggest something, and then turned to walk down the hallway, shaking his head. A moment later he returned. "Mr. Maxwell said he'll be right out. He said you could buy him all the food in the world and you still wouldn't get him to tell you anything. He said he was aware of all your feminine tricks and wasn't going to fall for them."

Morrow laughed and then stepped back to wait.

10

TWO KLICKS SOUTH OF
THE DMZ, SOUTH
VIETNAM

Kutnetsov was glad when they finally crossed the last of the ten-kilometer strip that was the DMZ. Although the Americans had cut back the jungle and had tried to defoliate parts of it, the vegetation was still thick, giving Kutnetsov and the North Vietnamese all the cover they needed. Besides, with the sun gone, it was hard to see more than five or six meters, especially since the moon hadn't come up yet.

They wormed their way through the jungle, crossing a small, shallow stream. On the far bank, Moskvin touched Kutnetsov's shoulder. "Leeches."

Kutnetsov nodded his understanding, but the party didn't slow. Leeches could be taken care of in the morning when they returned to North Vietnam. The parasites were inconvenient, annoying, but not something that had to be dealt with immediately.

As soon as they were across the DMZ, the jungle thickened again. Trees climbed to two hundred feet, their leaves intertwined, forming one layer of the triple canopy. Now the little light that had helped them cross into South Vietnam was gone. The patrol pulled together, and in places the soldiers had to put their hands on the shoulders of the man in front or they would have become separated in the dark.

Quietly they continued south, stopping and starting as the point man checked his compass. Eventually they came to a huge clearing. Toppled trees were piled up in the center of it, and the sky overhead was gray, not the black of the jungle. A breeze seemed to filter down into the clearing like wind through a chimney. It rustled the leaves and bushes, creating a rhythm of its own. None of the Vietnamese seemed bothered by the noise.

They skirted the edge of the clearing, staying inside the tree line. Once they were past it, they began to spread out. Then they came to a game trail, which was little more than a green tunnel with a muddy floor. The point man followed it until he came to a larger, man-made trail. Here he stopped and waited for the rest of the men to catch up to him.

Without a word, the men spread out along one side of the route. They took up positions near the trunks of trees, behind rotting logs or under huge flowering bushes. Fanning out quietly, each man moved away from his friends to avoid bunching up in one area.

Kutnetsov stayed close to one of the North Vietnamese, studying him as he placed his weapons in front of him. First he laid out the grenades, each set so that he could snatch it easily. Next he placed a flare beside the grenades, then positioned one magazine from his weapon at the end of the line. Kutnetsov wasn't sure about the wisdom of that, but then he had never been in a combat situation where he had to grab spare magazines from a chest pouch.

Once the ambush site was secured, they all fell silent. Where Kutnetsov had been able to hear the quiet rustling of bushes and the occasional scrape of a foot against the deep, moist vegetation, he now heard nothing. It was as if he had become lost in a stinking, wet cave without a light. He could see nothing and could hear nothing. Like the men around him, he settled back to wait.

The Soviet captain found the jungle to be strangely quiet. At first there were no sounds other than the wind through the upper canopy. Then he heard the soft scrapings of tiny claws on vegetation as insects searched for food. And finally he noticed a quiet buzzing. Initially he thought it was caused by flies, then realized the sound came from mosquitoes. He felt them on his skin, tickling and biting, but made no attempt to brush them away as he crouched on one knee, his AK in his left hand, and waited.

For the first few minutes after the long walk through the jungle, he was happy with the inactivity. His breathing slowed. Sweat that had covered his face dried, leaving an itchy, dirty film that he ignored. And then he became bored. Kneeling in the jungle, unable to see more than a foot or two ahead of him, there was nothing to do. Just listen and wonder. Listen and worry. Listen and wait.

He tried counting the seconds until he reached a full minute, but that seemed an impossible task. He lost track because he didn't care about it. He let his eyes roam right and left but saw nothing. He felt a tingling on his skin and realized it was one of the leeches. That almost made him sick, so he ignored it, forcing his mind to concentrate on the silence.

Finally there was a single cough. Somewhere in the distance was another man. Someone who hadn't sneaked into the jungle with them. One of the enemy.

Kutnetsov had the urge to pick up his rifle, but he resisted it. Slowly he reached down with his right hand and picked up one of his grenades. It was a smooth metal object fashioned in the style favored by the Americans. It wasn't the pineapple-type used in World War II, but the baseball designed for easy throwing. It was packed with bits of metal with a killing radius of twenty to twenty-five meters. A deadly baseball.

The noise of an enemy patrol came closer. There was a second cough and then a whispered order. Silence descended for a moment, and then he heard a scraping of feet. The sound approached, and Kutnetsov felt his stomach tighten in anticipation. The enemy was walking into his trap, or rather into the North Vietnamese trap.

He lifted his hand so that he held the grenade under his nose as if he were smelling it. He wanted to jerk the pin free with his teeth the way the movie heroes did, but knew it wouldn't work unless the pin had been loosened. So, lowering the grenade, he grasped the pin with the index finger of his left hand, keeping the rest of his fingers wrapped around the butt of his AK as he tried to spot the enemy.

There was nothing to do but wait. The sounds of the enemy stopped and then came again, louder. They weren't taking their patrol seriously. Through a gap in the vegetation he spotted a tiny glowing light. Someone was smoking.

That gave Kutnetsov something to aim at. He wanted to throw his grenade, but now was uncertain. Before they had left, he had told the men that this would be a North Vietnamese exercise. It was theirs to screw up or to make a success. He and the other Russians were there as observers.

But suddenly the decision was taken out of his hands. He heard something crackling through the trees. A moment later there was a bright flash and an explosion. Shrapnel tore through the vegetation. That explosion was followed in quick succession by others.

The jungle was suddenly alive. Shouts, screams and curses punctuated the roar of the detonating grenades. One rifle opened up and then a second. The grenades began to throw fountains of sparks upward. More shooting erupted. The enemy soldiers, standing or crouching on the trail, were suddenly visible in the flickering illumination of the muzzle-flashes. They were jerking around like the figures in a silent movie.

Kutnetsov aimed his rifle and pulled the trigger. He felt it kick back but didn't hear it fire. His hand found the selector switch, and he flipped it to full-auto. He burned through his magazine quickly, a tongue of flame stabbing into the darkness. Emerald-green tracers bounced and danced in the night. The men on the trail fell and died quickly, screaming in fright and pain.

In seconds it was over. The night was silent again, but this time amazingly so. There was no sound, not even the echoes from the firing. And it seemed blacker, darker.

But before he had a chance to let that soak in, they were all up and moving. No one swept the trail, checking the bodies or taking the weapons. Instead they moved back to the North, almost running away from the ambush.

Kutnetsov felt a strange bubbling in his chest and stomach, a feeling that he was a teenager who had committed some misdemeanor and was fleeing into the night. He glanced over his shoulder to see if anyone was chasing him, but saw nothing other than the blackness of the jungle.

They didn't stop right away. They alternately ran, jogged and walked until they came to the relatively open area of the DMZ. Without a thought to military strategies or disciplines, the North Vietnamese ran into the open. They loped across the ground, leaping bushes and fallen logs, ignoring everything around them until they arrived at the stream. Then they collapsed onto the bank, suddenly laughing like kids who had escaped early from school.

Kutnetsov wanted to shout at them, but knew it wasn't the right time. Once they were back in the camp, he could rebuke them for the things they had done wrong. He knew they would protest, saying they had killed the enemy. But he also knew they wouldn't be able to tell him how many, or worse, who the enemy had been. And then with horror gnawing at his gut, he suddenly wondered if they *were* the enemy. What if the men on the trail had been VC or NVA whom they knew nothing about. No one had taken the time to identify the target. The bodies of the dead could have answered all those questions for him.

Still, there was some merit to the exercise. They had gotten into and out of South Vietnam and none of them had been injured. Maybe he could learn something from these North Vietnamese soldiers if he kept his mind open.

Moments later they were on their feet, splashing through the water, hurrying northward. The sounds of jets overhead and artillery faded in the distance. From a high point close to where they had left the trucks, Kutnetsov saw an American jet bombing the jungle. There was an orange ball of fire, but never the sound of an explosion. The pilot made several runs at his target. Finally, having used all his ammo, he turned and streaked for the safety of the sea. Kutnetsov wished there was some way to shoot at the plane.

And when they reached the isolated jungle clearing in North Vietnam where they had left the trucks, as they approached, no one challenged them. No one had bothered with guard duty. It wasn't necessary because the Americans never came north. They threatened and complained, but all they ever did was send planes to drop bombs.

As they climbed into the trucks, Kutnetsov took a head count of the Russians. He found that both Moskvin and Salmonov were there. Salmonov complained because he hadn't been allowed to search the bodies for intelligence. Moskvin complained because they had fled rather than set up a second ambush, hoping to catch anyone who wanted to find out about the shooting.

Kutnetsov just shook his head. "We'll teach them more about this tomorrow. Tonight be happy that we've returned from the mission safely."

In the morning they would learn that two of the North Vietnamese had disappeared.

IN THE RESTAURANT, Jerry Maxwell, who hadn't bothered to change, sat across the table from Robin Morrow, pretending to be angry with her. It was a ploy to throw her off guard so that he wouldn't have to answer a lot of dumb questions.

Morrow, on the other hand, was smiling sweetly. She was waiting for Maxwell to drink more of the wine she had ordered. She felt certain the liquor would have the desired effect, then she could trip him up.

Maxwell toyed with his whiskey glass, shaking it so that the ice cubes rattled. He kept his eyes on the glass, not wanting to look up at Morrow.

"So, Jerry," she said, "just what *is* going on?"

He looked up and took a sip. "Nothing that would be of interest to you. Some pretty tame missions to check on the flow of supplies into South Vietnam."

"Midnight meetings for that?"

Maxwell drained his glass and held it up, shaking it until the waitress nodded. "Midnight meetings for that. Hell, Robin, you know the military never sleeps."

"Yeah. Especially the one in Saigon. Come on, Jerry, you people, well, not you, but most of the people here work nine to five and are annoyed if they're required to stay ten minutes late."

"Well," said Maxwell, picking up his menu. He pulled a pair of glasses from his inside coat pocket and put them on. They immediately slipped to the end of his nose.

"I didn't know you wore glasses."

"I didn't used to. Now, sitting in that damned artificially lit office of mine reading all that fine print, I find my eyesight is beginning to go."

The waitress appeared and they both ordered. Morrow opted for seafood, but Maxwell stuck with steak and baked potato. As the waitress hurried away, Maxwell took off his glasses, folded them and shoved them back into his pocket. "Now that we've ordered dinner and you've promised to pay for it, I suppose I have to submit to the interview."

"I think that's only fair," said Morrow.

Maxwell nodded slightly. "Then proceed."

"I want to know where Mack Gerber is and what he's doing."

For an instant Maxwell was going to deny any knowledge of Mack Gerber's whereabouts or what he was doing, but then he looked deeply into Morrow's eyes. He saw something there. Instead of the flip answer he had been prepared to give, he asked, "This on the record, or is it deep background?"

"How deep?" she asked.

"Couple of thousand feet, I would guess."

"You realize," she said, "that anything you tell me will only allow me to narrow my search. Maybe I can't quote you as a source, or use the information, but it'll give me a handle on the situation."

"Then I shouldn't say a word to you."

"Jerry, I have my job to do and you know that. But I've never done a thing to jeopardize the men in the field. You know that, too."

His fresh drink arrived. The waitress hesitated just long enough to snatch the empty glass and then she was gone.

"I shouldn't have to tell you the importance of secrecy," said Maxwell.

"Look, Jerry, I know something's going on. It's obvious from the late-night meetings." She held up her hand to stop another protest. "Don't give me a lot of shit about it being normal because I know it isn't. Now, you can give me something to tell my boss, or he puts a number of other people on it."

Maxwell took a long pull at his drink and then carefully set it down. "I don't like being blackmailed."

"I'm not blackmailing you. I'm giving you the facts of life. You can talk to me and work with me, or you can deal with some of my fellow journalists who feel that anything the military and the government does in Vietnam is wrong."

"There's not much to tell. Just that Captain Gerber and Sergeant Fetterman are in the field making a normal recon. It's nothing special."

Now Morrow smiled. "Then why is the CIA running it?"

"Where in hell did you get that idea?"

She stopped talking as the food arrived. As soon as the plates were set in front of them and the waitress had vanished, she answered his question. "Because you always know about the mission."

"Christ, Robin, I know about most of the Special Forces missions run in South Vietnam. There's nothing extraordinary about that."

"Then there's nothing special here?"

"Routine, believe me. So routine that it's boring. Had a hell of a time convincing Gerber and Fetterman to take it."

"I thought you weren't in on it."

Maxwell picked up his knife and scraped butter into the steaming potato. He kept his eyes on it and said, "I wasn't. That's what I heard. Gerber suggested that some guy with two months in-country could handle it. Didn't require a lot of brains or experience.''

''But he took it.''

''Under protest, sure.''

Morrow shook her head in disbelief. She picked up her fork and spread the food around to let it cool. She had heard Maxwell change his story and knew he was lying.

''Jerry, that sounds like the biggest load I've ever heard. Mack wouldn't be out if it was routine. Hell, the way it was put together suggests something more.''

''You going to keep digging?''

''I have to,'' she said. She stared at him and repeated, ''I have to.''

HALF A WORLD AWAY Alan Bates stood on the platform in front of the silver screen in the base theater, which was small, crowded, and hot. At the far end, at the top of the gentle slope that led to the rear, was the projection booth, a series of speakers painted light green and an armed guard. The guard was mainly for show. MPs had been stationed around the outside of the theater so that no one could sneak close to the exits and listen.

Bates stood in the shadows. A small spotlight was trained on the lectern at one side of the stage, but Bates was staying in the shadows until he was sure everyone was inside. He glanced at his watch, decided that everyone who was going to come had arrived, then nodded. The MP disappeared long enough to signal the others outside that no one else was to be allowed in, and then locked the front door.

Bates, his green beret clutched in his right hand, stepped to the lectern, flipped a switch and heard an audible click. The microphone was now on.

He bent closer to the mike and then stared at the flyer he had put up in a half-dozen mess halls only that morning. It requested men with one tour of duty in Vietnam to report to the base theater if they'd like to volunteer for special training. It said nothing more and was similar to a dozen other announcements posted all over. The only difference was the requirement for combat veterans.

As the crowd in the theater—Bates estimated there were three to four hundred men present—settled down, he said, "Good morning, gentlemen, I'm Colonel Alan Bates and I have a bit of a problem."

He waited for a response, and when there was none, he continued. "I'm looking to put together a small force with special training. Right now there's no mission for that force and no real reason to put it together. In the future, a week, a month, a year, it might become necessary for us to have a small elite team. That's what we're planning here."

The house lights had been dimmed, and all he could see was a sea of dark shapes in front of him, some with light skin that marked their positions, some with dark that concealed them. It was interesting that no one was talking, joking or coughing. He had their undivided attention. Unfortunately he didn't know what to do with it.

"There isn't much I can tell you now. Circumstances are such that I'm required to keep everything about this, ah, exercise a secret. All I can say is that no one has to make a decision now. We have a little time to think about it. At least until after lunch."

That got a reaction. There was a quiet murmuring and then silence again.

"Gentlemen, those of you who'd like to buy a pig in a poke please return here at 1300 hours. Bring a copy of your 201 file with you. If you have any special training or abilities that aren't listed in the file, please note those on another sheet of paper. Are there any questions?"

From the back someone shouted, "Will you be able to tell us any more after lunch, Colonel?"

Bates shook his head. "You won't receive any formal briefing until after the selection process." Now he grinned, but the men couldn't see it. "I can tell you that this is one time you won't be sorry you volunteered. Now if that doesn't sound like something a recruiting officer would say, I don't know what would. Anything else?"

When no one spoke up, Bates said, "Thank you for your time and I'll see some of you after lunch."

The men stood to go, filing out quickly and quietly. At that moment Bates was sure none of them would return. He had been too vague, and that was something he couldn't help. He had his orders, too.

11

JUST NORTH OF THE
DMZ
NORTH VIETNAM

The trucks started north, bouncing along the rutted jungle trail. Kutnetsov sat there quietly, listening to the noise of the laboring engines. He closed his eyes and let the rush of air caused by the motion of the truck cool him, feeling the sweat dry from his face and hair. His breathing became regulated, and he wondered if he had gotten out of shape during the months he had sat behind a desk in Moscow and then during the days teaching the North Vietnamese.

He let the thoughts come to him then—a random pattern of thinking that relaxed him after the end of an exercise or a battle. And then the jungle intruded on his mind. He didn't understand it. He had heard that it was hot and humid, and while he knew what the words meant, he had had no idea it would be like this. There was something about that combination that sucked the strength from the toughest men, leaving them whimpering in the dirt. It was a relentless feeling that made the heart pound and the blood seem to boil. Continued effort made you feel faint and sick to the stomach, wishing that you would either pass out or throw up.

To make it worse, the jungle held the heat. The triple canopy might block the sun's rays, but it didn't filter out the heat.

It was a place of perpetual twilight, a glowing green hell that was like living in a steam bath. Water filtered slowly through the canopies until it dripped constantly. Leaves filled slowly and then tipped, the water cascading through the jungle and sounding like a platoon that had suddenly decided to run. Rain from the monsoons didn't reach the ground: it trickled through the upper canopy until it watered the plants at the lowest level a day or two after the storm.

Kutnetsov thought about all this, and then about the Third World where new conflicts were taking place. The steppes of Asia and the urban areas of Europe were worlds apart from the jungles that wrapped the equator. In future the major conflicts would be in the jungles or deserts that straddled the equator, and troops not prepared to fight there would be in trouble.

The truck hit a bump, throwing the men in the air. Most of them laughed as they bounced back onto the wooden benches. Kutnetsov wanted to yell at the driver, whom he felt had a soft job—nothing to do except stay with the vehicles while the men went out to fight. But Kutnetsov said nothing. Instead he shook himself and told himself not to get too philosophical. The Soviet military didn't like it. Let the marshals and the generals make the high-level decisions. He would stay in the background where he belonged, learning all he could.

They reached the edge of the jungle and stopped. In the half-light filtering through a partially overcast sky, he could see the camp. The walls reflected the moonlight, but there was no sign of life inside. That was just as it should be. From the air no one should be able to tell that anyone lived down there.

Now that the mission was over, a short walk of a kilometer or two wouldn't hurt the men. It would take the edge off, give them a chance to use the nervous energy that built after the close of a fight.

Kutnetsov stood and slipped along the bench, trying not to step on the toes of the men there. He dropped to the ground and called out quietly, "Everyone out."

For a moment no one moved, then Moskvin picked up one of the Vietnamese and propelled him toward the tailgate. The man shouted in surprise but kept moving. In a minute all the men were on the ground, standing at the rear of the vibrating trucks, waiting for someone to give them more instructions.

Moskvin moved to do just that, but before he could speak Kutnetsov stopped him. "Let them do it. We'll see how they think."

It didn't take long. The North Vietnamese were home. And when no one told them to form up, they began to straggle down the slopes toward the camp. At first it was a cautious move, as if they were waiting for someone to order them to halt. But when the order didn't come, they began to run. A couple of men jogged out in front, and then a few more raced by until they were all running toward the gate as fast as they could move.

Moskvin watched them stumble over the logs and ruts hidden in the short grass. "Now what, Captain?"

"We do it right, of course. Salmonov, please take the point and I'll bring up the rear."

Salmonov jogged a few meters and then slowed, walking down the slope, his weapon tracking right and left as if he expected the enemy to pop up at any moment. Moskvin was behind him, only four or five meters away. Kutnetsov brought up the rear, keeping his eyes roaming and his ears cocked.

They reached the front gate, but instead of entering they hesitated outside, checking it for booby traps and ambushes. Once inside, they found the members of the patrol scattered around, drinking water and laughing about the ease of killing the Americans.

Kutnetsov stood near the trunk of the tree and watched. The North Vietnamese finally gave up on the water and found several bottles of wine. They passed these around, drinking and pouring the liquor on one another's head. They ignored the stone-faced Kutnetsov but tried to interest both Moskvin and Salmonov in the party. Both Soviet NCOs refused.

Finally Kutnetsov moved to the center of the group and stood there, hands on his hips, until the North Vietnamese fell silent. When he had their attention, he began telling them everything they had done wrong. He told them of their sloppy noise discipline, their lack of unit integrity and their assumption that everything was fine at the camp. Just because it had been that way when they had left was no reason to assume it would be on their return.

"But we killed the enemy and no one was hurt," protested one of the Vietnamese.

"We can do better," said Kutnetsov. "If we plan our raids, we can kill more of them."

"It was a good mission," said another.

"Yes," agreed Kutnetsov. "It was good. But we can do better. Do more damage to the enemy."

"How?" asked another. He held a wine bottle by the neck. The liquor had spilled to stain his shirt.

Kutnetsov turned. "By planning and training and learning how to mount a proper ambush."

"Ours was just fine."

Kutnetsov stared at the man but refused to be drawn into an argument. Instead he said, "One of the first things we should take care of is our weapons. On return, before we drink, before we piss, before we do anything, we clean the weapons so that they're ready again. We do that now."

No one moved. No one spoke. Kutnetsov stared at the men. One of them defiantly took a drink from a wine bottle and Moskvin advanced on him. Kutnetsov shook his head and stepped to the man. His weapon was lying in the dirt, the operating rod down. Kutnetsov snatched up the weapon, dropped the magazine from it and worked the bolt. There was a tiny grating of sand before the chambered round was ejected.

"This man," said Kutnetsov, "just killed us all. He ignored his training for his creature comforts. He fails to take care of his equipment and then curses because it won't work. This man is a hazard to the whole unit."

He turned and tossed the weapon to Moskvin, who caught it in a huge left hand. "You're a disgrace to this unit," Kutnetsov told the man.

He wanted to lecture them some more but knew the point had been made. From the moment he'd begun talking to them, he'd known one of them would get mouthy. Once someone sounded off, all Kutnetsov had to do was use the smartass's remarks to reinforce the lesson. The rest of the soldiers would end up being glad they hadn't said anything.

Kutnetsov waved to his two NCOs. Together the three of them returned to their quarters where they would clean their weapons and prepare for the next day's lessons. Kutnetsov had learned one thing during his military career and that was to lead by example. It was too easy to fall into the rut that many top officers did. They yelled and screamed and ordered, but they never did anything. They lost the respect of their men because the men couldn't understand why there were two sets of rules.

Kutnetsov could have explained why there were two sets, and the reasons for it made good sense, but the men would refuse to understand. So, rather than alienate them by telling them one thing and doing another, Kutnetsov followed his own orders and made sure each of the Soviet soldiers with him did the same. The North Vietnamese might believe they knew better, but Kutnetsov would show them the error of their ways. By doing so, he knew he would end up with the kind of soldiers he wanted.

Thirty minutes later he looked out the window. The North Vietnamese were no longer sitting on the ground drinking wine. They were cleaning their weapons and preparing for the next day's activities, just as Kutnetsov knew they would be.

ALAN BATES SAT in the back of the mess hall, away from most of the enlisted soldiers who were swapping stories of women in the nearby town. Women who liked soldiers even if the majority of the people in the country seemed to believe it was the soldiers who had brought on the Vietnam War. Women who had one thing on their minds, and it cost the soldiers nothing to help them out.

Bates just sat there quietly, eating the food that was something less than spectacular. At least there was a lot of gravy to mask the flavor of the meat.

The mess hall itself was pleasant enough—a long, low building filled with tables surrounded by four chairs so that it looked like a cross between a diner and a restaurant. There was a serving line in the front. Men grabbed a molded plastic tray and aluminum silverware and progressed through the line, while other men wearing white stood behind tables and slopped food onto the trays. Once filled, the men moved to the tables.

The windows were open and giant floor-mounted fans roared near the windows and doors, creating strong winds throughout the mess hall. The fans made it seem almost cool inside, and once Bates had gotten used to the noise, it was almost pleasant.

He paid no attention to the two Air Force officers who entered. Pope Air Force Base was close so that it wasn't unusual to see Air Force people around. It was unusual to see them in an Army mess hall, since Air Force food was better.

Both Air Force officers got trays, made their way through the serving lines and then retreated to the rear of the mess hall. The male officer approached and asked, "Mind if we join you, sir?"

"Suit yourself," said Bates.

"You want chocolate milk?" asked the female.

"Sure, Sheila. Chocolate's fine."

As she headed toward the aluminum milk machine near the door, Rawlings held out a hand to introduce himself. "I'm David Rawlings, and that's Sheila Halliday. We met in General Steward's office."

Bates nodded and took the officer's grasp. "I remember."

"I must confess, Colonel, that we knew you were here and were sent to talk to you."

Bates set his fork on the table and raised his eyebrows. "You were sent here?"

"Yes, sir. General Steward thought there might be some information we have that could be useful to you."

Bates scratched his head and then rubbed a hand through his short-cropped hair. "I'm not sure of what value you could be to me here and now."

"Well," said Rawlings, lowering his voice. He glanced around quickly to see if anyone was paying attention to him. "I have some inside knowledge about the intended target."

"Uh-huh," said Bates. He didn't like this because he didn't know Rawlings. The meeting in General Steward's office didn't count, as far as Bates was concerned. The military was becoming a big bureaucracy like other aspects of the government. Too many people knew too much about everything, and the last thing he wanted to do was talk to a first lieutenant who hadn't even bothered to present orders of any kind.

Halliday returned and set two full glasses of chocolate milk on the table, one in front of Rawlings. As she sat down, she nodded. "Afternoon, Colonel."

Bates ignored her. "I'm not sure I know what help you can be."

"When we finish here," said Rawlings, "I can take you over to the base Intel office and show you some pictures. New pictures of the target."

"I don't see the relevance of any more photographs, at least at this point."

Rawlings took a big bite, chewed it carefully and then washed it down with milk. "Well, sir, maybe the photos will give you a clue about your mission."

"Why don't you tell me if there's anything in the new pictures that wasn't visible in the older ones. Is there any reason for me to waste my time looking at them?" Bates asked.

Rawlings stopped eating and touched a napkin to his lips. He glanced at Halliday. "This is really awful." He grinned and turned his attention to Bates. "No, sir, there isn't anything new. Again there's—"

"I don't need classified details."

"Yes, sir. Well, without worrying about compromising anything, I can say there's nothing new. There's more evidence of construction, but that's it."

"Seems to me that some people at the Pentagon are jumping through their asses."

Halliday entered the conversation for the first time. "I think, Colonel, that you've hit the nail on the head. They're all running around, but no one has anything to prove, one way or the other—what we want proved anyway."

"In that case," said Bates, "I don't see any reason for me to look at your pictures. I think I'll just finish my lunch and continue to march."

"Yes, sir," said Rawlings. "We're supposed to stick close to you."

"I assume you have orders to that effect and that you have documents to prove you have the proper clearances."

Rawlings nodded. "Our orders come from General Steward himself. You can check with him or with Colonel Sheckley, who I believe has the liaison job."

"Then you have written orders?"

"Yes, sir. As soon as I finish lunch, I can provide you with copies of them."

Again Bates put down his fork and stared at the young lieutenant. He didn't know what it was about the man, but he didn't like him. Maybe it was his nine-to-five corporate attitude that suggested he knew nothing of the military or of military courtesies. Maybe it was the way he had asked to sit down and then launched into his conversation.

Finally Bates said, "Lieutenant, you should know that you're required to carry copies of your orders. You shouldn't arrive on the scene without them and then suggest you'll provide the documentation later."

"Well, sir," started Rawlings.

"How long have you been in the Air Force?"

"About two years."

"Then you must have had contact with the proper military channels. I would think you'd have learned that this isn't a college classroom. There are ways that things are done and they're not open to debate. Now, I'd like to suggest that you find a copy of your orders and supply them. If not, get away from my table."

He hadn't planned to go that far, but the blank stare on Rawlings's face had set him off. The longer he looked at it, the madder he got. It was as if Rawlings didn't understand the English language.

Now Halliday spoke up. She opened her black regulation purse and handed a single sheet to Bates. "My orders, Colonel."

Bates took the paper and read it quickly. It gave him all the information he needed, including her serial number. Bates nodded. "May I see your ID card?"

Halliday nodded and showed it to Bates. He checked it carefully, including the information on the back. He returned it to Halliday. "See, Lieutenant, that's the way it's supposed to be handled. You supply the documentation first and then we talk about the mission."

"Yes, sir. My name should be on the orders there. With Sheila's."

"And it was. Now, if you'll show me your ID card."

They went through the ritual again. Bates, satisfied that he'd taught Rawlings a lesson, said, "Now, I'm going over to the base theater to continue my job. You're welcome to join me there if you want. If not, I'll meet you at the officers' club at 1600 hours."

Halliday nodded, but Rawlings asked, "You don't mind if we sit in at the theater?"

"Not at all. Be there by 1300, or the MPs won't let you in." Bates slid his chair back and stood. "Now, if you'll excuse me, I have a few things to do."

Without waiting for a reply, Bates hurried from the mess hall, aware he was supposed to pick up his tray and return it to the front. As a colonel, though, he figured he was entitled to a few privileges.

Outside, he stopped and faced the bright midday sun. After the roar and the forced breeze from the big fans in the mess hall, the quiet and the sun were welcome. He let the rays wash over him and felt as if they were cleansing him.

Bates walked over to the jeep that had been assigned to him, climbed in and started it. Instead of driving to the theater, he turned down a narrow road lined with pine trees. There were soldiers in white T-shirts and fatigue pants who were involved in a policing detail. Sergeants in perfect uniforms, wearing Smoky the Bear hats, were watching the soldiers. One of them snapped to attention and whipped off a perfect salute.

Bates came to an area of single-story buildings, which was a company and battalion administration area. He parked in the adjutant's slot, knowing that he outranked the man, which meant there wouldn't be any repercussions. Hell, he outranked the battalion commander for that matter.

The inside of the building was hot and humid, but not the way it would have been in Vietnam. Several fans were stuck in corners and by windows, each turned up full and blowing across the interior. There was a bank of offices opposite the door and an open bay with several desks. A few clerks, again stripped to T-shirts and fatigue pants, worked at old manual typewriters or sat reading magazines. The linoleum floor was polished to an impossible gloss, and bulletin boards on the walls held posters that demanded everyone wear the uniform proudly, instructed soldiers how to wear their ribbons or advertised Fun, Travel, Adventure in the Modern Army. Next to that poster was one of a man skiing down a green slope, his M-16 slung over his shoulder, the words underneath proclaiming, Ski Vietnam.

Bates moved to the waist-high counter and leaned on it, waiting for someone to spot him. A sergeant leaped forward and asked, "How can I help you, Colonel?"

"I've got a minor problem. I need a phone with an autovon. Have to talk to someone at the Pentagon."

The sergeant looked over his shoulder. "I don't know, sir."

"Is Colonel Mendez here?"

"No, sir, he's gone to lunch."

"The colonel knows me."

"Yes, sir, I'm sure he does." Again the man looked around as if trying to decide what to do. Finally he shrugged, "Hell, sir, if you're calling the Pentagon, I don't see how it can hurt." He reached around and opened the gate. "You can use the colonel's office."

Bates followed the sergeant into the office. He walked to the desk and sat down behind it. The sergeant stood there for a moment and then closed the door as he left. Bates looked at the office. It was like a thousand other such offices—small with a single window behind the desk, cinder-block walls painted green, a bookcase with black binders full of army regulations, a couple of chairs for visitors, and a heavily waxed concrete floor.

Bates tried to ignore the papers scattered on the desk. They concerned the running of the battalion and were none of his business. He pulled the phone closer and dialed eight to get access to the autovon. When the line opened, he dialed the number he wanted, waited and then heard it ring.

"This is Sheckley."

"Bates here. One question. You send a kid named Rawlings down here?"

"Sure did. Thought he might have some information you should see."

"Okay," said Bates, nodding. "You might want to instruct him in military courtesy. His companion seems to know what she's doing, however."

"Anything else?"

"That's it. Thanks." Bates hung up and walked to the door. The sergeant was seated close to it, waiting. Bates thanked him and left. As he climbed into his jeep, he saw that it was nearly one o'clock. Rather than hurry to the theater, he took the long route, giving the men time to get there and find a good seat.

Bates parked in the theater lot and strode up to the MP sergeant standing guard. He told the man that after he entered no one else was to be allowed in. It would be the same deal as in the morning, though he suspected it would last longer.

With that he entered the theater. For a moment he stood at the rear where he could see the crowd. It looked as if about half of the men had decided they didn't want to buy a pig in a poke. The rest had returned and were now talking quietly among themselves. For a group of Army enlisted men they were almost too quiet. There was none of the normal joking around and speculation on the nature of the mission.

Bates walked down the aisle and felt the eyes of the men turn toward him. He took off his beret as he neared the stage and rolled it in his left hand, then climbed the four steep steps to the stage and walked to the lectern. As he did, the men in the theater fell silent, but no one called them to attention. One by one they all got to their feet.

Bates turned on the light and the microphone, then leaned toward it and said, "Please be seated."

He waited until everyone was settled. "Thank you for returning. I'm sure you'll be glad you made that decision. Now, I'm going to circulate a roster. I'll need your name, rank, serial number and current unit of assignment. For my convenience, I'd also like a phone number. Afterward, we'll set up a series of interviews."

One of the men stood. "When do we get to know more about this?"

Bates hung his head and thought. There was nothing he could tell these men. Not at this stage. He leaned both elbows on the lectern and spoke into the mike. "Once the final team has been selected and the training begun, it will become obvious to you what we have in mind. However, given the nature of the job, I can't tell you any more than that. If any of you have second thoughts, now is the time to get out."

He waited and watched. Two men worked their way to the aisle and hurried to the rear. A lone man in front stood and left. But no one else did.

"So," said Bates, grinning. "Years of experience in the Army and you still haven't learned not to volunteer."

That was an old joke. In Special Forces nearly every man had volunteered two or three times just to get there. They had to have volunteered for jump training and then for the Special Warfare School and most of them had volunteered for an additional hitch in the Army.

"Okay," said Bates when it was clear no one else was going to leave. "I want all sergeants major and master sergeants to move to the front. I'll have to ask you men to help me get this sorted out. Once we've done that, I can start the interviews. Are there any questions?"

From the back someone shouted, "Yeah, when are you going to start the movie?"

There were only a couple of nervous chuckles.

12

ISOLATION AREA AT
BIEN HOA, RVN

Gerber sat sweating in the dirty, smelly hootch stuck at the end of a runway. The hut was separated from the rest of the military complex by a series of barbed wire fences and guard shacks. After the initial rush to get him and his men to Bien Hoa, no one had bothered with them other than to tell them to be patient and not to stray outside the isolation area.

Fetterman, of course, took the whole thing with his usual attitude. He checked through the equipment and made sure they had everything they would need for a covert mission, paying particular attention to the radios.

There were a couple of small URC-10s, an ultrahigh-frequency radio with the range to cover all of South Vietnam. And there were smaller sets that had the unlikely name of handy-talky. With a range limited to a hundred meters, less in dense jungle, these would be used for intraunit communication. And finally there was an AN/GRC-109, nicknamed the Angry 109. It had a keypad for the encryption of messages to base. Bocker would be the one to work with it. After Gerber and his men strung an antenna in a tree, the enemy would have a difficult time triangulating. Bocker would use short-burst transmissions to reduce the likelihood of enemy eavesdropping, but in case the NVA did manage to get a fix, they would only find the antenna and not the transmitter.

While Tyme slept, Fetterman checked the weapons. He examined them all carefully. "The AKs are good," he told Gerber. "Solves one of our resupply problems."

Gerber nodded, knowing exactly what the master sergeant meant. Rather than having to hump the ammo through the jungle and then worry about burning through it in a firefight, they could pick up what they needed from the enemy. That wasn't something the bureaucrats in Washington thought about.

Gerber moved to the weapons rack. "Are there enough AKs for everyone?"

"Yes, sir." Fetterman reached out and patted the French-designed MAS 49. "Too bad about this. I'd like to take it, but it's still chambered for 7.5 millimeter."

"Let's keep it as simple as possible," said Gerber.

"I was just thinking that if we were required to do any long-range shooting, the AKs aren't the best for that."

Gerber moved to the rack and looked at the weapons. None of them had been designed with long-range work in mind. The assault rifles were good up to about two hundred meters. They could be used at longer ranges, but there were other weapons with better long-range characteristics.

"Given the nature of the mission," said Gerber, "I doubt we'll be doing any long-range shooting."

"You never know," said Fetterman.

"Right, Tony, you never know. However, let's try to keep the selection of weapons simple. Everyone carries an AK. If one breaks, we'll be able to find spare parts."

Again Fetterman patted the MAS 49 lovingly. "No one appreciates these old weapons."

Gerber returned to the table and sat down. He pulled one of the maps closer and studied it. Like everything else in the room, it wasn't of American manufacture; it was an old French map that showed Da Nang as a small coastal city with no mention of the American base there.

As he studied it, he realized that a parachute drop into North Vietnam was a risk they didn't have to take. They could be ferried by helicopter to the DMZ, hell, into the DMZ, and dropped there. The hike to the enemy location wasn't all that great, and it meant that it could be done in one or two nights—a much quieter way of entering the North.

He checked the map again and then called out, "Say, Tony, I need your opinion."

Together they discussed the helicopter plan and decided it was the way to go. If one of the others organized the resupply team properly, they could bring in huge amounts of supplies, using the same system. A hike of twenty or thirty klicks wasn't that much with the reduction in risk. Hell, they could truck the stuff to the DMZ and go get it.

Escape and evasion would work the same way: everyone flee south, and in a day or less they could be in South Vietnam. Looking closely at the map, Gerber felt the excitement build in his stomach. He could see it all laid out in front of him—a simple low-profile mission that didn't require complicated airdrops and resupply. They could stay in the jungle for months with no one knowing they were around.

"I'm going to have to coordinate this with someone," said Gerber. "Call Maxwell and tell him to call off the parachute drop. Tell him we need airlift to... Quang Tri, and then helicopters from there."

"Looks good, Captain," said Fetterman.

"The beauty of it is the resupply. If somehow our guys get picked up, there'd be no indication there was another team in there. With airplanes flying all around, we alert the enemy to something."

"So what are you going to do?"

"Get Maxwell on the horn and tell him what we want. Either have him come here to hear us out or we go and see him. But I'm not going to parachute into North Vietnam when I don't have to."

Gerber got to his feet and moved toward the door. It opened then, and the sergeant who had picked them up at the airfield stepped in. He stopped short and stared, finally saying, "I've got some hot grub in the jeep."

"Good," said Gerber. "Bring it in. Then you and I'll go for a ride."

"Excuse me, sir," said the sergeant, "but I was just told to bring the food. Nothing was said about you going out somewhere."

Gerber nodded patiently. "And now something has been said. I need to coordinate a few activities and can't do it here."

The sergeant looked uncertain and then shrugged. "Okay, sir."

Fetterman got up and walked to the door. "Let me give you a hand with that food."

Outside in the jeep were two regular-Army hot food containers, a box filled with tin cans holding various fruits and a case of warm Coke.

"Any ice?" asked Fetterman.

"You're kidding, of course," said the sergeant.

"Of course," said Fetterman.

They carried the food back into the hootch and set it on the floor. When they were finished, the sergeant said, "Any time you're ready, sir."

"Tony, keep an eye on things here. Don't let Justin get a wild hair and take off. You know how he can be."

Fetterman nodded, knowing that Tyme could be counted on to find a reason to break the isolation. Zeroing weapons was his favorite method, and the best. At least it had some merit. Others ranged from a need to find spare parts for the weapons to a desire to get new boots off the enemy.

Outside again, Gerber climbed into the passenger seat. The sergeant started the engine, ground the gears and then lurched forward, spinning the tires and kicking up a cloud of dust that hung in the air. There was almost no breeze and the humidity made it seem stagnant. The sunlight was no longer bright, but seemed dimmed, as if filtered through several layers of dirty plastic. The heat hadn't diminished—in fact, it seemed hotter—but it wasn't bright enough for sunglasses.

The sergeant took him to a long building with a tin roof.
Sandbags were scattered around the plywood-and-screen
structure to hold it in place. Inside, a ceiling fan turned slowly.
It was attached to a parachute flare that hung down through
the canopy. A desk was tucked into one side of the small room
and a settee was pushed against one wall.

"What do you want?" asked the man sitting behind the
desk. He was a burly man with sweat-damp hair. An unlit cigar protruded from between his teeth. To Gerber he looked
just like the stereotype of the sergeant in a hundred bad movies.

"Need to contact someone in Saigon."

The burly sergeant pointed down a short corridor. "Talk to
Specialist McGee at the switchboard."

Gerber nodded and walked down the hall. The switchboard was shoved into a tiny cubicle barely big enough for it.
A man wearing jungle fatigue pants and a white T-shirt stained
yellow by sweat sat there pushing wires into slots as he worked
the board.

"I need to put a call through to Saigon," said Gerber.

The man turned to stare up at the captain. He was a young
man, no more than eighteen, with light blond hair and an almost invisible mustache and eyebrows. There was a bruise on
his cheek that looked as if it had happened by falling out of bed
rather than in combat.

"Anyone special?"

"Office of Jerry Maxwell."

"You got a number, or you want I should guess?"

Gerber shook his head in disbelief. Why was it that all the
men with good jobs in the rear had the worst attitudes? "I have
a number." He gave it to the man.

A moment later the man handed him the receiver. "If I was
lucky, I got through."

Then there was an answer. Gerber recognized the voice and
said, "Maxwell?"

"I'm sorry, I didn't quite catch that."

"Maxwell, this is Gerber," he shouted. Self-consciously he looked down the hall, wondering if everyone was watching and listening.

"Gerber? You're supposed to be—"

"I know where I'm supposed to be," shouted Gerber. "What I need from you is a change in plans."

"Everything is laid on," said Maxwell over the squeaking phone. "Nothing can be changed now."

"You'd better change it," yelled Gerber. "There are good reasons for it. You hop on a chopper, get your ass up here and I'll explain it to you."

"I can't make it," said Maxwell.

"Jerry, things change. I looked at the fucking map and there's no reason for us to go with the original plan. In fact, I now veto it in favor of something simpler."

"You can't do that."

"Maxwell," said Gerber, his voice growing cold, "I sure as hell can do it. SFHQ in Nha Trang will back me up on this, especially when they look at the map."

"Okay, okay," snapped Maxwell. "I can be there in an hour. Remain in your quarters until I get there, and don't talk to anyone."

"Maxwell, I'm not under house arrest. And I know how to conduct myself. Before you come up here, why don't you look at a map?"

"You made your point, Gerber."

Before Gerber could reply, Maxwell hung up. Gerber handed the phone back to the specialist and said, "Thanks for your help."

The man looked startled. "You're welcome, sir."

Gerber returned to the front office and found his driver sitting there, his feet up and his eyes closed. He had one of the other sergeant's cigars. There was a cloud of blue smoke around his head.

"Let's go," snapped Gerber. He was now in a lousy mood. Dealing with all the rear-area idiots did this sort of thing to him. These were men who had it good and didn't realize it, men who could have been humping through the boonies or living at a fire support base that was little more than sand-bagged bunkers inviting a VC assault—places that didn't have electricity, hot food or regular mail.

Outside, in the jeep, he decided to ignore the situation. If he tried to explain the facts of life to these sergeants, they would resent it. He was making their tour seem less of a burden than it was. Each of them wanted to think he had it rougher than anyone else as he tried to find the easiest way to pass the year. None of them knew what it was like in the jungle with the enemy waiting to kill you.

And once they got back to the World they would begin with the war stories. After all, it was unlikely that anyone would know what these guys had done in the war. Whatever they said would be believed. Gerber felt like screaming. It gnawed at him, making him see red.

Instead, he put it out of his mind and concentrated on the mission. He had to find ways to make it better and safer, as if a mission into North Vietnam could be safe. Then again, given the way the North Vietnamese thought, it was probably safer than some of the recons he had pulled in the South. In the South you didn't know who the enemy was. In the North everyone was the enemy.

CAPTAIN KUTNETSOV STOOD in front of the slate blackboard in the makeshift classroom and felt his blood boil. He carefully explained everything that had been done wrong the night before. But the men refused to listen. They kept bursting into babbles of rapid-fire Vietnamese, laughing and joking with one another.

The Vietnamese sat on wooden benches that resembled pews. Each man was dressed in a clean khaki uniform and had a weapon leaning against the bench near him. They watched the Russian pace in front of them, sometimes windmilling his arms as if he were about to topple. He would stop and stare and then begin another long diatribe against them, which was laboriously translated by the man standing in the corner.

Now Kutnetsov stared but said nothing. He glanced at the rear where Moskvin sat shaking his head in disbelief. He grinned at his captain.

"You know," Kutnetsov said, shouting and then waiting for the translation. "Two men didn't return with us last night. Two men disappeared into the jungles in the South. None of you seem to worry about that."

They fell silent at that. Kutnetsov didn't know what had happened to the men. No one did. They had been on the trucks when the ambush party had gone out, but no one had noticed their absence during the return trip. Maybe they had stayed in the South, figuring to join another unit to kill Americans. Or maybe they had faded into the jungle on the northern side of the DMZ, thinking of a trip home to see the family. Kutnetsov didn't care what the answer was; he was angry that no one had paid enough attention to find out what had happened to them.

He had talked with Thuy that morning, and the Vietnamese colonel hadn't been concerned. He believed the men would come straggling back sometime soon. In the jungle, at night, the men sometimes got separated. He had told Kutnetsov not to worry about the missing men.

But Kutnetsov did worry about them. A man shouldn't be left behind simply because no one knew where he was. Each man was responsible for getting all the others out. The NCOs and officers were required to know where each man was at every moment. This was the kind of sloppiness Kutnetsov wanted to eliminate.

Now he had their attention. They wouldn't look him in the eye because they knew they had made a mistake. They had only wanted to think about the success of the ambush and had ignored the missing men.

"Today we begin a policy of regular patrols."

There was a groan. The men began to complain, but Kutnetsov cut them off. "We have a report," he said, "that there are Americans in this area."

It was a thin lie, but he also knew that training patrols accomplished little with men who already knew the basics.

Sending them into the steaming jungle to sit up all night often degenerated into slumber parties, the men guarding one another from the officers and not the enemy. By inventing the possibility of Americans in the area, it gave the training missions a reality they needed.

When the men quieted again, he added, "There have been several air raids into Laos and just north of here. The heroic gunners of the People's Army have downed several American planes, and it's the crews from those planes we can ambush."

Still the men looked skeptical. Kutnetsov knew that American flyers, if downed, wouldn't try to escape and evade to South Vietnam. It was a long, dangerous route. They would either move toward the coast where helicopters could sneak in to pick them up or head for Laos where there was a better chance of survival. A trip the length of Vietnam wasn't in the cards.

Kutnetsov had gotten Thuy to agree to the deception. The Vietnamese colonel must have figured the Russian captain knew what he was talking about. If it raised the level of training and the expertise of his men, then it was certainly worth it.

"Beginning tonight," said Kutnetsov, "we'll have three patrols out. Two will be standard ambush patrols that will slip into position before sunset and the third will be a roving patrol with a specific area to cover."

Again the men groaned, but this time it wasn't as loud as it had been before, not that they were reacting as soldiers were expected to react, which entailed complaining about the duty but actually looking forward to it.

"The Americans," Kutnetsov continued, "knowing that we're looking for them, will probably only travel at night. Searching for them during the day will have little benefit, although we're going to put out one daylight patrol to range the jungle north of here.

"Now, since these are actual combat missions with the side benefit of additional training, we're going to expect absolute combat discipline. We won't tolerate the nonsense that happened last night. Everyone is responsible for knowing where everyone else is. No one gets left behind.''

Kutnetsov stopped talking and looked at the men sitting in front of him—hot, sweating men dressed in khaki uniforms, their weapons beside them.

''Any questions?''

When there were none, Kutnetsov nodded. ''Then we'll move outside where Sergeant Moskvin will instruct you in the use of unarmed combat.''

The Vietnamese interpreter made the announcement, and the men rose as one, coming to attention. Quietly, orderly, they exited the room, filtering into the courtyard near the large tree.

GENERAL STEWARD SAT at his massive desk in the dimness of his office and studied the latest intelligence reports. Not one of the recon flights had been able to establish any kind of human presence at the small camp outside Lang Mo. He read the report again and then closed the folder. Standing, he walked around his desk and stopped in front of the drawn curtains.

''What do you think, Jim?''

''I think we've jumped the gun, General.''

Steward locked his hands together behind his back and rocked on his heels. ''Uh-huh. Central Intelligence and the Air Force have had us looking at the wall structures in the search for POWs.''

''Yes, sir,'' agreed the aide. ''But just because there's been activity in such an area doesn't mean they're going to use it as a POW camp.''

Steward turned and walked to the conference area. He sat down on the couch and leaned his head back. Pinching the bridge of his nose, he said, ''This is one of those things that's a hard call. If word leaks that we're planning a mission into the North, everyone and his cousin is going to be in the streets. The media will go nuts. If it's a false alarm, we've blown our chances. The enemy will know what we're doing and what we're planning.''

''But if we're right?''

"If we're right," said Steward, "then we have an opportunity to get some of those men out."

"If I might suggest, sir, there's an option we haven't discussed."

"Go ahead."

"Well, General, it strikes me that this sudden push to get things done is wrong. Hell, if the enemy is going to put men in there, it won't be a short-term thing. I mean, they'll be there for months, possibly years."

"The point?"

"Once we've identified that it's a POW camp, we'll have time to put this package together. We're doing it now with a projected date in three weeks. If we delay now, call everyone in and sit back, it's not going to adversely affect our plans."

Steward sat up and looked at the major. He nodded. "Okay, get on the phone and alert Bates. Put a message out to stop the team in South Vietnam from deploying. Get those Air Force people back here and I'll put them to work studying the photos and Intel as it comes in." He hesitated and then added, "Oh, and I'll advise the chairman that we're on hold."

"Yes, sir."

13

FORT BRAGG, NORTH CAROLINA

After the brief meeting in the base theater, Bates moved across the street and down the block to one of the small office buildings that dotted the fort. There he was given a cubicle that contained a single chair for visitors, a desk with a small lamp, a desk chair, and a cardboard box on the floor that held the office supplies and files Bates had picked up during the interviews.

Jeff Flagg, a Special Forces sergeant with one tour in Vietnam, sat opposite Bates. He was a tall, wiry man with black hair and dark eyes and had a pointed nose and chin. When he talked, it was obvious he had lost a few teeth, most likely due to the war. The large scar on his right arm, probably a bullet wound, also bore silent testimony to combat experience.

Bates had already flipped through Flagg's 201 File. He had learned about the special schools the man had attended while in the military, read the records of his performance on various assignments and reviewed a list of awards and decorations the sergeant had earned. It was a fairly impressive record for a man who had just turned twenty-four and who had dropped out of high school in his senior year. Of course after basic training he had worked to earn his GED, which meant he had the equivalent of a diploma.

As he had done with the others he had interviewed, Bates started the conversation by asking, "Why are you volunteering for this assignment?"

Flagg leaned back in the chair and looked out the window, which showed only a large tree. He thought for a moment and then said, "Because I'm tired of the training here. Into the swamps to practice and then into the forest to practice. I think it's time to put all the practice to use."

"But I've already said that we'll be entering a period of intense training. More practice."

"Yes, sir," said Flagg, "but this time I'll know we're going to put the practice to use."

"Why's that?"

"Hell, sir, it's simple. You wouldn't be here asking for volunteers if it was just to form another unit that might be used sometime in the future. There has to be a mission coming up very soon."

"Why don't you volunteer for another tour in Vietnam?"

Again Flagg was quiet for a moment. "I've been considering it, sir. The problem is that I can't see we're accomplishing a whole lot. I mean we spend lives and money to do something and then turn around and throw it away. We limit what we can do and let the enemy have all the advantages. Still, I've thought about going back because I'm a soldier and that's where the soldiering is being done."

Bates made a note on his pad. "I want you to expand on what you've said about not accomplishing much."

"Yes, sir. I mean, we send a division into a valley to clean out the enemy. Once that's been finished, we set up a camp in there to be sure Charlie stays away. Then six months later we close the camp because there's no enemy around. After we pull out, the enemy infiltrates slowly and we're back where we were before we even started."

"Uh-huh," said Bates.

"I know what you're thinking, sir, but it's not like that at all. I mean, if I can sit here and see these things, why can't the men running the show see it?"

"Maybe there are things the men at the top know that you don't."

Flagg nodded. "I've thought of that, sir, but I think they owe it to the men to tell them why they decide to pull out of a place. After all, it's the GIs who make the sacrifice to take ground and build camps."

Again Bates wrote a note. "I think that's all I need from you."

Flagg stood and came to attention, but before he saluted he asked, "I guess I blew it, huh?"

Bates set his pencil on top of his notepad. "What makes you think that?"

"I know I shouldn't shoot my mouth off, but sometimes I get so mad. There are men dying in the war and the people in Washington don't see that. They only see the political ramifications of this move or that, not the bodies of the men who made it possible."

"Sergeant Flagg," said Bates, "it's not our place to criticize our leaders. Our place is to carry out the policies they've dictated, but if it makes you feel any better, I agree with everything you've said."

Flagg couldn't contain his grin. "Then I take it I've been accepted?"

"The final decision hasn't been made, but given the circumstances, I think you've been accepted."

Flagg saluted, then spun and left the office rapidly. As he did, Richard Pierce, one of the master sergeants Bates had used to help round up the volunteers, entered. Pierce wore his hair so short that it looked more like fuzz. He was a stocky man who was beginning to develop a potbelly. He had been in the Army for nearly twenty years and the years were beginning to catch up with him. Still, he had a record that was hard to beat. The only "flaw" was that he had been recommended for the Medal of Honor but hadn't received it.

"There's two more waiting, Colonel," he announced.

"Two." Bates looked at his watch. "Getting late in the day."

"Yes, sir. How many you going to take?"

"Including you, I think fifteen. Couple of others I'll take if we can't find better qualified men."

Pierce closed the door and sat down. It was a breach of military courtesy, but the older master sergeants sometimes got away with such things.

"What's wrong with them?"

"Nothing," answered Bates. "Good, enthusiastic troops. They're just a little short on experience. I'd like to limit this to men who've had at least one tour in Vietnam. I want combat veterans."

"What if their combat experience is Korea?"

"A different kind of war. That was more like World War II, with battle lines, seaborne invasions and mass assaults. Not quite like the war in Vietnam."

"How about men from the Pacific Theater or from the Philippines?"

"Well, they'd be getting a little old for this kind of thing, but I believe their experiences would be of benefit to this mission."

"A little old?" asked Pierce. "You mean like you and me?"

Now Bates had to grin. "Exactly like you and me. I think I've one or two campaigns left in me, though."

Pierce stood. "That's kind of how I feel. I'd like to go out a winner, and I don't think the Vietnam War is going to be a winner."

Bates shot the master sergeant a glance. It was the second time in less than an hour that an NCO had expressed doubt about the outcome of the war.

"Now what's that supposed to mean?"

"Just that the brass hats in the Puzzle Palace and the dummies in Congress aren't going to let us win it. They're doing their best to ensure a loss."

"And you believe this volunteer assignment I'm talking about is going to be a winner?"

"That's exactly what I believe," said Pierce. "If I didn't, you wouldn't find me within a mile of this place, even if you were handing out free beer."

"That's nice to know," said Bates. "Now, let's get these last two interviews cleaned up and I'll let you buy me a beer somewhere."

"Yes, sir." He turned and left.

JERRY MAXWELL, still wearing a white suit and white shirt, sat in the steaming hootch and stared at the pile of equipment stacked there. With a huge white handkerchief that was already soaked with sweat, he mopped his brow. He breathed through his mouth, which made him look like a long-distance runner who had barely finished a marathon. His hair hung in strips and sweat dripped from his nose and chin.

As soon as he sat down, he demanded, "Now what's so all-fired important that you had to get me up here?"

Gerber opened the map he had been studying and set it on the table near Maxwell. "Jerry, when you and your friends planned this mission, did anyone look at a map?"

"I would imagine so."

"Okay, well, look at this. We can eliminate the need to parachute into North Vietnam by walking. The camp isn't that far north. This takes out two major problems. One is the danger of parachuting into the enemy's backyard and two, the overflight doesn't alert him because there's no overflight. We can sneak in. All it does is change the timetable, adding a day, two at most."

"Everything's already laid on, including a diversionary raid into the area."

"But we don't need it. In fact, it would be better if we didn't have it. We just slip into the area and no one wonders why all the airplanes were flying over, because there won't be any airplanes."

"I don't know about this," said Maxwell. "Some very intelligent high-ranking officers came up with this plan, and I would think they know more about it than you."

"Jerry," said Gerber, dropping into his chair. "Why would you think that? These guys are grounded in World War II where paratroopers were the advance men. You had to use airplanes. But this is Vietnam. We use helicopters, which are a hell of a lot more mobile than a plane with paratroopers. We don't need to jump out of an airplane to make this work. All we need is a ride to Quang Tri and then a helicopter flight to the DMZ. We'll walk from there.''

"When would you want to leave?"

"I'd say tonight. Stop off at Quang Tri and then into the field as quickly as possible. It's perfect."

"Resupply?" asked Maxwell.

"Put Tyme in charge of it. He, Davies and Santini can run that end of it."

"Which leaves you in the field with . . . ?"

"Fetterman, and Bocker to run the commo end. Hell, Bocker's already been to Nha Trang for the commo briefing there. I'll also want Kepler with me because of his Intel background, and Sergeant Van because he's Vietnamese."

"I don't know," said Maxwell.

"What's not to know? Just get us the flight out of here."

"Authorization for deployment has yet to come through."

"That's not a problem. We're just moving our staging area to Quang Tri."

"Okay," said Maxwell. "I'll alert the people back at MACV of the changes."

"And get rid of the cover raids. The less noise we make going in, the better off we're going to be."

Maxwell got to his feet and stood there looking down on Gerber. "You know, for a mere captain you take a lot for granted."

"There's one thing you should remember, Maxwell. It's this mere captain who's going to have his butt hanging out in the North, so my opinions count for something. You want this done right, you listen to us because we've done it before. Those brass hats in Washington and Saigon don't understand the fine points of covert missions into enemy territory."

With that Maxwell spun and left. There was a roar from outside as the jeep started. When they heard it drive away, Fetterman said, "I think Maxwell is beginning to hate us. He's lost his sense of humor."

"I don't know, Tony. I think he's getting worried. The nature of this conflict is changing and there's no one around with a full set of rules. Hell, man, he's right on one point. For a captain I *am* beginning to take a lot for granted. When was the last time you heard of a captain questioning his orders?"

"It's happened frequently."

"Okay," said Gerber, smiling. "When was the last time he got away with it?"

"Now *that's* a good question," said Fetterman.

"All right," said Gerber, "we've got a few minutes here. Is there anything we need to go over?"

Tyme, who had been in the next room listening to the exchange, entered. "I want to know more about this resupply team I'll be running."

"A legit question," agreed Gerber. He pulled the map closer and then started another briefing. This one outlined the possible rendezvous sites, likely routes of march and the probable site for the establishment of the FOB. He explained in detail how he wanted everyone to go in on the first mission. That had two effects. First, it showed Tyme and the others where Gerber and his team would be. And second, Tyme and his men could carry a great deal of the equipment that would then be left. They wouldn't need much when they pulled out.

They also worked out the codes they would use among themselves and even a schedule of resupply. These were the details that had been left to them in the first place. The important thing was that they would all have to stay flexible enough to meet the changing nature of the mission. Gerber, like most military leaders, knew that the moment he entered the field his carefully laid plans would begin to break down. He would be forced to roll with the punches.

As they went over the plan a third time, they heard a jeep approaching. Fetterman moved to the doorway and glanced out. He nodded and said, "It's Maxwell."

The CIA man entered, his face a mask. Gerber didn't know whether Maxwell was actually angry with them, or if he was just overworked. Like the Special Forces, the CIA was having a tough time finding qualified people.

Maxwell entered without a word and slipped into the chair that had been vacated by Fetterman. He leaned forward, elbow on the table, and asked, "There any beer around here?"

"You know the Army regulations on that," Gerber reminded him.

"I didn't ask about the regulations," said Maxwell, "I asked about the beer."

Tyme ducked into the back room and returned with a can in his hand. "It's not very cold."

"Who gives a shit?" He accepted the can, opened it and drank deeply. "Christ, that's really lousy."

"The fortunes of war," muttered Santini.

"Okay, Gerber, I talked to the people in Saigon. They agree with what you said. They're convinced you shouldn't airlift people in when you can sneak them in on the ground."

"Then it's a go?"

"It's a go. They've dispatched an Air America aircraft from Tan Son Nhut for the flight to Quang Tri. The ETA is about an hour. You'll need to get things packed and ready to move from here."

"Who's going to sign for the equipment?"

Maxwell shook his head. "It's all expendable. No one has to sign for it."

Gerber was on his feet then, excitement flowing through him. He clapped his hands once and said, "Let's get to it."

The men gathered in the outer room and began to strip off their American-made uniforms and equipment, donning the gear that had been purchased from a variety of military suppliers around the world. The fatigues, a camouflaged pattern in deep greens, browns and blacks, had been made in Yugoslavia. The maps were French, as were the boots. There were combat knives from Switzerland and combat rations from West Germany. Naturally the weapons and ammunition were from the Soviet Union and other ComBloc countries. The medical supplies for Davies had been manufactured in the United States, Great Britain, France and East Germany. It gave an international flavor to the mission.

When he was dressed, Gerber moved closer to Maxwell. "You really think this is going to fool anyone? If the enemy manages to kill us all, they're going to know we're Americans."

"Doesn't matter," said Maxwell. "As long as we can deny it and there isn't a lot of American-made gear to back them up, we're in the clear. It's the doctrine of plausible deniability. We can just shrug and say, 'Hey, we don't know who they are.'"

"What bullshit," said Tyme.

For the first time since he had arrived, Maxwell smiled. "Of course it is."

"I think that's got it, Captain," said Fetterman, who was wearing his camouflaged uniform and holding one of the AKs. He had a soft cap pulled low over his face, and in the shadows of the hootch only the whites of his eyes were visible.

"Equipment check?" asked Gerber.

Fetterman shook his head. "Completed, sir. Everyone and everything is ready to go. All we need is a truck to the airfield, then Mr. Maxwell's plane."

"Truck will be here in a couple of minutes," said Maxwell. He stood to one side, leaning a hip on the table that had been piled with gear. "I'm not sure what I should say at this point."

"Well," interrupted Gerber, "good luck is appropriate."

"I know that," snapped Maxwell.

"And good hunting," said Fetterman.

Maxwell stood and held out his hand. "Okay, then, good luck and good hunting."

"Thank you, Jerry," said Gerber. "One of these days we're going to get you acting like a human being."

From outside came the rumbling of a diesel truck. Fetterman moved to the door as the vehicle backed up, stopping short of the boardwalk. "This is it," he said.

The men slowly shouldered all the equipment, carrying it from the hootch and into the fading afternoon sunlight. The heat and humidity was as bad as it always was. Now that they were dressed for combat, sleeves rolled down and buttoned, it seemed hotter to them. In seconds they were all bathed in perspiration.

They loaded the truck, then jumped in, crawling to the rear where the shadows caused by the canvas cover over the bed of the truck concealed them. Diesel fumes from the idling engine drifted in, almost choking them.

Gerber was the last to enter. He sat at the end of the wooden bench where he could look out. As Gerber settled in, Maxwell swatted the side of the truck twice, telling the driver that it was time. The truck lurched once, stopped, then began to pull away.

As it did, Gerber yelled, "Thanks, Jerry. See you soon."

Maxwell lifted a hand to wave, then murmured, "And good luck to you. You're going to need it."

They arrived at the airfield a few minutes later, but everyone stayed in the truck. It took up a position at the edge of the field, and although they couldn't see the airplanes and helicopters, they could hear them. The roar of jet engines and the pop of rotor blades made conversation in the truck difficult.

Not that it mattered then, because the men were lost in their own thoughts. Thoughts that concerned friends and family or the mission to come. Thoughts about things done wrong and things done right. Or thoughts about the mission and what was expected of them. Or thoughts about the bureaucrats, both civilian and military, who thought up ridiculous missions without any consideration for the men who would find themselves involved in them.

And if that wasn't enough to worry about, there was always the heat, now intensified by the canvas cover. It was a heat that surrounded and threatened to suffocate them, a warm, moist heat that was held in by the canvas so that even when the truck was moving there was no breeze. It was a heat that caused sweat to slide down their faces and drop onto the collars of their already sweat-soaked fatigues.

Then, without a word, they were moving again, bouncing across the field. A moment later they stopped and then turned, backing up toward a C-130 painted a flat black with no markings on it. The engines were turning, roaring at them and filling the area with the stench of partially burnt aviation fuel.

When Fetterman saw the plane, he laughed. "Oh, that's good. Don't call attention to the mission by flying us north in a regular airplane. Send us a spook plane so that everyone will wonder about it."

"Let's get going," said Gerber, ignoring Fetterman's remark. He dropped from the back of the truck and stood in the sudden coolness of the airfield. A breeze blew on him, drying the sweat quickly.

The men joined him, and as they moved forward the rear ramp of the plane began a slow descent. Gerber turned toward it and entered.

The gloomy interior looked like that of all the other C-130s he had ever seen. There was red webbing along the fuselage over the benches that formed the troop seats, and gray soundproofing was packed around the walls but did little to muffle the noise.

Gerber moved forward, dropped his pack in the center of the plane as he had done a dozen times before and took a seat, twisting right and left, searching for the seat belt ends. When he found both ends, he buckled himself in. He watched the rest of his team do the same. As the last of his men entered, the loadmaster pressed a button to raise the ramp. When it was closed, he moved to the front, inspecting the men to make sure they were wearing their seat belts.

The interior of the plane heated up quickly, but then the noise from the engines increased and they began to taxi. They stopped once and then began to race down the runway. The ride was rough. A moment later there was a push as the aircraft lifted off and began a steep climbout to avoid any enemy gunners who might be lying in wait outside the Bien Hoa perimeter.

There was a whine and a vibration as the landing gear was retracted. Then the flight engineer moved around with a flashlight, checking various oil levels.

"Finally on the way," Fetterman yelled over the noise.

"Yeah," said Gerber. "I just wish I had a better feeling about this."

14

MACV HEADQUARTERS
SAIGON

Robin Morrow sat in an air-conditioned office filled with the articles of war. The paneled walls held captured weapons, rifles, machine guns and RPGs that were mounted like game fish. Under each was a small brass plate that described the date and circumstance of the capture.

Behind the giant wooden desk was an ornately carved combat infantryman's badge with two stars and beneath it was a watercolor depicting a jungle firefight. On the desk, among normal items such as a pen-and-pencil set, a lamp with a green shade, and an in and out basket, were the brass bottoms of shells used as ashtrays and pencil holders. On a bookcase that held the normal Army manuals and black binders were framed pictures of men in combat gear ready to participate in a great battle. Featured prominently in each picture was General Davidson—at the time he was Lieutenant Davidson or Captain Davidson or Major Davidson.

Morrow studied the man behind the desk. He was a sour-looking individual with a fading tan and receding hairline. The hair on the top of his head was dark, but graying around his ears. His eyebrows had turned salt-and-pepper. His nose was a network of tiny red lines, indicating he had done his share of drinking. There were dark circles under his eyes and he was sweating freely, but that seemed to be more an aftereffect of a night of drinking rather than the stress of Morrow's close questioning.

Morrow sat in one of the two large leather wing chairs. She could feel the skin of her thighs sticking to the leather and that made it hard for her to get comfortable. She sat with her legs crossed and her reporter's notebook propped on her knee.

Glancing at the things she had already written down, she realized that Davidson had talked his way around almost all of her questions, not answering them, but filling the air with noise that sounded like answers.

"Now," she said, "I understand we have a team preparing to go into the North."

"Such operations are illegal and not condoned by this office nor by this command."

"Uh-huh," she said. "I know the team leader is Captain Mack Gerber."

"In that case, I don't see the point of your being here to ask me questions."

"Then you admit that a mission is being launched?"

Davidson shook his head and ran a hand over his short-cropped hair. It sprung back into place like the bristles on a brush. "I admit to nothing. In fact, I can assure you that Captain Gerber isn't taking a team into North Vietnam."

Morrow jerked upright. She was used to the nondenial denials that talked around points without actually addressing them, but this was a flat statement, one that ran counter to the information she had gotten first from Gerber's strange disappearance and then from Jerry Maxwell. She had been around long enough to know what it all meant. She had seen it all before, and the path always led to a cross-border operation, sometimes into the North. But now Davidson was denying that Gerber was going north.

"Excuse me, General," she said, "but I know that Captain Gerber is on the mission. He isn't available for comment and hasn't been seen in a couple of days. In fact, he told people he was going to Hawaii."

Davidson smiled. "Then I suggest you wait for his return."

"So you're going to stick with that ridiculous cover story?"

"No," answered Davidson, "I'm not going to because you're right. The story's ridiculous."

Morrow was taken aback by the candor. She expected denials and evasions, anything but the truth.

"Captain Gerber was tabbed for a mission. Oh, not the melodramatic raid into North Vietnam you've dreamed up, but a covert mission nonetheless. Now, however, that mission's been scrubbed."

"Then where is he?"

Davidson rubbed a hand over his head again. "Still in isolation, I imagine. The orders have yet to filter down. Once they do, there'll be a couple of debriefings and other mop-ups to take care of."

"Debriefings about what?" asked Morrow.

"Well," said Davidson, "even when a mission's scrubbed, there are elements that have already been accomplished. The details of the planning will be examined to learn if there are ways to improve such planning. There'll be discussion about the procurement of the equipment and they'll explore some of the classified features that I really can't discuss here."

"Uh-huh," said Morrow, writing furiously. "Then Captain Gerber should be returning soon?"

"Yes, I would think so. Orders canceling the mission were issued only a short time ago so that, as I say, it might not have filtered down to the lowest elements in the field."

Morrow flipped through her notebook, looking for a contradiction, but there weren't any. Davidson had given her everything she'd asked for except the classified details of the mission. She knew that if the mission were still on, he would have clammed up tight.

"A final question, then, General. Why was the mission canceled?"

Davidson shrugged. "I don't know. Orders came down to me, and I passed them along the chain of command. A reason wasn't given." He stopped, stared at her and added, "I prob-

Terrorists, anarchists, hijackers and drug dealers—BEWARE!

In a world shock-tilted by terror, Mack Bolan and his courageous combat teams, *Soldiers of Barrabas* and our new high-powered entry, *Vietnam: Ground Zero* provide America's best hope for salvation.

Fueled by white-hot rage and sheer brute force, they blaze a war of vengeance against a tangled international network of trafficking and treachery. Join them as they battle the enemies of democracy in timely, hard-hitting stories ripped from today's headlines.

Get 4 explosive novels delivered right to your home

Return the attached Card, and we'll send you 4 gut-chilling, high-voltage Gold Eagle novels—FREE!

If you like them, we'll send you 6 brand-new books every other month to preview. Always before they're available in stores. Always at a hefty saving off the retail price. Always with the right to cancel and owe nothing.

As a subscriber, you'll also get...
- our free newsletter *AUTOMAG* with each shipment
- special books to preview and buy at a deep discount

Get a stainless-steel pocketknife—FREE

As soon as we receive your Card, we'll send you a stainless-steel pocketknife as an outright gift. This multifunction pocketknife with key chain is yours—FREE. *And like the 4 free books, it's yours to keep even if you never buy another Gold Eagle book.*

RUSH YOUR ORDER TO US TODAY.

DETACH AND MAIL CARD TODAY

BUSINESS REPLY CARD

First Class   Permit No. 717   Buffalo, NY

Postage will be paid by addressee

Gold Eagle Reader Service
901 Fuhrmann Blvd.
P.O. Box 1867
Buffalo, NY 14240-9952

NO POSTAGE
NECESSARY
IF MAILED
IN THE
UNITED STATES

ably shouldn't even say this, but the orders didn't originate in Vietnam. That is, the cancellation came from Washington."

"Is that unusual?" asked Morrow.

"No," said Davidson, "not really. Given the nature of this war and the state of communications that exist, it isn't that uncommon. Hell, if I want, I can pick up the telephone and talk to the Pentagon. If I knew the phone number, I could probably call the President."

"Then the people in Washington meddle in the direction of the war effort?"

"Still trying for something for the front page, Miss Morrow? You won't catch me in that trap, although I will say that we have a participation in the command and control of the battlefield that was unheard of during World War II."

"Is that good or bad?"

"No, Miss Morrow, I won't answer that, either. I like being a general."

"I think that answers the question for me." She stood slowly, feeling the flesh of her thighs peeling from the seat of the chair. Leather in Vietnam, for Christ's sake. "Thanks for your time."

"Feel free to return."

BATES WAS CLEANING UP the last of his paperwork in his tiny office, pleased with what he had accomplished. The list of names had grown, and if he was required to, he could have put the men into the field inside of two weeks. That would have given him just enough time to learn about the men and to rehearse the mission several times, first in the daylight and then in the dark. Two weeks wasn't the ideal, but it was enough.

He snapped the folder shut and dropped his pen onto his desk. He laced his fingers behind his head and put his feet up on his desk. As he did, there was a quiet knock, and he was sure that it was Sergeant Pierce wanting that beer he had been promised.

"Come!" he said.

Instead, Jason Sheckley, the liaison officer, entered. He was followed by Lieutenants Rawlings and Halliday. Bates sat up and waved at the single chair. Sheckley dropped into it while the other two leaned against the rear wall. "What's all this?"

"You can close up shop here, Colonel," said Sheckley. "Orders from General Steward. We're scrapping the plans."

"Why?"

Sheckley nodded in the direction of the two Intelligence officers. "We can't confirm anything. All we've really got is some evidence of construction at a very unlikely site. The general feels, and we all concur, that to continue could tip our hand. We don't want to alert the enemy to the possibility of a rescue attempt."

"I can understand that," said Bates, "but it's no reason to quit down here. We can build the rescue force without anyone knowing what we're doing. That way we can have it ready if the opportunity presents itself."

"The feeling is that any continued progress on this operation would be counterproductive. It's time to fold our tents and go home." Sheckley was quiet for a moment and then said, "Besides, if we decided it was a go and you had to start over, how long would it take to put your team together?"

Bates shrugged. "Two weeks if we cut corners, three if we didn't. Ideally we'd have six to eight weeks after the selection of the assault force for training and target familiarization."

"So you see," said Sheckley, "there's no reason to proceed. The general couldn't conceive of a situation where you wouldn't have the time you needed, even if we suspended operations now. From a security standpoint, it makes good sense."

Bates glanced at the stack of files and paper he had accumulated in the short time he had used the office.

"Get one of the sergeants to take care of it. That is, unless you wrote down anything that could give a clue about the nature of the mission."

"Colonel," snapped Bates, "I know enough not to do that. I just hate to see all this work go up in smoke."

"Then have the sergeant pack it up and send it to you. You can use it as a base from which to build if we ever find what we're looking for."

"What are we going to do now? What are our orders?" asked Bates.

"We return to Washington to debrief with the general." Again he nodded at the two lieutenants. "They're going back with us and will continue to look for the signs we all want. If we come up with nothing, I imagine they'll be returned to their normal assignments."

Bates stared at them for a moment, wondering how two lieutenants could cause so much trouble. People flying all over the place, only to be called back. A typical military snafu. Everyone overreacting. At least no one had gotten killed before the calmer heads had taken over. Hell, no one had even managed to get into the field on this one.

THE C-130 TOUCHED DOWN at Quang Tri, bounced once, then settled to the runway. The engines began to roar louder than before and the pressure shoved the men inside forward as the pilots fought to stop the plane before it rolled off the end of the runway. They taxied to the far end of the airfield and stopped.

Gerber sat quietly, waiting for something to happen. During the flight, at altitude, they had turned on the heaters to keep the interior of the plane warm. As they had descended for landing, those heaters had been turned off and the plane cooled. But then they touched down and opened the ramp. The hot, humid air boiled in, displacing the coolness in seconds.

Outside sat two trucks and a jeep. The officer from the jeep moved toward the rear of the plane, peered in and then entered. As the engines were shut down, the young officer asked, "Where's Captain Gerber?"

Gerber stood and moved toward him. He put a hand out to balance himself as he walked through the rear of the C-130. Facing the man, he said, "I'm Gerber."

"Yes, sir. We have the choppers waiting at the far end of the field near the helipad. If you and your men will accompany me, we'll get you over there."

Gerber ducked and looked out the rear of the aircraft. It was dark with a few stars visible through the wispy clouds overhead. A breeze blew a coolness into the plane now, and even though they weren't that close to the South China Sea, there was a hint of salt in the air.

Gerber turned and saw that Fetterman was getting the men ready to move out. He followed the young officer off the plane and stopped at the front of the jeep.

"Sir, my orders are to get you on the choppers as soon as possible. If we hurry, you can get into position about an hour before first light."

"And you know where we're going?"

"More or less, sir. Actually just the general location. You'll have to brief the pilots when you get to the choppers."

Gerber didn't say anything to that. Everything up to this point had been well coordinated. His changing the plans hadn't thrown the wrench into the works Maxwell had wanted him to believe. Knowing the way the military operated, Gerber couldn't see how it would take much effort to get everything into place in a couple of hours. The only aspect he didn't like was the young lieutenant knowing where they wanted to land. It seemed like a vital piece of information to be communicated nearly the length of Vietnam, but then there were any number of secret lines and codes that could be used.

As Fetterman headed down the ramp, Gerber said, "Toss the equipment into one of the trucks and have the men pile into it. I want you up here with me."

"Yes, sir."

The men trooped off the plane and disappeared behind one of the trucks. A moment later Fetterman reappeared. "We're all set, Captain."

Gerber climbed into the rear of the jeep and was followed by Fetterman. The officer took the passenger side and then held a hand in the air, waving it in a circular motion as if he were a wagon master ordering the Conestogas into a defensive ring. Instead there was a rumbling cough as the diesel of the deuce-and-a-half was started.

They drove across the darkened airfield, across the PSP taxiways and behind the control tower that looked more like a fortified FCT than a facility at an airstrip, although the top bristled with radio antennae. Passing a number of low wooden structures with tin roofs, they heard music drifting from some of them, music filled with static pops and chirps as if the station was a long way off and there was a thunderstorm somewhere close by.

They stopped close to the darkened helipad. Gerber hopped from the rear of the jeep and stood looking at two Huey helicopters. The aircraft sat quietly, their rotor blades lined up along the fuselage and tied down. From the interior of the closest came a bright orange glow, evidence that someone sat on the troop seat smoking a cigarette. Gerber hoped it wasn't one of the pilots because smoking killed night vision as quickly as exposure to light.

"We need both choppers, Captain?" asked Fetterman.

"I don't know. Seems like we'll be loading one down if we all try to climb into it."

"I was thinking, sir, that once we get into the area, if the two choppers separate and make a series of fake landings, it'll confuse Charlie if he happens to be watching."

"Yeah," agreed Gerber. He stepped to the closest and asked, "Where's the pilot?"

A man who had been lying on the floor, his head resting on the bulk of his chicken plate, sat up and said, "I'm the aircraft commander."

"Okay," said Gerber, "got a question for you. How big a load can you take?"

"Eight, if you don't have a lot of equipment. Six, if you do."

"And what if I want to get everyone on one chopper with all our equipment?"

The AC slid across the deck of the cargo compartment and then climbed out. He looked at the two trucks and the jeep and asked, "Exactly what do you have with you?"

Gerber gave him a list of the equipment and the men, including the fact that one of them was Vietnamese.

"Okay," said the pilot. "Since it's night and fairly cool, I don't think that will be a problem. Besides, by the time we're ready to insert, I'll have burned off about half the fuel. Yeah, it'll work."

"You have gun support on this?" asked Fetterman.

"Nothing is lined up, but I can have guns in ten minutes if you think we'll need them."

"A little suppressing fire in a couple of locations wouldn't hurt," said Fetterman. The master sergeant smiled as he realized the irony of his statement. "But then again, it might."

"Give Charlie something else to watch," agreed Gerber.

"I'll make the call."

"You know where we're going?"

"No, sir. Just the general area and that it's close to the DMZ."

"Tony, order the men off the truck and get the equipment loaded here." He pulled a map from a pocket and opened it, propping it against the side of the helicopter.

The pilot reached into the cargo compartment to retrieve a flashlight with a red filter over the lens. He snapped it on and pointed it at the map.

"The LZ we want to hit is in this area, about a klick south of the DMZ. There are several other landing zones in the region, and if you and the other ship dip down into them, that'll confuse the enemy. I think gun support on two or three would be nice, especially if we don't use it on the real one."

"Yes, sir. I'll coordinate. The guns can meet us once we're airborne."

The crew chief supervised the loading of the chopper with the heaviest gear as far to the rear as possible. He wanted it shoved under the troop seat so that it would be next to the transmission, but Fetterman refused, saying that it would be too hard to extract once they touched down in the LZ.

When the equipment was loaded, the crew chief insisted that the biggest men sit on the troop seat, their feet propped on the gear. He had Fetterman, Santini and Van sitting right behind the pilots' seats. Satisfied with that, he untied the blade, swung it around so that it was perpendicular to the aircraft's body and climbed into his well.

Gerber, finished with the briefing of the aircraft commander, climbed on board the Huey. He sat at the end of the troop seat, one foot at the edge of the cargo compartment. In the darkness he could see a puddle of water reflecting the little light available. The breeze that had cooled him earlier died and the humidity seemed to smother him. Mosquitoes, no longer inhibited by the breeze, began to swarm, and their incessant buzzing seemed to fill the air.

The AC, having briefed the other pilots, climbed into the left seat of the chopper. He took his flight helmet from its hook just behind him and donned it, letting the chin strap dangle. He then reached up to the panel over his head, flipped a number of switches and turned a couple of knobs. Finally, leaning over, he put his right hand on the throttle of the collective.

"Clear!" he shouted.

That was echoed by the crew chief and door gunner.

The whine in the turbine began. A moment later there was a roar, and the AC sat up, slowly rolling on the throttle as the rotor blades began to spin. In just under a minute they were at full rpm.

They broke ground, hovering in the popping of the rotor blades and the whirlwind the Huey created. The water in the puddle rippled, pushed to the far end by the downwash. They turned to the right, and then the aircraft seemed to leap into the air with a series of vibrations and an increase in the roar of its engine.

Climbing out rapidly, they watched Quang Tri fall into darkness behind them. Unlike some of the American bases where light marked the boundaries and interiors, there was no flood of light on Quang Tri. It was as dark and unremarkable as the rest of the Vietnamese countryside.

They reached altitude quickly and leveled off. The noise from the engine decreased. To the left and to the rear, the second chopper appeared, a faint gray smudge barely visible against the night sky. Because it was the trailing aircraft, it didn't need its lights. Only a dim red glow from the instrument panel was visible.

They continued north, flying over jungle. No lights were visible now. There were no roads and only occasionally did they see the silver ribbons that were rivers and streams. The jungle hid everything else.

Gerber turned his attention to the instruments wrapped in the red lights, but he couldn't see enough to tell anything from them. He studied the radio panel where one of the pilots had set his map. Feeling a tap on his shoulder, he turned.

The crew chief held a flight helmet out and shouted, "AC wants to talk to you."

Gerber took off his soft cap and put on the helmet, holding the earphones with his thumbs. When he had it seated comfortably, the crew chief handed him a small black box with a button on it so that he could use the intercom.

"Captain," said the AC, "we'll be airborne for about thirty minutes more."

"Okay."

"Wanted you to know that we've got a couple of reports of contact in the general area. Small firefights with Charlie breaking off quickly."

"How close to where we want to insert?"

"I figure a couple of klicks at least. Shouldn't affect us at all."

"Thanks." He took off the helmet but didn't give it back to the crew chief. Holding it on his lap, he watched as the blackened landscape slipped under the helicopter.

A few minutes later the crew chief tapped Gerber on the shoulder again and yelled, "AC wants to talk to you."

Again Gerber put on the helmet and told the man he was ready.

"We're about five out. Figured you'd want to hit your LZ first so that Charlie has as little warning as possible."

"Sounds good."

"All right, Captain, good luck on this."

"Thanks again."

As he took off the helmet, the crew chief reached over for it. He touched Gerber's shoulder with a gloved hand and shouted, "Good luck to you, sir."

Gerber nodded and glanced out the cargo compartment door. The chopper that had been close to them was gone now, off on its diversionary missions.

They started a slow descent, making a long approach toward the ground until they were just above the trees. They rushed forward, popped up once and then suddenly dipped down. The nose of the chopper came up until it was pointing skyward and Gerber could feel gravity forcing him down into the troop seat. The landing light flashed once, went out and then flashed again. The skids leveled and the chopper dropped to the ground.

"Get out! Get out! Get out!" shouted the crew chief.

Gerber dived out the doorway and into the knee-deep grass of the LZ. He turned, reached for a bundle of equipment, dropped it onto the ground, then took another. Quick as a cat, Fetterman was beside him, and the aircraft lifted. The rotor wash hit them and grabbed at their clothes. The dirt and debris in the LZ swirled around and sandpapered them. Gerber flattened himself on the ground as the chopper lifted off. He glanced at the Huey, the flame from its turbine reaching to the rear as if trying to burn off the tail rotor.

And then the night was quiet. Gerber got to his hands and knees, then crouched, one hand on his weapon, the other against the stack of equipment. A few feet away from him were the others, black silhouettes against a blacker background.

"Tony, let's get moving."

"Direction, Captain?"

"To the north, off the LZ. We'll hole up in the trees for a few minutes."

"Yes, sir."

Gerber bent down, picked up his rucksack and shouldered it. He seated it, adjusting the straps, and then moved forward. Tyme was crouched over some equipment. He handed a battery pack to Santini and said, "Slip this in."

Fetterman stepped off, moving north carefully, quietly, his AK-47 clutched in both hands. In seconds he was lost in the gloom, but by then Santini was behind him. One by one they filtered off the LZ until they were just inside the tree line, where they halted.

Gerber wiped at the sweat on his face and was overwhelmed by the desire to wait out the night where he was. It had been one of those rush jobs with long periods of riding in the back of aircraft. By the time they reached the ground, Gerber wasn't mentally prepared for a long hike. He wanted to put it off as long as he could.

But he was aware of the danger of remaining too close to the LZ, although they were still in South Vietnam. It wasn't like a covert drop into enemy territory where a scrap of paper could alert the enemy to their presence. Hell, anything found there could have been dropped by Americans sweeping through the day before or the week before. No, what he had to do was get moving, putting distance between his men and the landing zone in case Charlie wanted to explore it because someone had seen the helicopter landing.

He moved forward and touched Fetterman on the shoulder. "We've an hour or so until first light," he whispered. "Let's use it to get out of here."

"Yes, sir. Same course?"

"More or less."

Fetterman nodded, touched Santini and signaled him forward. He found Van and had him join the point element just in case they stumbled across a Vietnamese patrol. As the point moved off, the rest of the men stood and fell into line. Gerber stayed where he was until the last of the men had left, then he got to his feet and brought up the rear.

15

THE DEMILITARIZED
ZONE

It was like walking through a steam bath in the dark. The heat was bad, even long after midnight, but the humidity was relentless. It was a physical assault on the body that threatened to overwhelm and incapacitate. Within seconds of landing, as they moved to the tree line, they were all soaked. The sweat coated them, covering them with an itchy, gritty film that was hard to ignore. The perspiration dripped from the hairline, down the nose and chin and along the back and sides.

And the night didn't help. It was so dark that the men had difficulty seeing more than a couple of feet. Overhead were clouds, some of them wispy but others thick and huge, which blocked out the moon and stars. It made the jungle a black mass that concealed traps and pitfalls.

Gerber, at the rear of the tiny formation, could see only one man in front of him. The rest of the patrol was lost in the gloom. He moved slowly, rolling his foot from heel to toe, listening for the snap of a twig or the sudden shift that suggested a pressure plate of a land mine.

He touched his face to the sleeve of his uniform, trying to dry the sweat. He was breathing through his mouth, surprised that the strain of slipping through the vegetation was taking such a toll so soon. His head and shoulders ached, and already he was wishing for a rest.

Silently they continued forward. All they could hear were the sounds of predators and their prey, along with the usual incessant buzz of mosquitoes and flies and the rattling of monkeys in the treetops.

After an hour of the strain of trying to see and trying to remain silent, Fetterman halted. Gerber moved forward and realized the problem. In front of them was an open area that was at least a klick across and more than three wide.

Fetterman leaned close to Gerber, his lips nearly touching the captain's ear. "Take us an hour to cross and two or three to go around."

Gerber nodded and moved forward, crouching just inside the tree line. In front of him was a gray expanse. He slowly pulled out his binoculars and swept the area. There was enough light that he could make out black lumps concealed in the grass, but they looked more like tree trunks than men hiding. A light breeze rippled the grass, making it look like the gently rolling surface of a lake.

"What do you think, Captain?"

Gerber stepped back a foot and peeled the camouflage cover off his watch. He studied the glowing numbers, covered the watch, then looked at the clearing.

"I think we're a good klick, klick and a half off the LZ. Let's stay here and keep an eye on the clearing. If we see nothing in it, we'll cross it after sundown."

They retreated slightly and found the rest of the men, who had taken up firing positions, facing in opposite directions so that the enemy, if any were present, couldn't sneak up on them. Gerber touched Tyme on the shoulder and pointed to the rear. The sergeant got to his feet and slipped into position there. The men then broke up into two-man teams and spread out into a loose circle. Gerber and Fetterman took up a position near the edge of the tree line where they could watch the clearing. Gerber touched Fetterman's shoulder, and the master sergeant nodded, telling the captain he would take the first watch.

Sitting down, his back to the rough bark of a palm tree, Gerber shrugged off his rucksack and suddenly felt as if he were about to float into the sky. He pulled out one of his canteens and drank from it. The warm water tasted of plastic and halazone. Gerber poured some into the palm of his hand and splashed it on the back of his neck, surprised at its cooling effect.

For a few minutes he sat there, slowly inhaling and exhaling, tasting the humid air. He wished for a cold beer and a cool bed but only had the warm water and the soft, moist jungle. He slipped down onto his back, then turned onto his side. The last thing he wanted was to sleep on his back; he was afraid something might drop on his face—a snake, a monkey or one of the leeches that inhabited the undersides of leaves. They were ugly black things that found enough moisture in the nearly perpetual mist of the jungle.

From far overhead came the roar of a jet's engine that quickly faded. From farther away was the steady drone of a propeller plane, and near it the beat of helicopter rotors. The air war was beginning to heat up even before the sun rose.

Gerber closed his eyes and then opened them again. He had thought he had blinked, but now the jungle was gray-green and he could see the shapes of the bushes, vines and ferns near him. He shifted around, moving with great care. By staring into the vegetation, he could just make out the shape of Fetterman, who was stretched out on his stomach, watching the clearing. Through the veil of vegetation came a steady glow as the sun peeked over the horizon.

Gerber rested for another hour and then took over for Fetterman. He hadn't bothered to eat breakfast, figuring there would be time enough for that later and because the cardboard food from the C-ration meals just wasn't appealing. Instead he crept forward, into the spot vacated by Fetterman, and watched the jungle clearing.

The grass now looked about knee-high, and not all the black obstacles were logs. One looked like the drop tank from a fighter and another was the rusting remains of a fifty-five-gallon drum. Just like the Americans to litter everywhere they went, and if they couldn't drop beer cans and newspapers, they found a way to do it from the sky.

He used his binoculars to scan the jungle opposite. There was no evidence of bunkers or movement except for the monkeys swinging in the treetops. It was quiet around him.

Gerber watched and waited, but no one seemed to be alive in that one small part of the world. The war went on elsewhere. Life went on elsewhere. Around that clearing, only Gerber and his team existed. And that was exactly the way Gerber wanted it.

KUTNETSOV SAT IN HIS ROOM, exhausted. He was soaked with sweat. His hair hung in his eyes and he found that every bone in his body ached. He wanted a hot shower more than anything in the world, but he was too tired to move. There was something about the jungle that sapped the strength, something about it that made life more miserable than it would be under similar circumstances anywhere else. All he could do was sit there breathing heavily and wonder if he was going to die soon or if he would linger for a week.

Finally he leaned over and untied his boots, slipping them off his hot feet. He peeled the damp socks away and dropped them onto the rough wooden floor. Then slowly he massaged each foot, working out the kinks.

There was a soft knock at the door. It was Colonel Thuy. As usual he wore a freshly laundered khaki uniform. This time, though, he held a swagger stick in one hand.

"May I speak with you, Captain?"

"Of course. Please come in." Kutnetsov thought again of a shower or a bath, but knew that it was now a dream for the future.

"I'd like to talk about these patrols of yours."

Kutnetsov stood and stripped off his fatigue jacket. He let it fall to the floor, kicked it aside, then plucked a towel off the rack and dried himself.

"What about the patrols?"

"I think you should slow them down. The men are beginning to grumble."

"Soldiers always grumble. It's a fact of life in the army."

"That's true, but I think we've, you've, gone too far. All these attempts to find mythical Americans are taking a toll on our men."

Kutnetsov wiped his face and then dried his hair. He tossed the towel aside and sat down. "Colonel, I've learned one thing during my career and that's to make the training harder than the real thing so that when the men find themselves fighting for their lives they're prepared."

"Yes," agreed Thuy, "training is good. But you have the men chasing imaginary Americans in the jungle day and night."

"Because, for the training to be effective, there must be a goal. If the men believe there are Americans out there to find, they'll do better in the training."

"Then you don't plan to cut back?"

"No," said Kutnetsov. "We must keep the men out there in the jungle, setting up their ambushes and making their sweeps. It's good training for them."

"And where are you going from here?"

"First, I think I'll take a shower and catch some sleep. Then, tonight, we'll set out ambushes south of the camp. I think the thing to do is slowly progress south until we run into the Americans in South Vietnam. We're getting ready for that."

"How soon?" asked Thuy.

"A week. No more than that."

JERRY MAXWELL SAT in the air-conditioned mess hall of one of the aviation units based at Bien Hoa. He was still wearing his wrinkled white suit and looked as if he had slept in it. The CIA man had spent the night at a TOC, listening to the various military units talking to one another. It had been an interesting lesson for him since, as the CIA representative at MACV and a civilian, he rarely had the opportunity to listen in. There had been calls for Medevac choppers, calls for slicks and calls for artillery support, most of them directed to the fire support bases scattered around Three Corps. And he had heard someone turn back an enemy probe of his perimeter and heard various people arguing over who was the shortest.

Maxwell had sat there waiting for word that Gerber and his team had gotten to Quang Tri, then off to the DMZ. He had asked the NCOs who were working the blocks of radios behind the plywood counter if they would make the radio calls for him. He had stood in the half-light of the heavily sandbagged TOC, the smell of dirt in the air even with the airconditioning blowing constantly, and waited patiently. He had helped himself to coffee from the huge pot sitting on a table covered by battle maps and intelligence charts.

For a while he read the various unclassified reports lying around and then studied the charts. Periodically he asked if anyone had heard anything, and he answered the questions posed by a couple of lieutenant colonels, who eventually left him alone, happy that they didn't have to worry about him.

Finally, after he had given up hope that any word would filter back to him, one of the sergeants approached and asked, "You Maxwell?"

"That's right."

"Got something here for you. Came from a colonel up in Quang Tri. Said to tell you that the insertion's been made."

Maxwell nodded and stood up. He scrubbed at his eyes with the heels of his hands. "Yeah. Thank you." Then he glanced at his watch and realized it was now late enough for him to get something to eat.

He stepped out of the TOC and onto the wooden sidewalk that led away from it. The sun was up and the air already warm. Just standing there was enough to work up a sweat. Maxwell took out a huge red handkerchief and wiped the perspiration from his face. He inhaled deeply and nearly choked on the heavy, damp air.

Listening to the sounds of the aircraft operating on the airfield not far away, he walked away from the TOC. There were choppers, their engines roaring and their blades popping, and there was the high-pitched whine of jet turbines that built to a screaming peak and threatened to destroy hearing.

Maxwell hurried off, passing dozens of men in uniform. Many of them were armed and all of them were sweating. The sunlight was just beginning to beat down, making it seem hotter than it was. The steam rose from the ground, particularly from the puddles that stood in the depressions, and shimmered from the metal rooftops.

The CIA operative followed some of the soldiers to a mess hall, managed to convince the Spec Four at the door that he was authorized to eat in the military facility and got a huge breakfast of scrambled eggs, hash browns, bacon, toast and juice. A table sat vacant in the corner, and Maxwell chose it, content to be alone with his thoughts.

So, he mused to himself, bringing his mind back to the present, Gerber and his men were on the ground and moving slowly north. They would make a single radio report at six in the evening and then be off the air until they reached their objective. Maxwell smiled ruefully as he dug through the mound of cold scrambled eggs. He couldn't understand how the Army could screw up food so quickly and easily.

After he drank his juice, which was warm, he pushed the tray away. He sat staring at the plywood-paneled wall and listened to the hum of the air conditioner. It would be simple to get back to his office—in fact, he could be there in an hour—but for some reason he didn't want to do that. He wanted to stay at Bien Hoa, eat at one of the clubs and ignore his duties for the day.

Maxwell picked up his coffee and smiled at the cup. In three months he hadn't taken a single day off. Everyday, Monday through Sunday, he had been in the office. Now, after sitting up all night waiting for word that the mission was operational, he was tired and happy. He didn't want to go back to Saigon, because if he did, he would have to go to work.

That was it, he decided as he finished the last of the toast. He would check into one of the transient quarters and take the day off.

BATES WAS TIRED when the plane touched down at Washington's National Airport. He didn't want to get off and report to

Steward's office at the Pentagon. He just wanted to get some sleep. Sitting quietly, he watched as the other passengers stood in the aisle and waited for one of the flight crew to open the door.

In front of him were the two lieutenants, Rawlings and Halliday. They were standing. Rawlings, bent slightly because of the low-hanging luggage rack, was whispering to Halliday. She shook her head, turned and grinned at Rawlings.

"We should be able to clear up the paperwork in thirty or forty minutes," said Sheckley.

Bates closed his eyes and nodded slowly. "And then?"

"Then you're free to go back to your unit of assignment. Oh, you can of course take a couple of days to sight-see in Washington if you like."

"What I'd like to do is finish building the team," said Bates.

"Well, you're about to have a chance to build your case in front of General Steward."

The front door was opened and the people started to move forward, an inch at a time. Rawlings looked at the two colonels, who hadn't bothered to stand, then sat down himself. When the aisle was clear, Bates got to his feet, hesitated as Sheckley struggled from his seat, and then started forward. Once off the jetway and onto the concourse, they hurried toward the baggage claim area where there was another crowd. Two dozen people stood around the carousel waiting for luggage. Bates couldn't see the point of that, either. He stood at the rear of the crowd.

Off to one side was a Special Forces sergeant who was thin but well tanned. He sat quietly on a bench reading a paperback novel. Bates studied the rows of ribbons above his breast pocket. They were strangely colored. The reds were more pink than red and the yellow seemed to be more orange than yellow. Bates recognized the problem. The man was just back from Vietnam and had purchased the ribbons in one of the shops run by the Vietnamese, who never quite got the colors right.

As Bates began to move toward the soldier, two people detached themselves from the crowd of travelers. The man looked older than the woman. He had a scraggly beard and long dirty hair. His blue jeans were old, faded and frayed. He wore sandals and his feet were filthy.

The girl didn't look much better. Her long hair hung limply to her waist and needed washing. She wore a light blouse stained with mustard. Her jeans were in worse shape than her companion's and her feet were equally dirty.

They stopped in front of the soldier and stared at him. He finally glanced up, smiled and then began reading again. Bates moved closer.

The man stepped right up and said, "Hi."

"Hi," responded the soldier.

"You kill any babies today?" asked the girl.

The soldier shot her a glance and shook his head sadly. He turned his attention back to the novel, ignoring them.

The man kicked the soldier's boot. "Hey! She asked you a question."

The soldier closed his book, set it down and stood up. He reached out and touched the front of the man's shirt. "Why don't you get the fuck out of here before you get hurt."

"Yeah," sneered the man. "Just like you baby killers. Resort to violence to make your point."

Now the soldier grinned. "You came over and inflicted your point of view on me. I'm merely letting you know that I firmly disagree and don't want to hear any more. I'm asking you politely to leave me alone." He hesitated, the smile still on his face, "Or I'm going to break you in two."

The man stared for a moment and then dropped his eyes. He backed away, turned and said to the girl, "Come on, Susan, the Neanderthal can't understand."

The soldier sat down and picked up his book. Bates moved to sit beside him. "You showed admirable restraint."

The soldier looked up. "Yes, sir. Figured that if I beat the snot out of him, it would be all over the evening news and we'd have another story of a returning Vietnam soldier attacking the poor and innocent public. This way he goes away maybe feeling a little less sure of himself."

"Well, Sergeant," said Bates, "I was impressed. You just back?"

"Been in the World for, oh, twelve, thirteen hours now. Just trying to get home."

"Listen, I'm putting together a large team and I think you've got the qualities I'm looking for. If you'll give me a copy of your orders, I'll keep you in mind. And if you come with me, I think we might be able to arrange transport for you."

"Thanks, Colonel, but my ride will be here shortly. She got the flight times wrong, or I did, or something. Shit, what a way to begin, huh?"

Bates stood and read the man's name tag. "Well, Sergeant Green, if there's anything you need, give me a call." He accepted the copy of the orders that Green handed him.

The two shook hands, then Bates returned to his friends. The carousel had started to spin and the luggage was sliding down the ramp. Bates collected his, waited while Sheckley found his own suitcase and then asked, "We going to give the lieutenants a ride over to the Pentagon?"

Sheckley turned and saw the two of them sitting close together, trying to look as if they hadn't noticed each other. If they had been sitting any closer, they would have been sitting in each other's laps.

"I don't know," said Sheckley, "you think we should interrupt them?"

"What is it with them anyway?" asked Bates.

Sheckley shrugged. "I think they just discovered that one was a boy and the other a girl."

"Grab them and I'll find us a cab."

Outside the airport he had no trouble finding transportation over to the Pentagon. After a short taxi ride, Sheckley paid off the driver and then took them all inside. They made their way through the myriad corridors and hallways until they reached Steward's office, where the general was waiting for them. Comstock told them to leave their suitcases in the outer office and then escorted them into the the general's presence.

Steward ordered them to sit down in the conference area where the light was the brightest and then came forward from behind his desk. He stood there for a moment, studying them, then said without preamble, "Sorry about all the trouble we've put you through, Colonel, but I think it's best that we scrap these plans for now."

"Maybe we should continue on this," argued Bates. "The team I want to put together would be more than a one-time assault squad. It could be used in a variety of places for a variety of actions. Its mission could be expanded outward to include antiterrorist activities."

"I appreciate what you're saying, Colonel, but I think it's in the best interest of everyone to let it drop now. We've got the preliminary work done so that if we decide to go with it in the future we can put it together quickly."

"Sir—"

"No, Colonel, I think we're better off this way. Hell, man, the trained personnel exist. It's just a question of bringing them together and giving them the special assignment when the need arises."

Bates nodded, thinking that there were things he should be saying, but for some reason they weren't coming to mind. He wanted to tell Steward that a specially trained unit would be valuable in the future, but he couldn't think of the arguments. Nearly every advance in the military profession had grown out of a wartime need. Advanced thinking wasn't condoned. And now, sitting in the air-conditioned office of a general who had the power to make or break the unit, Bates found himself without an argument.

"General," he began, but didn't know what to say after that. "General," he said again.

"No, Colonel," interrupted Steward, "this is over for now. My orders have come down to me. I think it's because we were premature on it all. If we'd waited for confirmation, it would have been different."

"General, we know the North Vietnamese are doing construction at the site," said Rawlings.

"That's right, Lieutenant. Construction. But we have no information that POWs are going to be sent there, and without *them* there there's nothing for us to do. Premature."

"Then that's it," said Bates.

"I'm afraid so, Colonel. Right now we have no need for a special unit, so the money isn't there. Everyone goes back to their original assignments. One thing positive I can say, though, is that no one got into the field and no one got hurt."

16

**THE DEMILITARIZED
ZONE
VIETNAM**

Gerber lay in the steaming jungle, his uniform drenched with sweat. The ground under him, a moist mass of rotting, reeking vegetation, soaked his chest and legs, making his existence even more miserable. His gaze roamed the clearing, which was stretched out in front of him like a blanket for a picnic, but he saw nothing that would be of interest.

The jungle beyond it was a dark, steaming mass with wisps of white mist drifting in the shadows caused by the triple canopy. It was a silent, foreboding jungle that hinted at something more sinister than huge spiders and giant snakes. Gerber knew that his perception was being colored by the knowledge that the jungle was probably in North Vietnam. That was what made it sinister.

He spent the morning watching the clearing and jungle, switching duty with Fetterman. When not on guard, he lay quietly under a massive bush covered with pink flowers that filled the air with a sickly pungent odor that sometimes threatened to gag him.

He tried to rest, telling himself over and over that there were people who paid good money to sit in the hot, humid environment of a steam bath. It was good for them, baking the poisons out of the system. But Gerber couldn't convince himself of it.

At noon he ate a cold meal and drank more of his water. Again he poured a small amount onto his go-to-hell rag and wiped it across the back of his neck. He rested for a while longer and then pulled out his map. Checking it carefully, he realized they were about a klick to the east of where they wanted to be, but that was almost nothing. It wouldn't take them long to get back on track.

Then it was his turn on watch. He moved to the edge of the jungle where Fetterman crouched, touched the master sergeant on the shoulder and raised an eyebrow in question. Fetterman responded by shaking his head, telling Gerber he had seen nothing of interest.

That was the way it was for the whole patrol: no one saw anything of interest. There were no people in the DMZ other than NVA slipping into the South and Americans slipping into the North. The soil was too poor for farming and everyone used it for a free-fire zone. Anyone or anything caught moving was shot at.

The only sounds other than those generated by the animals or the wind through the top canopy were the indistinct rumblings of artillery and bombings in the South. Gerber wasn't sure he actually heard them, or if he was feeling the vibrations in the ground. Not that it mattered.

In the late afternoon he ate more of the C-rations and finished one canteen of water. He studied his map, trying to memorize the terrain features they would be able to discern in the dark—a wide stream or a high ridgeline, some physical feature that would give him an idea of the patrol's progress.

Of course it would be easier if he could navigate using the stars, but in the thick vegetation it was almost impossible to see the sky, and when there were glimpses of it, there were so few visible stars that it was next to impossible to identify them. In the jungle he had to rely on his compass and the terrain features he could find.

Again he rotated with Fetterman, letting the master sergeant eat and rest, not that it was demanding to watch an open patch of jungle. But the man on guard did have to stay alert while the other caught some sleep.

And then the sunlight seemed to dim slightly and the trees and bushes that had held a form changed into shapeless gray-black masses that concealed the jungle. Gerber watched the clearing mutate into something eerie and veiled, the logs, bushes and anthills turning into twisted, sneering enemy soldiers—tricks of the eye and the twilight.

He waited another hour, but still there was no sign of the enemy, and although Gerber knew a patient ambush could be waiting on the other side of the clearing, he didn't really believe there was. Charlie and the North Vietnamese had no reason to suspect Americans this far north. They wouldn't be laying ambushes that had no hope of killing the enemy.

When it was finally dark, so dark that again it was like the inside of a small cave, Gerber crawled to the rear. The men formed in a tight circle, their faces only inches apart. Each man knew his job then. Gerber didn't have to spell it out. To them he said, "Fetterman, point. Van with him. Tyme in the rear with Kepler."

Fetterman hesitated long enough to take his own compass reading, then he was on his feet, slipping forward to the very edge of the clearing. He stopped there, crouched and listened, his head cocked to one side. He held up a hand and then pointed at the ground near his feet, telling Van to take that position as soon as he had moved.

Slowly, moving in a crouched position, his shoulders hunched and his head bowed, Fetterman moved into the clearing. He walked slowly, carefully, setting his feet down precisely, trying not to break the grass and leave a trail. When he reached the first of the logs, he slipped from sight and waited.

The rest of the men moved out then, spreading into a long line at the edge of the clearing. Gerber had thought about making them all follow the same path so that the enemy, if they found this clearing before the grass sprung back, wouldn't know how many men had crossed. But he wanted the men spread out farther than that would allow. Besides, he could get them across faster.

Fetterman watched as they left the trees, black, indistinct shapes that detached themselves from the jungle and crept forward. When they reached his position, he was on his feet again, moving in a straight line. He kept the pace slow deliberately, averting his gaze from the jungle in front of him because it was too distracting. He glanced at it, looking for enemy movement, knowing if they were hiding in there, he would see no movement. The first clue would be an exploding grenade or a volley or enemy shots designed to kill and maim everyone in the clearing.

Halfway across he halted again, crouching among the tiny bushes and deep grasses there. For a moment he let the tension drain out of him, forgetting where he was and what he was doing. His senses were still working, searching for signs of the enemy, but his nerves were calm, his muscles relaxed. And then he was on his feet, moving forward more rapidly now. He stepped over a fallen log and felt his foot slide into a puddle of water.

Half an hour after he started, Fetterman was within thirty yards of the jungle. He halted a final time and crouched in the semiprotection of the clearing, listening to the sounds of the night creatures as they scurried through the jungle. The calls of the predators and the warnings of the prey came clearly to him. He listened to the natural sounds of the jungle and knew that if the enemy had been lying in wait all day, the animals would ignore them by now. No clue there.

At last he reached the edge of the jungle. He stopped, hesitating before he entered it. In the clearing there was a light breeze that touched his face and hands, drying the sweat. He could feel a slight chill as the back of his fatigue shirt dried. Once he entered the jungle, there would be no cooling breeze. The mass of vegetation was too thick for the wind to penetrate. It got lost in the upper levels, swirling around, promising relief that never came.

With an effort, Fetterman reached out and touched the thick leaves of a bush, pushing them aside. He turned his body as if passing through a heavy crowd on his way to the bar, and was back in the jungle, back into the steaming misery of the rain forest.

Moving deeper into the vegetation, he halted, then touched the smooth bark of a teak tree and let his fingers slide down it until they brushed the thorns of a wait-a-minute vine. He drew his hand back and turned, facing the way he had come. Behind him was the black, featureless dark that seemed to invade the jungle at sunset, a night so black that he couldn't see anyone with him. He caught the quiet rustle of cloth against vegetation or the sound of a foot crushing the decaying leaves. The men were there, behind him; he just couldn't see them.

Now that they had entered the jungle again, their tactics had to change. In the jungle, even in the daylight, you didn't set your weapon down to go around a tree to urinate because it was so easy to forget where you had set it. You held on to it.

With people it was the same thing. They couldn't move forward maintaining a normal patrol interval because it was so dark that the men could easily be separated and no one would know what had happened until morning. They had to travel together in a line.

Fetterman tied a piece of string to his little finger and handed it to the man right behind him, who did the same, passing the string to the rear. When each man was fastened to the line, Fetterman gave it a short, easy tug to let them know he was moving out again. A single tug told them to halt and two warned them of danger. It was a simple method to keep the patrol together in the jungle, and if one of them got jumped, the string would give silent warning.

Again they started off, moving carefully and quietly. Fetterman felt his way along with an almost supernatural ability. He would reach out at the last moment and touch the trunk of a tree that was in the way, then step around it and guide the remainder of the patrol to safety.

Slowly they wormed their way forward, crossing the DMZ, and entered the North without knowing it. There were no fences or guardhouses in the way. There was only more of the jungle, maybe thicker in places, but no man-made monuments marking the border between the two countries.

Gerber, who had memorized part of the map, didn't know the exact instant they had entered North Vietnam, but he suspected it had happened. For some strange reason he had expected something to change—sirens to go off or guards to begin shouting. But none of that occurred. He did think the jungle had turned darker and that there were fewer insects.

They halted a few minutes later. Gerber crouched near a lacy fern that dripped constantly. He could hear the quiet splashes as the water fell onto the jungle floor. He waited, wondering what was going on at the front of the patrol, knowing that Fetterman would call for help if he needed it.

Then they were on the move again. Gerber felt the jungle floor suddenly drop away. There was the quiet bubbling of a stream. He hesitated and then stepped forward. His foot sank into the water, which cascaded over the top of his boot. The water was cool, sending shivers up his spine, and Gerber had the urge to fall forward, letting the water wash over him. Instead he pushed on until he reached the far bank. He scrambled up and halted. In the inky blackness he could see a human shape and could hear the quiet breathing.

He leaned close to the man. "What is it?"

"Rest," said Kepler, his voice tight and strained. "We're resting."

MAXWELL FELT BETTER than he had in weeks, maybe months. He'd spent the day sleeping in an air-conditioned room with blinds that blocked out nearly all of the tropical sun. It was like being home in his own bed on a cool autumn evening. Best of all there was no phone to ring or people to drop by. He was as alone as he would have been if he had been lost deep in the forest behind his house in Maine.

He woke late in the day, having been able to sleep through the noise of men shouting to one another as they moved through the building. He had slept through the strains of Vietnamese music that the hootch maids listened to as they cleaned the rooms. He had even slept through an argument between two lieutenants about who was the best shot with an M-79.

Maxwell lay there for a long time, listening to aircraft landing or taking off at the nearby airfield, and to the men who were checking into the transient quarters. Finally he got up and took a shower. Fortunately there were a couple of towels, soap and even a toothbrush sitting in the room for whoever needed it.

Back in the room he sat on the bed, dreading the trip back to Saigon and the war. For a moment, sitting there, he was out of it. No decisions to make. No crisis to manage. Nothing to do but let the water evaporate from his body.

Soon, too soon, it was time to go. He dressed again in his dirty clothes, feeling that he was somehow doing something immoral. The underwear itched and his shirt smelled slightly of sweat, but there was nothing he could do about that. Had he been thinking, he could have had his clothes cleaned while he slept.

Outside, he walked from the quarters to the airfield and checked in at the ramshackle terminal next to the control tower. He strolled in and glanced up at the scheduling board. It was a huge white thing covered with acetate with aircraft numbers and destinations written in with a grease pencil. Two men, both wearing OD T-shirts and jungle fatigue pants, were working behind a counter made of plywood coated with peeling green paint.

"What can I do for you?" asked the older of the two.

Maxwell moved closer and leaned an elbow on the counter. "I need a ride into Saigon."

"Yeah, you and everyone else in this place. You in the Army or what?"

Maxwell looked at the man, taking in his sunburned face and graying hair. The man had to be a sergeant who was pissed at the world because he was stuck in Vietnam. To him, Maxwell said, "I'm a civilian employee of the government."

The man picked up a smoking cigar, chewed on its end, then dropped it back into the ashtray. "Well, Civilian Employee, I'm afraid I don't have anything available."

Maxwell stood there, his good mood evaporating. He blinked at the man and then took out his wallet, flipping it open so that his American embassy ID card was visible. Tapping on the counter in order to get the man's attention, he asked, "This good enough to get me a ride into Saigon, or do I call someone at MACV?"

The man glanced at the card, shrugged as he turned away and then whirled back. Suddenly the sergeant realized he was treading on thin ice. The wrong word in the wrong place and he could find himself at some fire support base waiting for Charlie to storm the wire. It didn't pay to piss off anyone who had even the slightest bit of power.

"I'm sorry, sir, but we get a lot of employees of contractors in here trying to push us around. All you had to do, sir, was show me your ID card." He turned again and consulted his board. "Chopper from Top Tigers is heading down there in twenty minutes or so. I can manifest you through on that if you like."

"Do you think you could get them to land at the MACV helipad before they go into Tan Son Nhut?"

"No problem, sir. Consider it done."

Maxwell nodded. "Thank you, Sergeant . . . ?"

"Winder, sir. Clarence Winder."

"You'll let me know when to board?"

"Yes, sir. You just have a seat and I'll personally tell you when the chopper's ready."

Almost before Maxwell could sit down, he was hustled out to the airfield where the helicopter was sitting. He crouched beneath the spinning rotor blades, and climbed up into the cargo compartment. As soon as he was strapped in, he lifted a thumb to tell the crew chief he was ready.

The chopper lifted and turned, then charged forward, nose low, as the ground raced by. An instant later the nose came up and they shot into the air, leaving Maxwell's stomach somewhere behind. He closed his eyes, but he hated that even more than seeing what was going on, so he opened them again.

Outside the chopper the night was beginning to engulf the countryside. The ground was dark just south of Bien Hoa, but farther away there was a sea of light. Saigon had shed its shabby daytime look and now glowed like the gem some people claimed it was. The darkness, chased by the sporadic neon and electricity of the capital city, looked like any city in the world. It was now a deceitful place, hidden behind the sparkling lights.

Maxwell sat quietly and watched the light show below him. Vehicles moved along the highway with their headlights blazing and calling attention to themselves. He wondered what the enemy thought about the glittering display. They were soldiers who had been warned about the decadence of the city, who were ass-deep in mud and who could see the city's glow. Then he decided he didn't care what the enemy thought. After all, they *were* the enemy.

Finally he did close his eyes, not wanting to see anything else. He heard the noise of the engine change and felt the aircraft begin its descent. Opening his eyes, he saw the lights on the helipad at the headquarters building. That was something he had never thought about before. All the lights. They would make perfect aiming points for enemy gunners. But then enemy gunners didn't shoot at the headquarters building. It was almost as if they were afraid that shooting at the building would piss off the generals who worked there. If that happened, maybe the war would heat up. No one wanted to make waves.

They kept the descent going until they were close to the ground. The pilot shallowed it out, then dropped the collective so that they bounced on the center of the pad. As Maxwell leaped to the ground, the chopper took off, engulfing him in a choking cloud of swirling red dust. He closed his eyes and held his breath until the noise of the helicopter was a distant throb.

As the dust settled, Maxwell hurried through the heat of the night, up the steps and through the double doors. He stopped there a moment, letting his body adjust to the air-conditioning, and then walked downstairs. The guard at the metal gate made him sign in before letting him enter. Once that was done, he walked to his office, figuring to clean up some paperwork before heading to his hotel.

The sheet of paper taped to his door caught his attention before he got there. He hurried forward and ripped it off, unfolding it. The note was simple and direct: "Maxwell, where in hell are you? Report to General Davidson soonest and you better have the right answers—Thomas."

And with that the last of the good mood was gone. Such a summons could only mean bad news. The only thing that could make it worse was if Davidson was still in the building waiting for him to show up.

Maxwell folded the paper and stuffed it into his pocket. The bounce in his walk was gone as he stumbled back to the gate.

The guard smiled. "That was quick, sir."

"Just needed to pick something up," mumbled Maxwell.

The guard unlocked the gate and opened it. "Hope it was nothing classified."

Maxwell bent at the table to sign out. When he finished, he straightened and said, "What? Oh. No, of course not. Can't go violating the directives."

"Well, have a good evening, sir."

"Thank you," said Maxwell absently as he headed back up the stairs. He stopped at the top and glanced down the corridor. It was dark, but light spilled into it from several offices that were still occupied. He hoped that one of them wasn't Davidson's, but as he walked down the hallway he could see that one was. He felt sick to his stomach and wondered what had blown up in his absence. Wasn't that always the way? Take some time off and everything went to hell in a handbasket. It was almost as if God were punishing him for neglecting his duties.

The outer office was empty, but the door to the inner was open and he could see several men, all in uniform, sitting in there. He hesitated, wondering if he should just run and hide, but he didn't understand why he felt that way. Instead, he moved forward into the pool of light that surrounded the door.

Davidson looked up and waved a hand, motioning him in. "Jerry, just a quick question for you."

Maxwell entered and stopped. He recognized most of the men by sight but didn't know their names. He'd seen them around the building, but there were nearly three hundred men assigned to MACV and another thousand or so who made regular visits.

"First things first, Jerry," said Davidson. "Where in hell have you been all day?"

"Taking care of business up at Bien Hoa. Just got back about ten minutes ago."

"Good. Now, I've got a directive here from the Pentagon that says our covert mission has been temporarily scrubbed. That going to present a problem?"

Maxwell felt his head spin and his stomach turn over. He wished he had eaten something and then was glad he hadn't because he might have lost it.

"Jerry?"

"Sorry, General, but I've got the men in the field. They were deployed last night."

"Well, shit," said Davidson, "you're going to have to recall them. Where are they now?"

Maxwell looked at the four other men in the room and shook his head. "Sorry, General, but I don't know these gentlemen and that information is classified."

"We're all friends here, Maxwell. I'll vouch for the integrity of these men and for the fact that each has the necessary clearance."

"Yes, sir, but they don't have the need-to-know."

"Maxwell, where in hell are those men?"

"In the field moving on the target." Maxwell glanced at his watch. "Getting close to it, I might add."

Davidson slapped a hand against his desk. "Then recall them. Get them back."

Maxwell shrugged helplessly. "I'm afraid I can't do that."

"Can't or won't?" demanded Davidson.

"Can't. They aren't scheduled to report in until six in the morning. And even that isn't a sure bet because we've built some slop into the schedule. They won't be considered to have missed a check-in time until midnight tomorrow, given the nature of the mission.''

"Shit," said Davidson.

"By the time we hear from them," added Maxwell, "they should be at the target. Recalling them at that point would be useless."

"No, it wouldn't," said Davidson. "It would be following our orders."

"Why not just leave them out there for a week or so and see what they discover?"

"Mr. Maxwell," said Davidson, his voice now icy. "I want those men pulled from the field at the first opportunity. They should never have been deployed. Someone overstepped his authority by getting them out there that fast. Heads will roll for this fuck-up."

"Yes, sir," said Maxwell.

"Right now our only problem is to see that we get the men back before the enemy discovers them, or someone around here learns they were out there."

Maxwell didn't respond. He stood and stared, waiting for someone to issue an order.

"You get those men recalled Maxwell and then you personally debrief them. They never left Saigon."

"We had them in isolation at Bien Hoa for a couple of days."

"Then they never left isolation. But they certainly never deployed. You got that?"

"Yes, sir," said Maxwell. "I got it."

17

NORTH OF THE
DEMILITARIZED ZONE
NORTH VIETNAM

The trip north from the DMZ was strange. The jungle was no different than that in South Vietnam. The ground underfoot was firm in most places, spongy in others and wet everywhere else. The trees, some as big around as houses, reached into the sky, hiding Gerber and his men under a layer of thick, intertwined leaves. The roots, moss-covered and poking through the rotting vegetation, were as big around as a man. But now that Gerber and the others were out of the thick undergrowth, the vegetation was sparse on the ground. Bushes and ferns blocked the way, but it was easy to get around them. Vines and moss hung from tree limbs. And just as in the South, the terrain was dark and dank and smelled of mold, freshly turned earth and death.

Fetterman increased the pace, dodging across the paths and trails that they came to. He stopped the men frequently, letting them all catch their breaths. But then he was up and moving again, taking them farther north. They crossed a single road that had been paved at one time but was now little more than a broken track overgrown with grasses and bushes. Huge chunks of concrete had slid into ditches at the side of the road.

They crossed the road quickly and then spread out into the damp swamplike areas that bordered it. When no one rushed out of hiding to shout or shoot at them, they started forward again, but now with Tyme in the lead and Fetterman bringing up the rear.

As the night continued, they stopped more frequently and rested longer. The strain of moving without noise was sapping their strength as quickly as the humidity and heat did. They were turned into sweat-soaked, tired machines who stumbled forward, making more noise the longer they were forced to walk. They rattled the leaves of bushes, snapped twigs and scraped against trees.

Gerber worried about it but knew there wasn't much he could do. It was a rule that eight men made more than twice as much noise as four men. He didn't understand it; he just knew it was true. Four men could almost glide through the jungle, but eight men couldn't. They made noise and left signs. But then, of course, Gerber had needed an eight-man team to make the mission a success.

They stopped once for about an hour before sunrise. Gerber dropped to the ground gratefully, feeling the sweat pour from his face and down his body. He tried to even out his breathing so that it didn't rasp in his throat and he tried to block out the odor of the jungle—a feral, almost evil smell that assaulted him with physical force. He knew it was a reaction to being in North Vietnam, but that didn't make it any less real.

And then they were up and moving again, sliding through the jungle between bushes and ferns, letting the thorn-covered vines grab at them, tearing their clothes and their skin, opening a dozen tiny cuts that itched and would soon be infected. They stumbled on the uneven ground and tripped over the unseen hazards in the darkness. They bumped their hands and elbows, knees and shins, but no one cried out in surprise or pain. They just kept moving steadily forward, northward, deeper into the enemy's backyard.

Gerber felt a tug on the string that held the patrol together and dropped to one knee, his hand on his weapon's safety. He waited for ten minutes, but there was no other signal. He slipped forward and found Tyme crouching among the bushes, ferns and grasses of the jungle, watching something far in front of him.

"What's going on?" Gerber asked.

Tyme turned and looked toward the voice. Nothing of his face or body was visible. It was wrapped in darkness and camouflage clothing. He leaned toward the sound. "I think we're here."

Gerber slid onto his belly and carefully crawled forward. He saw the vegetation suddenly thin until he was looking out into a dish-shaped valley a couple of klicks across. From the valley he could hear and see nothing. He took out his binoculars and swept them around until he spotted the dark gray smudge at the bottom of the dish. It looked as if it might be the walled village that had drawn them to North Vietnam.

He studied it carefully, looking for signs of life, a light, anything that would tell him there were people below. When nothing appeared he said, "I don't know."

But then Fetterman was next to him, his lips only inches from Gerber's ear. "Someone's coming," the master sergeant informed him.

"We avoid contact," ordered Gerber. "At all costs we avoid contact."

Fetterman slipped off, disappearing into the jungle. Gerber rolled to his right and put the binoculars into their case. He touched Tyme's shoulder and then moved to the rear, putting some distance between him and the young sergeant.

Fetterman crouched in the darkness, his left knee resting on the knobby, exposed root of a teak tree. Behind him, almost brushing his back, was the smooth bark of the teak, and in front of him was an open area sprinkled with short bushes, ferns and a carpeting of tiny plants.

He waited quietly, the string that had attached him to the rest of the team now cut and rolled up. He had pulled out his Randall Combat Knife, the blade blackened so that it wouldn't reflect any light.

Around him the jungle had fallen silent. The animals, insects and snakes had stopped moving, knowing that danger was near. It was as if he had been transported to a quiet, dark, steaming room where no one lived.

The first sound the enemy made was a quiet rustling of cloth against a bush. Fetterman didn't snap his head around, but turned it slowly, using his peripheral vision and his ears.

The first of the enemy suddenly appeared at the far end of the tiny area where Fetterman waited. The man, carrying an AK-47, was little more than a shape twenty feet away. Strung out behind him were more men feeling their way through the jungle.

For a moment Fetterman wondered if they were searching for him and his patrol, then realized they weren't. If it was a search party, they wouldn't be moving in a trail formation. They would be spread out and they would wait for first light, which couldn't be more than thirty minutes away.

The men weren't in a perfect line. They were drifting closer and closer to Fetterman. But the master sergeant wasn't worried because he knew that if he remained motionless he almost certainly wouldn't be seen. He let his eyes roam, watching the enemy patrol.

The men kept coming and passing by until the leader of the patrol disappeared into the jungle, heading more or less toward the walled camp in the bottom of the depression. The last man came out of the gloom, headed toward the village and then stopped dead in his tracks. He turned and stared straight at Fetterman, but didn't say a word.

He moved forward, one hand reaching out, as if feeling his way in a dark, unfamiliar room. He stopped, glanced at the retreating backs of his fellows, but remained silent. He turned his weapon toward Fetterman, and there was an audible snap as he took off the safety.

Again he started forward, stopped and probed with the barrel of his AK. That had been what Fetterman was waiting for. In a single, fluid motion, Fetterman snagged the end of the weapon and yanked it forward, stepping around it. As he did, he jerked it upward, wrenching the weapon from the enemy's hand. There was a startled gasp and the man released his AK.

Fetterman dropped it onto the jungle floor and stepped to the man. He grabbed his face, crushing one hand over the man's mouth and nose. As he did, he slashed with his knife. There was a whisper of ripping silk. The man sagged as his blood splashed over Fetterman's hand. There was an odor of hot copper and then of bowel. The man fell to his knees. A gurgling came from his mouth as he reached upward, his hands seizing Fetterman's arm weakly.

Fetterman turned, but before he could strike again the man died with a rattling in his throat. Fetterman eased the body to the ground and stepped away from it. His senses now sang with tension. He listened to the jungle and stared into it, but the rest of the man's patrol continued forward, never knowing that their comrade had died.

KUTNETSOV STOOD OUTSIDE of his quarters in the early-morning mist, sweating from the humidity that still hung in the air, and waited for the roving patrol. He believed that if he didn't actually go on the patrol, he should be around when they came back in. It gave the men an incentive to do their jobs well because the officers thought enough of them to await their return.

Moskvin led the men through the gate on the south side of the camp. He stopped to let them pass him, heading toward the debriefing area. At one time it had been held in a class-room, but somehow the heat of the afternoon lingered there, turning the enclosure into a sauna that neither the Soviets nor the Viets enjoyed. Now the debriefing was held outside under the huge tree that stood where the night breezes, when they came, could cool them.

When the last of the men entered the compound, Moskvin wasn't happy. He thought he had miscounted or that the rear guard was exceptionally slow. He stepped back through the gate and scanned the grass-covered slopes outside that led up to the jungles, but saw no one rushing down them.

He reentered the camp and hurried to the tree. Once there he counted the men again, now sure that someone had disappeared. He felt his anger grow like a red-hot coal in his stomach. He wanted to shout at these men, but instead asked, "Who's missing?"

They looked around and finally one of them stood. "I think Corporal Van Ngo isn't with us."

Kutnetsov heard the exchange and hurried forward. He leaned close to Moskvin. "You lose another?"

Moskvin stared at his captain, his face a mask, though the expression was lost in the dark. "One of the men has failed to return with us."

"That makes it twelve in the past few days," Kutnetsov said. He turned and thought about the dwindling force. In the old days, just after he had arrived, which wasn't all that long ago, he had laughed at the reports of the South Vietnamese deserting. He had gloated about it, figuring the Americans didn't understand the Oriental mind and that that was the reason their allies kept running off.

Now he found himself in the same boat. He had thought he was being given the best the North Vietnamese had, but as the training progressed, as it got harder, the men began to slip away. First only one or two, and then one night eight of them had failed to return from an ambush.

That had worried Kutnetsov, but not Thuy. Thuy had driven out of the camp and within three hours had located two of the missing men. They had decided they didn't like the Russians, even if they had better ways to kill Americans, and had elected to go home.

Of course Kutnetsov had raged at Colonel Thuy when the Vietnamese officer hadn't brought the men back. He had talked about poor examples and the breakdown in military discipline, but Thuy hadn't been impressed. The colonel had merely told the Soviet officer that the men would return when they were ready and that they would be better soldiers after their trips home.

And now another man had failed to return. He had just slipped off into the jungle so that he could go home. Kutnetsov stood there, enraged for a moment, and then asked Moskvin, "When was the last time you saw him?"

"As we started our inbound turn. Maybe an hour ago. Maybe a little longer."

Kutnetsov turned so that he could look south, but the walls were too high for him to see anything other than the treetops. He rubbed a hand over his face. "Maybe if we throw out a patrol, we could catch him."

"What for, Captain?" asked Moskvin.

"To make an example of him. Show these people there's more to soldiering than marching in straight lines and doing the duty when it suits them."

"Won't do any good, Captain," said Moskvin. "We'd never be able to find him in that jungle. Hell, we could step on him and never know it. Besides, what are you going to do, shoot him?"

Kutnetsov whirled on the sergeant. He shoved his face inches from Moskvin's and hissed, "Don't you ever talk to me like that, Sergeant. Don't you ever forget your place. Now I want you to get Baykal and Salmonov and get back out there. I want that little slope found and I want his body brought back here."

"What if he's not—"

"Sergeant, you've been given your instructions. The deserter died when he fell trying to get away. You understand me?"

"Yes, sir."

"Then you'd better get on with it. And don't come back here until you've located the missing man."

FETTERMAN WAITED IN SILENCE until he was sure the enemy patrol had continued on, never missing the dead man. When the enemy was gone, Fetterman carefully picked up the body, carrying him away from that spot. He moved deeper into the jungle, fighting his way through the thickening undergrowth, the tangle of weeds and the grabbing thorns of the wait-a-minute vines.

The body smelled. There was the odor of unwashed flesh, and in a few hours there would be the stench of decaying meat. It meant that Fetterman would have to move his people to another location. If the predators didn't get at the body quickly, the NVA would be able to find it, and it was obvious that the man had been killed.

Fetterman dropped the man onto the ground and rolled him over, shoving him into a depression that was partially concealed by a log. He pushed some of the decaying vegetation toward the body but knew that it wouldn't hide the dead man for long. That finished, he worked his way back to where Gerber and the rest of the team waited. As he moved through the jungle, he felt a crust on his hand—dried blood from the dead soldier, something he would have to live with until they came to a stream or a pool where he could wash. He found the others easily and moved through the perimeter until he could crouch next to the captain. "Ran into trouble with the patrol. Had to take one out."

"Kill him?" asked Gerber.

"No choice."

"Anyone hear anything?"

"I don't think so, sir. I stayed put and listened, but the patrol just kept going."

Gerber nodded and then pointed into the valley. "We watched them head down there. They all went inside. One man exited a while later, but then returned inside."

"Then they know a man is missing."

"They'd have to be pretty incompetent not to realize that," said Gerber.

"What are we going to do?"

"What did you do with the body?"

"Hid it the best I could, but I think they'll be able to find it in a couple of hours tomorrow unless we catch a real break."

"Okay," said Gerber. "Then we'll need to skirt this area, find our post and get everyone moving away from us. Get Tyme and his team out of here."

"And Galvin has got to make the radio check."

Before Gerber could respond, there was a commotion in the camp below them. A bright light flashed and then went out. A quick rumbling started.

"Generator," commented Fetterman.

"What the hell now?" asked Gerber. "You don't think they're going to launch a full-scale search, do you?"

"If that was one of your men, what would you do?"

"Yeah," said Gerber. He knew he'd turn out the camp, wait for first light, then sweep the jungle until he learned what happened. "Shit, Tony."

"Nothing I could do, Captain. He walked right up and looked me in the face. If I hadn't taken him, he'd have alerted the patrol."

"Then let's get the fuck away from here."

Fetterman retreated and made his way around the tiny perimeter, touching the men on the shoulder to get their attention. He told Tyme and Kepler to bring up the rear and then returned to the edge of the jungle where Gerber waited patiently, his binoculars on the enemy camp.

Fetterman crouched near the captain and waited. Gerber finally got to his knees and stuffed the binoculars into their case. He nodded and Fetterman climbed to his feet. He glanced over his shoulder, saw the men spread out behind him and realized the sun was coming up.

They moved along the edge of the jungle as it turned from deep, sinister blacks to shadowy grays that made it possible to see what the obstacles were. A light mist, a gray-white fog, clung to the low places on the ground, or among the leaves of the canopy, making the vegetation look as if it were on fire.

They came to a copse surrounded by bushes and bamboo. It was a thickness in the jungle that provided them with everything they needed—cover, good fields of fire and a source of water if they nursed the dripping from the thick leaves. Not a lot of water but some anyway.

Fetterman stopped and turned, aware of the men behind him now. They were no longer unrecognizable shapes hidden in the darkness, but people—sweat-soaked, tired men who wanted nothing more than to hide for a few hours.

As it got lighter around them, the jungle changed from grays to greens with a drifting white mist obscuring some of it. The men crawled into hiding, using different paths, trying not to leave signs. Fetterman followed them and Gerber brought up the rear. They fanned out into pairs so that they could keep watch around the whole perimeter while one of the men in each pair caught some sleep.

Gerber chose a vantage point so that he could keep an eye on the enemy camp. From their new position on the hillside, and in the growing light, he could see some of the interior compound. The binoculars brought the whole thing closer. There was nothing visible behind the windows and there seemed to be no one manning the guard towers.

As he watched, the gate on the south opened, but from his new position it was next to impossible to see anything there. A few men exited and headed up the slope toward the jungle. They angled away from him, and even in the growing light it was hard to see anything other than the silhouettes of the men.

Gerber watched them until the terrain and the vegetation concealed them. Then he turned his attention back to the compound. Smoke was coming from the chimney of one of the hootches now—probably a cooking fire. He glanced over at Fetterman and handed the master sergeant the binoculars. "Familiarize yourself with the camp."

Fetterman took the binoculars and scanned the ground below. He turned then, watching for the enemy patrol, checking out the portion of the jungle where they had disappeared. As he handed the glasses back to Gerber, he said, "They're close to where I killed the guy."

"You think they're going to find him?"

"Shit, sir, there are enough signs around that I don't know how they can help it. Even without the body, they should be able to find the blood. Nothing I could do about that."

"Garrote would have been better."

"Yes, sir, except I didn't have one, and even if I did I'm not sure I was in the position to use it."

"Maybe we'll luck out on it," said Gerber. He lifted the binoculars to his eyes and searched the compound again.

There was movement now, men walking among the buildings, many of them carrying weapons.

Gerber touched Fetterman's shoulder and pointed to the enemy compound. He leaned close. "Well, Intel got part of it right. It *is* some kind of military camp."

Fetterman borrowed the binoculars again and studied the camp. Gerber lay there quietly, his chin on his hands, watching the images below him. The sun had finally peeked over the horizon, and the shadows that had concealed much of the detail began to shorten.

Fetterman again turned his attention to the jungle, but the enemy patrol hadn't reappeared. He swung around and watched the enemy camp. Men tumbled out of the buildings. Some fell into a loose formation while one man inspected them. Others made their way to the building with the smoking chimney.

And then three men who weren't armed appeared in the center of the compound. They were taller, bulkier than the Vietnamese. Even without the aid of glasses, it was obvious the men weren't Vietnamese. Fetterman studied them for an instant and then whispered, "Got them, Captain. White men."

18

THE JUNGLES OUTSIDE
THE CAMP NEAR LANG
MO, NORTH VIETNAM

Gerber felt the words slice through him. He reached for the binoculars and focused them on the scene below. He saw two tall men, one with light-colored hair, surrounded by armed Vietnamese and being escorted into the building with the smoking chimney. Carefully he examined the rest of the compound but saw no other white men.

"What do you think, Tony?" he whispered.

"Looks like just what Maxwell told us. They're using it as a POW camp."

Gerber slipped back, letting the concealing branches of the ferns and bushes close in front of him. Now it was impossible to see the camp. For a moment he rested there, listening to the jungle as it came awake. He didn't hear the riot of noise that he had heard in some places. This time it was a quiet awakening—birds calling to one another as they lifted from the branches, a few monkeys chattering and insects buzzing into flight.

Maxwell and the Intel boys had pegged it right. The North Vietnamese had been working inside the camp, repairing and preparing it, and now they had begun to move the prisoners in. At least that was what it looked like.

He knew they had missed one check-in time, but he wasn't concerned. Provision had been made for that. He wished there was some way he could get down there and let the prisoners know that rescue was imminent.

The thoughts came to him quickly. He knew the depression the POWs had to be suffering. If they knew someone was near to rescue them, their depression would be gone. It didn't have to be much. One word to the POWs would be all that was needed.

Gerber looked around. The shadows, bushes and grass concealed his men so that he could only partially glimpse them—a foot and part of a leg, a single hand, or maybe a knee if he stared at it long enough.

"We've got to make check-in and alert them to this," said Gerber.

Fetterman didn't respond. Instead he began moving among the men, drawing them to the rear into a tight circle. He communicated with them by using hand signals, forming them into a tight perimeter. When it was done, he sat in the middle, waiting for the captain to issue orders.

There were a dozen things that Gerber wanted to say. He had worked with these men long enough to feel he owed them explanations when he changed plans, but here, in the bamboo-and-fern thicket, he didn't want to talk more than he had to. Quickly he told them he had seen white men in the enemy camp and that they had to tell Net Control in Nha Trang that they had confirmed the presence of prisoners.

He whispered to them, letting them in on the details. With the enemy patrol a klick or so to the east, he wanted to withdraw slowly and quietly to the south and west. They would make radio contact and then split the team. Tyme, Santini and Van would head back to the South, make radio contact and get picked up. They would arrange for the resupply. Gerber would remain behind with the others.

When he finished, no one asked any questions. Each man nodded his understanding as Gerber looked at him. Gerber then pointed at Fetterman, and the master sergeant turned, moving deeper into the bush, taking the point. One by one the men joined him, spreading out in a long, thin line.

They slipped through the jungle, easing around the big trunks of teak trees and avoiding fat, thorn-studded vines. Working their way through the thick, dripping vegetation, they moved south as they listened for the enemy.

After an hour or so Fetterman called a halt and the men spread into a circular perimeter automatically. They were on top of a slight rise that gave them a limited view of the surrounding jungle. Sitting quietly, they listened for sounds that the enemy was pursuing them, that the enemy had discovered they were in the area, but none came.

Gerber found Bocker sitting near the Angry 109. He was using the keypad and the cipher wheel to create the magnetic tape for a burst transmission. Bocker could set up the whole message on the transmitter, then push a button, and in two or three seconds the whole message would be sent. It gave the enemy no time to triangulate even if they happened to know what frequency Bocker was using and when he would be transmitting, assuming the enemy knew there was someone to look for in the first place.

When Bocker was finished preparing, he and Tyme set up the antenna. Normally Bocker would have tried to separate it from them by a hundred meters or more, but that was too dangerous to try. Instead, they hung the antenna in a tall tree, the four lengths of wire hanging down but concealed by the vegetation. Bocker connected the antenna to the radio, used Tyme to crank the generator and, once contact was established, pushed a button to send the main message.

Two seconds later he was packing up the gear. They pulled down the antenna and stored it. In minutes they were ready to move. As soon as Bocker signaled him, Gerber nodded to Fetterman and the patrol moved out. The plan was to put a little distance between them and the radio site just in case something had gone wrong.

THE MESSAGE CENTER called Jerry Maxwell an hour later and told him they had a classified document for him. Maxwell stared up at the ceiling, shivered and said he would be over to pick it up right away. That was a task he didn't want to perform because he knew what the message was and he would have to then report to Davidson for another ass-chewing.

Maxwell closed the file he was reading and stood, then moved to the safe in the corner. He crammed the file into the front, knowing he would have to read it again later. The last thing he wanted was to have to paw through the whole drawer.

He slammed the safe door shut, spun the combination lock and then tried the handle. It failed to move. He checked each of the drawers and found they were locked, too. Then he moved to the door, but stopped long enough to scan the office. When he was in a hurry, he sometimes failed to see a classified document, leaving it out for anyone and everyone to find. On his return he was always appalled by his sloppiness, but since he locked his door and there was never any sign that anyone had been in the office, he forgot about it. He wasn't following regulations, but locking the door covered his ass and that was the important thing.

He left his office, but instead of heading for the guard and the gate he turned in the other direction and walked down the cold hallway. The cinder-block walls dripped condensation.

The message center was around a corner and through a short hallway that ended in a wall. One side was a safelike door with a combination lock and next to it was a barred window that was closed. Maxwell stepped close and pushed the button that rang a bell inside the message center. Then he stood there feeling like an idiot, facing the peephole so that the operator would be able to see him.

A moment later the window opened and a strange face asked, "Yes?"

Maxwell looked at the young man. He had probably been in Vietnam for a week and this was his first day on the job. Maxwell gave the soldier his name and said, "You've got a message for me."

"Name and office symbol."

Maxwell told him and then nearly laughed when he saw the kid's reaction.

The soldier pulled a black loose-leaf binder from a shelf and flipped through it until he found a letter authorizing Maxwell to pick up classified documents. He closed the window but returned quickly, then checked the message time date group and wrote them on a form before pushing it toward Maxwell to sign. That ritual finished, he gave Maxwell the message.

Maxwell then returned to his office, unlocked the door and entered. Kicking the door shut with his heel as he opened the envelope, he extracted the message. As he sat down, he realized what he held—the first communication from the men in the field. He felt his heart flutter: he had yet to issue the recall order that Davidson had demanded be sent.

The message was short and contained added remarks by the Intelligence officer who had processed it at Nha Trang. Maxwell read it through twice and then leaped to his feet. He jammed it back into the envelope and rushed from his office. Stopping at the gate, he signed out and then ran up the stairs.

On the main floor he pushed by the dozens of men and women who worked in the building, ignoring them. He hurried to Davidson's office, stopped and took a deep breath. When he rubbed a hand through his hair and across his forehead, he was upset by the sweat that stained it. Then he pushed into the outer office and said to the major sitting there, "I've got to see the general."

"General Davidson is tied up in a meeting right now. You'll have to wait."

"Major, I think you'd better interrupt him because he's going to want to see this."

"I don't—"

"Well, I do," snapped Maxwell. He moved toward the door.

The aide stepped in front of him, blocking him. He put a hand up as if to ward off a blow and said, "Let me see if the general will see you." The man turned and opened the door, sticking his head into the office. Maxwell could hear the muffled words but couldn't understand them. The aide then stepped back and said, "Go on in."

Maxwell entered and then stopped. He glanced at Robin Morrow, who was sitting there, a notebook propped against her knee. She grinned at Maxwell but said nothing to him.

"All right, Jerry, what's so important that you have to burst in here?" Davidson demanded.

Maxwell moved forward, the envelope in his left hand suddenly weighing five pounds. He had trapped himself, insisting that the general get the message right away. If the damned aide had said the general was with a reporter, he could have figured something out. Now he was about to alert the press that something important was happening.

Davidson snapped his fingers. "Okay, Maxwell, let me have it."

Maxwell handed over the envelope and stepped back. He kept his eyes on Morrow, who continued to smile at him but remained silent.

Quickly Davidson read the message and then crammed it back into the envelope. He stood up. "Miss Morrow, I'm afraid something has come up that demands my immediate attention."

"Uh-huh," she said. "Would you care to elaborate on that now?"

"I'm sorry, but this is a classified matter. If and when I can release the details, I assure you that you'll be the first to know."

Still Morrow didn't move. She uncrossed her legs and bent at the waist to pluck her camera bag off the floor. Straightening, she brushed the hair from her forehead. "Does this have anything to do with Mack Gerber?"

"No, Miss Morrow, it does not." He held her gaze steadily.

In that moment she knew it did but couldn't think of a way to get at it. She scratched her knee and let the silence between them grow, hoping the general would blunder along trying to cover up.

But Davidson had been in the military too long and had been interviewed by too many reporters to fall into that trap. He let the silence build until it was uncomfortable, and still he refused to speak.

Morrow had run out of ideas. She got to her feet and held out a tiny hand. "Thank you for your time, General. Please stay in touch."

When she was gone, Maxwell dropped into the chair. "You got rid of her easily."

"Jerry, you never get rid of a reporter easily. We were almost finished and she knew I wouldn't give her anything more. Your running in here didn't help. Now she knows something important is going on and she'll be snooping around trying to discover it."

"Sorry, but your aide didn't tell me the circumstances. I thought you were meeting with people from MACV." He looked at the envelope. It reminded him of the reason for his visit. "You still want me to recall the team?"

Davidson sat down again and rubbed his eyes with the heels of his hands. He held out his hand then and picked up the message. As he read it, he said, "I think we need to keep this team in place. We need to get a message off to the Pentagon. Let them know we've got eyeball confirmation."

"Then we don't recall the team?"

"Use your head, Jerry. Of course we don't recall the team. The recall instruction was issued when we thought the camp was deserted. Now that we know there are people in it, we'll fall back to the original plan."

"Shall I draft the message?"

"No," said Davidson. "I'll take care of that, and of the coordination with them. You just monitor the team and learn all you can from them."

Maxwell waited for more, and when it didn't come he stood up. Without a word he left the office. Outside, in the corridor, he found Morrow leaning against a wall, playing with the lens on her camera.

When she saw him, she straightened. "What was that all about, Jerry?"

"Just some routine work that had to be taken care of right away."

"I don't know of any routine work that would require your interrupting the general." She smiled slyly.

"Well, Robin, then you're not as well versed as I thought. You know how we civilian types can get when we think the military is dragging its feet."

She fell in line with him as he walked by, linking her arm with his. "Tell me about it."

"Nothing to tell. Now, I've got some unimportant, uninteresting paperwork to play with, so I'll have to say goodbye to you up here."

"Jerry, you and the general haven't fooled me. I'm going to find out what's happening."

Maxwell stopped at the stairway. "Not from me you won't."

"Don't be too sure about that," she warned him.

The funny thing was that he wasn't.

RAWLINGS WAS FINALLY going to succeed in doing something he had thought he would never be able to do—gently and slowly peel Sheila Halliday out of her clothes. Not that she was putting up any resistance to the idea. In fact, Rawlings was sure she had engineered it. He was just surprised she had found him interesting enough to let him do it.

They had eaten a long, slow dinner illuminated by candles. After they had finished a bottle of wine, Rawlings had asked her to his room. The intention had been to go over some photos or papers or something. It was a standard excuse, but most of the time they just sat together watching something silly on television.

But this time, when they finally collapsed onto the couch, Halliday pulled him close, kissing him first. Rawlings wasn't slow to respond. He kissed her back, and in one of his bolder moves, forced his tongue into her mouth.

From that point on he thought he was leading her. As one of his hands brushed her breast, at first as if he was just trying to shift slightly, and then on purpose, she moaned her pleasure. She arched her back, forcing her body closer to his, forcing her breast into his hand. Naturally he squeezed gently and she moaned again.

Feeling bold again, he undid the top two buttons on her blouse and slipped his fingers inside. At any moment she was going to stop him, he was sure, but he wouldn't let that deter him. He felt her hot skin and slid his hand down inside the lacy cup of her bra until his fingers brushed her stiffening nipple. Her breathing was faster, heavier, as if she were running a long distance.

Encouraged by her response, he touched her knees with his other hand. The hem of her short skirt crept higher, and he could see the skin on the inside of her thighs. Gently he pushed at her knees and gasped as she let him force her legs apart.

Moving around, she leaned back on the couch and drew him to her. She let her hand dip to his belt, unbuckling it in one deft motion. Her fingers slid lower and grasped him. It was almost too much for him to bear, and he forgot what he was supposed to be doing.

To ward off his growing climax, he let his hand wander higher on her thigh. He touched her then, realizing that she was more than ready. With his free hand, pulled from her breast, he unbuttoned her blouse and then bent so that he was kissing her chest, letting his tongue taste her. All the while he kept his hand busy, rubbing her through her hose and panties, feeling the growing wetness.

He stopped long enough to unhook her bra and slip it and her blouse from her shoulders. As he bent to kiss her naked breasts, his tongue flickering over her rock-hard nipples, he unhooked her skirt.

Without waiting for him, she lifted her hips and slid the skirt and her panties down. Rawlings helped. He pulled her stockings and skirt from her and dropped them onto the floor, but left her panties around her knees.

"Now," she said, her voice husky with desire. "I want you in me."

Rawlings stared at her, taking it all in—her half-closed eyes and open mouth, the beads of sweat on her upper lip and between her breasts, the spread of her legs, hampered only by the panties at her knees. He kissed her belly, his tongue darting over her.

"Please," she whispered.

"No," he said. "I've dreamed about this for too long. I'm going to make it last."

She moaned then. One hand touched his head and the other touched herself. It played along her thigh and then across the darkness at her crotch. She shuddered at her own touch. "Please," she whispered. "Pretty please."

He let his fingers push hers to the side. He felt her carefully, rubbing her as she pressed herself against his hand, moaning in rhythm to the motion of her hips.

And then her hands were digging at him, clutching and clawing as her breathing came in short, explosive gasps. Her whole body stiffened except for her hips, which whipped back and forth as she cried out several times.

She collapsed, a red rash spreading across her chest. Then she pulled him close, shoved her tongue into his mouth and reached down, her fingers grasping and pulling at him.

Suddenly the phone rang.

Rawlings ignored it, but it rang a second time. He felt Halliday's hand loosen. Glancing at the clock, he realized it had to be something important, otherwise no one would have called.

He shifted around, his pants now around his thighs. Sitting there self-consciously, part of him still at attention, he reached for the phone as Halliday bent over and took him in her mouth.

"Hello," he squeaked.

"Lieutenant Rawlings?"

"Yes."

"This is Major Comstock. Your presence is required at the Pentagon now."

"Now, sir?" he asked, his voice strained as he tried to sound natural.

"Are you all right, Lieutenant?"

"Yes, sir," he managed to say. And then he knew it was too late. Halliday had moved around, dropping to her knees on the floor beside Rawlings as she worked on him. He stiffened, gasped and pulled the receiver away from his ear as he exploded. Halliday knew it was about to happen, but she kept at him, working with her hand and mouth. Rawlings fumbled the receiver. The tinny voice kept buzzing, but the words were lost. Halliday, still on her knees, grinned up at him.

Rawlings finally managed to retrieve the receiver. He picked it up and mumbled, "Sorry, sir. Dropped the phone."

"Are you sure you're all right?"

"Yes, sir. Never better." He noticed his voice was stronger, steadier now. "What can I do for you?"

"I want you and Lieutenant Halliday in here now—in the next twenty minutes. Do you know where the lieutenant is?"

"Yes, sir. I'll inform her." The line went dead.

Halliday stood but didn't pull up her panties. Instead, she let them fall to the floor and pool at her feet.

"We've got to get to the Pentagon," Rawlings told her. "Some big deal has come up."

She grinned lewdly. "Yes, I know. I saw it."

19

**THE PENTAGON
WASHINGTON, D.C.**

Alan Bates was angry. In fact, he was more than just angry. He was tired and angry and he hated phone calls in the middle of the night. He had leaped out of bed, thrown on a uniform and driven to the Pentagon. Then, to make it worse, there had been no parking near any of the entrances, so he'd had to brave the dimly lit expanse of concrete that had still radiated the day's heat, making it seem hotter than it was.

All this because of a message received from Saigon. That had been all he'd been told over the phone, and that had been given to him because he was a fairly senior colonel. The information itself had provided him with a clue about the late-night meeting, and that had made him angrier still.

Now, he entered through the basement, showed his ID card to the guard and worked his way up a flight of stairs. He stopped at the first landing and let the smell of the place—a rank odor that reminded him somehow of Vietnam—wash over him like a wave filled with sewage. Maybe it was the wet heat that had him sweating before the first landing, or maybe it was the locker room odor of sweat, urine and dirty clothes. He took out a handkerchief and wiped his face and then continued on up.

As he pushed himself out of the stairwell, a lieutenant hurried toward him and announced, "Colonel Bates, the general is waiting for you."

Bates wanted to tell the young officer not to get worried about it, but decided to let him stew. Rather than hurrying after the man, Bates slowed down so that he would have a chance to catch his breath.

Outside Steward's office, they stopped. The lieutenant looked at the clipboard he carried and found nothing on it concerning Bates. It meant that no preliminary briefing was necessary. He opened the door and said, "You may go in, Colonel."

Bates walked by him without a word. He found Steward sitting in his conversation area with two other men. The lights were bright and there were classified documents scattered on the coffee table near them. Bates could easily see the bright red Top Secret and Secret stamps on them.

"Ah, Colonel, come on in," said Steward, getting to his feet. "Sorry we had to drag you out here in the middle of the night like this, but that's one of the problems with fighting a war half a world away. When it's noon there, it's midnight here."

Bates mopped his face with his handkerchief again and stuffed it into his pocket. "What's this all about, General?"

Steward looked beyond him. "That will be all, Lieutenant." When the door closed, Steward said, "Have a seat and we'll fill you in quickly. Then you'll be on your way to Eglin in Florida."

"General—" began Bates.

"Sit down, Colonel." There was a slight edge to Steward's voice.

Bates shrugged and sat. He glanced at the documents on the table but couldn't tell anything from them.

"Now, Colonel, we've just gotten a message in from the boys in Saigon. Seems that not all of the mission was scrubbed. The field team there was deployed, and before they could be recalled they discovered the camp was being used." He let that sink in. "Used just as we suspected it would be. There are POWs on the site."

"You sure?"

"Colonel, I'm not accustomed to jumping through my ass without good reason. We're sure."

"Damn!" said Bates.

"Now, we want you to put together your team and get them deployed. You have one week."

"Wait a minute, General," said Bates, his head spinning. "There's no team. I've got a partial list of names of men who might work out, but I haven't got a team."

"Then you'll take your list and use it as a guide to recruiting a team. They'll be in place within twenty-four hours for briefing and possible practice. One week from tonight they'll be in Vietnam preparing to deploy."

Bates was silent, thinking about the logistical problems— finding the men, training them, briefing them, equipping them and keeping them quiet. Just getting the orders cut and the men to the training site could take a week.

"Sir—" ventured Bates.

"All the red tape will be cut," said Steward, anticipating the problem.

One of the other men, a full colonel whom Bates had never seen before, said, "We have a flight arranged and standing by at Andrews for you."

"For what?"

"To get you down to Eglin."

"General," said Bates, "right now there's no reason for me to go to Eglin. There's nothing there."

"Bates, in the next day your men will begin arriving and you should be there coordinating the effort."

"What men, General?"

"The team you interviewed at Bragg."

Bates shook his head. It was as if he had walked into the middle of an argument and had missed a vital piece of information. He just couldn't make them understand that he had put no team together.

"I want you to give the names to Major Comstock or Colonel Sheckley so that one of them can get orders cut."

"General, I have no names."

"You made a preliminary recon to Bragg. Get the names of the men from there. We'll get them down to you."

Bates could see there was nothing he could say to change anyone's mind. All he could do was go to Eglin and hope this would be scrubbed as the other one had been. If it wasn't, then he suspected a lot of people were going to die in the next week or so because people were jumping through their asses without worrying about the consequences.

Then he remembered the man he'd seen at the airport—the man just back from Vietnam. He was a levelheaded, clear-thinking soldier who would have no trouble becoming acclimatized to the environment in Vietnam.

"I can give you one name now and I'll have to make a phone call to get the others. Sergeant Pierce down at Bragg can get us what we need."

"Now that's more like it," said the full colonel.

"The weapons procurement for this is going to be a nightmare," said Bates.

"You let us worry about that. You just get your team ready to hit the target," Steward said.

"I'll need detailed information about the target," said Bates.

"Again, you let us worry about that. We have someone working the problem already so that by the time you hit the ground at Eglin, the models and maps you need will already exist."

There were a dozen things Bates wanted to say—reasons that this crash program wasn't going to work—but he knew better than to buck the trend. Steward had his mind set and there was nothing Bates could do to talk him out of it. Maybe someone else farther up the line would scrub the mission. Maybe Steward's boss would see the plan for the pipe dream it was and call it off. But, until that happened, Bates had no choice in the matter. He had to go through the motions. The only bright spot was that no one would die before they deployed. It gave Steward a week to change the higher-ups' minds.

"All right, General," he said, as if he had some choice in the matter.

RAWLINGS STOOD NEAR the gray-green wall of the tiny office and clutched the phone in fingers that were turning white. He glanced at Halliday, now dressed in a blue uniform and looking as if she'd just shown up for the beginning of the workday and hadn't had a tumble in the hay. Rawlings felt himself aching with desire for her. The trick on the phone hadn't satisfied him, although it had come close.

"Listen, Sergeant," he said, his voice level, "I want two forty-by-sixty blowups of the camp from photo A-407-1967 and I want them by morning."

"Sir, I told you our equipment is down and I can't get it fixed tonight."

"Do you have the phone number of someone who can fix it?" asked Rawlings.

"Yes, sir."

"Then I suggest you call him and get him in to do it."

"But, sir, I can't call him without authorization from Major Lewis."

"Fine," snapped Rawlings, "I'll have General Steward call him at home. That going to do you any good?" Rawlings didn't wait for a reply. "However, if you go ahead and get the man in, General Steward will be happy to square it with your boss tomorrow morning."

The sergeant hesitated, then said, "Yes, sir. I'll call when we have the prints ready."

Rawlings hung up and looked at Halliday. She glanced at the closed door, grinned and pulled her skirt up. Then she spread her legs. "You want to try it in the Pentagon?"

"My God," said Rawlings, "if we got caught, they'd send us to Thule or something. Maybe Minot or worse."

"Lock the door," she whispered.

Rawlings complied, and when he turned he saw that she wasn't wearing any panties. She had hiked her skirt up around her waist and was licking her lips. He felt himself respond suddenly, almost painfully, and decided that Minot wouldn't be so bad if she was sent there with him. Besides, he hadn't planned on making the Air Force a career anyway.

GERBER WAITED UNTIL the resupply team had been gone for
an hour before he ordered his men to move out. They had lain
in the steaming jungle, the sweat dripping down their faces and
sides and soaking their uniforms until it had created a sticky,
itchy mass all over their bodies. The main thing on his mind
was a shower, and Gerber knew that it would be a week, maybe
two, before he had the chance to take one. By then his uniform would be rotting off his body and the decaying vegetation would be ground into his skin so that it would take days
to wash it off.

Fetterman stood up and stepped off on the point. He slipped
between two ferns and brushed against the leaves of a vine,
which folded up and made itself look more like a rope than
something living and growing.

Gerber waited until all the men were up and moving as they
began their return trip north to where the enemy camp was.
He fell in line at the end, listening to the sounds of the jungle.
With the sun overhead creating occasional shafts of light that
penetrated the triple canopy, the jungle had changed into a
glowing green hell where it was rarely bright enough to see very
far, even if the dense vegetation would allow it.

The whole patrol moved in a sluggish, tired manner that was
made worse by the heavy, wet air. Breathing was difficult. It
was almost like trying to breathe steam. Gerber blinked
constantly. His eyes burned from a lack of sleep and from the
sweat washing over his face.

They pushed on, moving slowly, quietly, trying to hear and
see everything around them, afraid the enemy was going to
spot them first. Fetterman waved them into a defensive position once, but nothing came of it. Gerber figured he might
have seen a farmer or a hunter. He didn't complain because
he needed the breather.

It was midafternoon before they were back at the copse of
bamboo they had used earlier. Gerber wasn't sure he liked returning to the position, but then there was no evidence that
anyone had found it, or that anyone suspected Americans were
in the vicinity.

Once again they were spread out. Gerber slipped to the northern edge where Fetterman crouched, watching the activity in the camp below them. As Gerber approached, Fetterman turned a sweat-streaked face to him and whispered, "There's something wrong down there, Captain."

"What?"

"I'm not sure." He flattened himself out and studied the camp.

Gerber got down next to him and pulled out his binoculars. He tied an OD rag over them to keep them from reflecting the sunlight. With the sun behind their position, he didn't worry about the lenses flashing.

As he watched, he began to see what Fetterman had meant. The camp didn't have the appearance of a POW compound. There was no one in the guard towers and there were too many NVA walking around armed. The last thing you wanted was an armed guard in the compound where he could be overpowered by the prisoners and lose his weapon. An automatic weapon in skilled hands could literally wipe out the opposition.

The other thing that bothered him was the absence of any large numbers of Americans there. Given the number of guards, there should be several dozen prisoners, but he had only seen the two earlier that morning.

Fetterman was right. Something was definitely wrong down there.

Gerber felt a tap on his shoulder and turned. Fetterman was pointing to the northern edge of the clearing on the side opposite the camp. An enemy patrol had appeared, coming from the jungle, and was now working its way down the slope toward the camp. There were two white men with the patrol, and Gerber's first impression was that they were prisoners being marched to the camp. He was about to say something to Fetterman when he noticed that both white men were armed, too.

Carefully he took his binoculars and examined the patrol. It was exactly what he would have expected from the NVA working in South Vietnam. Although the men wore the uniform of the NVA, the khaki clothes with the boots modeled after the footwear of French paratroopers, they wore no badges of rank and no insignia. Each man carried an AK-47 and each wore a chest pouch with spare magazines. As well, they all had the usual oddly shaped, almost round canteens. One man wore a pith helmet and the rest had soft hats that looked like Australian bush hats.

The two white men were dressed in the same fashion as the Vietnamese. Both carried AK-47s. The only difference was that each of them had a pistol. In some armies that would mean they were officers and in others it meant nothing.

The white men looked hot and sweaty. Gerber passed the binoculars over to Fetterman and let him examine the patrol. "What do you think, Tony?"

"Look too young to be French."

"What the hell does that mean?"

"It means," said Fetterman, "that if the men were French, I'd expect them to be older—leftovers from the days the French were fighting the Viet Minh. Most of those French para guys were older than average then."

Gerber nodded. That made sense. If they were deserters to the NVA from the French paras, they would probably be forty or fifty years old. These guys couldn't be more than thirty.

"You don't think they're Russians, do you?" asked Gerber quietly.

"Shit, Captain, anything's possible."

Gerber took the glasses back and turned them on the compound, thinking they might be Russian interrogators working with the Vietnamese. The Soviets were sure to be interested in the tactics being used in South Vietnam by the Special Forces, or by the Air Force in their air war.

He scanned the camp. There was quite a bit of activity, but none of it suggested the presence of POWs. Too many men were wandering around with weapons. Gerber saw several weapons stacked near the large tree with no one there to guard them.

"We've blown it, Tony," he whispered.

"How so?"

"There are no prisoners down there and no guards in the towers. They've got weapons lying around all over the place." He handed the glasses to Fetterman.

Fetterman was silent, taking in everything below him. Finally he turned. "I think they're Russian advisers, Captain."

"Why?"

"I watched the patrol enter the gate and saw one of the white guys turn and hold his weapon in the air. I've seen old Boom Boom do that a dozen times. He was telling them they should have a weapons check."

Gerber took the binoculars and watched. A Vietnamese exited from one of the hootches. He was accompanied by another white man. This one wore a fatigue uniform that was vaguely familiar. Gerber had seen hundreds of pictures of the Soviet military in operation. He had seen them in their various roles at secret briefings where some Pentagon hotshot would talk about the buildup in conventional Soviet forces.

"There are no prisoners down there," Gerber repeated.

"No, sir, I don't think so, either."

Gerber lowered the glasses and studied the open area. The sound of a whistle drifted up to him, and he put the binoculars to his eyes. Below him, the men were suddenly running around. A few grabbed the equipment stored outside and fled into one of the hootches. The smoke that had been pouring out of the chimney got darker and then lighter and finally disappeared. Men rushed out of the field and disappeared inside. In less than a minute there was no evidence that anyone inhabited the camp. It had a deserted look to it.

"What the hell?" asked Fetterman.

"I don't know."

Everything was quiet for a moment, and then came the distant roar of a jet engine. Gerber turned and put the glasses on the speck that had appeared on the horizon. It grew rapidly until he could see the distinctive shape of an RF-101 Voodoo—a recon plane flown by the Air Force. The jet roared over the camp, its path never altering until it finally disappeared in the west.

"Son of a bitch," said Fetterman.

"Must be something pretty interesting down there if they go to all that trouble to convince us the place is deserted," whispered Gerber.

"We'd better alert the people at Net Control, so they can pass the information on."

Gerber looked at his watch. It was getting on toward late afternoon. There wasn't much he wanted or needed to do now, except make another radio transmission at check-in time.

"Let's stick here and see what happens," he said.

Fetterman nodded, rolled to one side and took out a canteen. He drank deeply, poured a little on his hat and then handed the canteen to Gerber.

Gerber took it and sipped at the hot, plastic-tasting water. It didn't do much for him. As he handed the canteen back to Fetterman, the camp began to spring to life. The men reappeared. A couple of them headed to the guard towers. Others formed up near the gate. There were three different patrols, each with at least one white man. The funny thing was how much it resembled the American Special Forces operations conducted from the camps in South Vietnam.

The patrols filed out the south gate. Two of them moved north, disappearing into the jungle there. The other stayed to the east, moving into the vegetation at the top of the ridge near the place where Fetterman had killed the Vietnamese the night before.

"Captain?" said Fetterman.

Gerber knew what he was asking. Fetterman wanted to know if they were going to withdraw to make the radio calls. He shook his head, telling the master sergeant they would lay low for the time being. There was no reason to make additional noise by trying to make radio contact before it was time. They'd done that once and it had turned out they had been wrong. There were no prisoners in the camp, just a bunch of Russian advisers doing for the North Vietnamese what the Americans did for the South Vietnamese.

He touched Fetterman's shoulder. "Alert the men that one, maybe two patrols are in the area. We have to be very quiet."

Fetterman didn't say a word. He slipped to the right, moving so quietly that Gerber couldn't hear a sound. In a moment the master sergeant was back.

For the next hour Gerber watched the routine in the camp as the men moved from building to building or stood in formations outside. At one point a Vietnamese officer, escorted by one of the Russians, reviewed a line of men who whooped loudly at the completion of the inspection.

There was no discernible pattern. Everything seemed to be random, which is just what a military unit in the field wanted. If a pattern could be discovered, that pattern could be used against them.

As it started to get dark, Gerber slipped deeper into the jungle. He handed the glasses to Fetterman and told him to take over. "It's time for something to eat," he added.

"And then we make radio contact with Net Control?"

"Right on schedule," answered Gerber.

20

EGLIN AIR FORCE BASE
FLORIDA

Alan Bates was tired. Hot, sweaty and tired. He stood in the terminal—Flight Operations, they called it—and wondered what he was supposed to do next. After the briefing at the Pentagon and the ride through Washington out to Andrews, he had gone as far as the orders directed. No one had thought beyond getting him to Eglin.

He stood there, his suitcase at his feet, and wondered who he should call, or if there was someone to call. Somehow this hadn't been covered.

And then it was.

A voice shouted, "Colonel Bates," and Bates turned to find Master Sergeant Pierce striding toward him, looking immaculate in his starched fatigues, his green beret molded to his head. He stopped short and threw Bates a perfect salute. "Welcome to Florida, sir. Sorry I'm late."

Bates returned the salute. "How long you been in Florida?"

"Couple of hours, sir. Got us a jeep and I'll drive you out to our staging area."

Bates picked up his suitcase and then had to fight off Pierce, who wanted to carry it for him. "I've got it, Sergeant," he snapped. "Now, where in hell is our staging area?"

Pierce turned and headed for the jeep. "Staging area is a run-down series of huts and buildings on the north side of the base. Real desolate country. Hot and humid like Vietnam but with pine trees and the like. Vegetation doesn't match Vietnam."

"What's the condition of the camp?"

Pierce opened the door of the terminal and stood back as Bates swept through. From the icy air-conditioning of Flight Operations they marched into the blast furnace heat of early morning. If there was one thing that reminded Bates of Vietnam, it was the uncomfortable humidity and heat of Florida in the early morning. No dew on the grass. No breezes off the gulf. Just a dampness that covered everything with a stickiness that made the skin itch.

Bates tossed his suitcase into the back of the jeep and climbed into the passenger's side. He waited as Pierce started the engine and backed out. "The base?" he prompted.

"Yes, sir. I'm afraid it's in pretty sorry condition. I don't think anyone's used it in a couple of months, and no one's been out to take care of it. Dirty. Trash everywhere. Buildings smell of mildew and rot and there are rats running around, although they seem to be afraid of us."

"Us?"

"Just two of us, now three. A Sergeant Green arrived with me. We've been trying to get things squared away."

Bates thought about the juice he had, the pull he could muster by dropping a certain name and phone number. "You having any trouble?"

"Oh, no, sir." He turned a corner and shot a glance at Bates. "Got the electricians out there getting us some power. Couple of the buildings have old air-conditioning units on them. There are lights. That's about it."

"Transport?"

"Have to make a call, but the motor pool promised me anything I wanted up to and including a tank."

Bates grinned, trying to figure out something to do with a tank.

They left the major part of the base and passed into rough country with woods that came up to the side of the road. He wondered if there were alligators around. He knew there would be snakes but that most of them would be harmless and that even the poisonous ones weren't all that dangerous. They'd have to be careful if they had occasion to hit the swamps.

The pavement ended and they bounced along a gravel road, kicking up a cloud of dust that rolled along with them as if it were chasing them. There were telephone poles along the road but no other signs of civilization. It both pleased and dismayed Bates. It meant he wouldn't be under the critical eye of some chairborne commando, but it also meant it would be difficult getting help. "What do we do in the way of communications gear?" he shouted over the noise from the engine and the roar of the wind.

"Right now we've got a Prick-25 and a field phone that's not hooked up to anything. Air Force promised to get someone out there so we could get plugged into the base switchboard."

He turned down a side road that was little more than a track through the trees. They came to a broken-down fence, drove through the gate and turned again. Then Pierce stepped on the brakes and they stopped.

It was worse than he had expected. The huts were unpainted shacks made of tar paper and plywood. Most of the windows had been broken and a couple of the doors stood open or hung by a single hinge. There were holes in the roofs and there were giant weeds growing everywhere. If murderers and rapists were confined to such an area, the public would be up in arms over inhumane treatment.

Pierce turned, a smile on his face. "It's not nearly as good as it looks."

Bates climbed out and felt the ground give under his feet. He looked down and saw that he was standing ankle-deep in water. "Shit."

At that moment Green appeared. He was in sweat-soaked, grease-stained fatigues. He approached, saluted and then with a smile asked, "This was the good deal you had for me, Colonel?"

"I'm afraid so."

"Oh, well, I suppose it's better than Vietnam."

Bates was going to tell him they would be there for a week at the most but decided it was a bit of information that didn't need to be shared.

"Sir," continued Green, "I got a radio message that some of our men will be arriving in the next hour and will need transport."

"They tell you how many?" asked Pierce.

Green shrugged. "Just said that it was a C-130 coming in."

Bates dug his suitcase out of the back and handed it to Green. "Find some place relatively dry to set this. I'll go in with Sergeant Pierce to arrange transport and messing facilities for our people."

"Sure, sir, leave me here on my own to rot."

Bates climbed back into the jeep and stared at his feet. They were dripping with mud and dirty water, but there was nothing he could do about it now. To Pierce, he said, "Let's get out to the flight line."

Pierce ground the gears, jerked into reverse, backed up, then slammed into forward and took off, heading back toward the base.

ON THE OTHER SIDE of Eglin, in an air-conditioned block-house that had no windows and only one metal door, Lieutenants Rawlings and Halliday were working on a long, low table. There were bright fluorescent lights overhead. The walls were made of cinder blocks and painted light blue. Around the table were six chairs. There was nothing else in the room.

Rawlings was leaning over the table, studying the photographic blowup that had been made the night before. He had brought it to Eglin rolled up in a five-foot-long tube. Now, spread out on the table, a piece of onionskin paper over it, it looked like a tablecloth. He was using a felt-tipped pen and a ruler to make an accurate map of the enemy camp drawn to scale.

He finished putting in one wall and stood up, stretching. As he did, he felt cool fingers on the back of his neck. He moaned in pleasure and closed his eyes.

"You almost done?" asked Halliday.

"Just about. What do you have in mind?" He twisted around and opened his eyes so that he could look at her.

"Obviously not what you do," she said. "I just wanted to get something to eat. We haven't eaten in quite a while."

Rawlings grinned evilly. "Sure you have. I watched you do it."

She pinched his nose sharply and pushed him away. "I meant real food and not that cardboard junk with exotic names they serve on airplanes."

"Okay, okay." He turned and studied the overlay. It was nearly complete. He wanted to take one of the other, smaller blowups and use it to make a model of the camp, putting cardboard buildings and walls on the photo to give it a three-dimensional look. That would provide the mission planners with something more than grainy pictures.

Rawlings looked at the spread of pictures and papers. Not much to go on when it came right down to it. He realized that mission planning would require weather information, terrain data, locations of population centers, details of the local flora and fauna and a dozen other things. Hell, the exact time of sunrise and sunset could be critical, not to mention the phase of the moon. There really wasn't time for eating.

He pointed all this out to Halliday. She shook her head. "That's not our function."

"As Intelligence officers," he responded, "I think it *is* our function."

"I mean," she said, moving closer to him, "that there'll be others who'll either have the information or who'll go get it. Our job is to provide the visual data on the camp with any observations we think are important."

Rawlings took a deep breath. He knew she was right. All he was wanted for was to put together the maps of the camp and anyone, the lowest airman basic even, could do that. He had been trying to make the job into something more than it was. He had gotten caught up in the flow and had forgotten that he was merely a ground pounder. He would never be able to fly in combat or lead troops into battle. All he could do was stay in the rear and provide information for the real soldiers. Halliday might not mind it, but it grated on his nerves.

He was going to snap at her, but knew it wouldn't do any good. It wasn't her fault that his eyes were so bad that he had had a hard time getting into the Air Force and that he was color blind as well. The silly military doctors didn't realize he could pick out the patterns in the pictures of colored dots, not by the colors, but by the shades of gray.

Finally, feeling his gut bubbling with anger and envy, he rolled up the larger of the photographs and stuffed them in the tubes. He collected all the pictures left over, stacked them on one side of the table and asked, "You going to buy breakfast, or am I?"

Now Halliday smiled. "Why, since it was my idea, I'll be more than happy to buy for both of us."

"You got a deal."

They left the room, locked the door and checked out with the airman who guarded the single entrance. Rawlings told him they had classified material on the table in their office, which was locked, and that they'd be back in an hour. The airman nodded and pushed the button that opened the gate in the fence surrounding the blockhouse.

BATES DIDN'T EVEN have to argue with the motor pool officer. He just told him that he needed seven deuce-and-a-halfs on the flight line and the man complied. No questions. No excuses. Just a "Yes, sir. They're on the way."

When the trucks arrived, Bates instructed his men to load their equipment into them and climb in after it. Pierce then pulled up in the jeep for Bates, and the convoy drove off toward the camp they would be using.

Once there they left the gear in the trucks and set about cleaning up the buildings so that they would have a place to sleep. Master Sergeant Gill, a bear of a man who had shaved his head, handed Bates a box with the records of the other seventy-four men who had been pulled in on the deal. Bates set the box on the hood of the jeep.

There was so much to do and so little time. They couldn't waste it cleaning the camp. He pointed at Gill, then thought better of it and called for Pierce.

"I'm sorry to do this to you, Pierce, but you seem to know your way around down here and we need some things taken care of."

"Glad to do what I can, Colonel, so long as I'm not cut out of the endgame."

"Don't worry about that," said Bates. "Okay, I don't want to waste time cleaning up this place. See about getting sleeping bags and air mattresses issued for everyone. Then check on box lunches." He held up his hand to stop the protest. "I know it'll be two stale bologna sandwiches and warm milk but that solves one problem for today. We'll worry about hot lunches, hot food, tomorrow."

"Yes, sir."

"Grab someone to help you, but rotate the duty. Next, there are two Air Force types running around loose here. Lieutenants Rawlings and Halliday. Find them and get them out here. Finally, find someone from Base Operations who has authority to schedule flights and get us a C-141 to fly us out of here. I'm not going to ride across the big pond in the back of a fucking C-130."

"Yes, sir."

"Now, finally, is there a place around here to get everyone inside for a briefing?"

"There are a couple of buildings where most of the interior walls have rotted away. We could use one of those."

Bates looked at the camp and waited for it to blow away. When that didn't happen, he said, "Okay. Get to work."

As Pierce started his jeep, Bates headed toward the orderly room. He knew where it was by the sign dangling over the door. He opened it, saw one desk covered with mold and shook his head. If someone brought in a couple of rolls of butcher paper, they could use the facility.

He found a chair and sat down. The floor was littered with papers, cans, rotting food and standing water. It smelled, but not too bad. He didn't see how he could use it for planning.

In fact, he couldn't see how he could put this thing together in under a month.

Gill entered and said, "I've got the troops ready, sir."

"Ready for what?" asked Bates.

"Well, sir, the orientation lecture, the welcoming briefing, that sort of thing."

"There any officers in the bunch with you, Sergeant?"

"No, sir."

"I didn't think so. Okay, have the men sweep through the buildings and locate the best places for their sleeping bags. Check out the latrines and see if they're working, and if not, have someone dig a couple of slit trenches. When that's done, I hope to have some idea about what's going on."

"We have shovels or E-tools?"

"Christ," said Bates, rubbing his head. "Oh, and find out, on the QT, if any of these heroes brought personal weapons."

"You going to confiscate them?"

"Hell, no, I just want to know if there are any. Might save us a hassle later."

"Yes, sir."

There was a tap on the door and then it opened. Green stepped in. "Colonel, we've got a jeep out here with a bunch of Air Force people in it."

"Fine." He looked at Gill. "Any questions?"

"No, sir."

"Okay, have Sergeant Green give you a hand. He's been here for a couple of hours and might have the answers to our questions." Bates stood up and looked at the dim light filtering in through the dirty windows. "That's it, boys. We've got a hell of a lot of work to do and not a hell of a lot of time to do it in."

"Yes, sir."

Together they stepped out of the building and then split up to see what they could get done before the whole thing unraveled.

STEWARD LOOKED at the classified message he had been handed and felt the blood drain from his face. He read it again, knowing it wouldn't change the text.

"Are they sure?"

Comstock shrugged. "That's exactly what they received in Nha Trang. CIA guy in Saigon got it and twixed it to us here."

"Shit," said Steward. "I guess I'd better call Bates and tell him the mission's scrapped." But even as he said it, he knew it wasn't right. The mission should go in.

"They're sure the men they saw are Russians?" asked Steward.

"They also reported that there were POWs there. Now they've changed their story."

Steward rocked back in his chair and turned so that he could look out his window, not that he had much of a view. All he could see was the blank wall of the inner ring. All he could tell was whether it was fair or raining.

Steward had tried to get the mission scrubbed, but somehow the men had gotten into the field. He hadn't worried about that because they had confirmed there were prisoners in the camp. Now they were retracting the information, saying that the white men were Russians. He didn't know how they knew, but decided to trust the judgment of the men in the field even if the preliminary reports did claim there were POWs present.

"Okay, Major, call upstairs and see if you can get me in to see the chairman. This is something we've got to talk about."

Comstock disappeared and returned ten minutes later. He peeked in the doorway and said, "The chairman will see you in fifteen minutes. His aide said not to show up if you have another problem. The war isn't going well."

Steward stood up and shoved the message into a leather folder. He headed toward the door but stopped short. "If I'm not back in an hour, send a rescue party."

"Yes, sir."

Steward started out for the office of the chairman of the Joint Chiefs of Staff. He passed dozens of people, most of them in uniform. Turning, he entered a new world, and finally, after walking on carpeted floors for a while, he stopped outside the huge wooden door that held a sign announcing the chairman's office.

He was ushered through the outer office, which made his look Spartan in comparison. There was thick carpeting, and huge wooden desks that almost glowed brown. The walls were paneled in teak and there were muted watercolors and oils hanging on them. Rather than a single secretary and an aide, the chairman had three secretaries and two aides. The remainder of his staff was hidden in other offices nearby and connected to him by intercom.

Inside the chairman's office it was even richer. The carpeting was thicker and the Great Seal of the United States was woven into it. One wall was lined with books. The desk was gigantic and there were ceiling-to-floor curtains along one wall. There were tables holding lamps and there was a wet bar in one corner.

The chairman stood near the bar, waiting. He held a glass in one hand, and when he saw Steward he said, "Come on in, General, and have a seat. Can I get you something?"

Steward shook his head. He opened the folder and handed the message to the chairman. "General, I think you better look at this."

The chairman put down the glass he held, wiped his hands on a towel and came forward. He took the paper, read it, glanced at Steward and read it again. "Well, shit. I thought we had this mission canceled."

"Yes, General, we did. Unfortunately the surveillance team was deployed before the orders were cut. Once they were in the field, they started relaying messages that suggested we might have been premature."

"And now we know there are no American POWs in the camp. Just some Russian soldiers. Some Russian soldiers who are working with the North Vietnamese."

"Yes, sir. My first instinct was to pull our people out and call the whole thing off, but then I got to thinking that we can't let those Russians stay there."

The chairman slipped into the closest chair and read the message a third time. He rubbed his face and then rocked back, closing his eyes.

"I think I understand what you're saying. We know there are Russians in North Vietnam. The assumption has to be that they're training the North Vietnamese. This is in opposition to our war effort. We can't let them get away with it."

"No, General," said Steward. "We let them ship in supplies and munitions. We pull our punches, letting the entire Communist world help North Vietnam, and pretend that it doesn't matter. But this is a step-up in the war. They're now sending troops into the North."

"Well," said the chairman, "we could alert the White House and register a protest through the United Nations."

"The Russians would deny they have anyone in North Vietnam, and we don't have any documented proof."

"But I think you have a plan."

"Yes, General, I do. We already have a recon team in place, and yesterday I initiated an activity that would have ended in the rescue of our men. I have a special team being assembled in Florida. Now we just change the mission scenario slightly. We send our people in just as we planned, but it's no longer a rescue mission."

The chairman cocked an eyebrow. "You're not suggesting what I think you're suggesting?"

"Yes, General. We go in and kill every fucking Russian in the place."

21

EGLIN AIR FORCE BASE
FLORIDA

Bates stood in the makeshift conference room and listened to the water dripping and echoing somewhere nearby. On the field table, which unfolded into a long, narrow affair that couldn't stand too much weight, was the map Rawlings had made. Next to it were half a dozen photographs of the enemy camp taken from different angles at different times.

There was no other furniture in the room. It was barren, with a dirty concrete floor and shallow pools of water standing in the depressions. The dirt on the floor had become dried mud and there were newspapers and beer cans scattered about, as if the place had been used for shelter by someone other than the military.

Rawlings stood at the end of the table, sweat pouring from him and soaking his uniform. He had taken off his flight cap and was twisting it in his hands as he stared at the map.

Opposite him, at the other end of the table, was Halliday. She didn't look any more comfortable than he did. She kept rubbing a hand over her face, trying to wipe away the sweat.

Standing near Bates were Sergeants Pierce and Gill and a young Special Forces captain who had walked into the wrong office at the wrong time and found himself on an airplane for Florida before he could refuse.

He was a tall, bulky man named Thomas Wansill. He had fair hair and a pale complexion. His mustache was barely visible because of his coloring. He had gray eyes that alternated between blue and green, depending on his mood. Wansill had had one tour in Vietnam and hadn't enjoyed it as some of his friends had. The major problem was that he could see all the waste, and it sickened him. He had always believed that if you were going to fight a war, you fought it. You didn't fuck around with a lot of stupid rules and regulations that gave all the advantages to the enemy.

"The major problem, as I see it," said Bates, "is that we have to take out the guard towers as we go over the walls. We have to hit damn near every objective at once or the NVA are going to have a chance to kill the prisoners."

"We know which building the prisoners are in?"

Bates looked at Rawlings.

"No, sir," he said. "In fact, we weren't even able to spot the prisoners until the field team confirmed them."

"There are some assumptions we can make," said Bates. "Each team will have to be prepared to rescue prisoners or shoot the guards as we hit the buildings."

"That means a medic with every team," said Wansill.

"It's going to be damn near impossible to hit everywhere at once," commented Pierce.

"Especially difficult without a great deal more information," said Gill, looking first at Rawlings and then Halliday.

"There's only so much information we can get from the photos," said Rawlings. "Without some intelligence from the ground, there isn't much more we can do. We can make a few guesses based on the data we have, but that's all they'll be—guesses."

"But we do have a ground team?" asked Wansill.

"Yes," Rawlings replied.

"Then I suggest we put together a list of questions we need to have answered. We can make some preliminary plans now and modify them when we get the final answers."

Bates looked at the captain. He was right, of course. This was one phase of the mission that couldn't be cut. If the planning was done right, then any changes, any variations thrown at them, would be eaten up by the plans. Without them, they would end up with a disaster like the Little Big Horn. That had been Custer's mistake. He had charged in without thinking about a plan. Just ride in with guns blazing and kill everything in sight. It hadn't worked.

But then Custer hadn't been under pressure to perform. All he had to do was get there by a certain date. Bates not only had to get there, but had to attack without knowing many of the things that were crucial to him.

He nodded at Wansill. "Captain, I want a list of questions from you arranged in order from most important to least important. Work with Rawlings and Halliday to set it up."

"Yes, sir."

Bates wiped a hand over his face and then rubbed the sweat on his fatigue shirt. He couldn't believe this assignment. He could see the need for a dozen helicopters, probably Hueys, which had the range. The size was important. Three of them could land in the compound, maybe four if they broke unit integrity and had one touch down near the tree. That left eight or nine to land right outside the walls, probably to surround the place. Then the men could go over the walls.

He snapped a finger at Rawlings. "How high are the walls?"

"Given our data, I'd say eight to ten feet. Probably no more than ten feet."

"How do you know?"

"Shadows on the ground. I can measure those. And given the angle from which the photo was taken, I can compute the height of the walls fairly accurately."

As Bates studied the map and then the photos, he could see exactly how to take the compound—a plan modeled after the German use of gliders to take the Belgium fort at Eben Emael, a vertical envelopment. The only problem he had that the Germans hadn't had was the prisoners. He had to ensure their safety. The Germans could shoot everyone inside the fort.

He could use the plan, though, and before the enemy would realize it, there would be soldiers inside the walls. It would be a bold thrust that would quickly lose its advantage of surprise unless they could kill most of the officers and set the buildings on fire to disrupt the lines of communication inside.

"Those guard towers bother me," said Wansill.

"Why?" asked Bates. "We'll have someone in each of the helicopters with a LAW or two designated to take them out as soon as we hit the ground."

There was a tap on the door and Green stuck his head in. "Sir, got a call from the command post at Eglin. We've got a VIP coming in here. They want us to provide transportation for him."

"Shit," said Bates. "That's the way it always is. Try to get some work done and the hotshots in Washington start dropping in, expecting you to show them around." He pointed at Wansill. "You work out the plans and the questions and be prepared to give them to me in an hour."

"Yes, sir."

Bates left the steaming hut and stepped into the fresh air. It seemed much cooler outside, and for a moment he was comfortable, but then the heat and the humidity there caught up with him.

"While we're doing this," he said to Green, "I want you to find me two more officers for platoon leaders. I can't go in on this thing with one captain, no matter how good the NCOs are."

"I'll do what I can. Maybe Sergeant Pierce would be better at this than I would."

"Then you get with him as soon as we have the VIP picked up. The two of you work it out. The only restriction I'll give you is that I want someone with a tour in Vietnam."

"Yes, sir."

They stopped at the jeep, and Bates stared at the mud-splattered vehicle. "You think we can pull this off?"

"I think we have a very good chance, sir."

Bates climbed into the jeep, wishing he shared Green's optimism. It would make his job that much easier. He put a foot up on the dash and said, "Let's do it."

KUTNETSOV SAT in the darkened hootch, clutching a can of beer. His feet were propped on the windowsill so that he could look out at the countryside. A light breeze that smelled of electricity or dust was blowing from the east. He knew it meant rain and could see the lightning rippling through the clouds far away.

That was the thing he hated most—keeping the camp dark during the night when there was so much he could be doing. There were nighttime exercises that would benefit the men who weren't deployed on the patrols. But the chance that an American recon aircraft, or a bomber returning from a mission, might see it made that impossible. They had to maintain a blackout because they didn't want the Americans to suspect the camp was being used.

He lifted the can of beer to his lips and drank, wishing it was cold. Leaning over, he set the beer can on the floor, then turned his attention to the lightning and heard a distant rumbling. Suddenly he didn't know if it was thunder or a bombing. The Americans could be attacking something on the coast, or one of the small industrial complexes that had been moved from Hanoi.

Kutnetsov got to his feet and leaned against the window, letting the breeze fan him. He hated this country and its heat, not to mention the Vietnamese themselves. They understood nothing of communism. They understood nothing of Lenin. They used what they wanted and perverted the rest. They had scoffed at his Lenin room and had asked questions that shouldn't have been asked. They claimed to have a classless society, but there were a dozen classes. It was a ridiculous contradiction, and he was getting tired of it already.

He turned from the window and felt his way though the room. Stopping at the door, he listened and then moved into the hallway. From one of the rooms came the unmistakable sounds of two people in passion, and he chafed at the noise. The Vietnamese soldiers had asked to have their wives, girl-friends and families join them, and Kutnetsov had refused. Now they sneaked them in when they thought he wasn't looking.

He reached the ground floor and exited. He saw two men, shadows really, sitting under the tree. One of them was smoking. He could see the orange glow from the cigarette.

As he walked toward them, Colonel Thuy intercepted him and asked, ''Are you enjoying the night?''

With an exaggerated motion, Kutnetsov wiped the sweat from his face. ''Is it always this hot?''

''This isn't hot, Comrade Captain. This is a pleasant evening with the possibility of rain.''

Kutnetsov stared at the Vietnamese officer. He was a strange mix of optimism and professionalism. He seemed to understand what fighting a war meant, and yet had time to worry about the weather, even when it didn't affect the mission. He understood the operation of weapons and tactics and yet he was an easygoing man who stood back and watched the war around him.

''I think,'' said Kutnetsov, ''that it will soon be time for a full-scale raid into South Vietnam, something that will not only be good training, but that will hurt the Americans.''

Thuy stopped walking and looked at the Russian. ''You have something in mind?''

''It's just a thought now, something to think about, but I'd like to see how many airplanes we could blow up at their base in Da Nang. A sapper team in, run down the flight line throwing satchel charges and then out.''

''That will make the men very happy,'' said Thuy.

''Good. Now, I have one other thing to talk to you about. Some of the men have been bringing women into the camp at night.''

Thuy grinned, his teeth bright in the darkness. ''Yes, well, the men must have their needs filled. All men must have their needs filled.''

''Colonel, we're fighting a war here.''

''But that doesn't mean we have to suffer when it isn't necessary. When it's time to fight the war, the men will be ready.''

Kutnetsov stared into the night and let his mind roam. This wasn't what they had promised him when he had volunteered for the Spetsnaz. They had talked about glorious missions behind enemy lines, harassing and killing them, making it easier for the regular forces to defeat them. Now he was locked in this sweatbox where he couldn't even talk to all his soldiers. It certainly wasn't what he had expected.

"Captain, why not come to my room? We'll light a candle and we'll have a drink. We'll discuss the war, philosophy and the ways of the world."

Kutnetsov shrugged. It would do no good to explain that officers shouldn't take privileges that the men didn't have. Thuy believed that as a man climbed the military ladder he gained more privileges. They were his due.

ALTHOUGH BATES MET the VIP at the flight line with his jeep, there was an air-conditioned staff car waiting for him already. As General Steward climbed out of the Air Force T-39 Sabreliner, the staff car, a large checked flag stuck on the rear bumper, left base operations. Bates stood next to his jeep and watched the whole show.

The car turned toward him and stopped near him. The driver's door opened and an Air Force sergeant got out. He hurried around to the rear and opened the door, saying, "General Steward would like you to join him."

Bates turned and said to Green, "Head on back to the camp and wait there." He scratched his ear and then stared at the ground. "It seems I should be giving you some orders. Have Captain Wansill have the men do something, but damned if I know what it is."

"I'll tell the captain to have the men work on getting their gear squared away."

"If it's not squared away, they don't belong in Special Forces," said Bates.

"Yes, sir. We'll think of something."

Bates nodded and then moved to the car. He dropped into the back seat and was immediately chilled by the air-conditioning. The sergeant closed the door and ran back to the driver's seat. He slipped into the car and started them off the flight line.

As they passed through a chain-link fence that separated the airfield from the rest of the base, Steward said, "We've run into a snag."

Bates felt his head spin. Here we go again, he thought. He wanted to ask questions but knew he couldn't. Not in the car because the information was all going to be classified.

"There a place we can talk?" asked Steward.

"The only place I know is out at the camp," responded Bates.

The sergeant glanced over his shoulder. "You could use the base commander's conference room. I'm sure he wouldn't mind."

Steward leaned forward, a hand on the back of the driver's seat. "Thank you, Sergeant, but I think we'll be better off at the base. Take us out there."

"I'm afraid I don't know exactly where it is."

Bates said, "Turn right at the next light and then right again. There's a highway that will take us out there."

"Yes, sir."

"How have things been going?" asked Steward.

Now Bates laughed. "You'll see when we arrive."

They rode in silence, Bates enjoying the air-conditioning. He closed his eyes and thought about how tired he was. In two days of running around he'd only managed a few hours of interrupted sleep on airplanes.

The driver glanced at the rearview mirror. "Colonel, I'm not sure where the turnoff is."

"I'll let you know." Bates opened his eyes and sat up, watching the trees flash by. "Next right will do it."

They turned and drove through the gate, then slowed. The gravel crunched under their tires for a short stretch and then they were at the camp.

"Jesus Christ," said Steward. He looked right at Bates. "This is what they gave you?"

"This is it, General. I didn't complain because I liked the isolation it gave us."

"Christ, Alan, I would have thought you'd have been on the phone to get a decent facility."

"No, sir. Too much to do too quickly to sweat the small shit. I figured we wouldn't be here that long anyway."

"Well, you've got that right." He opened the door and stepped out. "Christ, it's hotter than hell out here. And what's that smell?"

"I think that's the swamp. It's about two hundred yards to the north."

Steward leaned down so that he could talk to the driver. "I want you to stay here. I'm going to need you later."

"Yes, sir."

"Now, Alan, take me to your conference room."

Bates laughed again. "I'll take you to the hut we're using only because it's the one we're using." He started off, then said, "Follow me."

They entered the hut. Inside, Wansill, the two Air Force officers and Sergeant Pierce were still there, studying the photos and map. Wansill saw Steward and called out, "Attention."

"Carry on," said Steward.

"What you got now, Tom?" asked Bates.

"Well, sir, we've identified a number of problems and a number of questions."

"Before you get too far into that," interrupted Steward, "I probably should let you know that there are no prisoners in the camp."

Bates was suddenly sick. He glanced at Rawlings and saw the lieutenant blanch. Halliday moved to him, and they supported each other.

"What the fuck is this?" demanded Wansill, forgetting who he was talking to.

"Gentlemen," said Steward, "and lady. The mission is a go. We'll deploy within twenty-four hours."

"General—" began Bates.

"Hear me out, Alan. We've discovered there are Russian advisers in that camp. Not American prisoners but Russians. We're going after them. Going in to kill them and everyone else in that camp."

Wansill looked at the map and then picked up the yellow legal pad where he had listed his questions. He took a pencil and began drawing lines through them. "That certainly makes this easier."

"General, are you sure about this?" asked Bates.

Steward looked at the people standing in the room. "Are all these people cleared?"

"They've all been in on it from the beginning. I'd say they're cleared."

"All right." He turned, strolled to the window, his hands clasped behind his back. He stared out into the Florida forests for a moment and then whirled. "There are Russian advisers in North Vietnam."

He waited for a reaction, but he had already made the announcement, so no one reacted this time. He watched them and then said, "That's something we can't have."

Again there was no reaction, so he explained it to them. They could allow Communist assistance with arms and supplies, but they had to stop it there. If there were Russians on the ground, there would come a point where there would be a confrontation that could escalate.

"Which is exactly what you're advocating," said Wansill.

"But right now we're all pretending the Russians aren't there. We have to send a message to the Kremlin, tell them that we'll allow them to assist with supplies, but when they start sending troops, we'll do what we can to kill them."

"Wouldn't it be simpler to just bomb the camp out of existence."

"Simpler, yes," admitted Steward, "but it wouldn't send the message we want to send. A bombing attack leaves it open for discussion. The Russians could look at that and tell themselves it was a coincidence. If we put a force in on the ground, something that we haven't done, they'll know there was one reason—to get their men." Steward moved to the table and looked at the maps. "You have a plan, Alan?"

"Yes, General. We're going to use helicopters to land all around the compound and on the inside. Now I suppose we'll just kill everyone in sight."

"How long before you'll be ready to go?"

"You gave us twenty-four hours."

"Will that be enough time?"

Bates looked from face to face, as if polling them. He knew it was enough time. More than enough given the new mission. No worries about who might be there. Just land, shoot up the place, set it on fire and get the hell out. Executed properly, they would spend no more than five minutes on the ground. A good briefing, with the men shown the camp in the photos, shown a model that Rawlings and Halliday provided, would do it.

"If we get the weapons and each man has a chance to zero his," Bates said, "and given a proper range facility that shouldn't be a problem, we should be able to deploy inside twenty-four hours."

"You could always zero the weapons once you arrive in Vietnam," Steward suggested.

"Yes, sir, we could. So, given that, we could easily be ready in time."

"Excuse me, Colonel," said Pierce, "but most of these people are assigned to Fort Bragg and each has a weapon there. With a little coordination, we could locate those weapons and bring them down here. No one would have to zero anything."

"Why did they deploy without the weapons in the first place?" asked Steward.

"We didn't know what was happening. If this was a special briefing of some sort, we wouldn't need the weapons. No one told us what was going on. As usual," said Pierce.

"Let's get on that. Let me know what you need."

"Yes, sir. We can get our kits together easily and have them transported down here. That'll eliminate most of the equipment problems, especially for the type of mission we're contemplating."

"I'll leave it to you men to coordinate," said Steward. "Just remember the time frame. Now, if you'll excuse me, I'll go arrange for the transports to fly you out of here."

"Yes, sir," said Bates. "And I'll get Sergeant Pierce to start locating the weapons."

22

THE PRESS BUREAU
SAIGON

Robin Morrow sat in the partially lit city room and stared at her typewriter. She held her fingers poised over the keys, her eyes on the paper, and wondered what she wanted to write. The words marched through her mind, but she didn't put them on paper.

"Working late, aren't you?" asked a voice behind her.

Morrow jumped and felt her heart hammering in her chest. She glanced over her shoulder and saw Mark Hodges standing in the shadows. "You scared the piss out of me."

"Sorry. Thought you heard me come in."

"Obviously not."

Hodges grabbed the empty chair and pulled it close. He sat down, straddling it, an arm on the back. "What are you working on?"

Morrow glanced at the paper, saw that there wasn't much written on it and was unsure what to say. If she told Hodges her suspicions, he would demand she write the whole story, including her conjecture. He wouldn't see it as a military secret that needed keeping, but as a story that had to be published. There were no shades of gray. Just stories and nonstories. To Hodges the military was the enemy, not the North Vietnamese and the Vietcong.

She reached up, pulled the paper from the typewriter and wadded it into a ball, tossing it up and down in her hand. "Nothing," she said.

"Come on, Robin, I know better than that. You wouldn't be here working if you didn't have something to go on. With your contacts there must be something."

She leaned forward, her arms on her typewriter. Dropping the balled paper onto her desk, she stared at the darkened windows ranged along the front wall of the city room. There were flashes in the sky that looked like lightning. She turned her head and looked at Hodges. "I really don't have anything."

"Tell me what you have. Sometimes it helps to talk these things out."

Morrow nodded but didn't speak. She thought instead of Mack Gerber who was undoubtedly in North Vietnam. It was the only place they would send him that no one would talk about. If he had gone into Cambodia or Laos, there would have been a lot of denials, but there would have been a lot of winking, too. It was a "No, we don't operate in Cambodia" wink, wink, type thing.

What she had was a good story. One that would be splashed on the front pages of every paper in the country. One that could gain her the recognition she wanted and felt she deserved.

Still she hesitated because she also understood what it meant to the men in the field. She had listened to Gerber talk about just what the VC and NVA knew because of the media in the United States. The lowest of the Vietcong in the deepest of the jungles knew exactly what was happening in the United States, knew that students were in the streets protesting. And if she wrote her story, they would know there were Americans in North Vietnam.

"So talk to me," said Hodges.

Morrow sat up and looked at him. "I really don't have anything. Just suspicions, and I don't want to set those down on paper."

"Robin, we have an obligation here. An important job. We must see that the American people are informed about all aspects of the war."

She laughed. "That's a load of shit and you know it. You're more interested in the story than informing people."

"Don't go self-righteous on me," snapped Hodges. "You're in the same business."

Morrow didn't have a response to that. Hodges was right. She was in the same business and she had written stories without consideration of the consequences to the people named in them. She hadn't worried how the people named would be affected. She had gone after the story single-mindedly in order to report what the people had a right to know even when most of the people didn't care to know, even when the only people who wanted to know were the lowlifes others were trying to prosecute.

"I really don't have it worked out yet. That's my problem and that's why I'm in here. I thought that if I tried to write the story, it would give me some kind of insight into it."

"So what do you have?" pressed Hodges.

"Nothing yet. Nothing I want to talk about yet."

Hodges stood and shoved his chair back at the desk where he had gotten it. He leaned over and touched Morrow on the shoulder. "Tell you what. When you get it worked out, you let me read it. Maybe I'll be able to help."

"Yeah," she said. "Thanks, Mark."

She didn't notice that he took the paper she'd pulled from her typewriter.

PIERCE STOOD NEAR THE JEEP, blinking in the bright sun. Sweat soaked his uniform. To Bates, he said, "I don't think I've been this uncomfortable since I was in Vietnam. Man, it's miserable out here."

Bates took off his cap, wiped his forehead and wished he had a cold beer. That was the funny thing about the military. Everyone put down the beer, claimed it was for barflies and the unsuccessful, and yet everyone he knew in the Army drank it. An ice-cold beer, after several hours in the hot sun, couldn't be beaten.

"You got everything coordinated with Bragg?" he asked.

"You know, Colonel, I've been thinking about that. It seems to me that if we take a C-130 out of here, fly to Bragg to board the C-141 out of Pope, we'll have the men in a position to get their own gear and weapons. We won't have the nightmare we're about to design."

"Won't work," said Bates.

"Why not?"

Bates looked at the master sergeant and shook his head. He marshaled his reasons why it wouldn't work and realized they were all wrong. He was just trying to save the work that had been done at Eglin. There was no reason for sending them to Eglin. If someone had thought his way through the whole problem, he would have realized that deploying the men to Eglin because it was hot and sticky and had thousands of acres of isolated land wasn't a good enough reason.

Of course, everyone expected to stay at Eglin for a week working out the plan and then rehearsing it. Now, without the prisoners in the picture, there was no need. All they had to do was familiarize themselves with the camp, learn what was what and where and then go in with guns blazing.

"You know, Sergeant," said Bates, "I can't think of one reason why we shouldn't deploy from Bragg. I'll meet with Steward and get it arranged. We'll have to be careful that no one talks out of turn."

"Sir, these men are all professionals. No one's going to say anything that shouldn't be said. And, as a bonus, the return to Bragg will allow you the opportunity to pick up a couple of extra officers."

"All right, Pierce, let's get ready to pull out of here. Christ, what a wasted effort. Fly the men down here, fly them out. Just once I wish someone would think his way through the problem."

Bates climbed behind the wheel of the jeep. He started the engine and backed out, then turned and headed down the road. He gripped the wheel tightly, angry that he was running around all over the eastern seaboard, trying to get this thing started with people in Washington who changed their minds as often as the weather. It all made his life miserable and didn't help to ensure the success of the mission.

He got back to Base Operations and found that Steward was in the VIP suite, eating a steak sandwich and drinking the beer that Bates had wanted earlier. "General, I want to take the men back to Bragg before deployment overseas."

"You think that's a good idea?" asked Steward. He picked up his sandwich and took a huge bite.

"General, it'll save us the hassle of issuing equipment to the men and then having them zero the new weapons. We can pick up everything we need at Bragg. It'll be our equipment and not something someone else lets us have."

Steward picked up his beer and drank deeply, then patted his lips with a napkin. "Let me finish my lunch here and I'll get things cleared for you."

"Thank you, General."

GERBER HAD SLEPT FITFULLY, not tossing and turning, but jerking awake frequently, his nerves taut and his senses screaming. Each time he had done so he had wanted to grab his weapon and begin shooting and each time he had lain quietly, listening for the sound that had alerted him.

Fetterman was at the very edge of the jungle, lying there and watching the dark enemy camp. His foot was only inches from Gerber so that the two men could be in physical contact if it was necessary.

There was a sudden booming overhead and the jungle was alive with the sound of frying bacon. Gerber rolled onto his side and put an arm over his head. In seconds he was soaked by the downpour and was cool for the first time in days. He listened to the storm, the sound intensifying until it was impossible to hear anything but the rain.

The storm lasted for twenty minutes, but the rain lasted longer. After the storm had passed, the water, caught in the upper levels of the canopy, began to drip slowly to the ground. It dripped into the cup-shaped leaves until they spilled, letting the water cascade to the next lower level, sounding like a man stumbling through the vegetation.

Gerber found the noise comforting. The dripping was rhythmic, almost hypnotic. He concentrated on it, trying to hear nothing else.

As he drifted into sleep, Bocker loomed out of the dark, touched his foot and whispered, "Captain."

Gerber sat up so that his face was no more than an inch from Bocker's. "What you got?"

"Normal contact with Net Control. Timetable's been moved up. We can expect the raid to start in twenty-four hours, more or less."

"Jesus," said Gerber. He pulled the camouflage cover from his watch. "Twenty-four hours from when?"

"About an hour ago."

Gerber nodded and wondered what the hell was going on. With the fact transmitted that there were no prisoners on the camp, he had expected to be pulled out. Now that he was fully awake, he wanted a cup of coffee and his breakfast. He wiped his face and asked, "They give you anything else?"

"No, sir. Just that the raid is coming and we should be prepared to help. Provide pathfinder assistance. A homing signal for the helicopters."

"Christ," said Gerber.

"Yes, sir, that's kind of what I thought."

Bocker turned and slipped back into the jungle. Gerber rolled onto his belly and crawled forward so that he was right next to Fetterman. He put his lips close to the master sergeant's ear and told him what Bocker had said.

"That means we've got to take out the patrol that entered the jungle over here," Fetterman said.

"Quietly and one at a time. Then we've got to set up to stop the others from counterattacking."

"Who arranged this boondoggle?" asked Fetterman.

THEY TOUCHED DOWN just after dark. The C-130 taxied off the runway and pulled up on the ramp outside Base Operations where three buses sat, their engines running. As soon as the aircraft halted and the doors were opened, the men started filing off and entering the buses. Pierce had already told the men they had three hours to collect their gear and return.

Standing at the far end of the apron was the C-141 that would take them to Vietnam. It was preflighted, fueled and ready to go. The crew was standing by in Base Operations, waiting for the passengers. It just proved that generals could do anything they wanted when they set their minds to it.

Bates went with Sergeant Pierce and watched as the master sergeant drew his equipment and weapon. When he finished, Pierce asked, "Anything you'd like, sir?"

"Get me an M-16 and one of those .45s, and a bunch of extra magazines."

Pierce nodded and the armorer trotted off to fill the order. As he did, Pierce said, "There are some things around that are better than the .45. We could get you a Browning 9 mm if you'd prefer."

"Thanks, Sergeant, but I'll stick with the Colt. I've been in the Army long enough and used enough of them to appreciate them. I'm not that familiar with the Browning."

"Suit yourself."

The armorer returned, checked the serial numbers of the weapons and pushed them through the screen. Pierce took them, checked the numbers and then signed. "Make sure I get them back after the mission, Colonel."

"No problem."

With another two hours to kill and the prospect of a long flight ahead of them, they went to the NCO club. Pierce vouched for Bates, and they were both let in. Normally fatigues weren't allowed in the club, but with the number of men on call all the time, the surprise deployments and the war in Vietnam, the regulations had been relaxed in certain areas. Pierce took Bates down a flight of stairs and into a smoky room. There was a bar on one side, a jukebox in a corner and pictures of paratroopers painted on the walls. The lighting was strange, seeming to come from the floor. There were quite a few people packed into the room, most of them in fatigues, both men and women, and a few wearing civilian clothes.

Pierce pushed his way through the crowd, slapping a few of the men on the back, and then claimed a table. A waitress in a sweat-damp blouse and blue jeans materialized and asked for the order. Pierce told her he wanted two hamburgers in a basket and two beers. She disappeared into the wall of humanity.

Bates sat quietly, avoiding the stares of the men and women around him. He felt out of place because he was a full colonel in the haunts of the young enlisted. They had almost nothing in common except their green clothes.

"Don't let it throw you, Colonel. They don't like it when we master sergeants invade this place, but the hamburgers are good. Real good."

The food came and was as advertised. Bates took the first bite and smiled. "This has got to be one of the best burgers I've ever eaten."

"Guy who cooks them is an ex-con. Man's a wizard with a grill and hamburger. We're going to lose him, though."

"How's that?"

"The MPs are going to arrest him sometime in the future. He's been dipping into the till. Nothing much, just fives and tens, but they're going to get him. It'll be a shame. I think the club manager ought to give him a raise and not let him near the money."

They finished eating and Pierce said, "You want to get out of here so the young troops can let go. They're being good while you're here."

Bates wadded his napkin and tossed it into the basket. "I wouldn't want to spoil their fun."

They left the club and returned to the flight line. They found that most of the men were already back, waiting for the opportunity to board the aircraft. Their equipment and weapons were stacked all over.

As they entered, an Air Force sergeant came toward them. "Colonel Bates?"

"Yes."

"I have a classified document for you, sir. You'll need to sign for it."

Bates followed the sergeant and got the document. He took it to a corner and read it, then put it back into the envelope. He returned to the sergeant and said, "Thank you."

"Oh, no, sir. You're supposed to keep it."

"I don't have a safe."

"Not my problem."

Bates shrugged and returned to the men. He found Captain Wansill and asked him what was happening.

"I've got two lieutenants for us. Both of them worked with A-Detachments in Vietnam. And both those Air Force lieutenants are here and both claim they're going with us."

"I don't want to hear that right now. Where are the new people?"

Wansill took him over and made the introductions. The new lieutenants' names were Robert Diehl and Martin Farrow. They could have been twins. Both were six feet tall and had dark hair. Both wore mustaches. The only difference was that one was white and one was black. Farrow, the black man, also had a slight limp, but he claimed it was an injury from playing baseball and not very serious.

Bates nodded his approval. "Formal briefings will be on the plane. That gives us, with stops, twenty hours and should be enough."

Green appeared and said, "Everyone's here, Colonel."

"Then let's find the Air Force people, get the plane loaded and get out of here."

23

**THE CARGO AREA OF A
C-141
SOMEWHERE OVER
THE WESTERN UNITED
STATES**

Bates sat on the deck, the map that Rawlings had drawn in front of him. Around him were the officers who would be leading the raid. To one side were Rawlings and Halliday. She was having trouble because of her skirt. There was almost no way for her to sit in the briefing area without someone being able to see up her skirt. She wished someone had told her that she should wear trousers.

Unlike the C-130s that Bates had flown in, the C-141 was a jet aircraft. It was larger and more comfortable, having been equipped with airlinelike seats in rows of twelve. Those had been shoved up against the bulkhead at the front so that the rear two-thirds of the aircraft was empty except for a couple of pallets of equipment and the racks for the weapons.

Quickly Bates outlined the plan of attack as he saw it, including the deployment of the heavy weapons and the landing spots for the helicopters. He assigned each of the officers a specific target and then gave each a secondary. Everyone had more than one assignment, and Bates believed that if for some reason a target wasn't taken out as a primary, one of them would pick it up as the secondary. It was a plan with built-in redundancy so that nothing was overlooked. When he was finished, he asked for questions.

The men examined the map, asking Rawlings and Halliday for specific information about the camp. They inquired about the height and thickness of walls, the distances between buildings, the suspected armament of the enemy forces, the locations of enemy concentrations that could be called on for reinforcements, and the escape and evasion routes.

Rawlings knelt by the map, pointing to the various areas and answering the questions as best he could. Halliday opened up a large map of Vietnam and pointed out the known enemy troop locations and the best routes back into the South if it became necessary to escape and evade.

"We have a team in the area?" asked Wansill.

Bates looked at each of the men, hesitating with the answer. For some reason he was reluctant to give an answer, but didn't know why. Each of the men with him was cleared to have the information and each was trustworthy. He decided it was his security training. Never give out information that didn't need to be given, although if something happened the men might need to know.

"One team," confirmed Bates. "Call sign of Zulu. They're on location now, observing the camp."

"Radio frequency?"

Bates looked at Wansill, told him and then asked, "Anything else?"

Farrow looked up from the map. "The helicopter pilots are going to want to know about antiaircraft."

Halliday answered that. "Just small arms, possibly a fifty cal. or the Soviet equivalent, which is the 12.7 mm. Nothing other than that."

"Okay," said Bates. "That it?"

When everyone agreed it was, Bates said, "We'll have another briefing before we land and go over everything in detail. Then there'll be a final briefing prior to takeoff for the target. I want each of you to think about this mission now to see if there's anything I might have overlooked. Let me know about it at the next briefing."

As the officers returned to their seats, Bates found Pierce and asked, "You have the squad leaders assigned yet?"

"Yes, sir. I've worked out a whole TO&E for this mission and slotted the people based on both rank and experience in Vietnam. I've jumped a couple of people into squad leader and platoon sergeant positions over higher ranking men based on that experience."

"Then get them down here and we'll brief them on the mission. Then I'll separate them into groups and have them get to know the officers. That'll also make it easier to brief them on the final assignments."

Pierce nodded and went to alert the NCOs. They came forward and crouched near the maps. Bates explained the entire mission again, giving each of them the whole picture. When he asked for questions, they only wanted to know what they would be facing in the way of enemy weapons.

With that completed, they briefed the rest of the men, telling them exactly what would happen in all phases of the mission. Bates knew that more than one military operation had failed because the leadership didn't think the enlisted troops needed to know the details. When the officers were killed early on, no one knew what they were supposed to do. This way, the entire force would have to be eliminated, and Bates couldn't see that happening.

When the first round of briefings were completed, Bates stood and moved to the seats. He dropped into one and closed his eyes. He wanted to sleep for a while. Rest and not think about the mission or the men. Just relax.

Within a minute, Wansill was sitting next to him. "Colonel," he said, "I have one question. What was that classified document you received?"

Bates opened his eyes and looked at the young captain. He was about to tell him it wasn't any of his business when he realized Wansill was the second ranking officer on the flight. If something happened to Bates, Wansill would have to take over and would need to have all the information Bates had. That made it Wansill's business.

"It was a CIA report that the Soviet Union has deployed some special troops to North Vietnam. The men we'll be facing aren't the normal frontline troops but members of the Spetsnaz. You familiar with them?"

"Some."

"They're what the Soviets call diversionary troops, men who are parachuted or infiltrated into the front lines of the enemy with orders to disrupt the enemy through assassinations and sabotage. They're highly trained in unarmed combat and the use of small arms. The report said they're like a combination of our rangers and the Special Forces. They're supposed to be very good."

"How does the CIA know this?"

"About who's there? They don't. They picked up some rumblings that the Soviet Union was going to deploy some of these men to Vietnam. The chairman of the Joint Chiefs received the information in the course of his normal intelligence briefings and he forwarded it to me because he thought it might be of interest to us. We put two and two together."

"Marvelous, sir."

Bates couldn't help laughing. "That was kind of my reaction to the news."

THE SUN BROKE THROUGH the low-hanging clouds, changing the landscape from a dim gray mess to a brighter, clearer scene. A white, wispy fog, caused by the late-night rain, was drifting through the jungle and across the valley, sometimes obscuring the enemy camp. An early-morning breeze had picked up, chilling the men. Gerber ignored the discomfort, his binoculars trained on the jungle in front of him.

Just as had happened the day before, the enemy camp came alive slowly. One man turned out and went into one of the buildings to light a fire. Others stumbled from their barracks and headed to the building with the fire as if to get a hot breakfast. The Soviets were accompanied by a couple of Vietnamese who seemed to hold some position of importance.

Gerber noticed they didn't salute. It was as if they had taken a lesson from the Americans.

And just like clockwork the patrols came in. Gerber had watched three deployed the night before and watched three come in—one from the jungle on their side of the camp and two from the other. He studied them carefully, looking for something or someone he recognized, trying to determine if they were the same three he had seen go out. He thought they were but wasn't certain. He had to be certain. If the enemy had six patrols out at night, it would complicate the assault.

Once the patrols had reached the camp and were inside the walls, Gerber handed the binoculars to Fetterman. He whispered, "I'm going to eat breakfast."

Fetterman didn't speak. He held up a thumb, indicating he understood.

Gerber crawled deeper into the bamboo thicket. He sat with his back to a banana tree and used his P-38 to open his C-ration can. The boned turkey wasn't bad as long as it had enough salt on it. Somehow the salt, used in a quantity that would have seemed excessive in a restaurant in the World, made the turkey palatable. Otherwise it was nearly inedible.

He ate his meal slowly, peeling the meat out of the can with a plastic fork. It was only in Hollywood that soldiers ate with their combat knives. In the field such a trick dulled the blade and cut the hell out of a person's mouth.

When he finished, he buried the crushed can, then drank some water. Capping his canteen, he sat quietly, breathing through his mouth and wishing the heat would go away. His uniform, wet from the rain, wouldn't dry during the day. It would remain damp, first from the rain and then with his sweat. It would be a constant reminder of his situation.

He rubbed his face and felt the growth of beard. His face itched from a combination of the sweat, the stubble, and the camouflage paint that had been there for days. It was a hell of a way to make a living.

After an hour, he crawled back to the edge of the jungle where Fetterman watched the camp. He touched the master sergeant on the shoulder and nodded to the rear, telling Fetterman, without speaking to him, to take a break, eat and catch some sleep. Fetterman acknowledged the instructions by handing the binoculars back to Gerber.

The routine in the camp didn't change. The Soviets and Vietnamese went about their training, sometimes holding formations and other times just conducting informal classes where the men sat on the ground listening to the instructors. The thing that frightened Gerber was that it reminded him of scenes he had witnessed a dozen times at various Special Forces camps: the Vietnamese soldiers listened to the white men from the West explain the ways of war to them. He hoped the Soviets had the same kind of luck the Americans had—in one ear and out the other.

Other than that it was quiet. No one reported any Vietnamese in the jungle around them. No one had seen the patrols the night before. The camp gave every impression of being a training facility containing Soviet instructors and North Vietnamese students.

Gerber lowered his binoculars to rest his eyes. He rubbed them with the heel of his hand and raised the glasses again. Nothing had changed in the camp. Everything was quiet and peaceful and that was just the way Gerber liked it.

MARK HODGES STARED at the flattened piece of paper he had taken from Morrow and read the four paragraphs again. She was definitely onto something here and she wasn't pursuing it the way she should. Instead, she was Mickey Mousing around with generals and the CIA spook over at MACV. He wasn't surprised she hadn't found out anything else. When you wanted the straight poop, you didn't talk to generals or civil servants who had careers to protect. You talked to enlisted men and junior officers, men who were young enough not to have been brainwashed by the system, men who would have axes to grind and who would be happy to talk, thinking they would be doing something to improve the system.

Hodges stood up and walked around the littered edge of his battered desk. He stopped in the doorway of his glass-enclosed office and stared out into the city room. Nearly everyone was in, each sitting there waiting for either inspiration or an assignment.

Hodges reviewed the reporters like a general reviewing his troops, searching for the right man for a hard job. He rejected a number of them as too old or too soft or too immature or not smart enough. He needed someone who would dig deep and dig long, someone who knew his way around MACV and the military and who wouldn't hesitate to ask the right questions. Morrow had a misplaced sense of loyalty that caused her to let the good stories get away.

Jackson was the man he wanted. Jackson had been in Vietnam for a couple of years. He had even been thrown out once for writing stories the South Vietnamese government hadn't liked. Hodges thought the generals at MACV might have had something to do with it. Only after the ambassador had intervened had they been able to get Jackson back. He was the perfect choice because he hated everyone. He would dig long and deep.

Hodges raised a hand and hollered, "Jackson! Let me see you a minute."

"I'm busy," came the reply.

"Well get in here or you won't be busy. Ever." Hodges grinned to himself as he turned from the door. Just like Jackson to mouth off. The man didn't care about anything but getting the story. He had no friends, and with his attitude he wasn't about to make any.

Jackson entered the office but didn't sit down. He slouched against the metal bookcase provided by a colonel at MACV. The journalist was a skinny man with a normally light complexion that had been burned dark by the sun. He was losing his hair, the process having speeded up in the past few years so that he had a fringe around his ears and a thin crop combed across his balding pate. He wore it long, mainly to irritate the people he had to interview, knowing the military universally condemned long-haired hippies. Jackson had small, brown eyes and a habit of pursing his lips as if he were about to kiss someone.

"Got something for you, Jackson," said Hodges.

"I've got something."

Hodges held out the paper. "Take a look at this and then tell me you've got something."

Jackson grabbed at the paper as if afraid Hodges would try to snatch it away. He read it quickly, glanced up and then read it more slowly. "Where'd you get this?"

"Never mind that. You want to follow up on it, or do you want to do something else?"

"No, no," said Jackson. "I want to follow up on it. I know just who to ask. Should be able to get something for the afternoon feed."

"You got it on one condition," said Hodges. "You don't mention this to anyone. Not here. Not anywhere. You just go out and get to work on it."

"What are you afraid of?"

"Look at that again," said Hodges. "Study the son of a bitch. It's a hell of a story, and I don't want anyone to know what we're working on. The fewer people who know, the smaller the chance that one of the other news organizations will get hold of this."

"You telling me we're all alone?"

"As far as I can tell, we're all alone, but if you go shooting your mouth off, somebody's going to hear about it and then we're dead."

Jackson folded the paper and started to put it into his pocket, but Hodges snapped his fingers. "No, I want to keep that here. I may need it later."

Jackson shrugged and handed it back. "You want me to take a photographer?"

"For what? We won't get anything worthwhile and it's just one more person to spill the beans. No, you go out yourself and see what you can do. And I'm holding you to that afternoon feed. I want something by then."

"You'll have it."

BATES MOVED ACROSS the airplane and dropped into the seat next to Halliday. He stared straight ahead for a moment and then said, "We need to have a talk, Lieutenant."

"Yes, sir."

"Now that we've completed the preliminary briefings and we have nearly all the information we need, I'm going to have to put you off the plane at Okinawa."

"Sir?"

"Nothing personal, but we can't take you into Vietnam. Women aren't allowed into combat zones."

"What about nurses?"

"There we get into a gray area. Technically hospitals and MASH units aren't combat zones and the nurses are, of course, noncombatants."

Halliday turned toward Bates, her face a mask of rage. "Then I'll stay with the nurses at the destination. You can't just put me off the airplane like that."

"I'm sorry, Lieutenant, but if I had my way, I'd let you accompany us all the way to Da Nang, but we're dealing with regulations devised by Congress. It's a congressional, not a military ban that prohibits women in combat. I guess the men don't want to face the possibility that their daughters will end up in a war."

"That's shit, Colonel. How many congressmen's sons end up in combat? Not many, I'll wager."

"I'm not going to debate the point with you, Lieutenant. It isn't my decision to make. I'm going to put you off the plane at Okinawa. Now, when we're there, I can arrange to have you flown back to the World immediately, or you can wait for us to return."

Halliday shook her head and stared at the deck between her feet. "This is really great. I go through everything with you people, I provide some real help and at the very end you throw me off the airplane."

"If it's any consolation, Lieutenant Rawlings will be left behind in Da Nang."

"Now *that* is good news," she snapped.

"As I said, I'm sorry about the way this works, but that's the way it is."

Halliday stared at him but didn't speak. There wasn't anything she wanted to say. There wasn't anything she *could* say, because the whole problem had been laid out in front of Congress and they had voted against her. She would have to get off the airplane at Okinawa, and yelling at Colonel Bates wouldn't do any good.

She watched Bates nod, then stand and move to the rear of the aircraft. She felt rage burn through her, but knew better than to say anything. It wasn't the colonel's fault. She was caught in the bureaucracy. Getting up, she moved over to where Rawlings was talking to a couple of Special Forces troops. She touched him on the shoulder. "Can I talk to you for a minute, David?"

One of the men said, "You can talk to me for more than a minute if you like."

"No," she said, embarrassed. She turned back to Rawlings. "Please, David." They moved off and she said, "They're putting me off the plane at Okinawa."

Rawlings shrugged. "So?"

"Don't be an ass, David. I want to see this through to the end. It's not fair."

"I'm going to have to stay in Da Nang," said Rawlings.

"Sure you are. I have a life-size picture of that. You won't stay in Da Nang for long, not after the things you told me."

"What do you want me to do?"

Now she shrugged. "I don't know. I just wanted . . . wish that I could go all the way to Da Nang. I thought you'd understand about that."

And of course he did. He knew exactly what she was feeling; after all, he was being left in Da Nang. Somehow it didn't seem right. You started the ball rolling by seeing something in a photo no one else saw and then you were excluded at the very end. He didn't want to stay in Da Nang any more than Halliday wanted to stay on Okinawa, but he didn't know what to say to her.

They landed on Okinawa as promised. Since it was a refueling stop, everyone was forced off the plane. Actually no one had to be forced because the men enjoyed the opportunity to get outside. They spread out over the base, taking the time they had to see a little bit of the island, or as much as they could from the base itself.

Halliday ducked Rawlings, telling him she was going to the bathroom and then sneaking off. She went to the PX and bought a set of fatigues. Returning to Base Operations, she ducked into the bathroom and changed into the fatigues. After that she combed her hair out, then wrapped it up so that it was piled on top of her head. Pinning it there, she pulled on the cap, but had to rearrange the cap and her hair a couple of times until they both looked natural.

That finished, she folded her uniform carefully and stuffed it into the paper bag. Then she left, walked to the counter at the front and asked if she could get back on the plane.

The bored sergeant at the counter glanced at her, then at the scheduling board. "Be another twenty minutes or so, but the plane isn't scheduled out of here for three hours."

"Doesn't matter. I've seen all of this place I want to. Let me know when I can get on."

"You'll be more comfortable in the waiting room. I'll be sure to alert you in time."

"Just tell me when I can get back on, okay?"

"Suit yourself."

Halliday sat down in a chair near the front window and watched the activity on the ramp. Pickup trucks and crew vans cruised over the tarmac while fighters and cargo planes taxied back and forth. Because she was in the Air Force, she recognized some of the planes, but a few were new to her. She'd joined the Air Force, not because she was fascinated with planes and flying, but because it offered her the best chance for advancement. This was the first time she had been cut out of anything, and that was because of the Army, not the Air Force. She felt her anger peak and then forced it down. She clamped her hands onto the armrests, squeezing them until she felt the rage begin to disappear.

Picking up a magazine, she flipped through it, not really seeing it. She glanced at the clock, sure that Bates would return any moment and catch her. But the time passed and Bates didn't return. Finally the sergeant behind the desk yelled at her and told her she could board.

She nearly ran across the tarmac to the C-141, stopping at the rear where the loadmaster was standing. Over the noise from the other aircraft in operation on the field, she told him she wanted to board.

"It's going to be a while before we take off, and it's going to get hot in there."

"I don't mind. I just want to get on."

The man shrugged and helped her enter. As soon as he disappeared, she crawled into the far corner, away from the doors and the light, and tried to hide. She didn't want to overdo it. She just hoped Bates would scan the people and not see her because she had changed and was tucked into the corner. It wasn't as impossible as it seemed. Bates wouldn't expect her, and if no one said anything until they were airborne, she might just pull it off.

The loadmaster had been right about one thing. It was hot in the plane. Without air-conditioning, and with the sun pounding down, the interior quickly heated. There were no open doors, so there was no breeze. Halliday sat there quietly, the sweat pouring off her. It soaked her fatigues, staining the front, back and armpits. She wiped her face and pulled her shirt away from her upper body so that she could blow down the front. Then she picked up a discarded magazine and fanned herself.

Just when she thought she wouldn't be able to take it any longer, the doors opened and the rear ramp came down. The cooler air blew into the fuselage, and it was as if someone had opened a door to the arctic. It seemed so much cooler than it had been. Halliday fell back in her seat and let the breeze blow on her.

The men began entering the aircraft then. First only a few of them and then more as they straggled back before the departure deadline. Pierce came back early. He found a clipboard with a roster on it and set about checking off the names of the people who had returned.

Halliday watched all this from her corner, trying to pretend she was invisible. She sat still, not wanting to draw attention to herself. Finally Bates entered, scanned the men and then moved right to where Pierce stood. They talked for a few minutes and then Bates sat down. To see her, he'd have to turn far to the left.

Rawlings and the other two lieutenants entered a few minutes later. They were followed by a large group of men that included Wansill. As they came aboard, the loadmaster began to raise the rear ramp. With help from some of the other members of the flight crew, he buttoned up the rear of the aircraft.

Everyone sat down and strapped themselves in. Halliday talked to the men sitting near her, keeping her voice low, joking with them.

She tried to ignore the sound of the engines starting, but felt a thrill when they did. She crossed her fingers, hoping Bates wouldn't turn to see her before the takeoff. She kept glancing his way even though she was afraid she would communicate her presence through ESP.

But then they began to taxi and she relaxed. The ordeal was almost over. She was sure that once they got off the ground she would be safe. Bates wouldn't order a return just to drop her off.

She held her breath as they taxied into position on the active runway. They sat for a moment as the pilot wound the engines up. Then, after he released the brakes, they began the takeoff roll, reached transition and rotated.

They climbed out rapidly, and as each second passed she felt better. Finally the loadmaster told them they could move around if they wanted and she relaxed totally. One of the men whispered something to her that she didn't quite hear, but she laughed at it anyway, her relief unmistakable.

Bates stood finally, stretched and turned to face the men in the aircraft. His eyes roamed over them. He raised his voice so that it would carry over the sound of the roaring jet engines. "Let me have the officers back here one more time." Then he turned, froze and whirled. His eyes locked on Halliday. He stared at her, his gaze boring into her. Then he raised a hand and crooked a finger, motioning her to the front.

She worked her way through the maze of seats and walked toward him. She didn't look up, refusing to meet his eyes because she knew what was coming.

"So, Lieutenant, apparently in the Air Force they don't have to obey orders."

"You didn't actually give me an order."

"No," said Bates, shaking his head. "I didn't actually order you off the plane, but you knew what had to be done. I should have the plane turn back."

There were many things he wanted to say to her. He wanted to shout at her, make her stand at attention and answer in short, concise phrases. If she wanted to play juvenile games, he was ready to accommodate her, except that one officer didn't dress down a fellow officer in front of the enlisted troops no matter what the circumstances. Instead, the offender was taken aside and raked over the coals.

"Sir, I know I was wrong, but I couldn't stand being left behind."

"Sometimes we have to obey orders instead of doing what we want," said Bates. Although he'd never say it, he admired her for her stand. When they landed at Da Nang, he'd have to do something to cover his ass in case the shit hit the fan. If not, if no one said anything about it, he'd ignore it. He wouldn't tell her that, though. He'd just let her think she was going down hard because of the prank.

"You deliberately ignored my wishes on this, Lieutenant. I'm afraid there'll be repercussions." He saw that the officers had gathered around the map. "Join us now. Maybe you can be of assistance. We'll take this up later."

"Yes, sir."

Bates crouched next to the map and again detailed the mission for the officers, leading them through it slowly. When he finished, he asked each one to repeat the entire scenario to make sure they understood the whole picture. Then he quizzed each man on his specific function. Satisfied that they knew what to do and that there was nothing else to be done, he dismissed them and asked for the NCOs.

While they waited, Rawlings whispered to Halliday, "That was a pretty stupid stunt."

"Maybe, but I'm here and not sitting on my butt on Okinawa. That's something."

"Yeah," said Rawlings, "that's something." He didn't say anything more about it. He was thinking about the subdued reaction of Colonel Bates.

But then he had to turn his attention back to the briefings. Bates led the NCOs through it, then did the same with the enlisted men. Convinced that everyone knew his job, he brought the three groups together and they went through the mission a final time.

Almost as they finished the last briefing, the loadmaster told them that they were coming into Da Nang. Everyone had to sit down and strap in tightly because this was going to be a nonstandard approach. They were going to swoop out of the sky, spiraling in from overhead so that Charlie wouldn't have a good shot at them.

As she tightened her seat belt, Halliday took Rawlings's hand and squeezed it. "I hope this wasn't as dumb as it's beginning to appear."

"I'm afraid it's even dumber."

But before she had a chance to get scared the plane had landed and was taxiing toward the terminal. They had all arrived in Vietnam.

24

MACV HEADQUARTERS
SAIGON

Jackson sat in the office of Major Frank Taylor and was annoyed. He had been to every office he could think of and not one of his contacts had said a thing about a mission to the North. Jackson knew that knowledge of it would be restricted and that only a few people would have the information, but this was getting ridiculous.

"I'm afraid I haven't heard a word," said the major. He wore a fresh set of fatigues that had no evidence of sweat on them. It looked as if he had recently used talcum, and he smelled of Old Spice. He didn't give the impression he was a combat soldier. He was a paper pusher.

"Come on, Frank," said Jackson. "You going to tell me you're not in the picture on this? I thought you had a handle on all covert operations."

"Well, that's true if you're talking about an Army operation run through here, but then it could be Navy or Marine and running out of somewhere else."

Jackson opened his notebook and flipped through several pages. "Frank, it's an Army operation and it's being run here in Saigon."

"No," said Taylor. "I know better than that."

"The guys hit the field a couple of days ago. My guess is they staged out of Da Nang or somewhere else in the northern part of South Vietnam, but I haven't been able to run that one down yet."

Taylor leaned back in his chair and laced his fingers behind his head. He stared up at the ceiling, watching the fan spin slowly. "Can't see it," he said. "If they were Army, I'd have to know."

"How about this?" asked Jackson. "They're Special Forces working with the CIA."

"Okay," said Taylor, "that's a possibility. That would cut me out of the loop, but I still think I'd have heard something. These sort of things have to be coordinated through a half-dozen officers. Have to clear them, or we could end up with a recon team in the area of an Arc Light or artillery strike. Or we could end up ambushing one another."

Jackson looked up from his notebook. "So, then, you don't think there's anything to this?"

Taylor rocked forward, leaning his elbows on his desk. He steepled his fingers and touched the under portion of his chin as if he was deep in thought. "I wouldn't think so. Still, you never know the way some of these things are cobbled together. Let me check a few places and ask a few questions."

"I appreciate that, Frank. But I'm coming up on deadline and I wouldn't want to go with only half the story. Everyone looks bad in that situation."

"Whoa," said Taylor. "I wouldn't print anything we've discussed here. It's too dangerous. See, that's why we need to coordinate these things through the whole chain of command. We don't want a story being printed that might jeopardize the men in the field."

"Then you're saying there are men in North Vietnam on a clandestine mission."

"Don't go putting words into my mouth. I'm only suggesting that we check this thing out completely before we go off half-cocked. If something is going on, you could tell the enemy enough that the men might be endangered. Hell, you don't even have to be close to right. It would put the North

Vietnamese on alert and that would make it harder on the pilots trying to escape and evade.''

"I understand that, Frank, and I appreciate it, but if there *is* something going on in North Vietnam, we've got to tell the American people. This could escalate the war. They have the right to know.''

Taylor held up a hand. "I don't want to get into an argument about various philosophies. Just give me a chance to check around and see what I can find out. I'll keep you advised, and if I find anything, you'll be the first to know.''

Jackson stood up. "I'll give you a call before deadline, but you'd better have something for me or I'm going to file what I have.''

"THERE THEY GO AGAIN,'' said Gerber. "Three patrols out. Two to the north and one to the south.''

"Maybe we should put someone on them to see where they go,'' whispered Fetterman.

"No,'' said Gerber. "We've got to remain in place.''

Bocker appeared, crawling carefully through the vegetation. He hesitated and then moved closer. "Sir, it's tonight.''

"What?''

"Made normal check-in with Net Control and they had a message for us. Said it was a go for tonight. Coded transmission suggested the time for the attack will be two-thirty.''

"Okay,'' said Gerber. "I want you and Davies to remain here. Hold down the fort and prepare the NDB for the choppers.''

"Yes, sir.''

"Tony, you, Van and I will take out the patrol.''

"How so, sir?''

Gerber was silent for a moment and then said, "Quietly, one at a time if we can.''

"Maybe we should just ignore them,'' suggested Bocker.

"No,'' said Gerber. "I've thought this through and we've got to take them out. We can't have twelve armed men roaming the jungles here with the assault coming in.''

"What about the others, on the north?'' asked Fetterman.

"Yeah," said Gerber. "We take out the ones over here. As the assault goes in, we'll have to join it and take a position on the north to prepare for those men. Once they appear we can take them under fire."

"Good," the master sergeant said.

"We can get the squad on this side before the assault," Gerber continued. "Take them one at a time from the rear. We'll have to locate them and then take the rear guard. Once that's done, we'll just move down the line, killing them as we come to them, using a garrote or our knives."

"When do we go?" asked Fetterman.

"Galvin, get Davies in here. You'll have to watch the camp to make sure the enemy doesn't do something unexpected. You'll also have to monitor the radio."

"Yes, sir. No problem."

"Tony, get Van over here. Once he understands what we want to do, we'll head out and see if we can find the enemy patrol." He turned back to Bocker. "We'll return before two even if we can't find them. That way we'll be in a position to block them if they try to make a counterattack after the attack begins."

"Why not do that anyway?" asked Bocker.

"Because of the patrols to the north. This way we can get them all without them affecting us."

"Understood."

THE ONE THING Bates wasn't ready for when they landed in Da Nang was the weather. He told himself that the humidity and heat in Florida, or the sweltering weather in Washington, was as bad as anything he could remember, but one second in the Vietnamese environment was enough to convince him he had been wrong. Somehow it was hotter and more humid in Vietnam. There was something about the air. Maybe it was the wetness that made breathing difficult.

As he left the aircraft, a jeep, its headlights little more than slits, roared up and stopped near him. The driver, an indistinguishable man hidden in the darkness, waved at him and asked, "Where's Colonel Bates?"

"I'm Bates."

"Hop in, sir, and I'll take you over to the TOC where Colonel Jannish will talk to you."

"Colonel Jannish?"

"Yes, sir. The aviation commander. He has the air assets standing by but needs to know a little more about what's going on."

Bates stopped walking and looked back over his shoulder. The men were climbing out of the plane and moving away from its wings. But once they got out on the tarmac they were unsure of what to do or where to go.

"I've got to get the men off the field."

"There are trucks coming. They'll be taken to the isolation area until it's time to board the choppers."

"I don't like this. Too many people are getting in on this."

"Yes, sir," said the driver.

Bates climbed into the jeep, nodded, then settled back. The driver shoved in the clutch, pushed the stick forward, then spun the wheel and roared off the field. They weaved between bunkers and hootches, staying on a road that had been sprayed with peta-prime to hold down the dust.

After a few minutes they stopped in front of a huge bunker with an L-shaped entrance. Dim light tinged with red bled from the interior of the bunker. Bates stepped up onto the thick, rough-cut planks and moved to the bunker's opening. He opened a door, which had a wooden frame covered with dirty plastic that had once been clear but which was an off-white that let little light leak through it.

The interior of the bunker was a carbon copy of the TOCs on bases all over South Vietnam. There were maps on the walls showing, in bright red, the suspected locations of the enemy. As well, there were a couple of rough tables and a few scattered, wobbly chairs, and a bookcase held notebooks filled with unclassified intelligence documents.

But the radios were the dominant feature. There were banks of them, each glowing with tiny red and green lights. Covering all frequencies, they popped with static and buzzed with coded messages. Two giant fans blew on them, keeping them cool, while an air conditioner hummed above them.

Bates saw a tall, thin man standing near the radios. He was wearing a Nomex flight suit instead of jungle fatigues. Bates approached him and asked, "You Jannish?"

The man turned and grinned. He had a round face, a square chin and tiny eyes. Under his nose was the largest handlebar mustache Bates had ever seen.

"My God," Bates said. "How in hell do you get away with that?"

Jannish shrugged. "I stay away from lifers who'd have heart failure if they saw it and then order me to cut it off."

Bates liked the man immediately. The mustache said something about his character, about his personality. Anyone who would risk the wrath of lifers with that mustache had to be a fearless soldier who would do anything if he thought there was a good reason behind it.

"You Bates?"

"That's right."

Jannish pulled Bates aside, away from the NCOs working the radios and the enlisted men who were standing behind them ready to help. He dragged Bates into a corner of the bunker where the light was dimmer and they were insulated from the others.

"Got a special directive on you. Supposed to do whatever you say and take you where you want to go, regardless. And I mean anywhere."

"You have any idea of the mission?" asked Bates.

"I only know it's going to be hairy. I've lined up my best pilots."

"You have any Intel packages for me?"

"Nothing at all. I was told to have the flight on standby for Colonel Bates who would be arriving with a specially trained unit for a special mission. I'm to take my orders from you regardless of what those orders might be."

"Specially trained," echoed Bates. They had had no training, just a series of trips to various cities. Bates knew that if he was smart he would abort the mission on some grounds and then back off for a week or two. That way he could get the thing organized as it should be and not worry about the run, run, run nonsense that had been dreamed up in the Pentagon.

"Colonel Jannish, I'm going to give you a location. I have aerial photos of it and everything you need to plan your mission without telling you exactly where it is. If you need refueling, however, it will have to be done at Quang Tri because once we get airborne for the assault, we'll need to run straight in with no diversions."

"Christ," said Jannish.

"Once I brief you, Colonel, I want to join my people for the final equipment check. If you have questions, I can answer them on the flight line."

"I assume we're not going to stay in South Vietnam," said Jannish.

Bates looked at the pilot and then beyond him. No one in the TOC was paying attention to them. Everyone was busy with the radios and changing the maps so that they reflected the current state of the war.

"You may make that assumption. I assume you have the proper clearances."

"I was told that anything you wanted you got and to refuse would be considered desertion in the face of the enemy."

"Good." Bates opened the case he carried with him and took out the briefing package. Going through the plan once, he showed the aviator everything he had. He detailed the mission as he saw it, gave him the heights of the surrounding hills, briefed him on the terrain and then explained the extraction phase. When he finished, he asked if Jannish had any questions.

"Just one. Who in hell thought up this fucking nightmare?"

"I think it was the chairman of the Joint Chiefs of Staff, although I suspect he had help from various locations, not all of them aware of military limitations or requirements."

"I wish we had some help from those fuckers."

"Anything specific you want?"

Jannish stroked his chin as he thought. "Not really. Or at least not yet."

"Then I'm heading over to where my people are waiting."

Jannish turned and pointed at the driver. As the man approached, Jannish said, "Take Colonel Bates to his men and wait there. Stay in radio contact with me on the company Fox Mike."

"Yes, sir."

RAWLINGS AND HALLIDAY followed the men to the isolation area. The soldiers began checking their equipment slowly and carefully, taking extra care with the weapons, making sure they were the right ones and that they had survived the trip.

Rawlings felt left out. He knew Halliday could never sneak aboard one of the choppers for the flight into the North, but he could. No one would think twice about someone who had been with them the whole way, and no one had said Rawlings couldn't go.

Without a word, he slipped away from one of the groups and found a driver smoking a cigarette and sitting on the running board of one of the trucks. He approached him slowly and said, "I need to secure a set of jungle fatigues."

The driver looked up at him and said, "So?"

"You've got to take me to supply so I can draw the equipment I need."

The driver took a long pull at his cigarette. "Why don't you have what you need already? Everyone else does."

"Because I was pulled into this thing at the last minute. I was told I'd be able to secure the equipment I needed here. Now, who do I talk to so that I can get some help?"

The driver flipped away his cigarette and stood up to stretch, his hands high over his head. Reaching up, he opened the door to the truck and said, "Get in and I'll take you over to supply."

Rawlings did as he was told. They left the area, bounced down a couple of dirty roads and stopped in front of a long, low building that looked like a railroad warehouse minus the tracks. There was a concrete dock in front of it and a ramp leading up to huge white double doors.

"See the supply sergeant. Tell him Colonel Jannish knows about it. You'll have to sign for it and make sure it gets back here after the mission."

"Thanks," said Rawlings.

He climbed out of the cab and entered the building. There was one man sitting in front of a huge fan, letting the wind blow on him with the force of a hurricane. He fought it and the magazine he was holding, but looked happy in the breeze. Rawlings walked over to him and said, "Need to draw some equipment."

"Closed," said the sergeant without looking up.

"Colonel Jannish told me to come over here."

The sergeant glanced up and then stood, moving over so that he was behind a thirty-foot-long counter. Behind it were racks and racks of equipment. The sergeant leaned on the counter and asked, "What do you need?"

"Set of jungle fatigues, boots and a weapon."

"A weapon, huh? Deploy to Vietnam without a weapon. Great." The sergeant turned and disappeared into the stacks. His voice floated back, barely audible over the roar of the fan. "You look like a medium for the fatigues and what, nine, nine and a half on the boots?"

"Medium's fine on the fatigues. A ten on the boots."

The sergeant returned and dropped the clothes and boots onto the counter. He ducked and came up with a pad of forms, carbon paper stuck between them. Listing the pieces, he drew a line to the bottom of the form and spun it so that Rawlings could sign.

"The weapon?"

"What'd you have in mind?"

Rawlings shrugged. "Just an M-16 and a bandolier of ammo."

"I can get you the weapon, but I don't keep ammo here. Mortar round could set it off. You'll need to get the ammo at the re-arm point."

"The weapon then."

The sergeant grabbed a huge set of keys and disappeared again. He returned five minutes later carrying an M-16, which he placed on the counter. Then he found another form and wrote down the rifle's serial number. As he gave it to Rawlings for his signature, the sergeant said, "I figured you wouldn't want to clean it."

Rawlings took the weapon, spun it around like a drill sergeant inspecting it for a private while on parade, jerked the bolt and tried to look down the barrel. Failing that, he turned it again and stared at the safety on the side. He felt the barrel move and glanced at the supply sergeant, who was shoving the muzzle to one side so that it was no longer pointed at his stomach.

"Sorry," mumbled Rawlings. He picked up his fatigues and beat a hasty retreat. Outside he climbed back into the truck and they headed back to the isolation area.

When they arrived, Rawlings got out and then climbed into the rear of the truck. He stripped quickly, changed into the fatigues. When he was ready, he dropped back into the compound and searched for Halliday.

"Here," he said when he found her. "You hold on to my uniform. I'll need to change back into it when we return."

"You're really going through with this?"

Rawlings shrugged and then nodded. "Look, you didn't want to be left on Okinawa. I don't want to be left here. I might be able to supply information that will be beneficial when we hit the enemy camp."

"If you feel that way, why don't you ask for permission to go?"

"Because if I ask, I can be refused. If I just tag along, assuming all the way that I'm going, then no one can say I was ordered to stay behind."

"Like I was."

"Exactly. You'll be lucky if you don't get into real trouble for that. But me, I'm free and clear because no one has ordered me to remain here. The assumption by everyone is that I'll remain behind, but that's wrong." He grinned with false bravado.

Halliday took the clothes and turned away from him. Quietly she said, "I really wish you'd reconsider this. It's not like me getting on the plane for Da Nang. At least I knew no one would be shooting at me when I got here."

He reached out and put a hand on her shoulder. "Sheila, you have to understand why I need to go."

She nodded once but didn't speak.

Rawlings made her turn and face him. Her face was stained with tears. "What's this?"

She took his hand and kissed it, staring up into his eyes. "This is really stupid, David. You don't have to do this to impress me."

"I'm not," he whispered. "I'm doing this for me." He was going to drop it there, but knew he couldn't. "I've always gotten everything the easy way. Somehow, something always happens so that I obtain my goal without the work and effort most people need. Everything's been that way. Now I have a chance to be part of a mission, and once again I have it the easy way. Our friends at Wright-Pat are going to know we deployed to Vietnam on this and they'll assume we went with the mission to the final goal. All I have to do is keep my mouth shut and they'll believe we really participated."

"But we have," she said.

"To a point," he agreed. "But this time I'm not taking the easy way. I'm going to go all the way, the hard way, with the men who are going to fight the battle and win it. I won't stay behind."

She was going to protest further, but knew it wouldn't do any good since she knew exactly what he felt. Instead she dropped to the soft ground, hidden behind the shadows of the truck, and pulled on his hand. They sat there quietly, touching at shoulder, hip and knee, both not talking, sitting close together, while Colonel Bates went through the mission plan one last time with the men of the strike force.

The time passed for Rawlings and Halliday much too quickly. Bates finally appeared outside the briefing hootch and glanced up into the night sky. He then came forward and got into a jeep. The rest of the men exited the hootch and began filtering toward the trucks.

Rawlings stood up and pulled Halliday to her feet. He kissed her quickly, all too aware he hadn't brushed his teeth in twelve hours and hadn't shaved in twenty-four.

Without a word, the men started climbing into trucks. Rawlings moved toward the last one in line, Halliday with him. He touched her hand and then her chin.

"I'll see you around dawn," he said. He kissed her cheek. The men in the truck cheered and one of them said, "If she was with me, I'd have done more than kiss her cheek."

Rawlings laughed and turned, holding out a hand so that he could be helped into the truck. Once he was in, he looked back at Halliday and said, "The man is right. I blew that one."

There was a bark of laughter and someone slapped him on the back. At that moment he felt like one of the boys. The truck lurched once and then rolled forward. Halliday was a lone figure standing in the dark, watching them leave, and then someone joined her. Together the two of them walked to the hootch to wait for the results of the assault.

25

**THE JUNGLES NEAR
LANG MO
NORTH VIETNAM**

Just as Gerber had suspected, the enemy patrol didn't have complete noise discipline. He had ordered Fetterman and Van to slip along the edge of the jungle until they came to the place where the enemy had entered it. Then the three of them, following the path of least resistance, moved deeper into the vegetation, searching the area for signs of the enemy. It wasn't an easy task because the sun had set and the jungle was wrapped in darkness. That slowed the search. Van actually crawled on his hands and knees at times, his face inches from the rotting carpet of fallen leaves, dead ferns and decaying logs. He looked like a bloodhound on the trail of an escaped convict.

But it worked because they were able to find the trail and follow it. They moved rapidly and then slowed, checking again for signs. Before long they heard the quiet rustling of cloth against bark, or thorns or vines. Gerber and his people moved forward quickly, with Van leading them. He suddenly dropped to the ground and Gerber looked up. The shape of a man stood in front of them, facing away.

With a garrote Gerber had given him, piano wire with wooden handles, Fetterman stalked the man, moving like a jaguar about to pounce. He moved toward the man, sliding through the jungle, placing his feet carefully so that they made no noise. When he was only a couple of feet behind the enemy soldier, he rose to his full height, and crossing his wrists, flipped the noose over the man's head.

The man reacted immediately. He raised his hands but wasn't quick enough to slip them inside the loop. Before he could cry out in surprise or pain, Fetterman had swung a hip into the man and levered the man's body upward, off the ground, jerking the noose tight. Fetterman completed the movement by bringing the man over his head in a throw designed to snap the neck, and as a coup de grace he drove a knee into the man's chest. The North Vietnamese soldier died before he hit the ground.

With the rear guard dead, Van moved forward along the trail until he came to the next soldier. This man was walking slowly, following the barely visible figure just in front of him. Van crouched for an instant and then joined the formation.

He slipped closer to the target, and when the man glanced over his shoulder, Van struck. Holding his knife in his right hand, he wrapped his left hand over the man's mouth. Then he pinched the NVA's nose, swung his knife up in a wide arc and jammed it into the man's back just above the right kidney. The sharp blade penetrated the khaki uniform and soft flesh easily, and there was a trickle of blood from the wound. As the man spasmed, almost jerking himself free from Van's grip, the Vietnamese commando shoved the knife in deeper, piercing the lung and heart.

Van pulled the enemy soldier backward slowly, still holding him in a grip of steel, the knife lodged in the NVA's back until he was sure the man was dead. Then, slowly, he rolled him aside, pushing the body under the long, flowing branches of a fern.

Gerber stepped past Van and moved up the trail. He kept moving confidently in a half crouch. When he saw one of the enemy, he straightened and walked faster. He grabbed the soldier from behind, and before the man knew what happened, Gerber cut his throat. The blood splashed, covering Gerber's hand, and the smell of copper overpowered the other jungle odors. The man drummed his feet, and Gerber lifted him off the ground easily. The body seemed to tense once, shudder and then was still. Gerber caught a whiff of bowel and knew the man had died.

Like Van, he rolled the dead man into the vegetation at the side of the trail and then hesitated. Fetterman passed him, taking out the next member of the patrol. They worked their way forward until there were only three men left alive, none of them suspecting the others were dead.

Gerber was determined that they should take the last three at once if they could. It lessened the risk that someone would hear something and open fire. They trailed the surviving soldiers, with Van taking the fourth position in the enemy line. If anyone looked back, he would see a Vietnamese, just as he should.

For nearly thirty minutes the patrol continued, walking through the jungle, but staying first on the path and then moving to a game trail. The game trail was narrower, and the overhanging limbs of trees and bushes formed a tunnel that caused the men to walk hunched over. But the ground was clear and it kept them moving away from the camp.

They came to a wide place on the trail. The vegetation had been cut back and there were the remains of a lean-to hidden at the edge. The three enemy soldiers stopped. One of them turned and motioned to Van, as if trying to get him to hurry. The other two, one of them a huge man, dropped to the ground and slipped their packs from their backs. The smaller soldier rolled onto his side.

Van moved into the area slowly, his eyes on the man who had spoken to him. He walked toward him, shielding both Gerber and Fetterman from the man. As he did, the two Americans began advancing on the remaining two enemy soldiers, staying in the shadows as long as they could.

As Van approached the standing enemy, the NVA sensed something was wrong. He retreated a step and raised a hand, as if to ward off a blow. Again he spoke, his voice soft, but now there was a hint of fear in it. Before he could move farther or speak again, Van leaped at him, driving his knife into the man's stomach, twisting the blade and jerking it upward. The man gasped in pain, and a scream bubbled in his throat. He reached for the weapon and fought Van for it. As he fell to his knees, he triumphantly yanked the knife from his body, holding it over his head as if displaying a trophy until he finally collapsed facedown.

The patrol leader heard the commotion and turned toward the noise. He saw one man lying on the ground, another standing over him. He spoke, quietly and sharply.

Gerber recognized the words as Russian. He moved toward the voice, and as he did the Russian began to stand, asking quietly what was happening. Gerber leaped toward him, and the man turned at the last moment. The Special Forces captain slashed with his knife, but the Russian blocked the blow with a forearm, swinging at Gerber with his other hand.

Gerber brought his knee up sharply and connected. Pain ripped through his leg, but the Soviet soldier flipped onto his back, rolled right, then left, kicking out. Gerber avoided the blow and danced to the right. In the dark it was hard to see the enemy's shape. He was merging with the pools of blackness where light couldn't penetrate.

Gerber attacked again and felt the blow blocked once more. He sensed something and turned, taking a fist on the shoulder. His arm tingled and he lost sensation in his fingers. He kicked out and felt his foot connect. There was a grunt of pain.

Now Gerber used his knife. He felt it strike home. The Russian grabbed his wrist and twisted. Gerber didn't resist but used the motion to strike again. There was a loud grunt and a startled gasp. The pressure on Gerber's wrist disappeared and the man collapsed.

Fetterman attacked swiftly and savagely. Before the Vietnamese soldier could react, Fetterman was on him. He kicked the weapon out of the man's hands, and heard his adversary's arm break with a loud snap of bone. The NVA screamed, grabbed his arm and tried to roll away. Fetterman leaped over him. The man got to his knees and tried to reach for his rifle with his good arm. Fetterman kicked it aside and used his knife. He slammed it into the NVA soldier just above the belt, twisted and then pulled it out. With a gasp, the man crumpled into a heap and died.

Fetterman picked up the dead enemy's rifle, extracted the magazine, ejected a live round, then slung the weapon over his shoulder and crouched. He wanted to search the man for documents or insignia, but in the dark he could see nothing of importance. Besides, they already knew as much about the Vietnamese as they needed to. Fetterman dragged the body off the trail and concealed it in the bushes.

When he returned, he found Gerber patting down the body of the Russian soldier. Gerber looked at the master sergeant but continued to work, taking everything he could find in the pockets, which wasn't much. On a combat patrol, even inside one's own territory, it wasn't smart to carry much of a personal nature. Gerber found a few things and put them in his pockets. He cut the epaulets from the Russian's uniform, stripped him of weapons and then pushed the body into the jungle.

"Let's get out of here," he whispered to Fetterman.

The master sergeant nodded and moved to Van, who was waiting quietly. Fetterman leaned close to him. "Return to our camp."

Without a word, Van started back along the trail, moving rapidly and quietly.

THE HELICOPTERS SAT on the taxiway at Quang Tri at flight idle. The engines were running and the blades were turning, but not fast enough for flight. Bates had landed there to wait for a last-minute message, afraid that the mission would be canceled. But that message never came, and as the minutes ticked away and the fuel burned, he realized that it was a go. Everyone in Washington and Saigon had approved the mission and no one wanted to stop it. It was something that had to be completed.

Bates finally leaned forward and tapped the aircraft commander on the shoulder. He held up a thumb, telling the pilot it was time to take off.

The lead chopper lifted, then hovered in a swirling dust storm that reflected the red and green nav lights. For a moment the chopper hung in the air, the AC looking at the line of choppers behind, warning them that takeoff was imminent. Then he rotated again, dropped the nose, and sucked in the pitch. They began a slow climb out, first over the end of the runway marked with dim lights and burning barrels of trash, and then over the strands of concertina that sparkled and flashed in the moonlight as the cans hanging on it caught and reflected the light.

They continued the climb until the humid air in the aircraft became cool. The ground near Quang Tri, alive with light, was now a dark mass with only occasional lights. There were ribbons of black that marked roads carved into the hills and jungles and strips of silver that indicated rivers and streams. But mostly the landscape was an unbroken sea of black that stretched to the charcoal horizon, a blackness that hid the dangers of tall trees, deep ravines and lofty hilltops, a few of which had been scraped bare by bulldozers and were now artillery outposts marked with lights.

Bates leaned to the rear, his back against the armored seat of one of the pilots. He was able to see out of the cargo compartment, or he could stare into the camouflage-painted faces of the men with him. Each of the men, as they had sat on the ground at Quang Tri, had painted their faces with green and black greasepaint. When they had finished, they had straightened up, sat quietly and waited for the order to go.

Each man carried an assault rifle. Most had M-16s, although a few preferred the M-14. Each had a pistol. Again many of them had the Browning P-35, which held fourteen rounds rather than the seven plus one of the Colt .45. And each man was loaded with spare ammo and grenades. Only a few had grenade launchers and even fewer carried LAW rockets.

Bates had never been impressed with the LAW. It was an unreliable weapon, which, when it worked, could be helpful. Unfortunately it rarely worked.

Bates drove these thoughts from his mind and looked at the soldiers around him. The men were ready for this. Bates could sense it. Although they didn't joke with one another on the way in, part of that was due to the roar of the Huey's engine and the pop of its rotor blades. The din made conversation difficult at best. Besides, men who were about to enter combat, who knew that there would be fighting, didn't joke all that much. They were too often lost in their own thoughts, just as he, Bates was.

He tried to concentrate on the mission, projecting the outline of the camp in his mind, mentally seeing the helicopters landing and the firefight developing, but these thoughts were pushed aside by mental images of his family. In his mind's eye, he saw his redheaded wife, a woman who had the best body he'd ever seen and who had somehow retained her figure even after the birth of two daughters. She'd asked him once if he was disappointed that all she had given him were daughters, and he'd felt tears sting his eyes, unable to believe she could think such a thing.

"No," he'd told her. "I wouldn't trade the girls for anything. They're absolutely the best."

And he thought about the damned dog they had acquired somewhere. The dog loved the girls and protected them from everything, including him. Every time he walked in the door, the dog barked at him.

He thought about the girls in high school and then moving on to college. They were lovely young ladies who thought for themselves, and although they hated the war in Vietnam, they didn't hate their father for his part in it. They could see his point, and understood that a defeat in South Vietnam might mean a bloodbath in Southeast Asia.

For one horrifying instant Bates felt that he was never going to see them again, that this mission was his last, that he was going to die. And then he knew that it wasn't. The icy hand that had clamped his stomach, squeezing it so tightly that he thought he was going to throw up, let go. This wasn't his last mission. He grinned to himself and thought about all the Hollywood movies where someone like himself would now be obliged to die. Not so in real life.

There was a sudden change in the pitch of the engine as the aircraft began its descent. The crew chief peeked out of his well and said something to the man sitting on the troop seat near him.

That man leaned forward, his face close to Bates. "We're at the DMZ. Going down to about fifty feet or so. Another ten, I'd say."

Bates nodded and held up a thumb.

GERBER AND HIS TEAM trekked back to the bamboo copse, moving slowly and quietly. At the edge of the jungle, the land down to the enemy camp was clear. And, as on all the other nights, it was dark. No lights burned, at least none that were visible. The enemy was doing an excellent job of light discipline.

Gerber entered the copse first. He saw Davies sitting in the middle of the tiny clearing there, cranking the handles on the Angry 109. The antenna leads had been strung back and up into the trees. They were broadcasting a continuous tone that could be used as a nondirectional homing beacon by the helicopters.

"Choppers are inbound, Captain," said Bocker. He whispered it, but no longer as quietly as before. In a few minutes the attack would start. "How'd it go?"

"Got them all," he said. He handed the material he'd taken from the Russian to Kepler and added, "Something for you to play with when we get out."

Kepler held one of the epaulets up to his eyes, trying to see it in the almost nonexistent light. Not saying anything, he just tucked it into his rucksack.

Gerber rubbed a hand over his mouth and chin, feeling the stubble, dirt and sweat. He looked into the darkness, but there was nothing to see. Turning, he moved through the vegetation until he was close to the edge of the jungle. He then got down and crawled the rest of the way.

If he hadn't been there for several days observing the camp, he would have thought it deserted. He used his binoculars and studied every building, every shadow and each of the guard towers. There was absolutely no movement or light.

Bocker crawled up and leaned close. "About five out, Captain."

"Okay," said Gerber. As he stuffed his binoculars into their case, he reviewed the bare minimum he and his men should do next. First and foremost they had to get down the hillside and out onto the other side of the camp so that they could be prepared for the two enemy patrols in case of a counterattack. But that was all they needed to do.

In fact, they didn't even have to do that. They could warn the incoming troops of enemy in the jungle and let them deal with the problem. But then he wouldn't get a chance to see the interior of the camp, and he wanted to do that.

Gerber was joined by Fetterman, Bocker, Kepler and Van. Each of them crouched at the very edge of the jungle, staring down at the enemy camp. From far away came the first faint sounds of the choppers—the distant pop of rotors and the quiet, insistent hum of engines.

Davies approached and said, "Choppers are inbound now and have the camp sighted."

Gerber made one more check of the guard towers, but there was still no one in them. The enemy abandoned them at night. Gerber could understand the motive: the Americans would never attack them in North Vietnam.

They all began to move then, crawling forward out of the jungle. They worked their way down the hillside, using the tall grass to conceal their movements, just in case there was anyone watching. Halfway to the enemy camp, with the sounds from the choppers growing louder, they turned east and worked their way around the camp so that they would be ready for any enemy soldiers who might appear.

IN THE LEAD CHOPPER Bates chambered a round and switched on his weapon's safety. Then he knelt behind the console on the deck of the Huey so that he had an unobstructed view through the aircraft's windshield.

The AC cupped a hand over the boom mike of his helmet and pulled it away from his lips. "Camp's right over there," he shouted, pointing through the windshield.

Bates saw nothing at all except the black landscape stretched out in front of him like a lumpy blanket waiting on the beach. Then, in the center of all the darkness, he saw a circle of gray that looked like a bowl. There was nothing to distinguish it from the rest of the countryside except for its shape, which he recognized from the photos he had studied.

By staring at the bowl-shaped depression, he was sure he could see the camp tucked away at the bottom of it. The longer he stared, the more detail he could see: the walls, the guard towers, the buildings and even the tree that concealed part of the parade ground.

Bates slapped the AC on the shoulder and yelled, "That's it! That's it!"

They started a slow descent that carried them to within a few feet of the trees. The pilot had turned down the red lights on the instrument panel so that even they wouldn't inhibit the view outside the cockpit. Bates knew the red lights could sometimes be seen by the enemy, and a few pilots turned them completely off just before landing in an LZ.

The pilot looked over and shouted, "One minute!"

Bates nodded his understanding and turned to the men in the chopper with him. "One minute. One minute." He held up one finger and watched as each man nodded.

The men began the ritual of checking their equipment a final time, pulling out the magazines in their weapons and pushing them back in. They worked the bolts and chambered rounds. They touched their grenades, their spare ammo or the hilts of their combat knives. Then they looked at one another, each slightly embarrassed by the apprehension that he felt.

Then they stopped moving and sat quietly, staring into the night sky as the choppers roared a few feet above the jungle, racing toward the enemy camp. For thirty seconds they were silent, waiting and watching.

And then the helicopter banked suddenly, flaring out and hovering momentarily. The ground was lost in a swirling cloud of debris stirred up by the rotors and downwash.

26

**THE ENEMY CAMP
OUTSIDE LANG MO
NORTH VIETNAM**

The first few seconds went off like clockwork. Bates was out of the chopper and on the ground, running south toward the gate. The roar from the choppers drowned out everything. From the aircraft that had landed behind him, the men leaped out in rapid succession.

One of them split from the group, ran toward a guard tower and knelt on the grass. He ripped the cotter pin from the LAW rocket launcher, extended the tube, glanced over his shoulder to make sure the backblast wouldn't hit anyone, then sighted and fired. The rocket hurtled out of the tube, its roar lost in the noise of the helicopters, and the guard tower burst into a thundering blast of fire.

Another soldier broke from the group, ran west, then stopped. He aimed his weapon and fired. An instant later that guard tower erupted, too, the flash illuminating the camp as the fireball rolled skyward and debris rained down.

As soon as the guard towers were down, one of the choppers that had been holding back screamed over the top of the wall and disappeared behind it, landing in the center of the compound. It was followed by another and another.

Bates ran around the corner of the wall nearest the gate, slid to a halt and waited. The rest of his men joined him there, then two of them ran for the gate, hitting it with their shoulders. The gate crashed open and the men poured through.

As Bates entered the compound, he saw one of the choppers sitting on the ground to his left. He ran to the right, heading toward a low building. The men fell in behind him. He detoured slightly, avoiding the door. Two of the men jumped to either side of it and a third tossed a grenade in as he dived out of the way.

When the grenade detonated, the sound lost in the growing din inside the walls, the men leaped into the building. Bates followed them into the dark mass of hanging dust that was mixed with the smell of cordite. A shape loomed in the hallway and Bates fired once. The shape collapsed.

Outside, small-arms fire began to rattle—at first M-16s on single-shot. They were joined by AK-47s, some of them firing on full-auto. That was punctuated by grenades. There were a few shouts, cries of surprise and wails of pure agony.

Bates rushed down the hallway, came to a door and riddled it with M-16 fire. He stepped back to one side and waited for an enemy response. When there was none, he kicked in the door and sprayed the room with M-16 rounds.

All around him his men were doing the same thing. They were using their grenades and rifles, cutting down any enemy who moved.

OUTSIDE, WANSILL LEAPED from the cargo compartment of the chopper that had landed on the western side of the compound. He took one running step and dived for cover. As he hit the dirt, the doors on the building flew open and someone began firing. The green tracers from the enemy whipped overhead, slamming into the tail boom of the chopper, tearing at it with quiet, popping sounds. The door gunner, sitting behind an M-60, returned fire, his ruby-colored tracers arcing into the doorway.

As the AK fell silent, Wansill was up and running. He sprinted to the wall of the building and dived to the ground under one of the windows. Rolling onto his back, he pulled a grenade and jerked the pin free. He then let the safety spoon fly, sat up and tossed the grenade through the window. As he dropped back, he curled up against the wall, shielding his eyes and face from the flash.

Wansill was up with the explosion, climbing through the window. He held his weapon in front of him, the barrel pointed at the rear door of the room. Small fires, caused by tracers and grenades, burned in the room. Bodies were strewn about the floor. There was an underlying odor of fresh copper mixed with smoke and burnt gunpowder.

He wanted to head straight for the door, but there were too many enemy soldiers in the room. He set about checking them, making sure each was dead. As he swept forward, he picked up weapons that didn't look badly damaged, stripped the magazines and worked the bolts and dropped them onto the floor.

He reached the door and looked back at the seven Vietnamese in the room, all of whom had been killed by the blast. It had gotten them as they had scrambled out of bed, clawing at their weapons.

At the door he stopped and listened to the shouting that was beginning to boil through the hallway. He opened the door, saw a white soldier with an AK and ducked back. An instant later a burst ripped through the door near him. Splinters from the wood clipped him, some of them drawing blood.

Wansill scrambled to the rear and overturned a cot for protection. He waited a moment and then fired, putting his rounds through the door near the knob, angling the burst up toward the opposite corner. He heard a screech of pain and a thud outside as a body fell.

Now he moved again, heading for the other side of the room. He crouched as the door was kicked open and someone dived in, rolling toward him. Wansill hesitated and then pulled the trigger. The round hit the man in the middle of the forehead, snapping his head back and splattering blood and brains on the wall behind him.

Wansill got to his feet, his weapon aimed at the dead man. The body was larger than most of the Vietnamese and had white skin. It had to be one of the Russians.

Wansill heard a noise in the hallway and dropped to one knee. As he did, two men rushed into the room. They opened fire, their weapons spraying the room.

Wansill shot at them. One fell and died immediately. The other started to spin, still firing, but Wansill cut him down, pulling the trigger until his weapon was empty.

The enemy soldier was driven back, his blood spurting. Throwing his AK down, he wrapped his hands around his stomach and groaned in pain as he fell over. His feet spasmed, kicking at the flimsy walls, and then he died.

Wansill dropped the empty magazine and slammed a full one home. He slapped the bottom of it, making sure it locked in, and then worked the bolt to chamber a round. Normally he would have recovered the empty magazine, especially on a covert mission, but he knew Washington wanted no mistake about what had happened. The Pentagon wanted some evidence left behind, just not too much.

He moved to the doorway again, aware that time was ticking away. They only had a few minutes to spend in the camp. Around him the firing was increasing—AKs against M-16s. Grenades detonated as the men cleared the rooms, sweeping through the buildings they had been told to attack.

Carefully he opened the door, now a bullet-ridden piece of junk. It hung by a top hinge. Wansill crouched and glanced into the smoke-filled hall. Flames flickered at the far end and he could see shapes moving, but he didn't know who they were. They seemed to be small men, probably Vietnamese, but he couldn't shoot at them without being sure. He didn't want to cut down his own soldiers by accident.

He held his hand up, staring at the watch on the underside of his wrist. Three minutes had passed from the time he had leaped out of the rear of the chopper.

THE BLAST OUTSIDE the walls woke Kutnetsov. He rolled out of his cot and onto the floor. Without opening his eyes, he grabbed at the weapon leaning against the wall nearby. He inched toward the window and slowly rose to his knees. Through the open window he could see the guard tower burning brightly.

At first he thought it was some kind of exercise designed by Thuy to make him look bad—catch the Soviets off guard to prove they didn't have all the answers, didn't have the answers about guerrilla warfare and the Vietnamese way of fighting it. But then the helicopters swooped in and the firing began.

Kutnetsov ducked again and crossed the room. The flickering firelight illuminated the interior. He snagged a chest pouch filled with spare magazines and ran out. At the stairs he paused, glanced down but saw no one.

At the bottom of the stairs he stopped again, trying to figure out what was happening. Given the increasing cacophony of weapon fire and the roar of helicopter engines, Kutnetsov believed it was an American attack. He didn't know why they were attacking now, but it was the only thing that made any sense.

He ran to the front of the building, opened a door and ducked into the room there. He began to crawl across the floor, suddenly aware of how easy he would be to spot. His white skin stood out like a beacon.

He reached the window and peeked out. In the courtyard sat an American-made helicopter. There were men running through the shadows—tall men carrying American-made weapons.

He ducked below the sill and looked at the AK in his hands. He worked the bolt, ejected a live round and then whirled. Pushing the barrel through the window, he pulled the trigger and watched the green tracers dance out, some of them slamming into the rear of the chopper.

A couple of the men dived for cover and opened fire, the rounds hitting the window and wall near him. A machine gun began to hammer, and he heard slugs smashing into the building. He dropped down again. Beads of sweat broke out all over his body. He felt it dripping down his sides.

Carefully he rolled onto his stomach and began crawling across the floor. From the hallway came shouts in Vietnamese. They were screams of panic, and although he couldn't understand the words, he understood the emotion.

RAWLINGS HELD ON TO the edge of the troop seat, his eyes squeezed shut, and prayed silently. When the guard tower had blown up, he had suddenly realized what he was doing and it scared him. Now he didn't want to look at the battle scene, believing, irrationally, that keeping his eyes closed would protect him.

As the chopper descended toward the enemy camp, he heard the explosion as the second guard tower blew up. He knew he would be in the thick of battle in a few seconds. His stomach flipped over and drifted away from him, and he began mumbling over and over, "Oh, God! Oh, God!"

The chopper crossed the last few feet of open ground, popped up over the wall and then dropped. The rotor blades hit the branches of the compound tree, tearing through them like a lawn mower through weeds. Debris was scattered, sucked up in the rotor wash and thrown around.

The aircraft landed hard, bounced and came to rest, listing to the left. Someone yelled, "Let's go."

Rawlings felt the aircraft rock as the men leaped from the cargo compartment. The sound of sporadic firing came to him, but for the moment he was paralyzed, unable to move or even open his eyes.

Then suddenly there was a hand on his shoulder and someone yelled, "Are you hit?"

Rawlings couldn't respond. There was a lump in his throat, and he knew that talking would call attention to him and tell the enemy where he was so that they could kill him. His training in ROTC and the Air Force hadn't prepared him for the total terror he felt now, a terror that froze his muscles and numbed his mind.

He was shaken then, first gently and then harder until his head snapped back and forth. The voice continued to yell at him, "Are you hit?"

Finally, in anger, he swatted at the hand, pushing it away from him. He stared into the leering face of the crew chief, his features barely visible in the half-light. For a second he stared and then screamed, "I'm fine. Let go of me."

Still he hesitated. Outside there was more shooting. Red and green tracers danced through the night. There was a flash as a grenade went off. Rawlings believed he could hear the individual reports of the weapons over the roaring of the Huey's turbine and rotor throb. Human silhouettes leaped and ran.

With a herculean effort, Rawlings shoved himself from the troop seat. He crouched in the hatch of the Huey, watching the attack, listening to it. Then he took a deep breath, knowing he would have to do something soon. He couldn't sit in the rear of the chopper forever.

Rawlings sat down then, like a kid on a dock trying to convince himself to dive into a cold lake. He leaned forward out of the chopper. Around him the firefight raged. Crouching, he clutched at his weapon, his fingers curling and uncurling. His breath rasped in his throat as if he had run a long distance. Cautiously he slid one foot forward, and when no one shot at him, he jumped out. Glancing right and left, he began to trot across the hard-packed earth, thinking that it wasn't so bad after all. It had just been those first few moments.

He worked his way across the open area and crouched near the corner of a building. Along the front were a dozen Americans preparing to sweep in. They each held a grenade in one hand as the man in the middle counted down, using exaggerated hand motions. When his index finger stabbed out, the men turned and tossed their grenades into the building. A moment later, as the men flattened themselves on the ground, there was a series of detonations. Fire and smoke billowed out of the windows and doorway. From inside came screaming. One man, dressed in dark shorts, burst out of the building, his hair in flames. A single shot cut him down.

The men at the front of the building were up then, peering into the windows. One of them leveled his rifle and opened fire, the flame from the muzzle reaching into the window. He jumped to the side as his weapon emptied itself, but there was no return fire.

Rawlings inched his way toward the rear of the building. In the darkness he saw a shape running, his head down like a man in a heavy wind. Rawlings raised his rifle and tried to sight but couldn't find the target. He lowered his M-16, saw the man again and pointed his weapon at him. As he fired, the man disappeared into the deep shadows at the base of the wall.

Rawlings didn't know if he'd hit the man or not. There was no return fire.

Rawlings stayed where he was, his back against the rough material of the building's exterior. He felt the impact of bullets as they slammed into the building near him and the heat as the fire spread through it. The flickering light made the shadows dance and bob, giving them a life of their own. He'd have to move again soon, he knew, but for the moment he was happy right where he was.

Colonel Thuy was awakened by the roar of the incoming helicopters and the detonation of the guard tower outside the wall. He sat up in bed. Not the cot that everyone else in the compound had, but a real bed, with a wooden headboard and footboard. He knew immediately what was happening. The Americans were attacking. Something he had believed couldn't happen was, in fact, happening.

He climbed out of bed and moved to the window. Outside, not more than sixty feet away, one of the guard towers was burning furiously. In the flickering light one helicopter squatted on the grass like a giant insect ready to spring into the air. Men leaped from the sides, running around the front to form a single unit that moved south toward the gate.

Thuy couldn't help grinning at the scene. More helicopters materialized out of the darkened sky and more men ran across the hillside, attacking his camp. He should have known the Americans wouldn't tolerate the presence of his force so close to the Demilitarized Zone. He should have guessed the Americans wouldn't want the Soviets working so closely with the North Vietnamese Army. He was surprised by their response, but he should have known.

He turned from the window, and in the light filtering through he could see everything inside—the bed with the wooden headboard, the framed picture of Ho Chi Minh signed by the leader and given to him personally, the desk the French had brought to Vietnam so long ago, the bookcase with many volumes, including a French edition of *Huckleberry Finn*.

Using the light from outside, he stepped across his room and began to dress in his best uniform. He buttoned the shirt slowly. It had been tailored so that it fit his body like a glove. He pulled on his trousers, then buckled on his pistol belt, shifting it slightly so that the holster was at his hip. Then he sat down. His boots had been polished the night before and nearly glowed in the reflected light. He pulled them on, stamping his feet.

Dressed, he took his pistol, a Soviet-made Tokarev TT33 from the holster, checked to see if it was fully loaded and then half cocked it. Ready to face the enemy, he moved to the door and leaned an ear against it. Hearing nothing in the hallway, he opened the door.

The hallway was deserted but beginning to fill with smoke. He didn't know if it was from the burning guard tower or if the building was now on fire. He could hear shooting outside, some of it very close. The men were shouting at one another, screaming orders and prayers, many of them unsure of what to do. The commands were in English, Russian and Vietnamese.

It was time to take charge, thought Thuy. The Russians might be very good soldiers, had defeated the Nazis during The Great War, but they understood nothing about lightning raids and guerrilla attacks, something the Americans seemed to have learned well since their involvement in Vietnam. But this was Thuy's element, and he knew that a resistance had to be organized quickly or they would all be dead in minutes.

He reached the ground floor and found the hallway full of dust and smoke. The firing had increased steadily, and bullets were snapping through the air near him. Debris rained from the ceiling, making it hard to breathe.

He ran to the front of the building and looked out. The Americans were swarming over the ground in front of him, shadows in the flickering light of a dozen new fires.

His men were crouching in fear and hiding in terror. Few were trying to resist. Most were trying to live long enough so that they could flee to the rear wall where they hoped to avoid the Americans and then escape into the safety of the jungle.

Thuy whirled and saw two men in the hallway. He ran to them and jerked one roughly to his feet. "Where's your weapon?" he demanded.

The man failed to respond. He looked at the colonel with wide-eyed terror.

Thuy grabbed the front of his dirty shirt and yelled into the man's face. "You want to kill Americans? You want to go south to fight? Now you have to fight here and you want to run. You are a coward."

That seemed to jerk the man out of his state of fear. He pushed Thuy's hand away, then spun and disappeared into the smoke and dust. A moment later he was back with his weapon and spare magazines.

"Good," said Thuy. "Very good. Get to the front of the building and shoot. Kill the Americans who are invading your home."

The other man was up and moving now. He yelled at the others and the men began to respond. They appeared from hiding, some dressed in black pajamas, others wearing parts of their uniforms, a few almost totally naked, but each with his weapon. Thuy started placing them so that they could cover one another and hit the Americans with a devastating fire. Not all of them were at windows. Some stayed in the hallways behind the doors, covering the men at the windows. It would be very difficult for the Americans to get in.

Thuy ran back to his room, stumbling through the thickening smoke. He found a crate of grenades that had been stolen from the Americans and then brought north for training purposes. Thuy now had a more important use for them. He hoisted the crate to his shoulder and ran back into the hallway.

GERBER WATCHED the helicopters land. One man dispatched from the first chopper blew up one of the guard towers. Then helicopters and men were all over the place. Some of the men ran toward the south gate while others tried to scale the walls.

As soon as the helicopters were all on the ground, Gerber motioned his men forward. They skirted to the west, away from the action, and ran through the knee-deep grass, trying to get into position to form a blocking force. Gerber didn't know how long it would take the two patrols on that side of the camp to recover. He didn't know how long it would be before they were in a position to launch a counterattack.

Gerber and his men fanned out on the hillside, well away from the tree line, using the available cover. There were a few large rocks, one log and a couple of depressions. The men spread out, forming a ragged line to guard the assault force.

It was a difficult task. The firing in the camp behind them was a temptation. Each man wanted to run down the hill and join in the assault. But no one moved. Kepler positioned himself to make sure the enemy didn't somehow mount a counterattack from the enemy compound.

In what seemed like seconds, the jungle began to flicker and sparkle as if a thousand fireflies had been released. Gerber knew that it meant the enemy was there already, probing. It was a recon by fire, and none of his men shot back.

He kept his eyes locked on the jungle. The sweat was rolling down his face and dripping down his back and sides. He felt hot and his temples throbbed. He ignored the ache as he stared into the black jungle.

The enemy appeared moments later. First, a single man moved from the trees in a low crouch. He worked his way down the hillside, turned once and looked over his shoulder. Then he continued as others joined him. They fanned out so that they were almost in line.

Anchoring one end of the line was a big man. His white skin was easily visible even in the darkness. He raised his hand once and pointed. The line swept forward, angling toward the helicopter sitting in front of the burning guard tower.

Gerber sighted on the white man. He didn't care if the rest of the enemy soldiers survived or not. He didn't care if they fled into the jungle, as long as the white man, who had to be a Russian soldier, didn't live through the assault.

Gerber lay there quietly, letting the barrel of his weapon track the man. He waited as the enemy came closer. There was a shout, something in Russian, and then something else in Vietnamese. When the whole line stopped, Gerber pulled the trigger.

The Russian soldier didn't seem to react, and Gerber thought he had missed. Then the man dropped his rifle and clutched at his chest. He let out a bloodcurdling noise that ripped through the night. Two of the Vietnamese leaped to the Russian's side, but the others seemed unsure of what to do.

At that moment the rest of Gerber's men opened fire on full-auto. The AKs they carried ripped at the night. The Vietnamese began to drop, screaming and cursing. A few turned to run but were killed before they got close to the trees. One man threw his weapon away and stood still, his hands locked behind his head until a round struck him, knocking him off his feet.

In thirty seconds it was all over. None of the Vietnamese remained standing. From his prone position Gerber watched the ground where the Russian had fallen, but there was no evidence that the man still lived. Over the sounds of the firefight and the helicopters in the camp behind them, Gerber heard a quiet moaning and knew that someone had survived.

BATES LEANED AGAINST THE WALL to catch his breath. His heart hammered in his chest and his breathing was ragged. Sweat soaked his uniform and dripped from his face. He couldn't remember combat ever having affected him this way, but then it had been a while since he had been in the thick of it.

He dropped the partially used magazine from his weapon and reloaded, then crouched. Reaching out, he touched the doorknob and twisted it, throwing the door open. One man was facing out the window, firing an AK. Bates shot from the hip, and even over the noise around him he heard the bullets strike flesh. The impact propelled the man through the window.

Bates entered the room, searching it carefully. He found an overturned cot, a broken chair and another weapon. Near the window was a pile of empty AK casings and two empty magazines. The man had done a lot of firing from his position.

Bates leaped to the wall and eased his way to the window. The last thing he wanted to do was silhouette himself against the light filtering into the room from the hallway. He peeked around the edge of the window and saw the enemy soldier lying facedown in the dirt, his weapon partially under him. A pool of blood, which looked like oil poured onto a concrete floor, was spreading from the bullet holes in the man's lower back and side.

Bates moved back to the hallway and saw several of his men now standing outside of the rooms. They had cleared them all, killing the occupants or causing them to flee. Bates ran to the stairs in the center of the building and looked up. "Anyone upstairs?" he asked.

"Saw Jones and Hernandez heading up there."

Then, from the second floor, came a wild burst of firing. A grenade exploded and debris clattered into the hall, shaken loose by the detonation. A body fell.

Bates didn't wait. He took the stairs two at a time, thinking that he was getting too old for this shit. He stopped at the landing, spun and faced the second floor. He heard running footsteps and a burst that stitched the wall near him. A man appeared, whirled to fire, then started down the stairs.

The man was Vietnamese. Bates triggered his weapon once. The round hit the man in the stomach, almost doubling him over. He tossed away his weapon and sat down groaning. Looking down, he saw Bates there. He raised his hands, as if to fend off another shot. Then his body slipped down the stairs, stopping at Bates's feet.

Another shape appeared and spun, leveling his weapon. Neither he nor Bates fired. The man lowered his weapon first and said, "Jesus, Colonel, I could have killed you."

"And I you."

"Yes, sir. That's it up here."

"Let's get out then." Bates stayed where he was as the men fled past him. When the second floor was clear, Bates took out a thermite grenade, jerked the pin free and threw it onto the second floor. It detonated in a bright flash and started a fire that began to spread quickly. Racing down the stairs, Bates yelled, "Let's clear the building."

The raid had been going on for just under five minutes.

THE MEN WHOM WANSILL had seen disappeared into the smoke. When they were gone, he ran down the hallway, hurdled an overturned chair and slid to a halt. The hall in front of him was empty. He began to work his way along it, the smoke stinging his eyes and making it difficult to breathe.

With his back to the wall, he turned the corner, but again the hallway was empty. Wansill wiped the sweat from his face and continued forward. He found an open door and the body of one man. Wansill kicked the weapon away from the dead man's outstretched hand and exited.

Suddenly he was in the coolness of the night. He crouched, watching the firefights developing around him. Green and white tracers from enemy weapons snapped by him. There was a chattering of automatic weapon fire, staccato bursts from M-16s and occasional explosions from grenades. Few enemy weapons were firing now.

The courtyard was now empty except for the Huey sitting forty feet away, the engine still roaring. A crewman sat behind the M-60 door gun, firing bursts into the upper floor of a building.

The men should have been trying to break contact now, pulling back to board the choppers or getting out of the camp. Wansill got to his feet and took only a single step. From the side there was a noise, and he spun to face it.

An enemy soldier, dressed in nothing more than black shorts, rushed from the shadows. He held his AK in both hands. The bayonet was extended. As he rushed Wansill, he began screaming.

Wansill turned to meet the attack. He kicked out, stopping the man in midstride. Wansill clipped his adversary with the butt of his M-16. Since there was no weight behind the weapon, the blow did nothing more than push the man off balance. As the NVA fell, he lost his grip on his AK, and before he could recover, Wansill shoved the barrel of his own weapon into the man's face and pulled the trigger. The enemy spasmed, the muscle reaction nearly bending him double as his head sprayed blood in a black fountain.

FROM NO MORE THAN fifteen feet away, Kutnetsov saw the NVA soldier die. He sneered at the foolish attack, knowing that you never gave the enemy the opportunity to kill. Instead, you cut him down and went on to the next target.

Kutnetsov lifted his weapon and pointed at the American, but the man ducked and disappeared. Kutnetsov swore under his breath, but didn't let it concern him. He leaped from hiding, in pursuit of the enemy. At the building he stopped and peeked around the corner. The courtyard was filled with enemy soldiers and aircraft. Ruby-colored tracers filled the air. Kutnetsov was disappointed because he didn't have a decent target.

Lying near the building was one of his men. Kutnetsov recognized the body of Sergeant Moskvin. He had taken a round in the face, obscuring most of his features, but Kutnetsov knew it was the sergeant.

Without a second glance at the dead man, he moved forward and felt someone grab the barrel of his AK-47. The man jerked and twisted, and Kutnetsov let the rifle go. He turned to meet the threat and thought he recognized the American who had just killed the Vietnamese soldier.

Kutnetsov crouched slightly, turning so that his right side faced the American. He held both hands up as if to protect his head and face, then feinted and kicked out. The American blocked the kick and turned away from it.

Now the two men faced each other. Kutnetsov was surprised the American was such a good fighter. He had believed the propaganda that claimed Americans were weak-kneed capitalists who could easily be overpowered. That seemed not to be the case here.

Kutnetsov retreated a step, trying to draw the American away from the building, but the man wouldn't be fooled. Instead, he, too, retreated a step. Kutnetsov attacked quickly, first with a kick, then an elbow smash to the face when the American blocked the kick. But the American ducked under Kutnetsov's arm and came up quickly, catching the Russian by surprise and driving him back.

Kutnetsov stumbled and fell to one knee. He hoped it would give the American confidence and result in a foolish assault, but that didn't happen. Instead the American retreated again, clawing at his side. Kutnetsov suddenly believed that the American had been hurt. He leaped up to renew his attack and then realized his mistake.

The American pulled the pistol out of its holster and fired as it cleared leather. Kutnetsov felt a white-hot pain in his shin. He stumbled, dropped to one knee and raised a hand as the American fired again.

The second round caught Kutnetsov in the shoulder, spinning him. He fell facedown, but kicked out, trying to sweep the American's feet out from under him. The American rewarded him with a bullet in the back. Kutnetsov felt the explosion of pain, and everything around him lit up in a blinding white flash that was impossible to look at.

The Americans weren't supposed to be that ruthless. They were supposed to believe in giving an enemy an even chance. They weren't supposed to shoot a wounded man, even if he still posed a direct threat.

Kutnetsov tried to raise himself to his hands and knees, but he didn't have the strength. He pushed, the effort causing him to grunt in pain, but it did no good. He collapsed facedown, the rough ground digging into the flesh of his cheek. All the lights suddenly dimmed and faded to black.

WITH FIRES NOW BURNING in nearly every building in the camp, it was almost as bright as day. Rawlings stood with his back against one of the structures and felt the heat. He took a step forward. There was a flicker of motion to his left, and he spun to face it.

Without aiming, he opened fire, his finger tight on the trigger. The muzzle-flash seemed to touch the enemy soldier. He jerked and fell. After rolling once with his hand in the air, he didn't move.

Rawlings collapsed against the side of the building. He slipped to the ground, gasping for breath as his heart hammered almost hard enough to break out of his chest. Death, not fear, was driving him now. He had killed a man, shot him down as he had run through the night. Unlike most Air Force officers who had been forced to kill only from a distance during their career, he had seen the face of death, the agony etched on the dying man's features as his blood spurted.

But Rawlings wasn't sickened by the scene. He was exhilarated by it, exhilarated by the life-and-death struggle he had won by being quicker on the trigger.

As these emotions washed over him, he got to his feet. He wanted to run and shout but knew he had to be careful. The last thing he wanted to do was run into a bullet. The whole adventure would be something to tell Sheila when he got back to Da Nang.

The roof of the building was now in flames as burning debris drifted down. He shifted to avoid it, then dashed toward another building. Outside were a dozen men firing at the windows. Return fire was coming from the upper floor. Both the roof and the ground floor were burning, but no one seemed to notice.

Behind him there came a single shrill whistle. It pierced through the night, rising above the noise of the firing easily. A harsh voice demanded, "Break contact! Break contact!"

Rawlings halted as the men who had been shooting at the windows lowered their weapons. He couldn't believe they were just going to turn and run. Each man took a hand grenade, and almost as one they threw them into the burning building. The building shook with the explosions, then began to collapse. From the interior came screams of pain and fear until the roof broke apart and caved in. Then there was a fountain of sparks that looked like a solid wall and a whoosh as the flames billowed higher.

Rawlings realized it was time to make for his helicopter just as the other men were doing. It was all over. All he had to do was get clear.

As he approached his chopper, he noticed the blades were no longer spinning. He stopped short and saw two men climbing over it. One of them leaped clear and yelled at him, "We can't fly it out. We have to blow it up."

Now Rawlings was confused. He stood in the middle of the burning camp and glanced from side to side as the firefight still raged. When he saw a group of men running for the gate, he decided to join them.

They all reached the gate easily. Rawlings turned and looked back at the compound. Every building was on fire now.

Flames were shooting a hundred feet into the air. The fighting continued, but the firing had died down. Automatic weapons still ripped at the night. There were single shots and grenade explosions, but not the number there had been.

Rawlings spun and ran out the gate. Behind him someone called, and he stopped and listened. When the voice didn't come again, he was convinced that one of the Americans had been calling for help. He turned and ran back, but didn't enter the compound. He crouched near the gate, trying to find where the sound had come from.

Finally, convinced that one of the men had been hit, he entered the compound again. There was a single body lying in the shadows, and he ran to it. As he approached, he realized the man was too small to be an American. He slid to a halt and started to turn when a flicker of motion caught his attention. Rawlings opened fire almost instinctively, but his aim was bad. The bullets passed over the prone man, striking the wall behind him.

The man rolled and returned fire. Rawlings felt a pain in his side and thought he had walked into something. He tried to pull the trigger on his weapon, but no longer had the strength. He saw the enemy stand and then saw him hit by three or four rounds, driving him back to the ground. Rawlings tried to turn to see what happened next but couldn't. Everything went black.

WHILE THE FIGHT RAGED behind him, Gerber and his men stayed on the hillside, waiting for the second enemy patrol. Once or twice he glanced back and saw the continuing destruction of the camp.

Fetterman loomed out of the darkness. "We'd better pull to the rear, Captain."

"I know, Tony, but there's still one patrol out."

"Yes, sir, and they might be two klicks away."

Gerber nodded and waved a hand. "Fall back," he told the men.

They got up and began drifting to the rear where the helicopters waited. Each of them watched the jungle, but it was nothing more than a black smudge with no light or life.

And then, rushing them from the east, came the second patrol. Bocker spotted them first. He shouted a warning as he dropped to the ground and opened fire. The rest of the Americans did the same.

Despite the fusillade, the enemy kept coming. They didn't stop or slow down, but seemed intent on overrunning the Americans. But the return fire from Gerber and his men was too intense. It became a solid wall of lead and the enemy began to drop. They threw their weapons into the air, stumbled and rolled around on the ground screaming in pain. In an instant it was all over.

Fetterman stood and emptied the remainder of his magazine into the Vietnamese soldiers. As he slammed a new one home, he said, "It was like the banzai charges of the Japanese. No reason for it."

Gerber didn't care. It eliminated the problem. He yelled, "Let's fall back. Take it slowly."

They worked their way downhill. As they neared the helicopters, two men came forward cautiously. One of them yelled something Gerber didn't hear. He halted and waited. The man yelled again. "Seven."

Gerber knew it was a recognition signal. He looked at Bocker, who responded, "Five."

"Come ahead."

The men swept on down. They spread out and scrambled into the rear of the helicopters. As he sat on the troop seat, Gerber suddenly felt fatigue wash over him. He wanted to lie down and sleep. It was almost too much to stand. But then he heard the firing from the camp and knew it wasn't time to relax. Another ten minutes, once the choppers were off the ground, then it would be time. But not now. Not with the enemy still alive and shooting at them.

THUY THOUGHT HE HAD IT MADE. He had motivated the men for battle, but then saw that he was wrong. The feeble defense he had organized collapsed quickly. The cowards had fired a few rounds at the attacking Americans and then turned and fled.

Thuy didn't run. He hadn't run from the Japanese or the French, and he wasn't going to run from the Americans.

He retreated through the building and found the bodies of two Soviets killed by grenades. Their shredded flesh was mute testimony to their ineffectiveness against the Americans. He passed quickly, without much thought about them. He stopped at the side door and looked out. No one was there. He slipped through the door and ran across the open ground, trying to get into position to shoot at a nearby helicopter.

He took cover behind rubble that had tumbled from the top of one of the buildings. It was a small pile of smoking debris. There was nothing substantial in it, but it might turn a bullet if the angle was right. He stretched out behind it and took careful aim.

His first round snapped through the Plexiglass of the windshield, creating a small hole. The pilot ducked back, slipping down behind the small ceramic plate that was supposed to protect him from bullets.

Thuy aimed and fired again. The round disappeared into the night but did no damage. He popped up to fire again, but the door gun began to chatter. Thuy saw the muzzle-flashes. A line of tracers tumbled toward him. The Vietnamese colonel rolled away from the bullets. He burned himself on some of the debris, but ignored the searing pain. From his new position he could see the dark shape of the pilot. Thuy got to his knees to fire and was hit immediately. The M-60 rounds cut through him. His fingers went cold and nerveless as he died.

THE RAID WAS twelve minutes old. Bates was retreating. They had swept in as planned, set everything in sight on fire and shot everyone who moved. Now it was time to get out.

Sergeant Pierce ran toward him and slid to a halt. "Time to get out, sir?"

"Time to get out. Get a head count as we go through the gate and then on the chopper."

"Goes without saying."

Bates had known that. Each chopper had two men assigned to make sure everyone who had come in with them got out.

The last thing they wanted was to get clear, then realize someone had been left behind.

Together the two men rushed toward the gate. As they approached, they saw one man lying in the dirt. He seemed bigger than the Vietnamese. It might be one of the Russians, but Bates wanted to be sure. They detoured toward the body, and as they got close, Bates recognized the American-issue uniform.

Bates reached for the throat, but there was no carotid pulse. He turned the man over, but in the dark he couldn't recognize him. "Who is it?"

"Looks like that Air Force puke, Rawlings."

"Shit," snapped Bates. "What in hell was he doing out here?"

"Don't know."

Bates grabbed the dead man under one arm. "Give me a hand."

Pierce took him under the other arm and they trotted toward the gate. Green came up behind them. "Who is it?"

"That Air Force guy."

Green nodded and raced for the gate. He stopped to provide cover in case a Vietnamese survivor decided to snipe at them. When they reached the helicopter, Bates and Pierce lifted the body and rolled it into the cargo compartment. They followed it in and Bates collapsed on a troop seat. "Let's go," he said.

The chopper picked up to a hover. It turned, giving Bates a view of the hillside behind them. The men were filtering out of the camp and running across the open ground. The burning camp made it easy to see them now, and Bates tried to count. He knew that most of the men had gotten out, but he didn't know how successful they had been.

As the chopper lifted off, Bates turned and looked back. The enemy camp was a sea of flame. The compound, now brightly lit, was dotted with dark shapes. They were the bodies of the men killed in the raid, and there were dozens of them. From the interior he saw a couple of aircraft take off.

The AC turned in his seat and shouted, "Everyone's out. Count shows everyone who went in came out plus the pathfinder team. One chopper down and wired for demolition left on the ground, but the men from it were picked up by the others.'' He hesitated and then said, ''We did it!''

Bates fell back against the soundproofing and felt relief. They wouldn't really be clear until they crossed into South Vietnam, but the danger was over. They had done it. They had raided into North Vietnam and gotten out.

He glanced at his watch. The raid was twenty-two minutes old.

27

THE PRESS BUREAU
SAIGON

Robin Morrow sat at her desk, and felt sick to her stomach. She stared at the headline on the story—U. S. TROOPS IN NORTH VIETNAM—and knew Hodges had stolen it from her.

She crumpled the paper into a huge ball and tossed it at the wastebasket beside her desk. Then she turned and stared at the cubicle where Hodges now sat. In there with him was Jackson. They were laughing about something. Morrow couldn't contain her fury any longer. Not only had they stolen her story, but they might have jeopardized the lives of the men involved in the mission.

She got up and stormed across the room. She entered the cubicle, stopping where she could look at both men. Hodges wiped a tear from his eye, caused by his laughing so hard. He managed to choke out the words, "What's your problem?"

"You unbelievable bastard," she said.

The humor left Hodges's face. He sat up, his fists clenched on the desk in front of him. "I won't take that kind of shit from you, Morrow."

"Oh, no?" she said. "You steal my story, print a half-baked version of it and then get snotty with me."

"You weren't pursuing the story," snapped Hodges. "I assigned it to someone who had the ability to get the facts and who wasn't afraid to print them. I assigned it to someone who would take it all the way." He nodded at Jackson. "And a hell of a story it is, too. We've had a dozen calls from the networks. They all want more. MACV and USARV have been on the phone all morning, denying everything and demanding a retraction." Hodges rocked back and laced his fingers behind his head. He looked smug.

"Those men in North Vietnam are now in jeopardy because of that story."

"Oh, horseshit," said Hodges. "The military has pulled that old chestnut once too often. Those men aren't in any danger because we ran a story suggesting American soldiers are operating above the DMZ. There are no details that will put those men in jeopardy."

"That's all it means to you—a story. You don't care about anything else. Not the men up north, not the ethics of the situation, nothing."

"It doesn't matter what it means to me. All that really matters in the end is whether or not we're right, and I know we're right. The interest generated in the story, especially at MACV, shows we're right."

Before Morrow could speak, the phone rang. Hodges held up a hand to quiet her and picked up the phone. He spoke briefly, then listened as the blood drained from his face. "No," he mumbled, then hung up. He turned on Jackson and snapped, "I thought you checked your facts."

Jackson still looked pleased with himself. He nodded. "I'll stake my reputation on everything I wrote in that story. I can even give you the names of the men, at least some of them, who are on the mission."

"Give," said Hodges.

Jackson dug out his notebook and flipped through it. "One is Captain MacKenzie K. Gerber. Another is Sergeant Anthony B. Fetterman. I believe they're working with a Sergeant Tyme and a Sergeant Bocker."

"Uh-huh. And when do you expect them to return to the South?"

Now Jackson shrugged. "In a couple of weeks, maybe."

"Well, Mister Investigative Journalist, the men you mentioned are now en route to Saigon from Da Nang. I've been told they were operating on a special mission out of Quang Tri that ended last night. We're beginning to look like a couple of prize jerks.''

Morrow snapped her head up. ''Gerber's on the plane?''

''According to the man over at MACV. He said they brought him back to prove no one was in North Vietnam.'' Hodges held up a hand to stop the protest from Jackson. ''If they had people in the field in the North, there's no way they could have pulled them out this fast. Nor have them on a plane to Saigon already.''

''Now wait a minute,'' said Jackson, his voice rising.

''No, you wait, goddamn it. I gave you a perfect lead and you let some smartass over at MACV take you for a ride.''

''No one took me for a ride. The first thing they do when they detect a leak is pump bad information into it to taint all the information. I had a solid story.''

''You had shit. There's no way they could have gotten those men out of the North in time to have them on that plane. Not when they didn't know the story was coming.''

''You're right there,'' said Jackson. ''Which means they won't be on the plane. I'll bet money that when it arrives we'll find Gerber and Fetterman were detained in Da Nang for some reason. A couple of guys will get off who saw them in Da Nang, but Fetterman and Gerber will be among the missing.''

Hodges suddenly felt better. ''I bet you're right. Find out where the plane's landing, Tan Son Nhut or Bien Hoa, and meet it.''

''I'll go with you,'' Morrow said, ''and keep you out of trouble.''

''Good idea,'' said Hodges. ''You can temper his enthusiasm with a little levelheaded thought.'' He was quiet for a moment and then added, ''They'd better not be on that plane, Jackson, or we're all going to look like assholes.''

BEFORE THE PLANE LEFT Da Nang, Gerber had time to take a shower and shave. It felt good to wash off the accumulated dirt, sweat and camo paint. He stood under the long, hot shower at five in the morning and let the water run. He hadn't felt so good in weeks.

Finally Gerber changed into a clean, pressed set of fatigues. Someone had gone to a lot of trouble to get a full set of patches sewn on, including a name tag with his name stitched on it. Not that it was difficult to do, but it would make the press wonder.

Dropping into a chair, he rubbed a towel over his head and dried his hair. He glanced at the newspaper that claimed there were men in Vietnam and laughed. Although the story was correct, it was going to look wrong in a couple of hours. Someone knew what he was doing.

There was a noise and Fetterman entered, followed by Alan Bates. Gerber got to his feet, but Bates said, "Sit down, Mack. How've you been?"

"Hot and tired and miserable and I'm now looking forward to the plane ride to Saigon so I can get some sleep."

"Good." Bates looked around the room. There was an assortment of broken, dirty chairs. A card table held a couple of decks of cards and a Monopoly game while another table held a radio and a small black-and-white television. He dropped into one of the chairs and put his hands on his knees. "I don't suppose I have to tell you we can't talk about the mission."

"No, I suppose you don't."

"And you realize what was going on there, don't you?"

Fetterman, who had stayed near the door, said, "We have eyes. The Russians were training the North Vietnamese."

"So we went in and told the Russians that they weren't allowed to do that. They were allowed to send supplies, and they probably have people teaching the North Vietnamese how to use those fucking SAMs, but we draw the line at ground troops."

"I understand all that," said Gerber.

"There was a cover story prepared in case this thing blew up in our faces, but it doesn't look like we're going to need it. There was only one serious casualty. An Air Force officer got himself killed." Bates stopped talking and shook his head.

"What was he doing there? On the mission?"

"He wasn't supposed to be there. He was supposed to wait right here," said Bates. "Damn brave, stupid kid. Had no idea what he was getting into but couldn't stand the thought of getting left behind.''

"How are we handling it?"

Bates stared at the floor. "Killed in a plane accident. No mention of his being in Vietnam at all. Family will get his GI insurance and all. It'll be listed as a service-related death but not logged as a combat death."

Fetterman spoke up again. "Be nice if we could get him some kind of medal. A Purple Heart and maybe a Bronze Star."

"Yeah," said Bates. "The Bronze Star won't be a problem."

"Anyone else hurt?" Gerber asked.

"Not really," said Bates. "Everyone is accounted for. Couple of men took some shrapnel and one man has a flesh wound in the arm. Round went through the meat under the bone. More of a graze than anything."

"We get a count on their losses?"

Bates shrugged. "The whole camp burned. I'd say between seventy-five and a hundred and fifty dead. We'll have a recon over there by midmorning." He stood up. "I'd better hit the road. We're due to fly out of here in about two hours."

Gerber moved toward the older man and held out his hand. "It was nice to see you again, Colonel."

"You did a hell of a job up there, Mack." Bates glanced over his shoulder and said to Fetterman, "You, too, Tony. Without your part, this mission would never have come off. Too bad no one will be able to read about it."

"Isn't that always the way," said Gerber. He laughed. "A brilliant mission. We really hurt the enemy, but we can't tell anyone about it. If we'd fucked it up, it would have been all over the newspapers tomorrow."

"Unfortunately that's the way it has to be." Bates looked at his watch. "I really have to get moving. Thanks once again."

Fetterman shrugged. "Don't mention it."

COLONEL FYODOR TRETYAK sat at his desk and read the coded message again and again, but nothing changed the meaning of the words. It was a flimsy piece of paper torn from the teletype machine. Captain Yuri Kutnetsov and his entire team had been killed along with ninety-two North Vietnamese in a raid on their camp. A raid conducted by the Americans.

It was the last thing he had expected. The Americans had been so careful about not changing the war that everyone had thought they would ignore the Russian soldiers in North Vietnam. Everyone had thought the Americans would be afraid of offending the Soviets, but the first thing they did was attack with a vengeance. Tretyak knew that the raid had been designed not only to knock out the training program, but also to send a message. The Soviets were not to put ground troops into the North.

Tretyak stood up and walked around his desk. He stopped and returned to his seat. He was nervous because he didn't want to tell Bukharin about the failure and yet he knew he had to. Finally he got up, walked to the door and left his office.

Bukharin was waiting. He knew the message had been delivered to the colonel and he even knew the contents. There were no secrets, especially inside the Soviet Army. Without waiting for Tretyak to speak, he waved the colonel to a chair. "Sit and tell me what you have."

Tretyak nodded and collapsed into the leather chair. He held out the paper. "Our mission into North Vietnam has failed."

"Why is that?"

"The Americans, Comrade General. They attacked in force and eliminated our men."

"And how do we respond to this outrage, Fyodor?"

"Why, we must retaliate," said Tretyak, now unsure of what to do. The question had caught him off guard and his response had been automatic.

"No, Fyodor, we do no such thing. We close our files, we seal them and then we destroy them. We tell no one what has happened and we seek other methods of helping our North Vietnamese comrades. That is all we do."

Mixed emotions raged in Tretyak. One was relief because he wasn't being blamed for the failure. Careers had been ruined with smaller failures. And the other was anger. The

Americans had put one over on them and no one was going to do a thing about it. He slumped in the chair.

"I think, Fyodor, that you should return to your home, kiss that pretty wife of yours for me and take the rest of the weekend off. Then return here Monday morning ready for work. I may have another little project for you to work on."

Tretyak got to his feet. "Yes, Comrade General, I shall do that."

"And, Fyodor, I think it would be best if we didn't mention what has happened in North Vietnam. There are those around here who wouldn't understand the failure."

"Yes, sir."

"Good. I'll see you Monday."

Tretyak spun and headed for the door, unsure what was going to happen. He hoped to be alive Monday morning to report to work. He thought he would be, but there was a lingering doubt in the back of his mind.

GERBER'S PLANE WAS an hour late. It landed at Tan Son Nhut, taxied to the military side and halted. Gerber was one of the first men out, followed by Fetterman, Tyme and Bocker. Morrow stood there watching, dressed in a light cotton blouse and a short skirt, hoping that Gerber would take her out for dinner.

Jackson noticed that all the men he'd thought were in North Vietnam were getting off the plane. All of them, not just Gerber and Fetterman. "Now that's strange."

"Not at all," responded Morrow. She left him standing there and charged across the tarmac.

Gerber saw her coming, looked around frantically, as if wanting to duck her, and then grinned. "Robin."

She threw herself at him and kissed him wildly as the men stopped and stared. Fetterman edged closer, grinning. "You're making a spectacle of yourself."

"So what?" asked Gerber.

"So nothing. You want me to locate a cab? We do have a debriefing to conduct."

Gerber nodded. "You find us a cab. Robin, when this is over, I'll buy you dinner."

"Yes, sir," she said, beaming. She couldn't have been happier.

GLOSSARY

AC—Aircraft Commander. The pilot in charge of the aircraft.

ADO—A-Detachment's area of operations.

AFVN—Armed Forces radio and television network in Vietnam. Army PFC Pat Sajak was probably the most memorable of AFVN's DJs with his loud and long, "GOOOOOOOOOOOOD MORNing, Vietnam!" The spinning Wheel of Fortune gives no clues about his whereabouts today.

AK-47—Assault rifle normally used by the North Vietnamese and the Vietcong.

AO—Area of Operations.

AO DAI—Long dresslike garment, split up the sides and worn over pants.

AP ROUNDS—Armor-piercing ammunition.

APU—Auxiliary Power Unit. An outside source of power used to start aircraft engines.

ARC LIGHT—Term used for a B-52 bombing mission. It was also known as heavy arty.

ARVN—Army of the Republic of Vietnam. A South Vietnamese soldier. Also known as Marvin Arvin.

AUTOVON—Army phone system that allows soldiers on one base to call another base, bypassing the civilian phone system.

BISCUIT—C-rations.

BODY COUNT—Number of enemy killed, wounded or captured during an operation. Used by Saigon and Washington as a means of measuring progress of the war.

BOOM BOOM—Term used by Vietnamese prostitutes in selling their product.

BOONDOGGLE—Any military operation that hasn't been completely thought out. An operation that is ridiculous.

BOONIE HATS—Soft caps worn by grunts in the field when they weren't wearing their steel pots.

BUSHMASTER—Jungle warfare expert or soldier skilled in jungle navigation. Also a large deadly snake not common to Vietnam but mighty tasty.

C AND C—Command and Control aircraft that circled overhead to direct combined air and ground operations.

CAO BOI—Cowboy. A term that referred to the criminals of Saigon who rode motorcycles.

CARIBOU—Cargo transport plane.

CHINOOK—Army Aviation twin-engine helicopter. A CH-47. Also known as a shit hook.

CHOCK—Refers to the number of the aircraft in the flight. Chock Three is the third. Chock Six is the sixth.

CLAYMORE—Antipersonnel mine that fires seven hundred and fifty steel balls with a lethal range of fifty meters.

CLOSE AIR SUPPORT—Use of airplanes and helicopters to fire on enemy units near friendlies.

CO CONG—Female Vietcong.

DAI UY—Vietnamese army rank equivalent to captain.

DEROS—Date Estimated Return from Overseas Service.

E AND E—Escape and Evasion.

FEET WET—Term used by pilots to describe flight over water.

FIVE—Radio call sign for the executive officer of a unit.

FOB—Forward Operating Base.

FOX MIKE—FM radio.

FNG—Fucking New Guy.

FREEDOM BIRD—Name given to any aircraft that took troops out of Vietnam. Usually referred to the commercial jet flights that took men back to the World.

GARAND—M-1 rifle that was replaced by the M-14. Issued to the Vietnamese early in the war.

GO-TO-HELL-RAG—Towel or any large cloth worn around the neck by grunts.

GRAIL—NATO name for shoulder-fired SA-7 surface-to-air missile.

GUARD THE RADIO—Term that means standing by in the commo bunker and listening for messages.

GUIDELINE—NATO name for SA-2 surface-to-air missile.

GUNSHIP—Armed helicopter or cargo plane that carries weapons instead of cargo.

HE—High Explosive ammunition.

HOOTCH—Almost any shelter, from temporary to long-term.

HORN—Term that referred to a specific kind of radio operation that used satellites to rebroadcast messages.

HORSE—See *Biscuit*.

HOTEL THREE—Helicopter landing area at Saigon's Tan Son Nhut Airport.

HUEY—UH-1 helicopter.

IN-COUNTRY—Term used to refer to American troops operating in South Vietnam. They were all in-country.

INTELLIGENCE—Any information about enemy operations. It can include troop movements, weapons capabilities, biographies of enemy commanders and general information about terrain features. It is any information that would be useful in planning a mission.

KA-BAR—Type of military combat knife.

KIA—Killed In Action. (Since the U.S. wasn't engaged in a declared war, the use of the term KIA wasn't authorized. KIA came to mean enemy dead. Americans were KHA, or Killed in Hostile Action.)

KLICK—A thousand meters. A kilometer.

LIMA LIMA—Land Line. Refers to telephone communications between two points on the ground.

LLDB—Luc Luong Dac Biet. The South Vietnamese Special Forces. Sometimes referred to as the Look Long, Duck Back.

LP—Listening Post. A position outside the perimeter manned by a couple of people to give advance warning of enemy activity.

LZ—Landing Zone.

M-3—Also known as a grease gun. A .45-caliber submachine gun favored in World War II by GIs. Its slow rate of fire meant the barrel didn't rise. As well, the user didn't burn through his ammo as fast as he did with some of his other weapons.

M-14—Standard rifle of the U.S., eventually replaced by the M-16. It fires the standard NATO round—7.62 mm.

M-16—Became the standard infantry weapon of the Vietnam War. It fires 5.56 mm ammunition.

M-79—Short-barreled, shoulder-fired weapon that fires a 40 mm grenade. These can be high explosives, white phosphorus or canister.

MACV—Military Assistance Command, Vietnam, replaced MAAG in 1964.

MEDEVAC—Also called Dust-Off. A helicopter used to take wounded to medical facilities.

MIA—Missing In Action.

MOS—Military Occupation Specialty. A job description.

MPC—Military Payment Certificate. Used by military in lieu of U.S. dollars.

NCO—A noncommissioned officer. A noncom. A sergeant.

NCOIC—NCO In Charge. The senior NCO in a unit, detachment or patrol.

NDB—Nondirectional Beacon. A radio beacon that can be used for homing.

NEXT—The man who said it was his turn next to be rotated home. See *Short*.

NINETEEN—Average age of combat soldier in Vietnam, as opposed to twenty-six in World War II.

NOUC MAM—Foul-smelling sauce used by Vietnamese.

NVA—North Vietnamese Army. Also used to designate a soldier from North Vietnam.

P (PIASTER)—Basic monetary unit in South Vietnam worth slightly less than a penny.

PETA-PRIME—Tarlike substance that melted in the heat of the day to become a sticky black nightmare that clung to boots, clothes and equipment. It was used to hold down dust during the dry season.

PETER PILOT—Copilot in a helicopter.

PLF—Parachute Landing Fall. The roll used by parachutists on landing.

POW—Prisoner Of War.

PRC-10—Portable radio.

PRC-25—Lighter portable radio that replaced the PRC-10.

PULL PITCH—Term used by helicopter pilots that means they are going to take off.

PUNJI STAKE—Sharpened bamboo hidden to penetrate the foot. Sometimes dipped in feces.

PUZZLE PALACE—Term referring to the Pentagon. It was called the puzzle palace because no one knew what was going on in it. The Puzzle Palace East referred to MACV or USARV Headquarters in Saigon.

RINGKNOCKER—Graduate of a military academy. The term refers to the ring worn by all graduates.

RON—Remain Overnight. Term used by flight crews to indicate a flight that would last longer than a day.

RPD—Soviet 7.62 mm light machine gun.

RTO—Radio Telephone Operator. The radio man of a unit.

SA-2—Surface-to-air missile fired from a fixed site. It is a radar-guided missile that is nearly thirty-five feet long.

SA-7—Surface-to-air missile that is shoulder-fired and has infrared homing.

SACSA—Special Assistant for Counterinsurgency and Special Activities.

SAFE AREA—Selected Area For Evasion. It doesn't mean that the area is safe from the enemy, only that the terrain, location or local population make the area a good place for escape and evasion.

SAM TWO—Refers to the SA-2 Guideline.

SAR—Search And Rescue. SAR forces were the people involved in search and rescue missions.

SIX—Radio call sign for the unit commander.

SHIT HOOK—Name applied by troops to the Chinook helicopter because of all the "shit" stirred up by its massive rotors.

SHORT—Term used by a soldier in Vietnam to tell all who would listen that his tour was almost over.

SHORT-TIMER—Person who had been in Vietnam for nearly a year and who would be rotated back to the World soon. When the DEROS (Date of Estimated Return from Overseas) was the shortest in the unit, the person was said to be next.

SKS—Soviet-made carbine.

SMG—Submachine gun.

SOI—Signal Operating Instructions. The booklet that contained the call signs and radio frequencies of the units in Vietnam.

SOP—Standard Operating Procedure.

STEEL POT—Standard U.S. Army helmet. The steel pot was the outer metal cover.

TEAM UNIFORM OR COMPANY UNIFORM—UHF radio frequency on which the team or the company communicates. Frequencies were changed periodically in an attempt to confuse the enemy.

THE WORLD—The United States.

THREE—Radio call sign of the operations officer.

THREE CORPS—Military area around Saigon. Vietnam was divided into four corps areas.

TOC—Tactical Operations Center.

TO&E—Table of Organization and Equipment. A detailed listing of all the men and equipment assigned to a unit.

TOT—Time Over Target. It refers to the time that the aircraft is supposed to be over the drop zone with the parachutists, or the target if the plane is a bomber.

TRIPLE A—Antiaircraft Artillery or AAA. This is anything used to shoot at airplanes and helicopters.

TWO—Radio call sign of the intelligence officer.

TWO-OH-ONE (201) FILE—Military records file that listed all of a soldier's qualifications, training, experience and abilities. It was passed from unit to unit so that the new commander would have some idea about the capabilities of an incoming soldier.

UMZ—Ultramilitarized Zone. It was the name GIs gave to the DMZ (Demilitarized Zone).

UNIFORM—Refers to the UHF radio. Company Uniform would be the frequency assigned to that company.

USARV—United States Army, Vietnam.

VC—Vietcong, called Victor Charlie (phonetic alphabet) or just Charlie.

VIETCONG—Contraction of Vietnam Cong San (Vietnamese Communist).

VIETCONG SAN—Vietnamese Communist. A term in use since 1956.

WHITE MICE—Referred to the South Vietnamese military police because they all wore white helmets.

WIA—Wounded In Action.

WILLIE PETE—WP, White phosphorus, called smoke rounds. Also used as antipersonnel weapons.

WSO—Weapons System Officer. The name given to the man who rode in the back seat of a Phantom because he was responsible for the weapons systems.

XO—Executive officer of a unit.

ZAP—To ding, pop caps or shoot. To kill.

ZIP—Derogatory term applied to the South Vietnamese.

ZIPPO—Flamethrower.

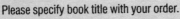

Mack Bolan's

PHOENIX FORCE

by Gar Wilson

The battle-hardened, five-man commando unit known as Phoenix Force continues its onslaught against the hard realities of global terrorism in an endless crusade for freedom, justice and the rights of the individual. Schooled in guerrilla warfare, equipped with the latest in lethal weapons, Phoenix Force's adventures have made them a legend in their own time. Phoenix Force is the free world's foreign legion!

"Gar Wilson is excellent! Raw action attacks the reader on every page."

—Don Pendleton

Phoenix Force titles are available wherever paperbacks are sold.

PF-1